MONARCH

an imprint of Amplify Publishing Group

www.mascotbooks.com

Monarch

Cover Image: Milosz_G

For more information, please contact:
Mascot Books, an imprint of Amplify Publishing Group
620 Herndon Parkway, Suite 220
Herndon, VA 20170
info@mascotbooks.com

Library of Congress Control Number: 2023924196
CPSIA Code: PRV0424A
ISBN-13: 978-1-63755-909-3

Printed in the United States

To Jill, for her unwavering love, support, and encouragement.

MONARCH

JOHN ARNETT

MASCOT BOOKS
an imprint of Amplify Publishing Group

CHAPTER 1

DANNY KERRIGAN STARED AT THE EMAIL as if it were a death sentence.

He was dazed and confused, as though someone had reached out from the screen and smacked him in the face with a two-by-four. As he reread the message, his throat tightened. His stomach knotted. His breathing became rapid and shallow. His pounding heart rattled his chest.

It was 6:30 p.m. Hoping his boss was working late, Danny frantically fired off a response. He wrote it with a firmness that he felt his value and seniority allowed:

Gary,

I can certainly understand why Nathan is upset. However, I must decline the assignment. I'm just a software support person. As always, I want to help the company any way I can, but that is really out of the question. It's not a matter of being unwilling. I simply cannot do it.

Thanks, Danny

After sending the message he was on his feet, moving his six-foot, 180-pound frame around his home office like a caged animal. He'd be a wreck all night if he had to wait until morning for a response. Much to Danny's relief, Gary's reply arrived in just a few minutes.

> I'm really sorry, Danny. I guess I didn't make myself clear. Nathan already knows you're the best we have, and hearing about the case you resolved today just reinforced that. When everyone said you were the best person for this job, the conversation was pretty much over. I told Nathan about your situation, but he didn't want to hear it. He's the president of the company. I can only push back so much. It won't be that bad.

"Damn," Danny whispered. He picked up his phone.

"Hi, Danny."

"Gary, I'm serious. I can't do it." His voice trembled.

"Calm down, Danny. I know you're serious, but there's nothing I can do about it. I'm sorry."

"Come on, Gary. You know about my issues."

"I know. Like I said, Nathan didn't want to hear it."

"Can't you just wait a couple of days for him to cool down and then tell him you all decided it would be best to get someone else? Or just have someone else do it and not tell him?"

"Can't do it. He thinks this is important. We get a ton of revenue from our department, and he's worried customers are going to start dropping support if things don't improve. I'm sure you've heard how he can be when he gets riled up."

"What if I just don't do it? He'd be pissed, but he'd get over it. I mean, come on, he's not going to fire me. Think of the impact that would have on the company."

Gary paused for a moment. "I'm going to be completely honest with you. He actually said that you'd better get your ass in here and do it or start looking for a job. It won't be that bad. Hell, you'll hardly have to prepare anything. And you already know most of the people involved. It'll be a very informal—"

"Thanks, Gary," Danny mumbled before abruptly terminating the call.

"Fuck!" he yelled as he grabbed a notebook from the desktop and threw it against the wall. "Fuck!"

Danny shuffled to his living room, still breathing heavily. His apartment seemed foreign to him. His comfortable, relaxing sanctuary was now just walls and furniture. He paced around the room trying to figure out what to do and cursing the fact that his perfect world had been shattered so abruptly.

His logical mind took charge. He could look for another job, but that would entail interviewing, learning a new product and company, dealing with lots of new people, and, worst of all, probably working in an office again. Two years of working from his apartment had made that prospect seem intolerable. He could quit, move back to his hometown, and probably get a job in construction or at a local factory. The thought of doing physical labor for the next forty years nauseated him. And he didn't relish the idea of returning to a small town. Everyone knew what everyone was doing. It would be terribly difficult for him to isolate himself.

After twisting the cap from a beer, he continued pacing like an expectant father waiting for an idea to be delivered. Maybe he could win the lottery in the next two weeks. Maybe someone would uncover some scandalous behavior by Nathan and the board of directors would fire him. Maybe the chain of management above him would band together and stick up for him, threatening to resign if Nathan forced Danny to do it. And maybe the whole department would join them.

The first beer, gone in a matter of minutes, was followed by a second. Danny entered his bathroom and took stock of himself in the mirror. He struggled to find the boyish good looks that had always been there. His light-brown hair, parted on the right side, was tousled. His normally bright blue eyes exuded sadness and anguish. He looked haggard; much older than his twenty-eight years. He disgustedly flicked off the light and headed back to the living room.

Danny stepped onto his balcony, where the chilly November air seemed to distance him slightly from the situation. As he stood and sipped his beer, the quiet slowed down his thoughts. There was no need to freak out. He had two weeks to figure out what to do.

The situation made him venture into painful memories that he rarely revisited. He thought back to his first day of kindergarten . . . the battle his mom had getting him out of the house, how he screamed and sobbed when they got to the school—clutching the door handle and refusing to leave the car. He replayed how his mom and teacher had to work to extract him, and how the teacher introduced him in front of the already-seated class. Everyone knew who he was and could see he'd been crying. The giggles he heard as he shuffled to his desk were seared into his psyche.

He jumped forward to the fourth grade, when each student had to sing a solo in front of the class. He recalled how for weeks his looming performance dominated his thoughts and blanketed him with dread. The memory of the solo was vivid. He could see the music teacher wheeling his piano into the room. He could feel how totally numb he was as he made his way to the front of the class, and the horror that filled him as he turned to face everyone . . . his throat so tight he couldn't swallow and beads of sweat trickling down his forehead. He could hear the teacher start the music three times before he tried to start singing. And worst of all, he could feel himself throwing up on the first row of his classmates before running from the room. It took the principal an hour to get him out of the bathroom and his mother a week to get him to return to school.

Danny shook his head and took a large gulp of his beer. He closed his eyes before thinking back to his crowning failure, Oral Communications class his sophomore year in high school, a class in which every student had to give speeches on topics of their choosing. He winced as he thought back to his first performance, a speech on the history of golf. He put himself back at his desk, his mind racing and his sweaty hand clutching his notes as he waited his turn and frantically searched for an escape. He remembered turning to face the class, then looking down to see his hands trembling uncontrollably. He could feel his perspiration-soaked shirt and vividly recalled the complete lack of moisture in his mouth. He felt like he was engulfed in flames. When he started his speech, his voice was quivering and was so soft his classmates had trouble hearing him. He wrapped up his planned fifteen-minute speech in five. He sat at his desk, exhausted, humiliated, and demoralized. He had two more speeches to give during the school year. The second and third didn't go as well as the first.

He scanned the countless moments when panic had struck out of nowhere, from grade school through his years of working in the office, any time he felt he was the center of attention or thought he might be getting into trouble, or felt confrontation was inevitable, or had to deal with an unfamiliar situation. Each one he replayed added to his anguish.

Danny took a deep breath, brushed aside a runaway tear, and pulled his mind back to the present. He thought about how content he'd been an hour before.

He had solved yet another high-profile customer issue, further cementing his standing as his software company's support guru. After work, he had gone for a jog and then to the grocery to stock up for the weekend. He had beer in the fridge, pizza in the freezer, some shows and movies waiting to be streamed, and an Ohio State game to watch Saturday night. All of that now seemed alien to him, like it was someone else's life.

He thought about his life, a life created with the sole purpose of having as little human interaction as possible. Since he worked from home, he didn't have to deal with co-workers or customers face-to-face. He had no friends, which meant he didn't have to constantly worry about what he did or said in social situations, whether he fit in with everyone else, or what other people thought of him. He had no family, so he didn't have to be concerned with nagging obligations. No tedious phone calls, painfully boring visits, or dreadful holiday gatherings. He had no girlfriend, which meant he didn't have to worry about what to talk about with her, how much attention he paid to her, what to buy her on special occasions, or where to take her on dates. His free time was his. He could do whatever he wanted any time he wanted as long as he was at his desk for work on time. Best of all, he had eliminated the debilitating, demoralizing anxiety attacks that used to strike from out of nowhere in countless business and social situations.

His life was simple. He kept his apartment, clothes, and car neat and clean. His activities consisted of working, running errands, watching movies and television, playing video games, jogging, and taking an occasional drive in the country outside Columbus. He paid his bills and taxes on time, never played music too loudly, and never intentionally made any automotive maneuver that could be considered the least bit hostile. He annoyed no one, stayed out of everyone's way, and was extremely polite during his limited personal interactions. He'd created the perfect world for himself.

That was one way of looking at it. Another, perhaps more realistic view, was that he was withdrawn from life. What he had actually built was a relatively stress-free but joyless existence. What he'd been considering his happy moments were actually just moments of relief from angst, stretches of time during which he felt no anxiety. But at no time did he feel any real happiness. When he felt content, it was really just a feeling of satisfaction that he'd kicked the world's ass by successfully building a life where no person or situation could get the better of him or make him feel out of control.

But he was trapped. Trapped in his job, trapped in his apartment, and, most of all, trapped by his issues. And now, the new assignment. It was too much to think about.

The second bottle was empty, and his jeans, tee, and quarter zip weren't standing up to the brisk breeze, so he went back inside.

"Son of a bitch!"

His scream echoed through his apartment. He banged the empty bottle down on the kitchen counter, grabbed another beer from the refrigerator, ripped off the cap, and took a large swig. Realizing he needed to get something in his stomach, he threw a frozen pizza into the oven. As he stood in the kitchen, unsure of his next move, he noticed a ladybug sitting on the kitchen counter.

"What the hell am I gonna do about this?" he yelled. "Huh? Help me out here."

Danny wandered back into his office and looked around as if he were surveying the scene of a train wreck. He stared at the screen for a few minutes before opening and rereading Gary's first email:

Danny,

I wanted to tell you again what a great job you did on the Caludyne issue. How quickly you resolve complex problems for our customers never ceases to amaze me. You are extremely valuable to this company and are appreciated by the entire management team.

I also need to let you know of a new assignment you've been given. I just got back from a meeting called by Nathan Forrester that included some VPs and directors. Nathan was fit to be tied. He's been getting bombarded the past few months with customers that have been irate about product quality. This Caludyne case was the last straw. Their president called him this afternoon and really tore into him. Nathan called the meeting to get to the bottom of it. What came out of it is that a lot of the newer programmers lack thorough product knowledge, especially in some of the more complex areas of the software.

Nathan wanted everyone's opinion on who in the company had the best knowledge of the product's functionality, history, code structure, database architecture, and how customers really use it. The consensus, with little debate, was that person is you.

I know you don't like to do this sort of thing, but Nathan wants you to do a series of training classes here in the office for our developers. The first, covering the production planning module, will be two weeks from today. Some of our newer consultants and support people will be attending too. It would be around twenty people.

Go ahead and start spending a couple of hours a day on the class format and materials. I'll see you here in the office two weeks from today.

Gary

As the reality of the situation hit him again, he sat quietly, sadly, with his arms folded, beer in hand, until the oven timer went off. The panic had been replaced with despair.

Danny decided it was time to escape, at least for a while, to the twenty-fourth century. After settling into his chair with his pizza and beer, he kicked off an episode of *Star Trek: The Next Generation*. The opening words were music to his ears: "Captain's log, star date 2531.3." The rich, distinguished voice of Jean-Luc Picard elicited a Pavlovian response. His shoulders fell. His jaw unclenched. His brow relaxed. He'd seen the episode at least five times, but it didn't matter. Danny wished he could go to Jean-Luc about his problem. He would know what to do and would advise Danny in a firm, fair, fatherly fashion.

Halfway through the episode Danny had finished his fifth beer and was considering whether to get another. He realized he had passed giddy relaxation and was on his way to becoming reasonably inebriated, but he knew it was making him feel better, or at least feel less. He also realized that if he continued, he was in danger of feeling like hell in the morning. Ultimately though, he didn't care, so he wobbled back to the kitchen and grabbed a sixth mind-numbing bottle.

Over the next few hours Danny ate most of the pizza, downed a few more beers, and watched three more episodes of *Star Trek*. The trips to the kitchen for each beer became treks of their own. Despite being more than a little inebriated, he was still disappointed when he pulled the last bottle from the fridge.

With each sip of beer his mind had gotten smaller. With his last smidgeon of mental activity, he convinced himself that something would happen to get him out of the assignment. Comforted by that thought, he let his brain go blank and his body go limp in his chair. His head rolled to the side, and he released the half-full bottle he had been clutching, sending it tumbling to the floor.

The ladybug left its perch on the television and flew toward him. After hovering in front of his face for a few moments, it ended its transmission, slid through the crack along the bottom of the apartment door, and headed back to its source, the spaceship hovering far above the passed-out Danny Kerrigan.

CHAPTER 2

Danny didn't move until bright sunlight pouring through the patio doors hit him in the face. Consciousness was followed ever so closely by incredible pain. As he reached for his throbbing head with both hands, a spike shot down the left side of his neck. A churning stomach added to his discomfort. He had yet to open his eyes due to the brightness of the sun when he realized that it shouldn't have been an issue. He distinctly remembered closing his curtains before settling in for *Star Trek*.

Danny slowly opened his eyes, blinking and squinting as they struggled to adapt to the direct sunlight. As he pushed himself out of the chair, he got his first glimpse of who had opened the curtains.

"What the hell?" he yelled as he stumbled over the arm of the chair. The two men sitting on his sofa didn't move.

"Hello, Danny," said the one closest to him.

"What . . . what the hell are you doing here? Who are you? What do you want?" A pounding heart, rapid breathing, and trembling were added to Danny's list of maladies.

"Please try to calm down. We only want to talk to you."

The person speaking was a large, distinguished-looking man with mostly silver hair and a well-trimmed, salt-and-pepper beard. His companion was a much smaller, much less distinguished-looking, mostly bald man. Both appeared to be in their seventies. They were dressed nearly identically in mock turtlenecks, pants, and jackets, all black.

"Then why the hell did you break into my apartment? You could have just knocked on the door."

"I'm sorry about that, but we felt it was necessary. We wanted to speak with you, and we feared that if we knocked, you might not have answered, much less let us in. We're not ruffians, so we wouldn't have forced our way in. This was really the best course of action. I do apologize for startling you so."

While he was speaking, Danny glanced toward the door and then at his phone.

"Danny, we're not going to harm you, and we don't want anything from you. You have nothing we could possibly want. We do want to discuss something with you, but we're not going to create a ruckus over it. If you try to dash out the door or call the police, we won't try to stop you. We will simply leave, never to return, which would be quite a shame, really. You'd be missing out on the experience of a lifetime, so I do hope you hear us out."

Danny had unconsciously relaxed and was becoming curious.

"Okay then," he said slowly. "I'll listen. What could you possibly want to talk to me about?"

"First," the man said as he rose from the sofa and approached Danny, "let's have some proper introductions."

As the man neared, Danny saw that he was indeed a powerful presence. He was at least six-foot-three, with broad shoulders and striking blue eyes that exuded wisdom, warmth, and confidence. He had a definite air of authority about him.

"My name is Kingsley Vortex," he said as he extended his hand. "You, I sincerely hope, are Danny Kerrigan?"

Danny cautiously shook his hand.

"Yes, yes I am."

"And this is my associate, Shey Gabink." Kingsley turned toward his companion.

The other man rose and finally spoke. "Hello, Danny. It's a pleasure to meet you," he said as he shuffled over and firmly shook Danny's hand before returning to his spot on the sofa.

Shey, who was nearly a foot shorter than Kingsley, exuded confidence but not power. And he had a smirk on his face, as if he was amused by the situation and was going to break out laughing at any moment.

"You guys sure have some unusual names," Danny said as he winced from the pain of an especially strong throb in his head.

Kingsley glanced around the apartment. "I'm guessing that's related to all the empty bottles I see scattered about?"

Danny felt slightly embarrassed. "Yeah. I had a few too many."

"Well, that happens. Perhaps this will help," Kingsley said. He reached into his jacket and pulled out a flat silver case. He flipped open the lid and held it out to Danny. "Take one of the green ones. It will eliminate your symptoms."

The case contained several rows of large capsules, each row containing a different color. Danny hesitated.

"Go ahead, take one. They're far superior to any remedies you have on hand. Not only will it make you feel better, but it would be helpful if you had a clear head for our discussion. It won't hurt you. If that was our mission, we could have done you in while you were sleeping."

Danny grabbed one of the pills, went to the kitchen for water, and swallowed it. In a matter of seconds, he experienced a sensation he'd never felt before, as if the entire inside of his body were being flushed with a cool, refreshing wave of . . . something. His headache dissipated, his stomach quit churning, and his mental clarity returned to almost normal.

"Oh my God," Danny said with wonder.

"Pretty neat, isn't it?" Kingsley said when Danny returned to the living room. "It looks as though you've got something going on in your neck, too. Shey is one of the best body workers you'll find anywhere. Mind if he takes a look at it? Shey, would you please relieve Danny of his neck pain?"

Danny didn't object as Shey hopped up, sat him down on the ottoman, and started prodding his neck, shoulders, and back. As he continued his examination, Danny's curiosity returned. "So what do you want to talk to me about anyway?"

Kingsley had wandered over to Danny's collection of DVDs and was reviewing the titles.

"Don't you have streaming services for watching such things?"

"I do. I bought all of those before streaming existed."

"*The Last Starfighter, Stargate, Mission to Mars, Interstellar,* six *Star Wars,* nine *Star Treks,* a dozen *Star Trek: The Next Generation.* It appears as though you have quite an appetite for science fiction."

"Yeah, I guess so. I like it a lot," Danny said just before gasping as Shey hit a tender spot.

"Ah. There it is," Shey said. "Now begin breathing slowly and deeply until I tell you to stop."

Shey pressed on a spot at the base of Danny's skull, close to his left ear, with one hand and a spot halfway down the left side of his back with the other. He pressed hard, with the tips of his fingers, for several seconds before taking a step back. "Okay, stop the deep breathing. That should do it."

"Oh my God. It's, like, mostly gone."

"Of course it is," Kingsley said. "Now tell me, Danny, what is it about space stories that enchants you so?"

"I don't know. I just like it. It's different than normal life. I like being able . . . hey, listen, I appreciate the pill and what he did for my neck, but I still have to ask, what the hell are you guys doing here? What do you want with me?"

"Danny, what would you say if I gave you the opportunity to experience the sort of things you see on these shows? I mean, really experience it?"

"You mean one of those simulations like they do at the studio theme parks?"

Kingsley chuckled. "Heavens no. I'm talking about the real thing. Going into outer space for an adventure, just like all of these people in these stories you watch."

Danny looked suspicious. "Okay, I know they're selling trips on space shuttles, but that's for a small number of people and costs millions of dollars. Why in the world would you ask me to go?"

"I'm not talking about a couple trips around Earth in a primitive shuttle. I'm offering you the chance to travel around the universe, see other planets, other species, on a real spaceship. Surely you've dreamed about such a trip?"

"Will you still leave if I call the police?" Danny asked.

"I'm about to tell you something that you'll find quite extraordinary, but I'm hoping you'll use your intelligence and imagination and have an open mind to everything you hear."

"Go on."

"Shey and I are not from this planet."

"I knew you were going to say that. Could you please leave now?"

"Hear me out," said Kingsley. "Why is this so hard for you to believe? Are you saying you watch hour upon hour of stories that depict space travel and life on other planets, but you totally dismiss the possibility when I tell you we are aliens?"

Danny glanced over at the still-smirking Shey. "Maybe I need more than two guys just breaking into my apartment telling me they're from outer space. Maybe I need to see a spaceship land and you get out."

"Our ship is hovering above your planet as we speak. It's much too large to land undetected, so we came down last night in a transport that is parked below your balcony."

Kingsley slid open the patio door and beckoned Danny outside.

Danny moved to the balcony and looked down at the vehicle parked below. It was slightly larger than a minivan, silver, with a sloped nose and curved front corners. In place of the front windshield were two dark rectangular panels.

"There it is," Kingsley said almost proudly, "the Star Hopper KX 300. Don't ask me what the KX stands for. But it's the state-of-the-art transport . . . fast, maneuverable, with a good defense system. Its most efficient mode is to glide along above the ground, but we do end up visiting many planets that are not yet aware. Most of them have vehicles with wheels, like Earth, so we use them so that we don't draw attention to ourselves."

"Aware of what?"

"Of life on other planets. It's one of four stages the inhabitants of planets go through. They are either *oblivious*, which means they have no concept that life may exist elsewhere, they *suspect*, which means that a sizable number of the inhabitants are open to the possibility and may actually believe it, they are *aware*, which means they have definitive knowledge of life on other planets but have yet to achieve significant space travel themselves, or they *travel*, which means they are sufficiently advanced that their population can travel about space freely and easily, as easily as you travel around your roadways, for example. It's called the OSAT system. Earth suspects. It probably won't be too long before you are aware. Now, tell me if you've ever seen a vehicle like that before."

"I can't say that I have."

Kingsley headed back inside, Danny following closely.

"Then there is the hangover cure I gave you. Have you ever heard of anything that can come close to doing what that pill did? We also have the technology to scan your planet's computer systems and acquire whatever information we like. For example, we know that you are Danny Kerrigan. Your parents were Bill and Sally Kerrigan, both of whom have passed away. You are an only child. You grew up in a small town in western Ohio, sought higher education at an institution called The Ohio State University, and have been working at a computer software company called Vertran Systems since you left school. Your social security number is—"

"You could get that information easily," Danny interrupted, "and the van and probably even the hangover pill if you worked for a government agency."

"Yes, well, we've heard that one before. What would a government agency want with you?"

"What would a couple of aliens want with me?"

"We'll get to that, but not until you believe, or at least believe it is possible, that we're aliens. Perhaps a further display of our technology would help."

Kingsley pulled a device from inside his jacket. It looked like a sleek, sliver pistol.

"This is the Zapper MR5. The MR stands for multi-ray. It is the state of the art in handheld weapons," he said as he pointed it at the wall and pulled the trigger. A thin green beam was emitted.

"It has a basic, five-level energy ray of varying strengths, the effects of which will range anywhere from temporarily disabling to vaporizing most known life-forms. Of course, there is some guesswork involved since you have to factor in the power and physical makeup of the being you are combating. For example, level one would knock a Trigillian out cold for several U-mins, while if you were zapping a Grugnok, you would have to be on level three before you'd even get their attention."

"U-mins?"

"Yes, a U-min. It's an increment of universal time, roughly one and three quarters of your minutes."

"Universal time?"

"Yes, universal time. U-time. Every planet has its own time-keeping system. The length of your day broken down into your increments would mean nothing to someone living on Zanum or Maltair. So, a universal time-keeping system was created by PUPCO to—"

"PUPCO?"

"Planets United for Peaceful Coexistence. PUPCO is an organization with representation from almost all planets that travel. It's not unlike your United Nations, I suppose. It's an arena for all planets to air grievances, work out differences, and learn about each other. It has several branches for such things as establishing policy for proper travel between systems, planet visitation protocol, dealing with cultural differences, and arriving at systems to smooth interaction such as U-time and a universal currency system. Anyway, tell me your government has such a weapon," Kingsley said as he tucked the MR5 back into his jacket.

"No . . . no, I don't suppose they do," Danny said with a pensive, per-plexed look. It was all starting to sound pretty cool. "If you're aliens, why do you look human?"

"Reasonable question. Roughly eighty percent of the beings in the uni-verse are humanoid. They'd be able to walk down any street on Earth and fit right in. There are exceptions of course. The Grugnok being the most prom-inent. They have humanoid characteristics but look more like large reptiles."

"And what is it you want from me?"

"Danny, we'd like to take you on an adventure. I am from the planet Yoobatar. Shey is from Drimmil. We are searchers, a cross between a private investigator and a treasure hunter. I am hired and paid, quite handsomely, to find and retrieve people, information, or precious things that have been lost or stolen. Shey is my assistant, my right-hand man. We have been doing this for a very long time and have never, I repeat never, failed on a mission.

"For most missions we recruit one or more beings from some planet that doesn't travel, usually from one that suspects but isn't aware. We find it is often very helpful to have another being along to help out with various simple, rather menial tasks. We've found that using someone from a planet that doesn't travel works out nicely since they don't demand a large portion of our fee. Plus, they tend to do what we ask with enthusiasm and wonder, since the entire situation is so new and exciting for them.

"The payoff for the recruit is that they get an experience of a lifetime, a chance to witness technology and visit worlds the likes of which they've seen only in science fiction. They also get to learn about the universe from two incredibly well-traveled individuals. Which reminds me of another benefit to us. Missions can have a lot of downtime when traveling from planet to planet and, quite honestly, Shey and I ran out of interesting things to say to one another long ago. We like to get a recruit from a different planet each time so that we can learn about it from someone who lives there. Reading all the intelligence gathered about a planet is one thing, but hearing about the experience of living on a planet from an actual inhabitant is much more interesting."

"You have intelligence on Earth?" Danny asked.

"We do. PUPCO has been monitoring Earth's planetary affairs and scientific advancements for some time. Our approach is to arrive at the planet and have our ship's computer scour the planet's information systems for beings who fit our model. Once we have the list of a few hundred prime candidates, we dispatch a swarm of iggies to keep each one—"

"Iggies?"

"Information-gathering devices. They are mechanisms that we send out in the form of some type of small insect that is native to the area in which the candidate resides. They keep each being under surveillance for a day or so, to see what else we can learn about them, things that would eliminate them from consideration. I believe your iggy was what you would call a ladybug. The iggies report back and load what they've acquired into our ship's computer. It analyzes the audio and video and comes up with a list of the top twenty candidates. Shey and I then make a visit to the one we feel is the most interesting, would be the most likely to accept our offer, and is the most suitable for the job."

"So I was the best person on Earth?" Danny asked incredulously.

"Not exactly," Kingsley replied. "You made the top twenty but weren't actually our first choice from the list. Scans of your internet told us that you do live alone and have no family. You are in reasonably good health. We found that you did well in school and that you're extremely interested in science-fiction, adventure, and espionage movies. You work from home and have no friends. And you are considered to be a top-notch employee and are a problem-solver by trade.

"On the surface you were a perfect candidate. However, the iggy's surveillance showed that you became quite enraged last night upon reading something on your computer. You apparently were upset the remainder of the evening, so upset that you emptied all of these bottles and passed out in the chair. The fact that you were upset is not necessarily bad. We assumed last night was an anomaly. However, it was enough to knock you out of the top spot. The competition is stiff in the top twenty."

Shey piped up. "I'd like to be stiff in a few of the top twenty."

"Shey," Kingsley said sternly. "I apologize, Danny. Shey fancies himself a ladies' man. His appetite for sampling the carnal offerings of the planets we visit has jeopardized more than one mission. I've considered having him fixed, but he puts up quite a fuss whenever I bring up the subject."

Shey sat quietly, his smirk having been replaced with a mischievous, somewhat silly grin.

"I didn't pass out," Danny said defensively. "I was a little tipsy and really tired, so I fell asleep in the chair. So others have turned you down?"

"Let's just say that we're finding earthlings to lack a spirit of adventure. We've never had so much trouble finding a recruit. We've approached seven others in the last ten of your hours, all of whom either didn't believe us or couldn't bring themselves to join us. In any event, we're starting to think that coming to Earth was a mistake. If you turn us down, we're going to have to dive into this case without an assistant. Back to last night. What was it exactly that upset you so?"

"It was nothing, really. It was just that my boss wants me to do this special project for work, and I don't want to do it. I was just on edge from a stressful situation I'd been dealing with all day, and my boss's request kind of set me off."

"I see. That's understandable. Am I correct that your little drinking binge was atypical?"

"Absolutely. I mean, I like beer, but I usually only have a couple. Sometimes a few."

"In that case I would like to officially extend you an offer to join us on our current quest. I know you'll find it to be easily the most interesting and exciting thing you've ever done, an adventure you'll never forget. What do you say?"

Danny had been playing along, acting as though he was seriously considering Kingsley's proposal. He took a step back to review everything that had happened and contemplate Kingsley's claims. He was still concerned it was all an elaborate ruse and that they intended to harm him. Even if it wasn't, even if it was truly an adventure in space, the thought of walking out of his apartment into something so unknown made his stomach churn again. What had happened so far was really enough of an adventure for him.

"Thanks, but I think I'll pass."

Kingsley was crestfallen. "What's the problem, Danny? Don't you believe what I'm telling you?"

"Actually, I think I might. But I can't just up and leave here for . . . how long would I be gone?"

"Probably about a week to ten days of your time."

"I can't just up and leave here for that long. I mean, I've got to go to work, and I've got bills that need paid, and . . ."

"And you've got beer to drink and movies to watch? I'm guessing that if you really wanted to, you could get off work for a couple of weeks. What's the real problem, Danny? What are you afraid of?"

"Nothing . . . I don't know. What's this mission you're on?" Danny asked.

Kingsley sighed. "You earthlings are a timid lot. I was hoping not to get into it, but if it will ease your mind, I'll elaborate."

CHAPTER 3

"Our current mission," Kingsley continued, "is special because it is for the royal family of my home planet, the Quilicants. I have actually been retired from the business for some time now, but the current queen, Vivitar Quilicant, coaxed me into one more mission. Our task is to find and return to the Quilicants the Tablet of Jakaroo, an item that has been the subject of folklore for a very long time.

"Legend has it that over two hundred Yoobatarian years ago, Shintar Quilicant was exploring the ancient ruins at Jakaroo when he discovered an amulet along with a tablet. The tablet explained, supposedly, that the amulet had mystical properties that dramatically boosted the charisma and appeal of whoever was wearing it, giving the person a great deal of influence over people. The tablet also contained instructions on how to recreate the amulet. Shintar, who had little experience in governing but had aspirations of being the leader of Yoobatar, wore the amulet constantly and it worked. He amassed a formidable number of followers and convinced the masses that the current ruling family needed to be replaced. The end result was that Shintar became the king of Yoobatar.

"Shintar's family never approved of the amulet. They felt that artificially enhancing your appeal to gain the loyalty and support of the people was deceitful and corrupt. Shintar had no such qualms and wore it until his death. At that time, his family destroyed the amulet but not the tablet. It was stored in a secure location on the family's compound. Shintar's eldest offspring, Balibar, became king after Shintar's death.

"Balibar and his descendants have ruled Yoobatar ever since, quite fabulously, I might add, without the use of the amulet. To this day, Shintar's descendants consider the entire episode a black eye on the family history, that it tarnishes their legacy. For that reason, they've never acknowledged the story as true and never admitted the tablet's existence. Until now. The tablet is missing. The Quilicants contacted me, explained what I've just told you, and hired us to track down the thief and retrieve it. I was reluctant, but then they offered what would be the largest fee of my career, five million U-bucks . . . PUPCO's universal currency. I've amassed quite a fortune already, but my wife and I enjoy a rather upscale lifestyle, so I took the job."

"Why don't they just send their military after it?" Danny asked.

"Because there will need to be a lot of searching for clues, deductive reasoning, playing hunches, and using contacts I've made over the years. A military operation, even if it were a small group of highly trained specialists, would be a bit clumsy and have a strong chance of being discovered. This needs to be an ultra-clandestine operation."

"Why do they want it back so badly?"

"One reason is the current queen, Vivitar Quilicant, does not want the existence of the tablet to be confirmed and become common knowledge. If that happened, thousands of beings would start looking for it, which would really muck things up. And, it would definitely tarnish their legacy. The people of Yoobatar could possibly demand the Quilicants be removed from power because they achieved their position unethically. But the main reason is that they suspect the tablet was stolen by an unscrupulous scoundrel who is planning on using it to overthrow them, in the same way Shintar Quilicant did when he first found it."

"If it's so important, why did you spend an entire night recruiting a helper? Aren't you in a hurry?" Danny asked.

"According to the legend, the amulet's special power is created by a very specific combination of five crystals imbedded in a particular metal. Each component is very rare. The tablet gives the exact location on the specific planet where each crystal can be found. However, it only gives the instructions one crystal at a time. When each crystal is placed on the tablet, the instructions, or hints, for finding the next one appear. We have one of the fastest ships around, so we have little doubt we'll be able to catch up to the thief long before he is anywhere close to creating an amulet. Now, the mission calls and I've grown weary of this recruiting visit. You have a lovely planet, but I'm working harder at this than I care to. I need an answer, Danny. Will you be going with us?"

Danny wandered over to the patio door, staring down at Kingsley's vehicle.

"It sounds kind of neat, it really does, but . . . I'm sorry, I just can't leave my life for something like that. You make it sound fun and interesting, and I think I actually believe you, but I don't know what's really going to happen or if I'll ever come back. It sounds like it could actually be kind of dangerous . . . and scary. I'm sorry. I can't go."

"I don't really understand, but I accept your decision. Shey and I will go this one alone. Shey, let's go. Danny, it was interesting meeting you and some of your planetmates. I'm glad we finally made it to Earth, even if it was a fruitless visit. I wish you well in your future endeavors."

Kingsley turned before exiting to throw him the newspaper that had been resting outside the door.

"Good luck with that special project at work that had you so upset last night. Goodbye, Danny."

They were gone before Danny could reply, leaving him alone with the dark cloud of the training class looming over him once again. He thought back to the events of the prior evening, his growing angst and anguish changing to anger as he thought of Nathan Forrester's decree.

"Son of a bitch!" he screamed as he flung the paper at the door. As he stood in his living room, trembling, he glanced over at the clock to find it was 8:30 and remembered it was Friday. "Oh great, now I'm late for work," he said before hurrying back to his office. As he opened his email and saw the previous night's messages, a wave of panic started building. He staggered back to the living room, somewhat lightheaded from the growing anxiety. His apartment seemed more quiet and more empty than ever before. Kingsley and Shey's visit almost seemed unreal, even though it had ended only a few minutes before.

In a flash Danny was out the door and running down the steps. As he landed at ground level, he ran into the parking lot and stared down the road leading out of the complex.

"Looking for someone?"

Danny spun to see the Star Hopper still parked below his balcony, a smug-looking Kingsley leaning against it with his arms crossed.

"You . . . you didn't leave yet," Danny gasped, trying to catch his breath and calm down.

"Very observant, Danny. You should be great at surveillance. I knew we had a winner when we picked you."

"I want to go with you. How soon can we leave?"

"Wonderful. We can leave as soon as you are ready. You don't need to pack anything. We have everything you could possibly need, but you can bring a few things if it would make you more comfortable."

"I think I will. I have to get approval from my manager. And I need to stop the newspaper and mail before we leave."

"You go take care of all that. Shey and I will wait here. Shey?" Kingsley looked around for his assistant to find him five parking spots away, his arm around the waist of a tall blonde as they walked toward the building.

"You won't regret this," he was telling her. "I've picked up some techniques in my travels that I think you'll find astonishing. If I showed you nothing more than a Darzillian Inverted Twister, you'd feel indebted to me for the rest of your life. And, if you're up for it, I could—"

"Shey! Get back here. We don't have time for that!" Kingsley yelled.

Shey froze in his tracks, visibly upset about his escapade being foiled only a few steps from the woman's door. "This won't take long, really. You guys go ahead and get Danny ready for the trip. I'll be along in, say . . . fifteen minutes."

"Shey, come along. Now!"

Shey offered an apology to the disappointed young lady and shuffled back to the Star Hopper with his head down. "I was just trying to use the knowledge I've accumulated to spread joy about the universe."

"Yes, I know what you were trying to spread. You know it would have taken me a good hour to get you out of there and I'm not in the mood. We're going to wait while Danny takes care of a couple of things, and then we're leaving."

As Kingsley and Shey waited by the Star Hopper, Danny threw some things in a duffel bag, put his mail and paper on hold, and made sure he had no bills coming due before calling his boss. Gary reluctantly approved the request after Danny convinced him that he could take the time off and still be ready for the training class.

As he reached the bottom of the steps and started toward the Star Hopper, Danny stopped and looked back at his apartment. Kingsley motioned for Shey to prepare the transport for departure and returned to a worried-looking Danny.

"Is there a problem?"

"I don't know about all this. It's so unlike me to up and do something crazy. It's so . . . unknown."

"Danny, it may be uncomfortable at times, but exploring the unknown, experiencing the unfamiliar, is what makes life interesting and exciting. Think of it this way: everything you currently know was unknown to you at some point."

"I guess it was," Danny said pensively. "Okay. Let's do it before I change my mind."

Kingsley led Danny around to the side of the transport. The door quickly slid to the side with a barely audible *whoosh*. Kingsley stepped in and motioned for Danny to do the same.

The ceiling was close to seven feet high. To his right were two plush, black leather seats. Behind them was a wall containing a door and several compartments. To his left were four more seats, the front two of which were occupied by Shey and Kingsley. Large windows lined the sides, and a glass panel dominated the ceiling. At the very front was a console containing display screens and touch panels. Shey was seated in the left of the two front chairs, studying a map on one of the screens. The walls and floor were black, accented with brushed chrome hardware and elegant wood trim. Small lights imbedded in the ceiling gave the interior of the vehicle a soft glow.

"Do you like it, Danny?" Kingsley asked.

"Yeah, sure," he mumbled, trying to take it all in.

"Do you like the colors? My wife wanted a white exterior with tan leather and taupe walls, but I like the silver with black. I think it's more sophisticated and masculine, and, after all, I'm the one who uses it the most. Now, take the seat behind Shey and we'll get going. Shey, take us back to the ship."

Danny looked out the windows and saw a handful of his neighbors out and about. "We're just going to take off with all of these people around?"

"Of course not. That would create more of a ruckus than we would like to leave behind, and PUPCO wouldn't be very pleased with us if we did that. We're going to move to an isolated area away from the city before departing," Kingsley said as Shey slowly backed the Star Hopper from its spot, stopped, and started creeping forward.

"Why don't you let Max drive? Max is the Star Hopper's computer, Danny."

"You know I like to have control when driving around a strange planet."

"Well then, let's pick it up."

"Leave me alone."

"You drive like a Maroovian swamp sloth!" shouted Kingsley.

"How many times do I have to tell you? I drive with extra care when we're on unaware planets because if we had an accident, the police would be summoned, and an unpleasant scene would ensue. Now leave me alone."

"That makes sense. Thank you for explaining. Danny, I'm afraid it won't be much of an adventure for you, since it appears we're going to spend the next two weeks getting out of this parking lot. The thief will have made an amulet, ousted the Quilicants, and will be ruling Yoobatar by the time we get back. And of course, I'll have to explain to my wife why we're out the five million U-bucks. If I survive that conversation, we'll spend the rest of our lives in reduced circumstances. Shey will have to look for new employment, since I certainly won't be able to afford an assistant."

Shey abruptly stopped the vehicle and sat defiantly with his arms crossed.

"Shey, now is not the time to pout. We've got to get started on the mission. And, we've got a guest. I asked you to be on your best behavior. Now make this damn thing move," Kingsley said firmly.

"Yes, we do have a guest, in front of whom you just insulted me. The only way this damn thing is moving is if you drive it out of here or apologize."

Kingsley sighed. "I'm sorry I criticized your driving in front of the earthling."

Shey was appeased if not pleased by the apology. He exited the lot and headed out of town, stopping on an isolated stretch of road.

"This looks good," he said while examining one of the console's view screens. "There are only seventeen people in a three-mile radius. Twelve of them are indoors, which leaves five potential spotters. The closest is just over a mile away. There are currently no aircraft in the area. Shall we?"

"Proceed," Kingsley replied.

Danny clutched the arms of his chair as he sensed the craft leaving the ground.

"Wait! Let me out!" he blurted as the ship accelerated straight up.

"Too late, Danny. We're on our way," Kingsley said without looking back.

Danny glanced out the window and saw the ground rapidly dropping away. As the ship smoothly shifted from moving straight up to ascending at an angle, nose first, he saw his neighborhood, then Columbus, then the United States all get smaller at an incredible rate. As he doubled over and wrapped his arms around his stomach, he took another peek out his window.

"Oh God, what have I done?" he moaned as he saw a good deal of the planet below.

"Everything okay, Danny?" Kingsley asked over his shoulder.

"I don't feel so good."

"That's quite normal. Your first trip into space can be a disorienting experience. Put your head back, close your eyes, and do some slow, deep breathing. It'll make you feel a lot better."

Danny followed Kingsley's advice and quickly unclenched. He was brought back by Kingsley announcing that they were approaching the ship.

"There she is, the *Aurora*, named after my wife."

Danny leaned up between the front seats to see. They were headed directly for a ship that sat motionless above them. It appeared to be enormous, as large as a football field. Like the Star Hopper, it had a sloped, rounded nose with several large panels across the front. The body of the ship was rectangular. The top and back end were flat, but the sides curved slightly. Rows of windows lining the side told Danny that there were four floors.

As they drew nearer to the *Aurora*, the transport moved directly under it, came to a stop, and started moving straight up again. Danny looked up through the ceiling windows to see that they were moving toward an opening in the bottom of the ship. He glanced out the side at distant Earth and again wished he was back at his apartment.

As the Star Hopper disappeared into the ship, Kingsley yelled back to him. "Ready for your adventure, Danny?"

"I guess so," he said, as the *Aurora*'s door slid shut beneath them.

CHAPTER 4

As the transport came to rest and the faint hum of the propulsion system ceased, Danny wasn't nearly as anxious as he would normally feel in much less unfamiliar situations. The reason was Kingsley. He had immediately felt comfortable around the stranger with the fantastic story. Danny trusted him. And liked him. He had the feeling, a very comforting feeling, that Kingsley would take care of him, that he would not let anything bad happen to him. As Shey shuffled past him toward the exit, Kingsley rose and looked down at Danny.

"After you."

Danny cautiously stepped out of the transport, bag in hand, into a huge, well-lit room, probably fifty feet front to back and a hundred feet wide, with fifteen-foot ceilings. He noticed banks of windows on both sides of the room and was confused by what appeared to be trees and blue sky visible on one side, with sunlight streaming in from the other.

"I thought we'd start with a tour of the ship and then get a bite of lunch," Kingsley said. "Does that sound good, or would you prefer to clean up and get into some fresh clothes? Or would you like to lie down for a while first? The hangover remedy I gave you does wonders with the symptoms, but your body will still need some rest to recuperate from what you did to it."

"No," Danny said, still gazing around the room.

"No what?"

"I'm not tired."

"You're not tired and . . . ?" Kingsley asked.

Danny looked puzzled. "I'm not tired and . . . and so I don't want to take a nap?"

"And so you'd like to . . . ?"

"I guess I'd like to see the ship," Danny said, with all the enthusiasm of someone choosing between a prostate exam and an IRS audit.

"You guess? That gives one the impression you don't know the correct answer. Is that it? Or is it that you really have no strong preference? Why don't you wait here and think about it? If you get tired, you can stretch out on the floor. I'll be back for you in a few hours."

"No," Danny shouted, as Kingsley headed for a pair of sliding doors. "I'd like to see the ship."

"That's more like it. Danny, you are now officially a member of my crew. I'm not a mind reader, so I expect you to state your preferences when asked and interject your opinion when not. It also would impress me if you showed the proper excitement when presented with something that obviously should excite you. Do you not find the prospect of touring a genuine space vessel to be exciting?"

"Yes, I guess I . . . yes, yes, I do," Danny said.

"That's better. At least a little. Allow me to show you my ship, or as I prefer to think of it, my home in space. My people determined long ago that extended space travel is more palatable if ships simulate being at home. Our military vessels are rather utilitarian, probably something like you are used to seeing in your science fiction, but privately owned ships are quite the opposite. The architecture, decor, and technology are completely geared toward making you forget you are on a spaceship. For the most part, we refer to everything on the ship using terms that relate to a house. For example, we are in the garage, which is in the level we call the basement," Kingsley explained as he and Shey strolled past and around the front of the transport. "It is where the Star Hopper is kept and . . ." Kingsley backtracked toward Danny, who hadn't moved. "Danny, in case you missed it, this is a tour. Where I come from, a tour consists of a guide and participants, with the latter typically following the former. I would be the guide in this situation. Is there a problem? Are your feet stuck to the floor?"

"Uh . . . no, no problem. I didn't know if I was supposed to follow you. I thought maybe I probably should, but you didn't say anything. I just wasn't sure if I was supposed to, and I didn't want to . . ."

"Think, Danny! Think clearly and act assertively. I encourage you to be bold. If you don't know, ask. Timidity won't cut it around here. Now try to keep up."

Though his words seemed harsh, they felt more to Danny like encouragement than a scolding.

"The garage is in the middle of the lower level and extends from one side of the ship to the other," Kingsley continued. "It's by far the largest room on the ship, if you don't count the yard. It's a three-transport garage. Along the back wall are a number of small vessels called Solo Treks. They're used for individual trips from the ship. I saw you staring at the windows. That's the feature of this ship that makes me most feel like I'm at home. All of the exterior windows can be in either space mode or Yoobie mode," Kingsley explained as he made his way toward one of the windows.

"In space mode, they are true windows that allow you to see the space outside the ship. In Yoobie mode, the views out the window are exactly what you would see from the windows of a building on Yoobatar. It's a complete simulation, right down to the sun rising and setting and an estimation of the weather on Yoobatar, based on the current season. The view can be controlled room by room." Kingsley had slowly made his way to the window. "This is the view from the east side of my country house in the Ontaga region. It's late spring right now on Yoobatar."

Danny looked out the window and understood immediately why Kingsley liked it so much. Once his eyes adjusted to the bright sunlight, what he saw reminded him of the western United States. Stretching out from the window were acres of gently rolling land dotted with small patches of trees and wildflowers. In the distance was an enormous, crystal-blue lake, and beyond that a row of snow-capped mountains.

"All in all it's an amazing system. It really does keep you from being homesick, and the day-night simulation keeps your body in its rhythms. I keep the windows in Yoobie mode most of the time. So what do you think?"

"It's . . . it's pretty neat," Danny said softly.

"I see we still need a little work on the enthusiasm. Oh well—we've plenty of time for that. Come along."

Kingsley headed toward their starting point. "There are four floors on the ship. As I said, we were in the middle of the lower level. Through the doors between the Solo Treks is the back third of the lower level, home to storage rooms and engineering."

Kingsley motioned to three sets of doors along the opposite wall. "The middle set of doors lead to the front third of the ship, which contains the main kitchen, food storage, and the greenhouse. There's a kitchen on the main floor that we use most of the time. The one down here is a larger, commercial-style kitchen that we only use if I know I'm going to be entertaining important clients with large entourages. In that event I often bring along my personal chef and his staff. That area also has extra bedrooms and common living spaces they use. The doors on the far right lead to where we store the heavy weaponry. The ones on the left lead to the lift. We'll be heading through those."

As the doors closed behind them, Danny saw that they were in a wide hallway. He felt as though he had stepped into a someone's home—and an elegant home at that. The floor was gleaming marble, mostly cream, with streaks of gold and black, with a beautiful Persian-looking rug running the length of the hall. The walls, a deep shade of red, were home to several large landscape paintings hanging over a pair of gorgeous, upholstered chairs.

"This is the entrance hall. Those are exterior doors at the end," he said, motioning down the hall to the left. "Most visitors I receive dock their ship there and enter through those doors. They use this lift, which takes them up to the reception area on the main floor. I end up doing a lot of business dealings on the ship, so I had to buy a ship that was designed for accepting, entertaining, housing, and hopefully impressing potential clients."

Kingsley entered the lift with Danny on his heels. It was about eight feet square and decorated in a similar fashion to that of the hall, with paneled walls, crown molding, and another elegant rug covering most of the hardwood floor.

"Foyer," Shey said, before they began to ascend.

"This is one of two lifts." Kingsley's zeal told Danny that he obviously loved showing off his ship. "There is another one at the very back of the ship."

As the lift came to a halt, the set of doors behind Danny opened. Danny turned and stepped from the lift to find himself in a brightly lit, circular room. Around the curved walls were several open doorways. On the walls were paintings, along with niches that were home to small sculptures. The marble floor was cream and gold, with an enormous black V in the center. Danny looked up to find the source of the room's light, a domed ceiling that depicted a bright blue sky with white puffy clouds, one of which was blocking a sun.

"We call this the foyer. It's where we greet all arriving guests," Kingsley explained. Danny's attention and gaze, both fixed on the ceiling, were interrupted by a rapid-fire clicking sound. He looked down just in time to get a glimpse of a furry black blur before it hit, and hit hard, knocking him back into the wall. As Danny tried to fend off the beast's attack, he realized the creature was licking his face, not going for his jugular.

"Abby!" Kingsley shouted. "How many times have I told you not to jump on the guests. Now leave Danny alone."

The blur backed off far enough for Danny to see it was a dog, a large black dog that backed off but remained excited, prancing around in front of Danny with its tail going a mile a minute. It appeared to be a Labrador retriever.

"Sorry about that, Danny. This breed is supposed to be mellow as well as extremely loyal and friendly. Unfortunately, I'm still waiting for Abby to grasp the mellow part. She's been an adult for some time now, but she still exhibits the exuberance of a puppy from time to time, especially when we have a visitor." Kingsley bent over to rub and accept a few licks from the enthusiastic dog. "Hello, sweetie, did you miss me? Are you okay, Danny?"

"Yeah, I'm fine. It scared me more than anything."

"Now, if I may proceed, the foyer is the hub of the front half of the main floor. All of the living and entertaining spaces are situated around this circle. At the front of the ship is the living room." Kingsley motioned to a large wall that was directly across from the lift's doors. The wall was framed by two doorways that mirrored a pair on each side of the lift. "It's home to the bridge, casual dining, and kitchen. We spend most our time there when not in our rooms.

"The next doorway to the right leads to the great room. It's a huge room with multiple conversation groupings, large television screens, and tables for game playing. It's where my guests can go to relax during travel time or breaks between meetings. But my guests aren't always here for business. I have a rather large extended family, so I often take them all on holiday. When I do so, the great room gets heavy use. To the right of that is the conference room. Any questions yet, Danny?"

"Nope."

"My, you're just a fountain of curiosity, aren't you?" said a lurking Shey. He had been so quiet that Danny had forgotten he was following them. He gave Shey a what's-your-problem look but said nothing.

"Shey, why don't you get started on some lunch?" said Kingsley.

Once Shey disappeared into the living room, Kingsley continued. "Danny, I want to apologize and warn you about Shey. Shey is Drimmillian. Drimmillians have a well-deserved reputation for being arrogant, sarcastic, stubborn, and brutally honest. Some consider them caustic. But, even with their annoying side, the Drimmillians make the finest assistants of any species in the galaxy. He has been with me since shortly after I started my career as a searcher. Drimmillians can excel at so many things because of a photographic memory and an uncanny ability to immediately comprehend the intricacies and nuances of anything to which they are exposed. He's also been my best friend for many years."

As Danny listened, he felt something wet and slightly slimy on his left hand. He looked down to find Abby lapping away.

"Hey," he said, as he pulled his hand away and wiped it on his pants. Abby ceased the licking but stayed at Danny's side.

"Looks like you've got a new best friend," Kingsley said before pointing at the door to the left of the living room. "That's our main dining room. It's where we have the formal meals with clients and where we often eat when I have my extended family aboard. To the left of that is our theater. We use it for entertaining our overnight guests after dinner with movies, sporting events, or readings from poetry or fine prose."

Kingsley motioned toward the hallways on each side of the lift. "Those lead to the back two-thirds of the main floor, which consists of our individual living suites and several guest rooms. Let's proceed."

Kingsley led Danny across the foyer, through a doorway, and down a short hallway that opened into the living room. Danny immediately liked and felt comfortable in the huge room, certainly the most casually decorated of those he'd seen. It was divided into three levels, each one step lower than the next. On the top level, to the right of the hallway from which they had emerged, was a kitchen that shared a wall with the foyer. It was separated from the rest of the room by a large island, one side of which was curved and lined with six stools that faced the kitchen. The stainless-steel appliances, antique white cabinets, and granite-looking counters were all less futuristic than Danny expected. Shey, busy creating a meal, paid no attention to them. He was whistling along to the upbeat classical music that played softly over the room's speakers.

"This is where we spend a good deal of our time. This next area is for casual dining," Kingsley said as he stepped down to the middle third of the room. The dark hardwood flooring of the kitchen continued on to the next level, the focus of which was a round pedestal table. Surrounding it were four upholstered dining chairs, all in red. Covering much of that level was a large, rectangular, multicolored rug. Along each wall, facing the table, was a taupe sofa, each framed by end tables with lamps. Abby broke away from Danny's side, leapt onto one of the sofas, rolled onto her back, and let out a couple of barks.

"The front of the room is the ship's bridge," Kingsley explained as he crossed the dining area and took another step down after throwing his jacket on one of the sofas.

The third level was home to four dark green leather chairs in two rows of two, all facing forward toward an enormous screen that curved along the nose of the ship. Separating the chairs from the screen was a control console. It was the first thing Danny had seen since they left the garage that reminded him he was on a ship. The area was covered in a short, beige shag carpet, which gave it a casual feel. The room's walls were a warm gold, accented with white baseboard, crown molding, and a barrel-shaped ceiling. Each side of the sun-drenched room had multiple windows, each framed by white, gauzy draperies.

"I love this room because it is so open. The levels create a feeling of three distinct living spaces, but you can still view the screen or talk easily to someone in another area. Shey, how are we doing on lunch?"

"Five minutes," responded Shey from the kitchen, again without looking up.

"Danny, I think it's time you met another member of my crew who you'll be spending a lot of time with. Hello, Gracie," Kingsley said.

"Hello, Kingsley. Welcome back. How was your trip?" responded a soft, pleasant, female voice. Danny glanced around to find that no one had entered the room.

"A bit frustrating but in the end, fruitful. I'd like you to meet Danny Kerrigan. Gracie is our ship's computer."

"Hello, Danny. Welcome aboard the *Aurora*."

"Hi."

"Shey does a lot around here, but Gracie really runs the ship," Kingsley said. "She controls everything from the temperature, music, food service, and mode of the windows to the ship's navigation, shields, and weaponry, all via voice command. You can ask Gracie anything you like. She's a fine conversationalist. If you need advice or just want someone to talk to, just ask her. All of our transports and devices have voice assistants. We refer to them as Gracie's kids. When on board, they sync with her and she keeps them up to date. Our guests are assigned an access level, from one to five, that controls what Gracie will do for them and where they can go on the ship. Gracie, Danny will have an access level of three. Any questions, Danny?"

"No."

"Well, make sure to ask anything that comes to mind. Ask any of us, including Gracie. One of the main points of this setup is for us to learn about one another. I'm willing to bet that this may be the only chance you have to ask questions of space travelers, so I urge you to not squander the opportunity. Shey?"

"It's ready," Shey answered as he loaded plates with the food he had been preparing on the stove. Kingsley sat in one of the chairs surrounding the dining table and directed Danny to another. As Shey carried over a couple of plates, Danny suddenly became anxious about what kind of unusual food Shey was about to place before him. He didn't want to offend them, but he had never eaten anything he didn't want to eat, and he wasn't going to start now. He was relieved, slightly, to see what appeared to be chicken and some vegetables.

"This looks like chicken," Danny said cautiously as it dawned on him that it could be some strange Yoobatarian creature.

Shey responded, "It is a grilled boneless chicken breast with a lemon tarragon sauce and assorted vegetables sautéed in olive oil, garlic, and a touch of balsamic vinegar, topped with crumbled gorgonzola cheese."

Danny was still tentative. The basic ingredients were harmless enough, but he was wary of the tarragon, balsamic vinegar, and gorgonzola, all of which he had never had.

"Is there a problem, Danny?"

"Uh . . . no. Well . . . kind of. I've just never had some of this stuff before . . . like this cheese."

"Well, then, this is a great opportunity for you. It's exciting to try new things."

"I'm just used to eating certain things that I like and I'm comfortable with," Danny said as he flicked a couple of chunks of gorgonzola off the vegetables with his fork.

"Danny, trying new foods is one of life's great pleasures. There was a point in your life when you had never tried any of your current favorites, correct?"

"Yeah, I guess so."

"There you go guessing again. You certainly take guesses at some of the oddest things."

"It's just a figure of speech," Danny said.

"I understand, but the figures of speech that we utilize, the tone we use, the strength with which we speak . . . all of those things contribute to the persona you convey to others. If you make a habit of speaking confidently and assertively, you will feel confident and assertive, and others will perceive you as such. It's a minor change that is really simple to make. For example, using *yes* instead of *yeah*, which you use a lot, sounds bolder, more educated, and less apathetic. Does that make any sense?"

"Yeah, I guess . . . Yes, yes it does," Danny said, increasing the volume for his second attempt.

"Much better. Now, try that gorgonzola."

"I think I'll pass."

"What are you afraid of?"

"I'm not afraid. I'm just not in the mood to try it."

"Oh yes, mood is very important when determining if one is up to tasting cheese. I don't understand your reluctance. What's the worst that could happen? It's not poison. It won't kill you."

"I know it won't kill me," Danny shot back.

"No, it won't, but I might if you don't eat the meal I prepared you," interjected an obviously annoyed Shey.

Danny ignored him. "It just looks kind of weird with the blue in it. What if I find it so disgusting that I throw up, right here on the table?"

Kingsley smiled. "Now I see. You're reviewing all possible outcomes, focusing on the worst—a worst that has almost no chance of occurring—and concluding that if it did occur, it would be so horrible that it isn't worth the risk. Do you approach everything like that? If so, that's a terribly timid, unadventurous way to go through life. You ought to try focusing on the best possible outcome and affirming that it will occur. It's really a much better mindset. To answer your question, if you throw up, you will not be banished from the ship. We will clean it up and encourage you to not eat any more gorgonzola, but we won't think any less of you."

"Seems like we're spending a lot of time talking about a piece of cheese."

"It isn't the cheese, Danny. I'm speculating that the way you are dealing with the cheese is a microcosm of how you live your life. I'm just trying to understand you so I know what you are capable of and what to expect of you as the mission progresses. I don't really care if you eat the cheese."

After thinking about Kingsley's analysis, Danny took another look at the small chunks of cheese, speared a couple with his fork, and slowly put them in his mouth. He was at first taken aback by the strong flavor of the pungent bits, but as they dissolved, he decided he liked it, so much so that he quickly tried a couple more.

"Okay, it's really good," he said softly.

"I'm glad you had a pleasant experience, Danny. Well, that concludes our adventure. We'll be taking you home now. I don't really see the point of continuing with the mission. Nothing we could accomplish could possibly surpass getting you to taste a new kind of cheese. I'll now consider this one of my greatest triumphs."

"That's very funny," said Danny.

The mood for the rest of the lunch was much lighter. Kingsley expounded more about the capabilities of his ship, Shey made a handful of sarcastic remarks, and Danny let his guard down a bit, mentally if not verbally.

"I think it's time we all got some rest," Kingsley said as they wrapped up lunch. "I'll take you to your room. Grab your bag."

Danny followed Kingsley from the living room across the foyer and down the hallway to the right of the lift. They emerged into a perpendicular hall, this one running across the width of the ship, with a window on each end.

"The hall contains guest rooms and two restrooms. Over here is the center hall," Kingsley said as he veered to the left toward a wide opening directly across from the back doors of the lift.

Danny was surprised by the hall's size. It was quite wide and quite long. It had the feel of the living room, with gorgeous rugs complementing dark hardwood floors, white woodwork, and a barrel-shaped ceiling. The cream walls were lined with paintings, a couple of sofas, pairs of chairs, and large floor plants.

"In case you're trying to get your bearings, we're directly above the garage," Kingsley said as they strolled down the hall. "Along here are our personal suites and three guest suites. The guest suites are along the right side. The first one will be yours." Kingsley paused by a door, to the right of which was a small black screen that displayed Danny's name.

"Shey's suite is directly across the hall. The remainder of the left side of the center hall is my suite." Kingsley continued down the hall and motioned to another corridor to the left. "The two doors on the right of this hallway lead to our offices—one is mine, and the other is my wife's. The door on the left is across from my office and is also a back entrance to Shey's suite. The main entrance to my suite is down on the center hall on the left. Let's get you settled in, shall we?"

"Sounds good," Danny mumbled. He was more than tired. He was so exhausted he could hardly think clearly.

Kingsley led him back to his suite's door. "When you approach the door of your own room, it opens automatically. If you would like entrance to someone else's room, you can either touch this rectangle that's below the nameplate or tell Gracie that you'd like to enter. Anyone with an access level of five can override an entrance refusal and have Gracie open the door. However, she will only do so after two minutes have elapsed. After all, we don't want to catch anyone in a position that may unnecessarily damage their dignity. Step on up and touch the panel, Danny."

Danny did so, and the door slid open. He tentatively entered and turned to his right to find a large living room, which contained a stylish sofa, a coffee table, and matching chairs, one on each end of the table. The sofa faced the long opposite wall, in which was imbedded a large rectangular screen. Along the right wall was a round table with four chairs. The room was beautiful but inviting, slightly less elegant than the rest of the ship. On the opposite end was a wide opening through which Danny could see a large bed.

"This is your living room. Over here is one entrance to your bath," Kingsley said, pointing to a door in the wall opposite the screen.

Danny had already wandered into the other room and was examining the bed, which was on a platform that extended from the wall. On the wall across from the bed was a desk and monitor. On the wall above was another flat screen.

"This door leads to your closet. Come along, Danny. I need to explain this to you before you sleep."

Danny followed Kingsley into the closet.

"In here are all of the clothing and shoes you will need for the trip. Exercise clothing is in the drawers. I think you'll find all fabrics and designs much more comfortable and functional than what you are wearing. All of the shirts are designed to be worn untucked. We're comfortable and casual around here. Gracie acquired your dimensions when you came on board and stocked the closet with items in a variety of colors."

Kingsley strode briskly back through the bedroom and into the living room. "Tell Gracie if you'd like anything changed, such as the temperature, window mode, or the firmness of your bed. If you want to watch anything on one of the view screens, just tell her, and she will turn it on and walk you through selecting a program, movie, or sporting event. You can also access the U-net through this screen or the one on the desk. Everything you watch or do on the computer is completely confidential. If you're not awake after sleeping two hours, I'll have her wake you. See you later, Danny." And with that Kingsley was gone.

Danny stood in the opening between the rooms and looked around, adapting to the feeling of being alone for the first time since he woke up that morning. It felt good. No, great. And comfortable. As much as he liked Kingsley, he relished the silence and solitude in which he lived most of his adult life. He was dead tired, but he needed a few minutes to unwind and gather his thoughts before sleeping. He walked around the rooms, closely examining the configuration and furnishings, and then approached one of the windows as Gracie spoke up.

"Danny, what would you like the default room temperature to be for waking and sleeping hours?"

"I'd like seventy-two during the day and sixty-seven for sleeping," he replied. "Can I see outer space out the windows?"

"Certainly." The view of the rolling fields and woods of Yoobatar was replaced with the star-encrusted black of deep space. Danny's throat tightened, his stomach knotted, and his legs wobbled. He reached out and placed his hand on the window to steady himself. For the first time since the transport entered the ship, the reality of the situation became apparent to him.

"Oh my God. What the hell have I done?" he whispered.

"Danny, my periodic scan of your system indicates that your vital signs have all increased to well above normal levels in an unusually short time. Are you in need of medical assistance?"

Danny tried to compose himself. "Uh . . . no. I'm fine. Thanks."

Danny yearned for the comfort and security of his apartment, but those feelings were closely followed by, and obliterated by, thoughts of the previous night's drinking binge and the situation that sparked it. The training. The creature working on his stomach gave it another wrench. As Danny stared into space and considered the uncertainty of the situation, he actually softened to the idea of doing the class. He told himself he could do it.

Why not? After all, he knew the material inside and out. He was smart. And articulate. And he was fooling himself.

Danny took a couple of steps back and sat on the edge of the bed. Though exhausted and slightly rattled, he had the mental wherewithal to realize how horrible he would feel at that moment were he sitting in his apartment, trying to work with the training looming over him. It came down to a battle of fears: facing the unknown versus doing the training classes. It was no contest. He told himself that everything would be okay and that the adventure would be fun. After all, Kingsley was there to take care of him and counsel him. Maybe they'd really hit it off and Kingsley would ask him to stay with him and be a second assistant.

Danny inhaled deeply and exhaled loudly. "Well, I'd better get used to this," he said before rising and approaching the window again. As he stared into the darkness, a calm came over him. It was peaceful. And quiet. It was Danny's kind of place.

He shuffled over to the bed and let out a soft moan as his head hit the pillow. Gracie took her cue. The lights in the ceiling were extinguished, and sconces on either side of the closet door began to glow softly. Continuing to comfort himself by affirming that Kingsley would be his guardian, Danny effortlessly drifted into a deep slumber.

CHAPTER 5

"Follow me," said Kingsley. "We'll take the lift at the back of the ship."

Danny followed, still groggy from a two-hour nap. Kingsley, who had changed into black exercise pants and a long-sleeved, maroon tee, had entered his room and piqued his interest by asking him if he wanted to go for a run. After Danny changed into some athletic clothes—a white shirt and heather-gray pants—he followed Kingsley from his room and made a right turn.

Several seconds later they emerged from the lift into a hallway, Spartan in design compared to the rest of the ship. There was no crown molding, no art, and the flooring was a tight, durable-looking carpet. Light came from multiple sconces along both walls.

Kingsley went into tour guide mode once again, alternately walking and stopping as he spoke. "On the right is the medlab, where Shey does examinations and treatments. On the left is the Mermetec lab. Next on the left—"

"What's Mermetec?"

"It's a government agency that does research involving the merging of metaphysics and technology. It blends science and spirituality, looking for ways to improve our knowledge of each using the other. My sister, Kayla, has been the director of Mermetec for over thirty years. That lab contains some equipment we acquired from the agency. You don't need to be concerned with that. Next on the left is a room we use for meditation and for practicing yoga and other such disciplines. Next on the right is a multi-purpose sports arena. Gracie can change the configuration so that you can play basketball, racquetball, tennis, or you can bowl if you like. My favorite is the golf simulator."

Danny had perked up when he heard basketball. He became almost excited when Kingsley mentioned golf. "Golf? You can play golf in there?"

"Why yes, yes you can. Do you play?"

"I love golf. I just haven't had the chance to play much the last few years," said Danny, longingly looking at the arena door.

"Well then, we'll have to tee it up when we have some down time during the mission. The last room on the left is the exercise room. Through the doors at the end of the hall is the two-story yard, which covers the front half of the ship. There is one more floor, which we've nicknamed the attic. It covers the back half of the ship and holds guest bedrooms and a small living and dining room combination. Ready for that run?"

Danny stared at the door at the end of the hall. "What's that yard area like?"

"The yard is a large outdoor simulation area. It satisfies our desire to be outdoors, to connect with nature, while we're in space. Let's take a look. After you."

Danny walked toward the door, which slid open when he got close, revealing blue sky and trees. He was stunned by the realism of the surroundings. Where he knew there must be walls, there appeared to be none, just blue sky above him and horizon all around, as far as the eye could see. The floor, or ground, had gentle slopes and was mostly grass covered. Paths went to both his right and left as well as straight ahead, the latter dead-ending into a large rock formation. Sprinkled about the area were shrubs, bushes, vibrant wildflowers, and small groupings of trees, their leaves softly rustling in a gentle breeze. A couple of benches and a pair of white chairs were spread about.

"Incredible," he whispered.

"Yes. Yes it is." Kingsley was obviously still captivated by the room, even though he'd seen it countless times.

Danny bent over to stroke the grass beside the path. "This feels like real grass."

"It is real grass. There is no synthetic flora in here. That's real grass with real soil under it. The flowers, trees, bushes—they're all real, growing plants. This room simulates the time of day and seasonal climate on Yoobatar at all times. There is no other mode. The walls and ceiling emit the precipitation and wind to match that on Yoobatar. The sun you see in the sky actually emits rays that replicate our sun's rays so closely that they nourish the plants and can give you a sunburn. It's the middle of our summer, so everything is alive, but the seasons change in here just as they do on Yoobatar. In the winter this is barren and quite cold. It even snows.

"The rock formation straight ahead houses the front lift shaft—the one we took from the garage to the foyer. There are some small bridges in the path that go over a stream that meanders through the yard. At the opposite end is a lovely patio. Sometimes I just come up, stretch out in a lounge chair, and take it all in. If you want to forget you're in space, you can certainly do it here. Now, how about that run?"

"Okay." Danny followed Kingsley back into the hall and into the exercise room, a large area containing many sleek exercise machines.

Kingsley went past all of the machines toward the far end of the room. "I rarely use all of these things. Shey does though. He works out like a maniac."

"Really? He doesn't look like it."

"Drimmillians are naturally a very strong species. Without any lifting, he would be twice as strong as the typical humanoid. With the working out he does, Shey is probably three times as strong. Here we are, Danny." Kingsley stopped in an area divided from the rest of the room by a wall. "These are the Ped-Rite machines, which are designed to simulate the experience of being outdoors while running in place. You stand on one of these rectangles, facing the wall, and tell Gracie if you'd like to walk, jog, or run, along with the difficulty you would like, using a range from one to ten.

"The walls, floor, and ceiling all display an outdoor scene that moves as you run. The Ped-Rite surface will slant up or down at various points to simulate the inclines in the scene in front of you. The system will vary the duration, the wind speed, the give in the surface, and the frequency and number of inclines based on the difficulty level you choose. Are you in reasonably good shape?"

"Yep," Danny said, confident that his running regimen of two to four miles several days per week would easily allow him to keep up with the old man.

"Great. Take the one on the far left. I'll take the second one. It will start slowly and build up to the target pace. Gracie, give us twenty-five minutes on the ocean course at running level seven."

When both were in place, the neutral room became a panoramic view of rugged terrain, woods, and a large body of water in the distance. The initial pace, that of a brisk walk, lasted only a minute, after which it increased to a speed slightly less than that at which Danny generally jogged. He acclimated quickly to the Ped-Rite surface and settled in for a comfortable run down the gently rolling path that lay before him. The scenery was spectacular: brilliant blue skies, rich green foliage, wildflowers, and occasional rock outcroppings. The shimmering ocean was off to the left, the same direction from which came a fairly strong breeze. Two minutes into the run, Danny had yet to break a sweat and was feeling a bit cocky.

"I forgot to mention that the first couple of minutes are a warm-up period," Kingsley said.

The Ped-Rite surfaces, as if on cue, started moving more briskly, forcing Danny to run at a faster pace. Determined to show he could keep up with Kingsley, he said nothing, even though he was mildly concerned. After several minutes the scene became darker as the trail led them into a forest of towering pines. Danny's attempt to continue breathing at his normal rate was a lost cause. As he gave up and started gulping air, Kingsley looked surprised.

"I thought you said you were in good shape," Kingsley said.

"I . . . I . . . am," said a panting Danny.

After emerging from the pines and running along a cliff for several minutes, the path turned sharply left and plunged toward the beach. They were soon running where the tide had been, with smooth, sun-hardened sand stretching out before them. The pace slowed slightly, and Danny collected himself again. Ahead was winding coastline, as far as the eye could see, with glistening white sand separating the water from rugged cliffs. Large, lazy waves came tumbling onto the beach, stopping just a few feet from their feet. The wind coming off the ocean was strong, strong enough that Danny's sweat-soaked face and forehead were dry in no time. The sounds and smells were all there too, adding to the reality of the scene. Danny was mesmerized.

As the coastline curved gently to the right, the system took them slightly left off of the firmly packed sand and into what was another new running experience for Danny, the fluffy white sand closer to the cliff. The next several minutes were laborious, with the previously firm surface becoming soft and mushy, giving significantly with each step and requiring a good deal of effort to push off. Danny struggled.

"Push, Danny!" Kingsley shouted over the sound of the surf. "You can make it. This builds your character as well as your legs."

"Character . . . my . . . ass," gasped Danny. "This is . . . ridiculous."

The path mercifully returned to the hard-packed sand, but only long enough for Danny to catch his breath and for his legs and stomach to cease burning.

"Oh no," he moaned as he saw the path turn toward the cliff.

"Oh yes, Danny. This is the last challenge," said Kingsley.

"I can't make it. Make this thing stop."

"Nonsense. You can do it, Danny. It's mental toughness. Tell yourself that giving up is not an option! Don't think of the size of the hill. Focus on taking one step at a time."

Danny took a deep breath and reached down deep, looking for enough resolve and determination to beat the hill. He was helped by the feel of the strong wind at his back.

"One step at a time," Danny told himself repeatedly as the nose of the surface raised sharply. His feet feeling like lead, his thighs burning and eyes stinging from his forehead's runaway beads of sweat, Danny fought through one gut-wrenching step after another. The surface abruptly leveled out after a three-minute climb.

The pace slowed to that of a light jog as it gently curved along the edge of the cliff. Danny's exhaustion was overshadowed by his exhilaration, an I-kicked-its-ass satisfaction, the likes of which he hadn't felt in many years. He looked over at Kingsley to see a large grin and an outstretched hand, palm up. Danny reached over and swatted it with all the strength he could muster. They finished the run in silence, taking in the glorious view, basking in the sunshine, and savoring the moment.

The path led them to a point where the land jutted out into the ocean. The Ped-Rite surface slowly came to a stop, leaving them on the cliff, high above the water that surrounded them on three sides. They stood silently for several minutes, catching their breath and taking in the magnificent view.

"We're done, Gracie." The scene melted away, leaving shockingly mundane off-white surfaces on all sides. Kingsley glanced over at the sweat-soaked Danny. "I think you've earned a beer."

"Beer? You have beer on the ship?"

"Of course we do. We have the finest beers, wines, and assorted other libations from all about the universe. What do you think we are, Banga-nese Monks?"

"I figured people as advanced as you guys didn't drink alcohol. You know, like it was primitive or something."

"Nonsense," Kingsley said as he turned to leave the exercise room. Danny followed closely on his tail in the hopes of being led to the beer. "Go shower up. We'll meet back in the living room for dinner and drinks."

Danny strode across the foyer with a spring in his step. After a long, hot shower, he had thought of putting his own clothes back on before looking closely at what Gracie had put in his closet. Everything was black, blue, white, or gray—matching his own wardrobe at home—and the fabrics were luxurious and stretchy, so he decided to give them a try. He emerged from his room in sleek, comfortable black loafers, deep blue slacks, and a black, long-sleeved polo shirt.

His upbeat mood was dampened by a feeling of uneasiness, almost mild panic, that grabbed him when he entered the living room and found only Shey. He hadn't counted on Kingsley not being there. His first reaction was to retreat to his room and reappear later, hopefully after Kingsley had arrived.

"Hello, Danny," said Shey in a rather cheerful fashion from behind the bar in the kitchen area. He was in black slacks and a charcoal shirt with buttons down the front and a pointed collar.

"Hi. Where's Kingsley?"

"He'll be along in a few minutes. Have a seat at the bar. Did you have a good run?"

"Yeah. Sure. It was tough but good."

Danny struggled and strained to find something else to say, each passing moment becoming more and more uncomfortable for him. He needed a life preserver.

"Can I have a beer?"

"Beer?" Shey said incredulously. "There's no beer on this ship."

Danny felt his world collapsing, his life preserver being ruthlessly pulled away from him just before it was in his hand. "But Kingsley said I could have a beer after the run."

"He must have been yanking your chain. We advanced beyond the need for alcoholic beverages long ago. Really, Danny, needing to ingest a substance to make you feel good, or to make you feel nothing, simply to cope with your life. How terribly unenlightened. There's not a drop of alcohol on this ship."

Danny was crestfallen. He was licking his wounds as Kingsley walked in, Abby in tow. Upon seeing Danny she broke away, ran to him, went up on her hind legs so that her front paws and head were in his lap, and started nuzzling his right forearm. Kingsley was dressed similarly to Shey, but with a black shirt and dark gray slacks.

"Good evening, everyone. Shey, I'm in the mood for a martini. How's it going, Danny?"

"Martini?" said Danny, looking up at Kingsley and then over at Shey, who had moved to an open wall panel. He turned and headed toward the counter carrying two sizable martini glasses.

"Tranbo gin martini. Up. Two olives," Shey said as he handed one of the large glasses to Kingsley. "Danny, can I get you anything? How about a beer? Or a glass of wine perhaps?"

"You ought to try one of Gracie's martinis, Danny. If a better one is made anywhere in the universe, I haven't found it yet. Cheers," toasted Kingsley as he and Shey tapped glasses and took a sip. "Ah, piercingly cold. Perfect. Don't you want anything, Danny? You seemed so excited when I mentioned we had beer."

Danny stared icily at Shey. "I'll have a beer."

"Coming right up."

"Let's have our drinks down at the bridge level, shall we?" Kingsley asked.

After taking a couple of huge gulps from his beer, Danny followed Kingsley and Shey past the dining table, which had three places set, all with white china, sleek silverware, and wine and water glasses. Danny glanced out the windows. It was early evening on Yoobatar, a lovely summer evening, with a soft, cool breeze ushering in the fragrance of wildflowers.

"Happy hour, Gracie," Kingsley said matter-of-factly after all three were seated.

Danny nearly spilled his beer as all four chairs slid backward. When they came to a rest, the floor between them slid away, revealing a round table that rose slowly, stopping when the top was knee-high. On it were cocktail napkins, two platters of hors d'oeuvres, a stack of small plates, and three lit candles.

"Music, Kingsley?" asked Gracie.

"In honor of our guest from Earth, let's hear some Sinatra."

"A specific collection or randomly selected songs from various collections?"

"How about *Sinatra at the Sands* with Count Basie?"

"Excellent choice."

As the big sound of the Basie band started and Sinatra began belting out "Come Fly with Me," Danny's face scrunched up as if he had bitten into a lemon.

"Sinatra? Frank Sinatra? You mean like 'New York, New York' Sinatra?"

"One of the benefits of monitoring planets that aren't aware is that we can glean bits of their popular culture that we deem to have entertainment value. Mr. Sinatra is one of the most revered performers ever discovered on a non-traveling planet. What a voice. Not to mention the beauty of the accompanying music from this era of your planet's history. If the only song of his that you know is 'New York, New York,' you're in for an education, my boy."

Danny was skeptical but said no more on the subject. He looked around and took in the moment, a handsome room with views of tremendous natural beauty, a cool breeze hitting his face, a cold beer in his hand, an endorphin high from the rigorous run, and for company, two entertaining aliens who were feeling less and less like strangers. For the first time since before he read his boss's email the previous night, he was relaxed. Vertran Systems was a million miles away, literally and figuratively.

Kingsley raised his glass. "I'd like to propose a toast. Here's to our newest crew member, Danny Kerrigan. I'm sure you'll enjoy the experience as much as we'll enjoy having you around. Welcome aboard, Danny," Kingsley extended his glass and touched it to Danny's. "Do you have anything you'd like to say about your experience to this point?"

"Uh . . . no," he responded, shaking his head slightly.

"Nothing at all?"

"Can I have another beer? The first one went down kind of fast. I guess I was thirsty from the workout."

It wasn't exactly what Kingsley was looking for. "Certainly. There's a service bay over here in the wall behind me. Help yourself. Just tell Gracie what you want. But take it easy. You will be expected to carry out duties, possibly as early as tomorrow, and I won't stand for having a hungover crew member. I should also mention that you shouldn't expect to drink all you like and then wipe away your hangover with one of the pills I gave you this morning. Those are very expensive."

"I'll be careful," Danny said as he made his way to the service bay. "So where are we going, anyways?"

"Good question, Danny, but I've been dominating the conversation since we met. It's time for you to hold up your side of the bargain. My favorite part of recruiting crew members is learning about another world from one of its inhabitants. So tell us, what's it like being a citizen of planet Earth?"

Danny froze with the mug to his mouth. The room was silent save Sinatra singing "Fly Me to the Moon." Danny slowly lowered the mug, looking down at the table. Kingsley and Shey were gazing at him with a look of eager anticipation. Abby was sitting in the fourth chair and also seemed to be staring at him.

"It's okay."

"No, seriously," Kingsley responded. "We can study the media reports we gather, but who knows how accurate or unbiased they may be? Tell us what you think of Earth's history, popular culture, world events, political climate, religious practices. Just expound of one of those subjects, and the conversation will take off on its own. It always does."

"I really don't know much about all that stuff," Danny replied in a voice that quivered a bit.

"Nonsense. You can't live on a planet all of your life and not know anything about the experience of living there or have any thoughts about the culture. We can start with your country. What's your interpretation of your system of government?"

"I . . . I don't follow politics."

"Tell us about your popular forms of entertainment. You know, sports, films, television, music."

"I, uh . . . I don't . . . I don't know."

"Don't tell us you don't know anything about it. I know you watch television and films."

"Danny's vital signs have increased to well-above-normal levels," Gracie chimed in.

"Are you feeling okay?" Kingsley asked.

"Yeah. I'm fine," Danny replied as he wiped his forehead and took another gulp of beer. "Just a little woozy. Guess I'm still getting used to being in space. I don't really feel like talking right now."

"I understand if this is all a bit much for you at the moment. Let's start smaller. Tell us about yourself, your life up to this point."

"You seem to already know everything about me."

"Again, that's just information gathered from records. I want to hear about your life from you. Tell us about your childhood."

"Actually, I don't remember a lot about my childhood."

"Really. Is that typical for your species?"

"I don't know. I don't think so."

"Okay, then, we'll stick to your current life. Tell us about your profession."

"I work for a software company."

"Yes, Danny. I know that. I'm looking for a little more than that. What kind of software is it? What exactly do you do? Do you like it? How did you come to be in your current position? Or what about hobbies? Everyone has hobbies. How do you spend your time when not working?"

"I . . . it's, ah . . . I . . . I need to go to the bathroom. Can I go to the bathroom?" Danny stammered, his head spinning from all the questions.

"Of course you can go to the bathroom, Danny. You don't have to ask."

Danny headed to his suite. After splashing some cool water on his face, he sat on the edge of his bed trying to regroup before returning to the living room to find Kingsley sitting at the island chatting with Shey. The dining table now held several lit candles as well as a bottle of wine. The room was dimmer. The simulated natural light from the windows had faded, and a soft glow shone from behind the crown molding. As he slid onto one of the barstools, Danny thought of getting another beer but decided against it.

"Good timing, Danny. We're about ready to eat. Shey has prepared a wonderful meal in your honor. It's our tradition to do so on the first evening that we host a new recruit."

"What are we having?" Danny asked, bracing himself for the answer.

"I went to the far reaches of the universe and spared no expense for your first dinner," Shey boasted. "We are having broiled Grutopian Moose livers in a spicy ferret sauce, candied Lampuscan pig's knuckles, and breathing root vegetables from the lush plains of Triboika Tan, served in a lovely goat juice marmalade. The name comes from the fact that they continue to expand and contract for weeks after they've been harvested, and they occasionally let out an ever-so-tiny yelp when you cut into them. But don't let that bother you—they really aren't alive, and they stop moving within a few minutes after entering your system."

Danny had instinctively grabbed his stomach as Shey spoke, his throat tightening as he fought nausea.

"Shey, you know Danny isn't feeling well. Tell him you made that all up," said a mildly annoyed, mildly amused Kingsley.

"Okay. I made it all up!" Shey exclaimed gleefully.

Though Danny had visions of climbing over the island and popping the little bastard, he quietly stared at the bar and tried to calm down, taking deep breaths and reminding himself of Kingsley's warning about Drimmillians.

"Danny, you sit over there," Kingsley said before taking the seat facing the front of the room. "Do you like red wine?"

"I've never had it."

"Really? Well, you're going to try some tonight. A beer or two is just fine in certain situations, but wine is certainly much better with a fine meal. Tonight we're having a wonderful Pelitas from the Frangiano region of Srantham. Let's dine under the stars. Gracie—space mode, windows and ceiling."

While Kingsley filled each of the glasses with the dark liquid, the off-white of the barrel-shaped ceiling and the Yoobatarian vistas out the windows were both replaced with the deep black of space, the countless stars softly illuminating the room. Coupled with the candles, it created a magical atmosphere. Shey approached with two plates and cleared his throat.

"Dinner is served. For tonight's meal, I scanned the typical offerings of what are considered fine restaurants in Danny's locale and, at Kingsley's request, selected something that is considered to be less-than-exotic so that our guest feels comfortable. We are having filet mignon in a morel mushroom and red wine reduction, grilled asparagus, and garlic and leek mashed potatoes," Shey announced, placing the plates in front of Danny and Kingsley.

"How does that sound, Danny?"

Danny stared at the plate with a look of mild discomfort. "I don't know. I'm not really all that hungry."

"Don't tell me you've never had steak before?"

"Of course I've had steak. And mashed potatoes. But I've never had asparagus. Or mushrooms. What else did he say? Leeks? I don't think I've had those either."

"You've never had asparagus? Or a mushroom? Now I know you're playing games with us."

"Nope," said a tight-lipped Danny as he stared at his plate.

"My God, boy, what have you been consuming all of your life? Bread and water? I'm incredulous! I'm appalled. Shey's done research. He's used nothing up to this point that isn't a common food item on your planet. Will you at least try?"

"I'll try, as long as it doesn't look or smell too disgusting."

"Okay, then. Shey, you have a standing order to not make anything for Danny that is excessively disgusting."

"I'll see what I can do, though it may be difficult. Much of my training was at the Drimmillian Culinary Institute of the Repulsive and Disgusting."

"Gracie, random Sinatra ballads," Kingsley said. "Lower the volume a bit also, please."

As "All the Way" spilled from the speakers, Kingsley took a sip of wine and continued. "Let's get back to business. You asked me earlier where we are going. We are going to Kronk."

"Kronk?"

"Yes, Kronk. What's the problem? You've been to Kronk and you don't want to go back?"

"It just seems like a funny name for a planet."

"As opposed to Pluto? Or Uranus? I'd be willing to wager that if I had a U-buck for every time someone on your planet made a joke about Uranus, I wouldn't even be on this mission."

"Okay, we're going to Kronk. What for?" Danny asked as he began an exploratory mission of his own, jabbing an asparagus spear with his fork and lifting it to his nose before taking a small bite. "Hmm. This isn't bad. It's really different."

"Yes, it's one of the more exotic items you'll find anywhere in the cosmos," said Shey, rolling his eyes. "As a matter of fact, I think we should nominate you for the Cramoreekan Badge of Courage for just trying it. We'll swing by Cramoreeka to pick it up once we've finished on Kronk."

"That's enough, Shey." Kingsley said. "We've got a mission to discuss."

CHAPTER 6

Kingsley took a deep breath. "We are going to Kronk because we think that's where the thief is from. The Tablet of Jakaroo was housed in a deep cavern beneath the Quilicant compound, protected by the most sophisticated security system available. Not even the family's Top Royal Guards, known as Trogs, know the tablet room's exact location."

"So someone in the royal family took it?" Danny asked.

"Certainly not. The odds that a Yoobatarian, especially a member of the royal family, would attempt to steal an artifact are unfathomable."

"So how did it happen?"

Kingsley noticed that Danny had sampled the wine. "How do you like the Pelitas?"

"The first sip reminded me a little of cough syrup, but it's growing on me."

"Excellent. Anyway, it *was* an inside job. One of the Trogs, Chase Claxon, is believed to be the thief. The tablet was stolen three days ago. They cannot locate Chase anywhere on the planet, and one of the security force's transports is missing. Interrogation of the family members turned up that one of Vivitar's younger sisters had developed a secret relationship with Chase over the past few months. Apparently they often met in the most private place on the compound, the underground caverns, and the young lady ended up showing Chase the tablet room. So all evidence points to him, which was a tremendous shock to the family. Chase had been a loyal member of their security force for over twenty years."

"Why would a security guy steal the tablet?"

"It turns out he isn't who they thought he was. Before he was hired, Chase was interviewed and background checks were done, friends and family were contacted, employment records were verified, and he passed his physical. Once hired, he dazzled everyone. He was the complete package for a security specialist: extremely intelligent, powerfully built, with impressive combat skills, unflinchingly loyal, assertive, and clever. Within a couple of years he was quite valued and trusted. Within ten he was in the upper echelon of the security force. Three years ago he was named a Trog. After the theft, a check of his DNA taken from his home turned up that Chase was actually not Yoobatarian at all. Our experts determined that there was an excellent chance that Chase came from one of three planets: Nymoo, Azadrupia, or Kronk."

"So he traveled to Yoobatar from one of those planets over twenty years ago with the plan of someday stealing the tablet?" asked Danny.

"We don't think so. At least, not exactly. You see, none of those planets travel. Nymoo and Azadrupia are both aware and will probably be traveling in the near future, possibly any month now for Nymoo. Kronk was oblivious until about twenty-five years ago, and they now suspect. It will probably be at least a couple hundred years before they travel," Kingsley explained.

"So how did he get to Yoobatar?"

"We think he was recruited, trained in Yoobatarian culture, given a manufactured background, and placed as a candidate for the security force for the sole purpose of determining if the tablet existed and, if so, acquiring it."

"Recruited by who?" asked Danny.

"The dreaded Dank Nebitol," said Kingsley, his voice dripping with disgust. "At least, that's who we suspect was behind all of this."

"Dank Nebitol? Who's Dank Nebitol?"

"He has been, for the past thirty years, the number-one nemesis of the Quilicant family. For the most part, Yoobatar has had an idyllic society for over two hundred years. There is almost no crime, certainly no violent crime, and the society is practically void of deceit, cheating, prejudice, or hatred. It is one of the most spiritually advanced cultures you will find. Integrity, honesty, hard work, tolerance, love, and peace are the hallmarks of life on Yoobatar. Yoobatarians welcome visitors, but to preserve our way of life, aliens are not permitted to take up residence.

"Dank wanted to change all of that. He appeared on the scene as an angry young man who didn't have the same qualities as most Yoobatarian youth. The reason, it was later discovered, was that he was only half Yoobatarian. Dank's father was Klabanite. The Klabanites are an unscrupulous, hedonistic, egocentric race that live to achieve power at all costs. Unfortunately, Dank ended up being more like his father than his mother. While growing up, he was constantly getting into trouble, everything from harmless mischief to relatively serious crimes, at least for Yoobatar.

"The main problem," Kingsley continued, "was that he tried to influence other young people to follow his lead. He worked hard to convince them that the lifestyle they were being raised to lead was boring and would make them wimpish and weak, that they would be much better off bucking authority and being aggressive, insolent, deceitful, and even corrupt. When Dank found a vulnerable soul, he pounced, using his considerable charm and guile to get them to see things his way. He was so successful in such a short time that he began to think bigger, much bigger. He started thinking of himself as a leader, his work as recruiting, and the group's actions as a movement. Members began calling themselves Nebbers."

"Nebbers? Kind of a cute name for such a rebellious group," said Danny.

"Believe me, no one thought of them as cute. The group became so large and so vocal that it gained the attention of the government and the Quilicant family, though much of the population was unaware of the movement, or they knew of it but paid little attention. Dank had set his sights high, too high, as it turned out. He was so young and brash that he started making noise about overthrowing the Quilicant family and taking over Yoobatar. While he had amassed several thousand followers, he was way out of his league.

"They investigated him, and that's when they discovered he was half Klabanite. They considered banishing him, but that would make them seem intolerant. Instead, the family gave the story to the media, which presented it to the masses as a huge threat to the Yoobatarian way of life. They splashed pictures of Dank all over the papers and television, pointing out that he was half Klabanite and emphasizing what Klabanite society was like. The population was outraged and turned against Dank and the Nebbers."

"Sounds like a band," interjected Shey.

"Once the movement was exposed, it went nowhere. Dank was considered to be poison and was treated like an outcast. Dank was arrogant but he wasn't stupid. He and his staunchest supporters realized that it would be in their best interest to fold, or at least to give the public the perception they had folded. He made a statement in which he claimed to have seen the error of his ways, that his group was just young and impetuous, and that they realized that, of course, the Yoobatarian way of life was best. He pledged his support to the Quilicant family and apologized for any distress he had caused the society. That was twenty-five years ago."

"What did he do after that?" asked Danny.

"He became a fine citizen, at least on the surface. He laid low for a while and reinvented himself. He portrayed himself as a changed man, took up good causes, and didn't utter a bad word about the Quilicants. But the Quilicants received bits and pieces of intelligence that indicated Dank had slowly and quietly begun recruiting again, this time taking a more charming and less rebellious approach. They even suspect he was behind several manufactured scandals surrounding the family, even though he publicly supported them. Now the Tablet of Jakaroo has been stolen, and they fear he was behind the theft. If so, and in the unlikely event that he can create an amulet, he could be a force that would be difficult to stop."

"How would he do it? Would he, like, attack the compound?"

"Oh, heavens no. He may be unscrupulous, but he's not a barbarian. Every ten years, the people of Yoobatar vote on whether they are happy or not with the status quo. It's known as a satisfaction election. Since the Quilicants took over, the vote has been a formality, really, with anywhere from 95 to 98 percent voting to keep them. If 30 percent or more ever voted against the status quo, a second general election would be held three months later between the current ruling family and whoever wanted to run against them. The next satisfaction election is less than a month away. Vivitar Quilicant does not want that second election. Between the scandals they've been enduring and Dank having the amulet, they fear he could possibly pose a serious challenge."

"Okay, do they have any evidence that Dank was behind it, or are they just guessing it was him?"

"A little of both," responded Kingsley. "How about some more wine, Danny?"

Danny, absorbed in the story, was mildly surprised to see that his glass was nearly empty. "I guess I kind of like it. Sure, I'll have some more."

Kingsley poured everyone's second glass while continuing. "The Quilicants planned to question everyone that had been interviewed when Chase was hired, and not a single one of them was found. They looked for his parents, siblings, friends, and previous employer. There is no record of them ever existing. If Chase was planted, the only person they knew of that would be capable of such treachery was Dank. The closest they have to hard evidence is that there is a record of Dank sending three messages to Chase's personal comnum in the past week."

"Comnum?"

"Communication number. Gracie?"

"It is similar to what Danny would know as a cell phone number."

"Plus, Dank is nowhere to be found. No one has seen him since a couple of days before the theft, and his personal ship is gone. The theory is that Dank found someone on another planet who was qualified, someone who had never heard of Yoobatar or the tablet but was trained in the ways of security and espionage and perhaps disgruntled with his current life. Dank probably promised him a chance at adventure and riches if his mission was successful. Perhaps even a high position in his government. He then took the person to Yoobatar and gave them crash courses in the planet's history, culture, and customs. Finally, he manufactured this false background for the person."

"Why did Dank pick someone from another planet instead of one of the Nebbers?" Danny asked.

"He probably wanted someone with no history on Yoobatar. Plus, he wanted a seasoned professional who was skilled enough to get promotions. My guess is that, regardless of what he promised this person, he also specifically wanted someone from a planet that didn't travel so he could dump him back on his planet after the mission with no concern that he could ever come looking for him. That's why we think Chase is from Kronk and not from Nymoo or Azadrupia. Dank wouldn't take someone from a planet that he thought would reach travel status during his lifetime. If he used one of his own people, there would always be the chance that they would someday tell the world what he had done, that the tablet does exist, and that Dank utilized the amulet to achieve power. I wouldn't be surprised if Dank hasn't told any of his followers about Chase and is now on this quest by himself."

"And we're going to Kronk because you think Chase is there?" Danny asked.

"Correct. At least, we hope he's there. It's really our only lead. We're hoping that Chase can tell us where Dank is going and how he is planning on reading the tablet. The instructions on the tablet are written in an ancient language called Quontal. There are only five known Quontal experts on Yoobatar, and all have been accounted for."

Danny absorbed the story with no stress, no anxiety, and no concerns about how he was being perceived by the two men sitting across from him. The starlight ceiling, the candlelight, the delicious food, the wine, and the intriguing tale told by Kingsley—it all contributed to the feeling of total peace he was experiencing. He had moments of relaxation when drinking beer and watching a movie or sporting event, but it was always a restless relaxation, with frequent, faint thoughts of how the tenuous, delicate world he had built might be shattered at any moment. This moment was different. There was no blanket of dread, no worries of what was waiting around the corner, no fear tugging on his pant leg like an angry dog. His mind was free and clear and rapidly processing the story.

"How long will it take to get there? How are you going to find Chase once we do? What are you going to do if he's not there?" Danny asked.

Kingsley, mouth full, looked at Shey and motioned toward Danny with his fork.

Shey spoke up. "We'll be arriving at Kronk in about thirty-six hours. Based on his physical makeup, we have a good idea that Chase is from a country called Hanaba. How are we going to find him? We doubt Dank would just pick someone off the street for such an important mission. We are going to find him by scanning the government computers for a record of an intelligence or military officer that left the agency within a year or so before Chase appeared on Yoobatar. Hopefully, we'll also find that he's been missing in the years since."

"What am I going to do while you guys go look for Chase?"

"Finding and questioning Chase should be a quick, simple operation, so you'll probably have no mission-related tasks," Kingsley said. "I'm guessing he'll be more than happy to tell his story to someone who will actually believe him and who is trying to catch Dank. You'll wait here on the ship for us."

"I have to be alone on the ship?" asked Danny.

"You won't be alone. Abby will be here. And Gracie. Besides, what are you concerned about? You live alone."

"This is different. I mean, what if something happens to you guys and you don't come back?"

"I see," Kingsley said. "You're visualizing the worst possible outcome again. I can assure you the chances of us not coming back are next to nil. Even if something happened, all you have to do is tell Gracie to take you back to Earth and then use a Solo Trek to get to the surface. So you see, there's nothing to worry about."

"I guess not."

"Do you like living alone, Danny?" Kingsley asked.

"Uh, yeah, sure," Danny responded after thinking for a moment. Abby slid off the sofa and sat beside him, resting her head on his thigh. Danny began stroking her absentmindedly.

"What do you like about it?"

"Hmm . . . I guess I just like the solitude. You know, being able to do whatever I want whenever I want. I just like the freedom, not having to deal with people in general."

"Our research shows that people on Earth have often found a mate by age twenty-eight. Why is it that you have yet to do so? Is that not something that appeals to you?"

"Kind of, but I've just never been real good with girls. I have trouble talking to them. I get all flustered and start stumbling over my words, and what I do get out ends up sounding stupid. My life's a lot less stressful if I just avoid the whole thing."

"I see," said Kingsley, as Shey delivered a tray of mugs filled with steaming coffee and a pitcher of cream. "Well, that's certainly understandable. It's not unusual for the mating ritual to be awkward and uncomfortable. It would be a shame, though, to see you give up on it if sharing your life with someone and having offspring is really something you desire. Why is it that you work from home rather than in an office building? This is decaffeinated, so don't worry about it keeping you up."

Danny put cream in his coffee and took a sip. "Wow, this is really good. I worked in the office for several years. I just got tired of it. I'm in a position where people frequently need me for help, and it got to be too much. There was, like, a steady stream of people coming into my office all day, and I was being pulled a hundred different directions. I can do the same job from home, but it's a lot less stressful, since most of my interactions are electronic."

"Our research on you shows that you don't seem to have a lot of friends. Is that the case?"

"Yeah, I suppose," said Danny as he gazed into the deep space visible through the windows. "I used to have some. Back in high school I had a group of guys I hung out with, but I lost touch with them after college. There were a few people at Vertran that I thought of as friends, but after a while it got to be less and less fun doing things with them. It was just easier to stay home."

"Do you ever get lonely?" Kingsley asked.

"Lonely? Not really. Well, maybe a little on a Saturday night or on holidays—you know, times when you're supposed to be around people and having a good time. But even then, if I really think about it, really imagine myself somewhere with a lot of people, I realize that if I was there, I'd be having an awful time and wishing I was home alone."

"Well, it sounds like you've got a very low-stress life. You must be very happy."

"Happy? I never really thought about it in terms of being happy. I guess I'm happy. Sure . . . I'm happy," he said.

"Well, that's wonderful. You'd be surprised at how difficult it is to find beings that are truly happy. One other question. If you have no friends, with whom do you play golf?"

"I don't really play anymore. I'd like to, but I haven't for a few years."

"We're going to have some downtime tomorrow. We'll have to tee it up in the simulator. How's that sound?"

"Great. I'd really like that."

"Okay then, let's plan on it. With that, I must bid you good evening. I'm still recovering from last night. I used to bounce back from those all-night escapades quickly, but I'm not a young man anymore. Danny, you're welcome to sleep in tomorrow. Good night, everyone. I'll see you all in the morning."

"Night," said Shey and Danny in unison, Shey from the kitchen, where he was still straightening up.

As Kingsley made his way from the room, Danny looked around and realized that if he stayed up, he would be alone with Shey. "You know, I'm really tired too. I think I'm going to turn in. Thanks for dinner, Shey."

"You're welcome," he said, not looking up from the counter he was wiping.

Danny entered his suite with Abby in tow. Once again, it felt good to be alone. He wandered back to the bedroom and checked his watch to find it was 9:40 Ohio time. Too early to go to bed, even though he was tired and a little tipsy. He plopped down on the living room sofa, where Abby joined him, her head on Danny's right thigh. Danny asked Gracie to find him a golf tournament to watch. He soon realized something was missing.

"Gracie, can I get a beer?"

"You can, but my scans indicate that if you consume any more alcoholic beverages this evening, you would run the risk of having unpleasant side effects tomorrow."

Danny hesitated, but only for a moment. "That's fine. I'd like one of the beers I was drinking in the living room."

"Your beverage is in the service bay behind you."

Danny grabbed the beer and returned to the sofa. Over the next two hours he was totally absorbed in the tournament. His first beer was followed by another. Once it was over, Danny told Gracie to put the windows in Yoobie mode and crawled into bed. The lights slowly faded, the curtains closed, the temperature quickly dropped several degrees, and a sleep-enhancing herbal scent was emitted into the room. Danny let out a big sigh as he closed his eyes. He thought of what lay ahead, worrying about what it was going to be like to be alone on the ship when Kingsley and Shey went to Kronk. Fighting back the fear by focusing on the next day's round of golf with Kingsley, Danny drifted into a deep sleep.

CHAPTER 7

DANNY SCURRIED DOWN the arena's wide, curving, dimly lit corridor, desperately looking for some place he could stop to catch his breath. Seeing a dark concession stand, he ducked into the doorway, dropped to the floor, and leaned against the wall under the counter, trying not to make too much noise as he gasped for air. After a dozen or so chest heaves, his breathing slowed, and he turned his head just enough for his ear to be facing the hallway from which he had just come. Silence. He listened for another minute. Still silence. He dropped his head in relief, but it was temporary. He still had to find his way out of there.

His quiet contemplation was shattered by the sudden squeak of rubber-soled shoes on the marble floor. It was obvious they were being made by a large number of people. He panicked. He thought of staying put, but they were sure to check the concession stand—and then he would be trapped. He had to find the arena's exit.

In a flash he was back in the corridor, sprinting away from the squeaks, which grew louder. He stopped for a moment and frantically scanned the area before seeing an exit sign marking a stairwell.

Danny hurried down the steps as fast as he could without falling in the dim light. After three flights he hit the ground floor and looked around for an exit from the arena. He paused briefly to note that there was no pounding of footsteps on the stairs above him, then walked briskly along the outer edge of the curved hall looking for another exit sign. He finally found one, probably fifty feet ahead, and made a beeline for the opening below it. Halfway there he was stopped by a noise in front of him. It was the sound of doors being opened by their metal crossbars being pushed hard, and it was coming from the opening for which he had been heading. Danny froze and listened. The doors slammed shut. There were more of them. Damn it. He had been seconds away from freedom. He thought of giving up, of just standing there and letting them catch him. But he couldn't. His urge to flee was too strong.

Danny ran back toward the stairwell, but when he got close, he heard the thunderous racket of a horde coming down the steps. He raced down the hall and came to an opening, this one on the interior wall. Instinctively he ran into the opening and up a ramp. At the top he stopped to find that he was in the arena, an enormous basketball arena, in an aisle about ten rows from the floor. It was empty and mostly dark, the only light coming from dozens of illuminated exit signs that marked each opening back to the corridors. He heard rapid squeaks at the bottom of the ramp. He decided he had to get to an exit on the other side of the arena, so he ran down the aisle and jumped onto the floor. When he was halfway across, he heard loud clicks, immediately followed by the arena's lights coming on, flooding the floor while the seats remained in the dark.

Danny cringed and attempted to shield his eyes while they tried to acclimate to the brilliant white lights. With his anxiety spinning out of control, Danny sprinted for one of the four openings found at the corners of the court. The one he chose led to another dimly lit corridor.

There were several doors on both sides. After hesitating a moment, Danny entered one and found himself in a large locker room. Looking around for another exit or a good place to hide, Danny passed several rows of metal lockers until he came to an area containing several shower stalls. He desperately needed to rest and regroup, so he entered one, closed the frosted glass door, fell into a corner, and slid down the wall until he hit the floor. He sat there, panting and plotting his next move.

His rest was short-lived. He soon heard the locker room door open, followed by footsteps, followed by the sound of lockers being opened and slammed shut. Danny decided he was out of options and resigned himself to being caught. As the sound of the banging metal continued, he relaxed slightly. It almost felt good to give up. He was tired of running.

As he sat waiting with his head in his hands, he heard another sound, the sound of classical music competing with the clanging of the lockers. The music became clearer and louder. Danny looked up at the glass shower door to see a shadow looming on the other side. As he held his breath and braced himself for the door to swing open, he thought he heard a voice, a female voice, calling his name. He strained to hear the voice, which he somehow knew was not coming from one of his pursuers. The shower door and the shadow slowly faded to black. The music was all he heard until the voice called him again.

"Danny. Danny, it's time to wake up."

His eyes fluttered open, and he sat upright, chest heaving and forehead damp with sweat, as he frantically looked around the room, trying to get his bearings and identify his location.

"Kingsley is requesting admittance."

"Kingsley? Um . . . okay. That's fine."

"Let's go, Danny. Time to get up!" Kingsley shouted as he strode briskly into the bedroom. He was wearing black exercise pants, a heather-gray shirt, and black sneakers. "Are you okay? You look like you've seen a ghost."

"I'm good. Just woke up from a bad dream. It's still dark," Danny said, looking over at the windows. "What time is it?"

"A little after six."

"But you said I could sleep as long as I wanted to," whined Danny.

"Yes, well, I changed my mind. I decided that we should get an early start on the day. Do you always have so much trouble getting up in the morning?"

"Sometimes, especially when I haven't had much sleep. I watched a golf tournament for a couple of hours before I went to bed because you said I could sleep in."

"And had a beverage, I see? How do you like your coffee?" Kingsley approached the room's service bay.

"Just cream. I had a couple more beers. What's so important that you woke me?"

"Here you go," Kingsley said as he handed a mug of coffee to Danny. "What's so important is starting our day. We're going to do some yoga before breakfast."

"Yoga?"

"Yes, yoga. It's a system of movements, stretches, and postures. It gets your blood moving and muscles stretched, and, most of all, it gets your energy flowing."

"I know what yoga is," Danny said disgustedly as he put the mug on the nightstand and dropped back onto his pillow. "Why don't you do all of that, and I'll go back to bed and meet you for breakfast?"

"No, you're not going back to bed. On this ship, you have to be prepared for anything, to deal with the unexpected. Once the mission starts, you never know what you'll have to do and when you'll have to do it. Your mistake was staying up late and drinking more because you counted on what I said being an absolute certainty. The only absolute certainty is that nothing is absolutely certain. Gracie, will you assist Danny in getting out of bed?"

"Damn!" Danny shouted as he scrambled off the side of the bed and onto the floor. "What the hell was that?"

"That is Gracie's way of making sure you don't sleep the day away. She reduced the temperature of the sleep surface to something that I'm sure is quite unbearable unless you're a Lipyanbian ice monster. It's most effective. Don't you agree?"

Kingsley disappeared into the closet and reappeared with some clothes in hand.

"Here. Put these on."

Danny took the clothes and stepped into the closet.

"I'm ready," Danny said as he slid on the footwear Kingsley had given him. He emerged in a navy long-sleeved tee, stretchy, dark gray pants, and shoes similar to Kingsley's.

"Excellent," Kingsley said as he strode briskly from the room and down the hall toward the back lift. It was all Danny could do to keep up. "Second floor, Gracie."

After exiting the lift, Kingsley led the way into the yoga studio. Expecting to see a room similar to the main exercise room, Danny was taken aback by the atmosphere as he followed Kingsley and the door closed behind him. A pair of bamboo trees framed the entrance and set the tone. Once he stepped past them, they crossed a short bridge that spanned a small stream through which water trickled over gleaming black stones. More bamboo trees were scattered about the room, seemingly growing out of the floor, which was covered with a tight but soft beige carpet. Groupings of small boulders were nestled against the walls in a handful of spots. From one cluster along the left wall came the water that fed the stream. Large billows of sheer fabric hung from the ceiling, creating a breezy, flowing feeling. Soft light was emitted from sconces along the left wall. Simple, soothing music filled the room.

"I don't know about this. I've never been very flexible. I don't think I can do it."

"Don't worry, Danny," said an already-seated Kingsley. "You don't have to be flexible to do yoga, especially at the beginner level that we're going to do. The instructor will tailor the session to match your capabilities as we go. Trust me. I think you'll enjoy it, and I know you'll feel great afterward."

"What instructor?"

"Mara. Just have a seat facing this wall." Kingsley pointed to the right wall.

The screen was suddenly filled with a tropical ocean view. As a warm breeze caressed Danny's face, a life-sized holographic woman appeared in front of the screen. She was a young, attractive blonde dressed in loose-fitting black garments. Danny was smitten with her the moment she appeared.

For the next hour, Mara gently led them through a series of positions, starting with some simple seated stretches and building up to more difficult postures, all the while emphasizing the appropriate breathing technique and giving Danny direction and corrections. By the time she moved them into the last position, lying flat on their backs, arms relaxed at their sides, Danny felt wonderful. A peaceful energy seemed to fill him, as if every cell in his body was buzzing slightly.

"Danny. Danny," Kingsley said gently.

"Yeah," he said, slowly coming back to awareness.

"That wasn't so bad, now was it?"

Danny opened his eyes and looked over to see Kingsley facing him, sitting cross-legged with a rather pleased expression.

"No, not bad at all." Danny pushed himself up onto his elbows, still processing where he was and what he was doing there.

"Let me see," Kingsley said. "You've tried several new foods, drank some red wine, and done yoga, and nothing catastrophic has happened; no tragedy has befallen you. I dare say you've actually enjoyed it all. I'm starting to think that trying new things isn't such a bad thing. What do you think?"

"Okay, okay. So far I've liked what I've tried. But there certainly may be something that I don't," Danny said while staring at the frozen image of Mara.

"Danny, am I wrong, or did you get nervous when she appeared?"

"I might have been a little nervous."

"And it is kind of dark in here, but I believe your face turned red. All that just from seeing an image of a beautiful woman?"

"I get really nervous around good-looking girls."

"That's not all that unusual, Danny. When I was young, I was a little apprehensive around young ladies. But to react so strongly to a video image . . . this issue must be deeply engrained. Why do you think you get so agitated?"

"I suppose it's because I may have to talk to them."

"And?"

"And I'll mangle what I try to say and get more rattled. Or I'll try to be really funny or sound smart and end up sounding like an idiot."

"And?"

"And what?"

"And then what would happen?"

Danny thought for a moment before answering. "I guess I'm worried that when they see how nervous I am, they'll think it's because I like them, and that would be embarrassing."

"I see. So you think someone is attractive, physically or personality-wise, and you would be embarrassed if they knew you thought that. It sounds like they should consider it a compliment. Why would that be embarrassing?"

"Because they are probably way out of my league. They'd think it was funny or pathetic that I was interested in them, and then I'd feel humiliated."

"Ah, now we're getting down to it. It all comes down to potentially being rejected. My, you play all of that out in your head merely upon the sight of an attractive female. It's the same thing as when you avoid trying a new food. You're playing out the worst possible scenario in your mind before anything even happens."

"So I'm supposed to envision that everything's going to go perfectly, she'll think I'm wonderful and we'll end up getting married?"

"Of course not. There's nothing wrong with affirming that all of your interactions with other people will go well, but you shouldn't go into the interaction with an image of exactly how the conversation is going to flow. If you do, you'll lose your train of thought or get flustered the moment it deviates from your preconception. What I'm saying is that you shouldn't think that far ahead. Focus on the moment. Be authentic. Be sincere."

"I think you're making it sound a lot easier than it really is."

"Actually, you've been making it much more difficult than it really is. Ready for some breakfast?"

As they entered the living room, they were greeted by the smell of freshly brewed coffee and food cooking. Shey was in the kitchen, hard at work on the food, and what appeared to be a newscast was on the room's main view screen.

"Have a seat, Danny," Kingsley said as he headed into the kitchen and filled two mugs with coffee. Danny followed directions and turned his attention to the gentleman on the screen, a handsome young man sitting at a desk. On the wall behind him was a large logo depicting several planets and their orbital paths, with the letters *UNN* in the center.

"What's this?" Danny asked, after taking a sip of the coffee Kingsley had handed him.

"UNN. The Universal News Network. It's produced by PUPCO. We watch the local news from Yoobatar occasionally, but quite honestly, it's usually somewhat boring."

"In other news," said the anchor, "PUPCO media liaison Huppa Nanstrom held a press conference late yesterday to announce that Wallabus has been admitted to PUPCO, ending a long and controversial entrance process. Several members of the council of senior planets were strongly opposed to the admission based on the fact that the last war on Wallabus ended only eighty-three U-years ago and because it was only eight U-months ago that the planet reached the requisite CUSTAR of one hundred."

"What's a CUSTAR?" Danny asked.

"CUSTAR is a planet's cultural, spiritual, and technological advancement rating. PUPCO monitors a planet's development in these areas from the time they suspect, even before in some cases, and they are assigned a CUSTAR. The rating is an average of the ratings of the three areas. When they reach a CUSTAR of forty, the PUPCO delegation visit typically occurs and the planet becomes aware. When they reach a CUSTAR of one hundred, they are considered for admittance to PUPCO."

"What if they have an average of a hundred but are really high in one area and really low in another?"

"Splendid question, Danny. On most planets, the three ratings are fairly close. It's rare for the beings of a planet to have the intelligence to be technically advanced but not to have grown culturally or spiritually. I suppose

Grug is the best example of that. Don't you think, Shey?"

"Absolutely," said Shey as he approached the table with two plates of scrambled eggs, toast, and fried potatoes, which he placed in front of Danny and Kingsley.

Kingsley continued. "The Grugnok are an unscrupulous combination of pirates and searchers. They're quite advanced technologically but not by their own ingenuity. Their civilization advances by trading for, purchasing, or stealing technology. They travel about the cosmos acquiring anything of value they can get their hands on, by force if necessary, and then trade their bounty for technology. They are smart enough to learn it and copy it, but they rarely make any advancement on their own. The governments of respectable planets won't do business with them, but there are beings, mainly those interested in financial gain, who have no qualms about dealing with them."

"Are they dangerous?"

"They can be. They are not a warring race and don't go out of their way to look for conflict. They actually try to keep a low profile so they don't get PUPCO or any specific planet too annoyed with them. But their loose morals and nearly state-of-the-art technology can make them dangerous.

"I brought them up because their technology rating is well over a hundred but their spiritual and cultural ratings are well below that. They may average a hundred, or close to it, but they wouldn't be considered by PUPCO for a minute. Not that they'd want to join. They're not interested in peaceful coexistence."

As Kingsley and Shey proceeded to eat in silence and watch the newscast, Danny took it all in. The morning sun was streaming in the windows on the right side of the room along with a light breeze that was warm and refreshingly cool at the same time. He took another sip of the coffee, the best coffee he'd ever had, and subconsciously let out a deep sigh. He felt good. A little tired from staying up late and having one, or two, too many beers, but good. He could get used to this, he thought. Good beer, great meals, cool workouts, interesting company, and what was shaping up to be a fascinating adventure. He felt satisfaction, almost cockiness, from having escaped the looming training. He liked Kingsley, possibly more than anyone he'd ever known, and Shey seemed annoying but harmless. The thought of not going back, not returning to what he had considered his comfortable existence, was starting to appeal to him.

"In news from the Polaqui sector," reported the anchor, "Endoophar president Javo Jamison has announced that he will not be running for what would have been a record seventh term. Between joking with reporters during a lighthearted press conference, President Jamison said that he had treasured serving his planet but that it was time for him to pass the baton to someone younger, someone who could lead Endoophar into their thirty-second century with energy and enthusiasm. He also indicated that he wanted to retire while his health allowed him to travel, spend time with his eighteen grandchildren, and, as he put it, 'smack the little white ball around.' Javo Jamison's humor, integrity, compassion, and insight will be missed at PUPCO functions. Let's go to the cosmic weather desk for an update on that nasty meteor shower that is threatening the Clabeena system."

"Screen off, Gracie. So the old son of a bitch is stepping down. I thought that might happen," said Kingsley, slightly sadly.

"Do you know him?" asked Danny.

"Oh, yes. He's one of my oldest and best friends and a great, grand man. I'm sure he's quite melancholy. I may have to give him a call so we can hook up after we're done. If I had a U-buck for every golf ball we hit, laugh we shared, and glass we tipped together, I wouldn't be on this mission and you'd be back in your apartment doing whatever it is you do."

Danny thought for a moment while Kingsley stared into space.

"It's Saturday," he said. "I'd be getting ready to watch the Ohio State football game. Do you think I can pick that up on your television system?"

"No chance," answered Shey. "The U-vision system only broadcasts signals from PUPCO member planets."

"Perhaps Shey can see later if he can still access Earth with our scans and, if so, find out who won the game. If you're done eating, what do you say we clean up and have the round of golf I promised you?"

"Kingsley, there is an incoming call for you," interrupted Gracie.

"Who is it?"

"It is Queen Vivitar Quilicant, and the call is labeled urgent."

"Really?" Kingsley asked rhetorically as Danny tensed. "I'll take it here."

Danny held his breath and cocked his head toward the ceiling, waiting for the voice of Vivitar Quilicant. He got more than he anticipated. The screen came back to life with an image of the queen, sitting at a desk in an ornate, high-backed chair, wearing an emerald green and gold brocade jacket. She was a breathtakingly beautiful woman, who appeared to be in her mid-thirties, with lustrous, flowing chestnut hair that came to rest on her shoulders, remarkably green eyes, and flawless, radiant skin. Danny was mesmerized.

"Hello, Kingsley," she said in a voice that was both strong and friendly.

Danny froze in the hopes of not being noticed, as if she were a predator that could only see its prey if it moved.

"Greetings, Queen Quilicant. I hope you are well, Your Highness."

"I appreciate the effort, Kingsley, but you've known both me and my family much too long to be using such formalities. I'm going to tell you once more to call me Vivitar. How are you, Shey?"

"I'm fine, Your . . . Vivitar," Shey said with a hint of respect, perhaps even reverence.

"And who is this gentleman?" she asked, staring directly at Danny. He didn't know if he was supposed to answer, but there was little chance he could have even if he had wanted to due to the incredible tension in his throat and jaw.

Kingsley spoke up. "This is Danny Kerrigan. He's my newest crew member."

"Hello, Danny," Vivitar said pleasantly.

"Hi," he managed meekly, with an astonishing amount of trembling for such a short response.

"What can I do for you, Vivitar?"

"It's about the mission, Kingsley. We've uncovered some information that, if true, changes things dramatically."

"What did you find out?"

"Perhaps it's best if we spoke in private."

"Danny is privy to the mission details and is a trusted member of my crew. He can hear anything you need to tell me," Kingsley said, as Danny broke his gaze at the screen to look over at him. He was surprised at being called trusted. It made him feel important. "Please proceed."

"It was luck, really. We'd been having no success interrogating Nebbers. They either don't know anything or are extremely committed to Dank, because few of them acknowledged even knowing him, but last evening one of our intelligence people started chatting with someone in a drinking establishment. The person, it turns out, was a Nebber. He proceeded to expound on the Nebber movement and Dank, I assume due to being somewhat inebriated. He claimed that my family's rule would be coming to an end in the next election, that Dank was on the brink of making a huge leap in popularity, and that soon almost everyone on the planet would see things his way. He made no mention of the tablet, but in my view this confirms our suspicions that Dank was behind the theft."

"We've felt certain all along that Dank was responsible," Kingsley said. "I'm afraid I don't see how this changes the mission."

"I'm getting to that. It seems we've terribly underestimated Dank's ranks. He's apparently done a remarkable job of amassing followers while keeping his activities from being discovered by our intelligence. He's recruiting members by presenting himself as less of a rebel this time, more of a mainstream politician who is convincing people that it's time for a change. The bar patron said that the number who have promised their allegiance to Dank in the upcoming election is close to fifty million, with another hundred million who are at least considering Dank as an option. Plus it seems many of them are respected individuals, including law enforcement officers, local government officials, and other professionals."

"Oh my," Kingsley said.

"That's putting it mildly," Vivitar continued. "If Dank is successful in creating an amulet, I'm afraid my family's rule is all but over. If his natural charm and persuasiveness can convince that many people to vote for him, that will increase tenfold if he has the power of the amulet on his side. Kingsley, you know that I would step down gracefully if I were challenged and defeated fairly, but I won't stand by while someone like Dank uses the power of the amulet to push my family out while my popularity is in a temporary dip."

"One thing we still have on our side is that he probably won't be able to read the tablet. Without a Quontal expert, he'll have little chance of deciphering the text. Are all of our experts still accounted for?" Kingsley asked.

"Yes, they are, but that brings me to my next piece of news. A thorough investigation has turned up that there is someone on Fraleeza, a brilliant young linguist by the name of Dr. Jillian Falstaff, who has been studying Quontal for the past couple of years. She may be able to read the tablet, at least well enough to glean the meaning. Our people have had no luck contacting Dr. Falstaff. She hasn't been heard from in a week. Our concern is that she left with Dank, either by force or voluntarily at the promise of a large sum of money."

"Your points are well-taken, Vivitar. I will adjust my efforts accordingly, and I promise you that I will find Dank and the tablet as quickly as possible," Kingsley said. "Is there anything else?"

"Well, yes, there is," she replied. "I'm afraid that Chase Claxon isn't the only security problem we have. Despite our efforts, word has leaked out that you visited the compound recently and that the location and logistics of our meeting gave the appearance that it was not a social call. Those that acquired the information have also noted that you have not been seen at your golf club and favorite restaurants for almost a week. The word is spreading through the searcher community that you have been hired by me to find something. Since no members of my family have been reported missing, the assumption is that you are looking for an object. Some are even jumping to the conclusion that the Tablet of Jakaroo does exist and that it's been stolen."

"Well, that certainly makes things more difficult," said an obviously discouraged Kingsley.

"What's the problem?" Danny whispered to Shey.

"The problem, Danny," Kingsley explained, "is that Queen Quilicant is worried that my celebrity will now hinder the mission. Am I not correct?"

"Kingsley, you know that you are revered in the searcher community and fairly well known among the general public, and not only on Yoobatar. We knew you were the best person for the job and took the chance that it had been so long since you retired that anyone recognizing you wouldn't think anything of it. But these developments change everything, dramatically. Every searcher in the universe, amateur and professional, is going to be looking for you. Any report of your whereabouts will result in hundreds of them flocking to whatever planet you're on and getting on your trail. Kingsley, we cannot allow that to occur, given the nature of this matter. I now feel, and my family agrees, that our risk would be lower and our chances of finding Dank higher if we used a clandestine military operation. I'm sorry, Kingsley, but I must cancel your mission. We will pay you fifteen percent of your fee for your trouble."

Danny's head was flooded with images of his adventure coming to an end, of going back to his apartment, watching television, doing his job, and . . . preparing for the training class.

"I understand your concern," Kingsley said after pausing for a moment, "but what if I told you I could accomplish my mission without any chance that I would be recognized?"

Vivitar looked skeptical. "You're a very recognizable figure with striking features. An elaborate disguise may help, but someone may still recognize you. Plus, if you are investigating and asking questions of people, someone could become suspicious and identify you from your fingerprints, a DNA scan, or via voice recognition. I think it's still too risky. I'm afraid the same is true for Shey."

"I'm not talking about disguising myself. I'd like to take you up on your offer and continue this conversation in private. Will you hold for a moment?"

"Certainly," replied Vivitar before her image faded from the view screen.

As Kingsley hurried out of the room, Shey held his napkin out to Danny. "She's gone now. You can wipe the drool from your chin."

Danny reached for his chin but stopped short of touching it. "Okay, so she's good-looking. What? You don't think so?"

"She's reasonably attractive, but I like taller women, over six feet."

"So you have to carry around a step stool to kiss them?"

"I don't need a step stool to kiss them when they're horizontal, which is generally the case within a short time after I set my sights on them."

"Uh-huh. I hear you. You remind me of guys from high school that bragged about how lucky they got when they really went scoreless."

"Believe what you will," Shey said calmly.

"It's kind of a bummer, the mission being cancelled, huh?"

"The mission won't be cancelled."

"But you heard what she said."

"The mission won't be cancelled. She will see things his way."

After a few more awkward, silent minutes passed, Kingsley strolled back into the room and took the seat he had vacated, taking a sip of his coffee, seemingly oblivious to the stares.

"That's awful," he said. "I can't stand cold coffee. Cold coffee or warm beer. Isn't it interesting that beverages can taste so good at one temperature and so bad at another?"

"What happened?" Danny finally blurted out.

"With Vivitar? She's considering my proposal. I'm confident our mission will continue."

Danny tried not to show his jubilation. "How'd you talk her into it?"

"I simply convinced her that we could complete the mission successfully with no chance of me being spotted."

"How are you going to do that? Shey is going to do all the mission stuff while you run it from here?"

"No," replied Kingsley. "That wouldn't work either. You see, Shey has become fairly well-known from being my assistant for so long. He's certainly not as recognizable as me, but there is definitely the chance he could be identified. But you're on the right track."

"What are you going to do, send Abby out to do the work?"

"No," Kingsley said slowly.

"Unless you're hiding someone else on the ship, I'm the only one left. So what are you going to do?"

His query was met with a pair of stares, a smirk, and a smile.

CHAPTER 8

"Oh no! No, no, no, no, no!" Danny exclaimed as a mini-Mardi Gras started in his stomach.

Kingsley was unfazed. "Congratulations, Danny. You've been promoted from mission lackey to mission lead."

"No! I can't do that. I'm serious. I can't do it!"

"Nonsense, you can do it. It's not quantum nano-thermonetics. It's just detective work—questioning people, following leads, looking for clues. The difficult part is interpreting information, deciding the next step, and figuring out the best approach to take to get beings to cooperate, and I'll help you with all of that. We'll be in constant communication. I'll hear everything going on, including what you say, and will be able to give you guidance through any and all situations. You'll be my eyes and ears. The mission will still have my know-how and insight; it will just be executed through you."

"No, I mean it. I can't do all that stuff. You have to come up with another plan!" Danny yelled as he wiped his sweaty forehead with his napkin and tried to find enough moisture in his mouth to muster a swallow.

"There are no other options. I assured Vivitar that we can make this work, that we'd have a better chance than a military operation. She's conferring with her family now and will be making a decision shortly."

"Why don't you just recruit someone else, another person who can be the lead?"

"Danny, the mission has obviously taken on a new urgency. We don't have the time to find a suitable planet, even if there is one nearby, and go through the recruiting process again."

"You don't understand. I just . . . I can't do it."

"What's the problem? What don't I understand?"

"I'm just not good at . . . I don't deal with people very well."

"It's obvious that you're a bit on the shy side, but you can work through that with my help. No kidding around here, Danny. I need you to take the lead on this. If you don't, the mission will end. We'll be out our fee, and you'll be dropped back onto your world."

"I'm not kidding around. I'm telling you that I—"

"Kingsley, Queen Quilicant is calling for you again."

"On the screen, Gracie."

"Vivitar," Kingsley said pleasantly.

"I've decided to let you continue with the mission, Kingsley. I don't think I can emphasize enough how critical this is to my family and to the future of Yoobatar."

"Thank you, Your Highness. We won't let you down."

Vivitar turned her attention to Danny. "Mr. Kerrigan, I understand you are now my champion."

The words made Danny melt. He stared back, mesmerized by the gorgeous green eyes now focused on him, until Shey kicked him under the table. "Uh . . . yes, ma'am. I guess so."

"I certainly hope you undertake the mission with more confidence than you are currently exuding. I'm counting on you, Danny. Don't let me down."

"He won't. I'll make sure of it. He's just a little overwhelmed by meeting you," Kingsley said.

"Let's hope so. I'll expect progress reports every couple of days, with any major turn of events being reported immediately, regardless of the time of day."

"Certainly."

"Gentlemen, may you remain focused, fearless, and in the flow," Vivitar concluded before her image melted away.

"There, crisis averted," said Kingsley. "Gracie, maximum speed to Kronk."

"What did she mean by 'in the flow'?" Danny asked.

"It's just an expression my people use. It means to flow with the universe."

"I don't understand."

"No, of course you don't. Everything in the universe is a constantly moving stream, a stream of energy that takes the shape of information, situations, beings, and tangible and not-so-tangible objects. Everything and everyone you encounter comes through your life for a reason. It's either something you've created or something the universe has placed in your world as an opportunity for you to learn or as subtle guidance down a particular path.

"To flow with the universe is to flow with life rather than fight it. To fight life is to get into a negative, pessimistic mindset, to complain, mentally or verbally, about everything that occurs. You question why each situation is happening to you, not with objective contemplation but with anger and frustration. You view life as a struggle. Your other option is to flow with life, to trust the universe. You make the best of everything that is presented to you. You view nothing as a setback; you let nothing faze you. You learn and grow from your experiences. You let go of fears, worries, obsessions, and no longer desperately cling to desired outcomes. You go through life, as Vivitar said, focused and fearless. You move along gracefully with the flow of the universe. Does that make sense?"

"It sounds hard to do."

"It only seems difficult if you have been in fight mode for a long time. If you make an effort to flow, it soon has the opposite effect of fighting. Everything seems to start working out, good things start happening to you, and you stop feeling like life is a struggle. Danny, your stream has led you to this point. It has presented you with an opportunity to lead our mission.

Are you going to flow or fight?"

Danny stared into space for a few moments. He suddenly shook himself. "What am I doing? No, Kingsley, I can't do it. I just can't. I mean, I don't want to let everyone down and I really don't want to go home, but me leading the mission just isn't an option. I'm a guy from a small town in Ohio. You're talking about going to planets by myself and dealing with aliens."

"I'll compromise a bit. Kronk doesn't travel, and we'll quite possibly end up going to other planets that don't as well. Shey will go with you to any planet that doesn't travel since there is little chance of him being recognized. He'll have to stay in the shadows though. There's always the chance someone will begin following us. If they find and question the same beings that we do, we can't have them describing Shey."

"That would help, I guess, but there's still too much I'd have to do by myself. I didn't agree to this in my apartment," Danny said, although the idea of someone going with him, even Shey, sounded much better than going alone.

"Danny, I'm going to let you in on a simple universal truth. Things change. People, situations, material possessions. They all change. It's part of the stream of the universe I was talking about. When things change, you evaluate, adapt, and move forward. Don't retreat back to your life because it's the easy way out. It may be comfortable now, but it can change also. Your world changed when you stepped into the Star Hopper. Now it's changing more. Are you willing to adapt?"

"I don't know. It's not that I don't want to do it. I'd like to help, really I would. It's that I *can't* do it."

"That's where you are blatantly wrong, Danny. You can do anything you put your mind to. If you commit to the mission, you will be able to do it. You are incredibly intelligent and have tremendous deductive reasoning and problem-solving skills that you use every day at your job. You may not think they translate to other situations, but they do. With your skills and my guidance, I know you can do this. You don't want to let Vivitar down, do you, Danny?"

"Did you see the way Danny was looking at Vivitar, Kingsley?" Shey asked. "I think he's got a crush on the queen."

"I do not," Danny shot back.

"And you know," Shey continued, "I think she thought he was kind of cute too. I'll bet she would thank him personally if he were to present her with the tablet. She might even give him a kiss on his sweet little cheek." Shey reached over and pinched Danny's face.

"Knock it off!" Danny yelled as he swatted Shey's hand away.

Kingsley seemed to enjoy the interaction, as if he were watching two of his sons playfully tussling with each other. "Danny, why don't you take a step back and let all of this soak in. Go take a shower and change clothes and think about it for a bit."

"Okay," Danny said.

He returned to his room and looked around. It felt different, less like a sanctuary and more like a strange hotel room. Abby was on the sofa. He sank down next to her.

"Damn it, Abby. This isn't what I signed up for. If I wanted to deal with this kind of crap, I'd have stayed home. What the hell am I going to do?"

He went to the bedroom and peeled off his clothes. After a long, hot shower, Danny put on a robe and sat on the bed beside the dog.

"Gracie," he continued after a pensive pause, "what's Kingsley's fee for the mission?"

"Five million U-bucks."

"About how many United States dollars would that be?"

"Currently, approximately 8.6 million of your dollars."

"There's no way for Kingsley to exchange U-bucks for US dollars, is there?"

"No, there is not. Currencies can only be exchanged for other currencies through the PUPCO bank. Both planets must be PUPCO members."

"About how many U-bucks would I need to invest to make, after taxes, an amount that would assure the same quality of life on Yoobatar that one hundred thousand US dollars per year would on Earth?"

"Seven-hundred and eighty-two thousand."

"Thanks, Gracie."

Danny got dressed and headed back to the living room.

"Welcome back, Danny. What did you decide?"

"I'll do it for part of your fee," Danny said, much more meekly than he had intended, while looking at the floor.

"Part of my fee? Danny, that won't do you any good. There's no way to convert U-bucks to your dollars."

"I won't need to. I want to live on Yoobatar," Danny said. "At least, I want the option. It sounds like a really great place, peaceful, very advanced, nice people. And they have movies and golf and beer, right?"

"Yes, all of that is true," said Kingsley, slowly rubbing his beard.

"I want enough money that I can live there comfortably without working. I figure I'll need eight hundred thousand U-bucks to do that. When the mission's over, I want to go there and have you show me around, help me find a place to live, learn about the culture, and set up my investments. I won't be a burden though. Once you've helped me set up, you can forget about me. But if I get there and don't like it, you'll take me back to Earth."

"Danny, you seem to be forgetting that Yoobatar has a rule against aliens taking up residence. I would be willing to consider your plan, but they simply won't let you live there."

"There are exceptions to everything. I'll be a hero if we take back the tablet, and you've got a lot of pull with the royal family. I think you'd be able to convince Vivitar to let me stay, especially if you give your word that I'll be a good citizen."

Kingsley stared at Danny for a minute before replying. "I don't relish the thought of giving up part of my fee, but I've little choice at this point. Okay, you've got a deal. Agreed?"

"Agreed," said a relieved Danny.

"Well then, let the mission begin. That round of golf will have to wait. You are now officially the mission lead. We have to prepare you for your duties, and we don't have much time."

"What are you going to do, like, teach me how to fight?"

Kingsley chuckled. "Oh, heavens no. There shouldn't be any need for violence. We're going to teach you how to go about being the mission lead and how to most effectively carry out my direction. But first, we need to determine your capabilities, identify any areas in which you may need some work, and get a better feel for the true nature of earthlings. We will start with a thorough psychological examination, to be administered by Shey in the conference room."

Danny looked over at Shey with a slightly nauseous look.

"Don't worry, Danny; we're going to have a wonderful time together. It's been some time since I've had a new subject to examine," said Shey in his best mad scientist voice.

"Shey," Kingsley said sternly. "Let's play this straight. This is important stuff."

"Okay. Come on, sport."

Danny followed Shey from the living room, looking back at Kingsley on his way out the door as if it were the last time he'd ever see him. As they entered the foyer, Shey spun to face Danny.

"I'm glad we're finally alone. I've been wanting to talk to you. I'm taking the ship, and I need to know if you're with me."

"What?" asked a bewildered Danny.

"I'm taking the ship, and I need to know if I can count on you. Are you with me?"

"What are you talking about?"

"What am I talking about? I'm talking about a mutiny, a coup, a rebellion against Kingsley's tyranny! I've had enough of his arrogant attitude . . . thinking he's always right, telling me how to behave. It will be simple, really. I'll sneak something in his drink at dinner tonight that will incapacitate him. Once he's restrained, the ship is ours! Of course, we'll need to stop him from giving voice commands to Gracie until we can deposit him on some non-traveling planet. Let's see . . . I know. You can eat something really exotic in front of him, say, a piece of broccoli. That will keep him speechless for days."

Danny's shock quickly turned to anger. "Damn it. You scared the hell out of me! Why do you do that?" he shouted after Shey, who had turned and walked briskly into the conference room.

"Why? Because it's fun. It's entertaining, at least mildly, and it's certainly more interesting than typical, mundane chatter," Shey explained. "Now have a seat at the table."

Danny took a moment to have a look around before complying. The room definitely had a more businesslike feel than the rest of the ship. It was long and narrow, with a gleaming, reddish-brown wood table in the center, surrounded by a dozen black, high-backed chairs. A large screen dominated the far wall.

"That mutiny stuff you were doing, didn't Kingsley just tell you to knock it off?" Danny asked as he took a seat.

Shey chuckled. "What's he going to do, fire me? I don't think so. He's got people skills, but without me he wouldn't be able to find a drink at a cocktail party. He may be in charge, but I run things. I execute the plans. We're more like partners really. He'd be lost without me. He knows it, and he knows that I know it. He tells me things like that in the hope that I'll tone it down a bit, which I have done by the way, but he knows I'm going to do what I want."

As Danny listened, he realized he wasn't as uncomfortable with Shey as he thought he'd be. It even crossed his mind that he might actually like him.

"Gracie, give me a display with the exam questions," Shey said. A beam of light rose from a hole in the table and created a virtual display.

"I'm going to ask you a series of questions," Shey continued. "All you have to do is answer each one honestly without giving it too much thought. This test works best if you go with your first reaction. Gracie will record your answers, combine them with everything you've said and done since boarding the ship, and formulate the results. Are you ready to begin?"

"I guess so. It sounds easy enough."

"Look me in the eyes and state your name, address, and age."

Danny looked at Shey's face, wincing slightly.

"Danny Kerrigan," he said as he moved his glance to the floor. "2122 Warren Place, Apartment 2D, Columbus, Ohio. I'm twenty-eight years old."

"If you had to be one of the following objects, a television, a work of art, a mirror, or a garden hose, which would you choose to be?"

"Excuse me?"

"You're excused. Now answer the question."

"I don't see what . . ."

"Answer the question."

"I don't know. I guess a garden hose."

"The Ohio State Buckeyes have an undefeated season and make it to the national championship game in collegiate football. Thirty minutes before the game is to begin, you lose your television signal. What do you do at that point?"

"I hope like hell it comes back on before the game starts."

"And if the problem is not remedied five minutes before the start of the game?"

"I guess I'd listen to it on the radio."

"Prior to boarding this ship, when was the last time you tasted a food you had never tried before?"

"I can't remember. Many years ago, I guess."

"You are going to a social gathering for which you feel you do not have the appropriate attire. You are shopping in a clothing store and find the perfect shirt, the only one you like in the entire store. You pick up the only one they have in your size. While you are looking at other items, you place the shirt on a display table a couple of feet away. Another customer, a middle-aged woman, picks up the shirt and begins to walk away with it. What do you do?"

"Look for another shirt."

"You find out that the wife of a good friend has left him and will be asking for a divorce. Do you plan to go see him as soon as feasible, call him to offer your support, wait until you see him again and discuss it at that point, or do nothing?"

"I don't really have any good friends."

"I'm sure you did at some point. Use your imagination."

"I don't know, I might mention it if I saw him. I might not say anything. It depends on the situation."

"You are driving on a highway when the car ahead of you careens off the road into a ditch. Do you stop and go back to see if you can help, call for help using your cell phone, or continue on and do nothing?"

"I'd probably do nothing. Someone else would help them."

"When was the last time you struck up a conversation with a stranger?"

"I've never struck up a conversation with a stranger," Danny replied.

"How long ago was your last intimate contact with a female?"

Danny shifted in his chair. "I've never had . . ." Danny cleared his throat. "I've never had intimate contact with a woman."

Shey glanced at him for a moment before turning his attention back to the display. "You have a very serious personal problem with which you are struggling mightily. With whom, specifically, do you choose to discuss it?"

"I wouldn't discuss it with anyone. Like I said, I don't really have any friends or family."

"Same scenario, only it occurred when you were sixteen years old. It could be anyone. Friends, family, a physician, teacher, or therapist."

Danny thought for a moment before responding. "I wouldn't discuss it with anyone. It's my problem. I'll figure out what to do."

"When was the last time you hugged someone or were hugged by someone?"

"What in the world does this have to do with the mission?" Danny said in a raised voice. "This is a waste of time."

"Such outbursts serve no purpose and only hinder the examination. Kingsley ordered you to answer all questions. Shall I let him know you are unwilling to cooperate?"

"No. Never mind. I don't remember ever hugging anyone. Been hugged?

I don't know. I guess my parents probably did when I was growing up, but I don't really remember."

"Consider this carefully. You are offered two million dollars to give a one-hour speech to the United States Congress, a speech which details your life up to this point. Do you accept the offer?"

"No," Danny said without hesitation.

"As I instructed, consider the question carefully. I believe that amount of money would—"

"No."

"Next scenario. There is a young lady working for your company that you think is quite attractive. She works on another floor, but you see her a couple of times a week on the elevator. One day, she hands you a piece of paper before exiting the elevator. On it is a phone number. What do you say when you call her that night?"

"I wouldn't call her."

"The next morning, you enter the elevator to find only her. What do you say?"

"Nothing."

"You have fifteen thousand dollars in the bank. You are presented with an investment opportunity that requires an investment of ten thousand dollars. There is a 95 percent chance of tripling your money with a 5 percent chance you would lose it all. Do you invest?"

"No."

"Would you rather be stuck in an elevator with a pregnant woman who is about to give birth, just you and the woman in the elevator, or spend six months in prison?"

"Come on. I've been trying to cooperate, but this is getting ridiculous."

"Answer the question."

"Six months in prison."

"Would you rather be a successful professional golfer, a vice president in your company, or a janitor?"

"None of them."

"Select the least objectionable."

"I guess a janitor."

"List what are currently your top three goals, personal or professional."

"Goals?"

"Yes, goals," replied Shey. "Things you'd like to accomplish, areas in which you'd like to improve, a position in life you'd like to achieve."

"I guess I don't really have any."

Shey continued on, peppering him with several dozen more questions, none of which seemed the least bit mission-relevant to Danny.

"Okay," Shey said casually. "That concludes the exam. Good job. We'll discuss the results with Kingsley over an al fresco lunch. He's waiting for us in the dining area of the yard. You go on ahead. I'll be along in a few minutes."

Danny made his way to the yard, where he found the simulation of another glorious summer day. He took the path to the right and soon caught sight of Abby, bounding down the path toward him.

"Hey, girl! How you doing?" After a few moments of rubbing her and fending off her exuberant licks, Danny continued down the path to the patio area, where he found Kingsley, sitting quietly with his eyes closed. Danny froze, not wanting to disturb him.

"Come have a seat, Danny," Kingsley said before opening his eyes. "I was just meditating."

"Meditating?"

"Yes. Don't you meditate?"

"No. I mean, I've heard of it, but I always thought it was kind of . . . weird."

"You say that as though it has a negative connotation."

"Yeah, I guess so."

"Nonsense. It's easy and convenient to classify something with which you are unfamiliar as weird. Meditation is a good example. People dismiss it because they don't understand it and have never tried it. It clears your mind of the clutter and worries of day-to-day life, which, left unchecked, can accumulate and generate stress, which in turn generates illness. Clearing one's mind also leads to awareness of and connection to spirit, the universe, the energy that makes up everything you perceive, and that which you cannot. In fact, I think later you should give it a go. It would help calm you for the mission assignments."

"I don't know. I suppose I could try it."

"Have a seat and some lunch," Kingsley said, motioning to a covered plate and the empty chair in front of it. "So I trust the exam wasn't too unpleasant?"

"It was okay."

"And did Shey behave himself?"

"I wouldn't say that exactly, but he wasn't too bad. He sure thinks a lot of himself," Danny said while scrutinizing the turkey sandwich, greens, and vegetables that were under the lid.

"Yes, he has quite the ego, but I've learned to deal with that over the years. I don't come down on him too hard for his sarcasm because he's so damn sensitive. I also let him think he's a lot more in control around here than he is because it keeps his spirits up. Don't get me wrong; he's very talented and extremely valuable, but he wouldn't be able to find a book in a library without me around to analyze information and make decisions. Speak of the devil," Kingsley finished as Shey strolled up.

"Good afternoon, gentlemen," said Shey, taking a seat.

Kingsley lifted the cover from his plate. "Okay, Dr. Gabink. What's the verdict?"

"Before I get to that, I want to pass along some information that Danny may be interested in. I just tapped back into Earth's communication systems and found that Ohio State won their game today, 38–17."

"Really? Don't joke around about that, Shey."

"I'm not joking around. I swear on the Great Book of Troosec that I'm telling the truth."

"That's awesome! We're still undefeated!"

"I'm very happy for you, Danny. Now, if we can get back to business. Shey, the verdict?"

"The verdict is that, based on this examination along with observing him for a full day, we have to scrub the mission."

"What? Why?" Kingsley asked.

"Why? I'll tell you why. Because we have no one to lead it. If we let him do it, the Quilicants might as well start packing and Yoobatar can say goodbye to its civilization."

"Hey!" Danny yelled as Kingsley put down his sandwich and sat back in his chair.

CHAPTER 9

"Shey," Kingsley said. "Such overly-dramatic statements serve no purpose. Now, seriously, what's the problem?"

"The problem? I wish there were only one."

"You said I did good!" Danny was reeling.

"What I meant was that you cooperated without putting up much of a fuss. I wasn't referring to the results."

"Damn it, Shey. Explain," ordered Kingsley.

"It seems we've overestimated Mr. Kerrigan's abilities. To be more precise, his antisocial tendencies and dearth of people skills are more than alarming."

"I'll admit I'm a little shy, but once I get used to somebody, I'm okay."

"A little shy? That's like saying an Opzillian mountain beast is a little aggressive."

"Shey, we knew Danny was shy. All of our recruits live alone and have loner tendencies. It's what makes them good candidates. What makes you think we can't coach him through this?"

"Coach him through it? Fergo Woolnut couldn't coach him through it."

"Fergo Woolnut?" asked Danny.

"He's a famous basketball coach from the planet Hunderpa, probably the most famous coach in the universe. Shey, you still haven't told me why you're so adamant about this."

Shey continued. "Mr. Kerrigan's condition can be summed up in one word: *fear*. His life is ruled by fear. He has a tremendous fear of unfamiliar or unknown situations that keeps him from trying anything new or unusual, even if the perceived payoff is quite pleasurable. He is terrified of confrontation or conflict, so much so that he will avoid any interaction that he thinks has any possible chance of leading to either, no matter how important the issue. It's clear he has an acute fear of intimacy that makes him uncomfortable with even the slightest physical or emotional contact with another living being. And speaking of emotions, he's also afraid to express them, at least anything beyond anger, which he only lets slip if he is extremely upset.

"Vivitar's champion also has a fear of expressing opinions and making decisions, which results in him refusing to give opinions even when solicited and causes him to obsess over the smallest of personal choices. Probably linked to that to some degree is a tremendous fear of getting into trouble, dealing with authority figures, and an acute fear of failing. Last, and most certainly not least, is that he has the worst case of performance anxiety and fear of public speaking that I've ever witnessed, a fear so deeply engrained that the mere thought of talking in front of people invokes severe physical symptoms."

Danny had stopped eating and was sitting motionless, staring at the table.

"All of these issues bundled together have resulted in him having a tremendous fear of dealing with and connecting with people," Shey continued. "It's why he avoids human interaction unless it's absolutely necessary. When forced to deal with people, he is always apprehensive, talks very little, gets flustered easily, and makes almost no eye contact. If he perceives that he is the center of attention among several people, if an authority figure questions him about something, or if he finds himself in an unfamiliar situation, he has what would be best described as a panic attack. I think we probably witnessed a mild one last night when you asked him to expound upon life on Earth."

"Well, this certainly changes things," said Kingsley as Shey paused.

"I'm not done yet. I'm just catching my breath. If he manages to move past the initial anxiety and gets used to a person or situation, as he apparently has with us, he is friendly, with a pleasant demeanor, but he's also timid, indecisive, risk averse, reticent, and void of charisma. He shows no emotion, lets no one close physically or emotionally, and is only comfortable when he is safe within the confines of his own little world. After examining him, I'm astounded that he agreed to join us. The only possible explanation is that he was trying to escape something that he considered horrible, something more frightening than the prospect of going off into space with two strangers.

"In summary, we didn't just get a mildly shy loner, Kingsley, we got a trembling mass of fear and insecurity who is nearly void of the talents required of someone to lead the mission, even with your hand-holding. Aside from his complete lack of personal interaction skills, he has none of the assertiveness, charm, sense of adventure, decisiveness, or self-confidence needed to properly handle a task of such great importance. I think we'd have a better chance if we took Danny's advice and had Abby lead the mission."

Kingsley let the analysis sink in for a few moments. "As Shey was speaking, my first reaction was to chastise him for jumping to so many conclusions and being so hard on you, Danny, but I decided to hear him out and then get your side of the story. So? What do you have to say about his assertions?"

Danny too had changed his view as Shey spoke. His initial outrage slowly melted, giving way to curiosity and finally contemplation. No one had ever analyzed him, at least not to his face. Oddly enough, he wasn't offended in the least by Shey's rather blunt assessment and harsh words. On the contrary, he had quickly detached himself from the drama of the situation and slipped into a clinical mode, as if he were a colleague of Shey who was listening in on a patient's diagnosis. It was as if he had been waiting all his life for someone to notice all of this, someone to understand him, to see how he really viewed the world and what he went through on a daily basis. He wasn't offended. He was relieved.

"Danny?" Kingsley said cautiously.

Danny slowly lifted his head and stared at Shey with a sad serenity. "I think he's right on the money."

Kingsley was dumbfounded. "What?"

"I said he's right. Everything he said is right," Danny said, shifting his glance to Kingsley.

"Why didn't you tell me any of this when I was recruiting you?" asked Kingsley, his voice gaining volume.

"You didn't ask."

"I didn't ask?" His voice went up another notch. "Don't you think it would have been worth mentioning?"

"It's not the kind of thing I really talk about. As a matter of fact, I've never discussed it with anyone other than my mom. And I'm not sure she ever really understood how bad it is."

"But why did you agree to go if you're so damn afraid of everything?"

"Shey was right. I was trying to run away. They're going to force me to teach a bunch of training classes. If I don't do it, I think I might lose my job. I didn't know what to do, so I guess I thought I'd run away."

"But why did you agree to lead the mission this morning?"

"Oh, I don't know. I guess I still thought it was better than going home and facing the training. In some cases an unknown is better than a horrible known."

Kingsley looked at Shey, who was sitting silently, looking at Danny with . . . with . . . was it compassion?

"Well, I suppose that means we scrap the mission," said Kingsley. "Gracie, get me Vivitar Quilicant."

"No, wait," Danny blurted.

"Hold on, Gracie. What is it, Danny?"

"What if . . . what if I tried to be the lead like we told her?"

"I think we've established that you are not psychologically suited to handle that role," replied Kingsley.

"I think I can do it."

"Danny, just saying you think you can do it because you want to avoid what's waiting for you at home is not really good enough. We can't afford to spend more time on this only to have you turn into a puddle when the mission is on the line. If I called Vivitar in two or three days and told her we were backing out, she would be beyond livid."

"But why can't you help me? You said you could coach me. I've never had anyone work with me on any of this stuff. I'll bet with your help I could get through it. It's not like I have to do a presentation or anything, right?"

"Not a presentation, but you'll need to talk to people, perhaps multiple people at times, and you might have to pitch them a story in order to get information," said Kingsley.

Danny swallowed hard. "That's fine. I can do that, with your help."

"Danny, I've certainly accumulated some wisdom over the years, but I'm a searcher, not a psychologist. I just don't think I'm equipped to supply the kind of help you require."

"But I like the stuff you've been teaching me since I got here. It makes a lot of sense. I don't need a psychologist."

"Shey?" Kingsley asked, looking over at his assistant.

"It would be difficult, but he does have two things on his side: his intelligence and his problem-solving skills. The former would help him understand what we'd be trying to accomplish with our coaching, and the latter may be of some assistance, particularly if he thought of his situation as a problem that needs to be solved."

"Shey may be on to something, Danny," Kingsley said. "Perhaps we could leverage your existing skills to overcome your issues. It wouldn't be easy, but it might just work. Could you do that?"

"Yeah, I guess so."

"There's no guessing about it. We would have to cram into a couple of weeks what may normally be handled in months if not years of therapy. Think of it as a psychological boot camp. And I want to emphasize that this is not a game. We're dealing with not only my legacy and reputation but quite possibly the direction of Yoobatarian society over the next several hundred years. So there will be no quitting. If the mission's a go, once we leave this table, there's no bailing on us if things get unpleasant. If you try to quit on us mid-mission, I'll put you in a Solo Trek and jettison you into space."

Kingsley's threat got Danny's attention, awakening his sleeping anxiety. But he didn't let it deter him. He had made up his mind.

"Let's do it," he said.

Kingsley sighed deeply. "What the hell, no one has ever said Kingsley Vortex ran away from a challenge. The mission's a go."

"Danny, Kingsley requests your presence in the guest gathering room."

Danny had just awoken from an hour-long post-lunch nap. "Tell him I'm on my way, Gracie."

As Danny headed down the hall and across the foyer, his apprehension grew. The concept of dealing with his issues, which had seemed good, even grand in theory, now seemed rather foolish, even ludicrous, as he crossed the foyer. When he arrived at the entrance, he paused, took a deep breath, and stepped through the doorway. It was an enormous room, as long as the conference room and more than twice as wide. The wall at the left end was angled, giving the front two-thirds of the room a triangular shape. The lengthy wall was home to several windows, so the room was drenched in sun. Each window was framed by cream draperies, which accented the dark taupe walls. There were three levels containing several distinct conversation or entertainment areas. He found Kingsley sitting at a small, round table in the back right corner of the room.

"Danny," Gracie said, "you should be consuming substantially more water than you have been since boarding the ship."

"I'm not thirsty."

"Please proceed to the service bay and begin consuming the bottle of water that is waiting there. I don't want to have to tell you again."

"What the hell is up with her?" Danny asked as he looked at the ceiling.

"You've shown signs of not being terribly concerned for your own well-being at times," Kingsley replied. "Left on your own, your tendency is to make hedonistic choices over what is best for you in the long run. Since the mission is now riding on you, we can't have that. I've placed Gracie in mother mode."

"Mother mode?"

"Yes, mother mode. Until further notice, she will constantly monitor your activities, vital signs, speech pattern and tone, and overall health. If she determines that you are about to do something detrimental to your well-being or if there is something you should be doing that you aren't, she will give you direction, at first gently and then more forcefully if you don't comply."

"So what's she going to do, spank me?"

"Not exactly, but you're on the right track. There are thousands of microscopic holes in the floor, walls, and ceiling of every room and hallway. From those holes, Gracie can emit the same stun rays that can be generated from the MR5. It's mainly for defense, in case a guest becomes hostile or the ship is attacked and boarded. She also can emit what we like to call the tickle ray. It gives you the sensation that you are being tickled all over your body. If she hits you with a few seconds of that, you'll comply."

Danny swallowed hard. "And if I don't?"

"Not to worry. She's not going to start zapping you with stun rays. If you still don't comply, she will report to me that you are being uncooperative, and then we'll have a talk about your commitment to the mission. Now pick up the bottle of water and come and sit down across from me.

"When dealing with beings on the planets we'll be visiting, you'll need to present an image of strength and confidence. There are all kinds of beings out there, Danny. If an aggressive or unscrupulous one senses that you're indecisive or timid, they may view you as weak and try to take advantage of you, perhaps even physically intimidate you. Or worse. You need to make strong, clear statements so they respect you and take you seriously. In case you didn't realize it, the training has started, so I hope you're paying attention and taking this all seriously."

"Absolutely," said Danny.

"That's better. When dealing with kind, moral beings, which will more than likely be the case the majority of time, they are more likely to cooperate with you if they sense strength. People are drawn to strong, confident, high-energy people. Your style of speech conveys your personality and your attitude. Yours could be viewed as one of apathy. Would you consider yourself to be apathetic, Danny, honestly?"

"Yeah, I guess I am about a lot of things."

"You can't let them sense apathy. If they sense you don't really care, why should they bother helping you? The quickest remedy for apathy is to have a goal. When you have a clearly defined goal, and you care deeply about achieving that goal, you focus and act with purpose, perhaps even passion. Do you care about finding the Tablet of Jakaroo?"

"Yes, yes I do."

"Do you *really* care?" Kingsley asked slowly.

"I really care. I want to help Queen Quilicant and Yoobatar."

"Then make retrieving the tablet your goal and work toward it with passion. If you focus all of your energy on that, many of the things that you would normally get anxious about will seem insignificant. So starting right now you are to begin speaking with more definitive words and a stronger tone. No more beginning sentences with 'I guess,' 'I suppose,' or 'Oh, I don't know.' Incorporate more words like *certainly*, *definitely*, and *absolutely*. Use *yes* instead of *yeah*. Does all of this make sense to you, Danny?"

"It does."

"Good. For the remainder of the day and when on Kronk, concentrate on choosing your words carefully before speaking. On to the next issue."

"Gracie, since Danny sat down across from me, what is the total time he has looked directly at my eyes?"

"Four seconds."

"Four seconds," Kingsley repeated. "That won't do. Danny, this is something that needs correcting immediately. When you are talking to someone, you either look down or at some point off to either side of their head, as though you are glancing off of them rather than connecting with them. When you do happen to lock eyes, it looks as though it's a shock to your system, and you quickly look away, as if you've seen a terrible accident. Do you realize that you do this?"

"I suppose I do, but I didn't really know it was that bad. If I look right at a person, I feel really uncomfortable and often lose my train of thought."

"Well, you need to work hard at correcting this for the mission. Otherwise, I guarantee you that the people you encounter will think you're lying or trying to hide something. They will become suspicious and defensive. They simply won't trust you, which is not terribly conducive to getting them to help you or give you information. Almost as important for the success of the mission is that when you make eye contact, you can read people. Being able to tell that someone you encounter is not to be trusted can make or break the mission. Does that make sense?"

"Yes."

"It all comes down to connecting with people and being in the present moment, focusing your energy on the person and perceiving their energy. When you interact with someone, stay in the moment, stay connected. It will take practice, so I want you to start working on this immediately, making strong eye contact with Shey and me whenever we are engaged in conversation."

"I can certainly try."

"Wonderful. Start with me. Now."

"Okay," Danny said, slowly lifting his eyes until they locked on Kingsley's. After a second or two, he blinked rapidly and looked off to Kingsley's side.

"Good God, boy. You're not looking into the sun," Kingsley exclaimed before catching himself and softening. "Try again."

Danny once again focused on Kingsley's face.

"Now take a slow, deep breath, clear your mind, don't blink fast, don't try to guess what I'm thinking, don't grimace, don't think of what you're going to do when we're done here. That's better. Now glance away for a moment and then back. Okay, good. That's what I'm talking about. It isn't so bad, is it?"

"No, no it isn't," Danny said, before looking down at the floor.

"You can make anything second nature if you work at it. Making eye contact needs to be your primary thought when interacting with anyone. Got it?"

"Sure. Can I go to the bathroom before we keep going?"

"We're done."

"That's it? That's my training?"

"That's all you'll need for Kronk. If I overload you, you won't be able to retain it all. Over dinner we will discuss the details of the excursion to Kronk. Now I'd like you to go back to your room and think about what we discussed. Integrate the concepts into your being. Good work, Danny."

As Kingsley exited, Danny stared out the window. He was relieved by the simplicity of the session but had an uneasy feeling it was just the tip of the iceberg.

———

"Graham, I'm worried about Brisby," Marsha Flondike said as she flicked and picked her way through the pile of earrings in her jewelry box like she was looking for the cashews in a bowl of mixed nuts.

"Graham, did you hear me?"

Graham Flondike emerged from his dressing room, making a final adjustment to his bow tie. The tanned, blond-haired, blue-eyed, fifty-two-year-old looked dashing in his tuxedo. He always exuded power and success. The tux only added to his aura.

"We've got to get going," Graham said. "The benefit starts in thirty minutes. I'll make sure Winthrop has the car ready while you finish up."

Marsha stopped her digging and stared at her husband. After twenty-three years of marriage, he still occasionally managed to make her weak-kneed.

"Did you hear me?" asked Marsha as she refocused on finding her earrings.

"Hear what? Wow, you look fantastic. Great dress."

"Thank you. I said I'm really worried about Brisby. He isn't coming out of this . . . this funk."

"Oh, honey, there's nothing to worry about. He's a teenager. He's just going through normal teenage stuff."

"I don't think it's normal, and he's been going through it for a lot longer than he's been a teenager. It's just been worse the last couple of years."

"Okay, okay. I'll tell you what. After I get back from the club tomorrow, we'll sit down and have a serious discussion with him. Like I said, we really have to get going."

Appeased but still uneasy, Marsha gave up on finding the perfect earrings and settled for her second choice. Despite Graham's insistence that she join him in the lift, she stopped at a closed door and touched the illuminated panel to its right.

"Brisby, honey, we're leaving for the evening. Are you okay?"

Her query was met with silence.

"Come on, Marsha," said a perturbed Graham. "He's fine. He's got everything he needs in that room. Let's go."

"Brisby, make sure you eat something, and don't stay up too late."

Marsha finally gave in to Graham's pleading and joined him on the lift. Within minutes they were being whisked away to sip cocktails, laugh politely, and engage in lighthearted conversation at what anyone who was anyone considered to be the social event of the season, the Wanderwill Ball at the Pinclucker Center for the Arts.

Brisby Flondike sat on the edge of his bed and stared at the round yellow pill sitting on his nightstand, not changing his expression or break-ing his gaze, when he heard his mother's voice. It looked innocuous enough, like a cold remedy or headache pill. It certainly was easy enough to obtain. He just searched the internet using the right key words, found a reputable-looking site that promised a product that worked swiftly and painlessly, punched in his card number, and voila, his mother was placing it outside his door. He thought about the fact that his parents would have to pay for it after he used it, his mother possibly breaking down when seeing the charge on the monthly statement and realizing its source. The thought made him feel bad, but it passed quickly. He was too numb to let it bother him too much or too long.

Brisby looked around the room, the room in which he'd spent such a large portion of his life. His eyes came to rest on his large view screen, and he thought about what he would be missing on television that night or if there were any movies he wanted to see. He decided there weren't. He'd seen all the good ones at least three times. Still expressionless, he rose from the bed and made his way into his massive walk-in closet, where he slowly dis-robed and put on his favorite black shirt, a pair of jeans, and black socks. No shoes though. One shouldn't lie in bed with shoes on, he thought. Next, into the bathroom, where he brushed his teeth, combed his hair, and reviewed the state of his complexion. Not bad. Good enough, at least. He stepped in some water that he'd splashed onto the floor while brushing, causing him to return to the closet to change socks. One couldn't lie in bed with a wet sock.

He headed back into his room, over to the wall of windows that gave him a panoramic view of the pristine Flondike property: the enormous pool, sculptured hedges, countless flowers, and manicured lawn as far as the fading daylight allowed him to see. Returning to the edge of the bed, he hesitated before glancing down at the yellow pill. One more trip to the bathroom for a cup of water and quickly back to the bed, where he sighed and stared off into space.

"Music. 'Blue Flame' by Maleena Zeena. Repeat . . . ten times."

As the haunting opening bars of the song filled the room, Brisby closed his eyes and lost himself in the music, softly singing along, nearly inaudibly, to a few of his favorite parts. When the song started for the second time, he opened his eyes, wiped away a single runaway tear, went over to his monitor, typed several letters, and returned to the bed where he quickly picked up the pill and popped it into his mouth. He took a gulp of water and stretched out on the bed, making sure his favorite pillow was the one under his head. He focused on the second play of the song but never heard the third.

Darkness soon dominated the room, the only light coming from the monitor.

"Tired of fighting."

CHAPTER 10

"Come on in, Danny. Don't be shy," shouted Kingsley.

Danny, who had been standing motionless in the doorway, entered the room and joined him at the kitchen bar. Shey was once again busy in the kitchen preparing the evening meal. Anxiety about the Kronk trip had been building since his brief training session. Being alone caused his mind to start racing unchecked. Sliding onto a seat, Danny wondered how these two could be thinking about eating and drinking at a time like this. The gentle rumbling of thunder got his attention. He turned to see that the gorgeous Yoobatarian summer day was being threatened by some ominous storm clouds that appeared in the distance on the right side of the room.

"Do you sense the excitement, Danny? There's just a certain feeling in the air just before the start of a mission. You probably didn't play organized athletics, did you?"

Danny perked up a bit. "Actually, I did."

"Really? What sports?"

"A little baseball and golf, but mainly basketball."

"Were you good at them?"

Danny took a gulp of the beer Shey had set in front of him and considered how to answer. He thought fondly of those days—some of the best of his life.

"Just at basketball. I was a scorer. A pure shooter."

"Really? Given the results of Shey's exam, I wouldn't think you would have played sports. Playing in front of crowds didn't bother you?"

"Not at all."

"You know, that's actually not all that surprising. People were watching you, but you didn't have to connect with them, and you certainly didn't have to talk in front of them. And if you were skilled, that would have helped. My point was comparing the start of a mission to the feeling you have before a game. It's the flow of adrenaline, the slightly nervous energy that builds before the game begins, the energy that helps you focus and perform at peak levels."

"Sure," Danny said softly while thinking quite the contrary. The way he felt wasn't the way he had felt before a basketball game. It wasn't even close. This was dread, not adrenaline. It was more than being slightly nervous, and it was causing his mind to race, not focus.

"Did you work on the issues we discussed?" Kingsley asked.

"Um. Not exactly," Danny said before taking another swig.

"Then what exactly?"

"I didn't really think about them."

"Danny! I give you a couple of simple things to think about and you didn't do it?"

"I didn't feel like it."

"You didn't . . . did you hear that Shey? Danny didn't feel like it. Isn't that wonderful? Danny, I'm all for free will, but this is not the time or the place to be exercising it. If you've got a rebel streak that's rearing its ugly head, decapitate it. Now. This is serious business, and you need to get with the program. Excuse me," Kingsley said before rising and exiting.

Once Kingsley stormed from the room, Danny headed for the service station, asked Gracie for another beer, plopped back down on his stool, and hunkered down over his mug.

"You're not going to win, you know," Shey said matter-of-factly, his arms splayed across the bar.

"What are you talking about?"

"I'm talking about this defiant stance you're trying to take. It isn't going to work. He won't stand for it, and he'll break you down. Now isn't the time for it. You committed this morning to being the lead on this mission. Now isn't the time to throw a tantrum. Now's the time to reach deep down and show some character, some maturity. That is, if there's any in there."

Shey turned away and continued his work. Danny sat quietly, staring at his beer until Kingsley reappeared, grabbed his drink, and took a seat at the dining table behind Danny.

"Sorry about not working on that stuff," Danny said, spinning in his stool to face Kingsley. "I guess I . . . sorry. I mean . . . what happened was when I got back to my room, I got really churned up about the whole thing and was too worried about what was going to happen to think about the training, so I just watched a movie. It won't happen again."

Kingsley took a sip and thought for a moment before speaking. "That's very big of you to say, Danny. I know that took some effort. I know this all—"

"Pardon the interruption, Kingsley, but you asked to be notified immediately when we arrived at Kronk. We have done so and taken up orbit."

"Thank you, Gracie. Let's see it."

The Yoobatarian summer evening depicted in the room's windows was replaced by the black of space. The room took on the look and feel of a ship's bridge. Appearing on the view screen was a planet with land formations, several sizable bodies of water, and patches of cloud cover. The fact that it was very similar to a view Danny had seen hundreds of times in movies and shows didn't help. He became slightly disoriented and a little nauseous looking down at the massive world.

"Have you accessed the computer systems for the government of Hanaba?" Kingsley asked.

"I have. There are several hundred beings named Chase Claxon. None have been reported missing."

"Is there a record of anyone who was reported missing approximately twenty years ago who may have recently reappeared? Dank might have had him use a different name on Yoobatar."

"There are seventeen such accounts. Twelve are male, and five are female."

"Did any of the males work in the area of law enforcement or espionage?"

"One of the males, Jarrison Opal, served for nine years in the Hanaba Falcon Force, a branch of the government responsible for espionage, covert operations, and the security of top elected officials."

"Did he leave the force before his disappearance?"

"According to the records of government agencies, media outlets, and the Hanaweb computer network, he was released from the force under charges that he leaked sensitive information to an acquaintance, who in turn sold it to a media outlet. He maintained that he was the subject of a personal vendetta, held against him by a high-ranking member of the Hanaba government as a result of Jarrison having a sexual relationship with the official's daughter."

"Well, that seems to be his style," Shey interjected as he shuttled back and forth from the kitchen to the table with the evening's meal.

"Gracie," Kingsley said. "What happened after he was dismissed?"

"He was reported missing approximately four months after the ordeal."

"And he recently reappeared?"

"Yes, according to published reports, he contacted a television station two days ago with a story of living on another planet for the past twenty years. The slant they gave the story was that of a possibly disturbed individual with a wild imagination. They also re-reported his episode with the agency. At a minimum, he was viewed as someone who was just trying to get back in the spotlight, probably for financial gain. The story spread rapidly, and he has quickly become national news, with Jarrison being criticized and ridiculed by almost every media outlet in Hanaba. He has terminated all contact with the media and gone into hiding."

"I think we have our man. Gracie, do photographs of Jarrison match those of Chase?"

"Pictures on file for Jarrison and Chase indicate there is a 98 percent chance that the two are the same person."

"Gracie, start a DNA scan for Chase and review security and traffic video, focusing on hotel rooms closest to his last known address and moving outward. Also, scan the residences of everyone listed in his file as an acquaintance or family member."

"I have started the search."

"Well," Kingsley said while motioning for Danny to join Shey and him at the table, "that was easier than expected. Now all we have to do is find him. After hearing his story, I think he will be more than happy to tell us everything he knows about Dank, especially once you drop the name Chase Claxon. Dig in, everyone."

Danny again was looking skeptically at the shallow bowl that was in front of him, tilting his head from side to side to look at its contents from all angles.

"Shey, please let Danny know what's in his bowl."

"Penne pasta with asparagus, shitake mushrooms, sun-dried tomatoes, and grilled shrimp. Topped with grated cheese. All very exotic."

"Think you can handle that, Danny?" Kingsley asked.

"I suppose I can try it."

"Very brave. So tell me, Danny, could you embrace the concepts I explained in this afternoon's session, or did you think them rubbish?"

"Oh no, it all made sense, it's just . . ."

"Eye contact!"

Danny looked up from the table and at Kingsley. "Sorry, it's just stuff I've never thought much about, so it'll take me some time to get used to it."

"With some conscious effort and practice, it can become so natural that you don't have to think about it. As a matter of fact, at some point you may even enjoy truly connecting with people. Shey, I must say you've outdone yourself once again. This pasta is fantastic."

The group dined and chatted until Gracie broke in.

"Kingsley, I have located Jarrison Opal."

"Really? That didn't take long. Where might our wandering Trog be hiding?"

"He is currently in a residence located in the northeastern section of Vee Jimpa, a large city in southeastern Hanaba. The residence is owned by an acquaintance of Jarrison who, according to transportation records, is currently out of the country. The address is 4232 Wyndoggle Way."

"Splendid. Thank you, Gracie."

Hearing that their man had been located, which inched him closer to his first trip to another planet, jumpstarted Danny's anxiety. He finished his beer and headed to the service bay for another, half expecting Kingsley to chastise him for drinking so much.

"Let's talk about the details of the Kronk excursion, Danny," said Kingsley. "This is important mission strategy, so it's vital that you pay attention and absorb this."

But Danny, who was staring at his mug with a rather puzzled look, already wasn't paying attention.

"Something wrong, Danny?" asked Kingsley.

"Oh, uh, no, nothing. I was just wondering about this beer."

"Wondering what? Why you've had three beers and aren't in the least bit inebriated?"

"Well, yeah. I mean, I hardly feel a buzz."

"Yes, that should be the case. You didn't really think I was going to let you escape into drink the night before the mission started, did you? I instructed Gracie not to let you get drunk as part of her mother mode responsibilities. She is monitoring your blood alcohol level and serving you beers with varying amounts of alcohol based on her readings. She's allowing you enough to relax a bit, but not so much that you won't be able to focus on and retain what's discussed. This mission is much too important to be ruined by a hangover."

"I want a regular beer!"

"Why?" Kingsley calmly replied.

"Because I want it, that's why!"

"Because you want to numb your mind so you don't have to think about the mission. Well, that's simply a fear-based reality-avoidance tactic, and I won't allow it!" Kingsley boomed. "It's not going away, Danny. At five tomorrow morning we will wake you up, and you will go to the surface of Kronk and interrogate Jarrison Opal, and no amount of beer you drink is going to change that. Got it?"

"I got it," Danny replied sadly as he pushed his beer mug away.

"Good. Now let's discuss what you'll need to do on Kronk. Once night falls, you and Shey will head down to the planet in the Star Hopper. Wear a black mock turtleneck and black slacks, standard excursion attire. You will land just outside Vee Jimpa and drive to the area in which the residence is located. You will have in your ear a device called an EZ-Comm. It's a thin film that Shey will install in your ear canal. It will allow me to be in constant communication with you. It will also serve as a tracking device, allowing us to locate you at any time. You can toggle it off and on by simply saying 'EZ-Comm off' or 'EZ-Comm on.' You will approach the residence and request admittance. Based on what Gracie told us about Jarrison's situation, what do you think may happen when you do so?"

"He probably won't answer the door, because he doesn't want to talk to anyone."

"Correct, but that shouldn't be difficult to get by. Just say you're there to see Chase Claxon. Once he hears that name, he should answer, but he'll probably be suspicious. You'll then introduce yourself using your alias for the mission. You will be Inka Alibar, from the planet Ipnokia."

"*Inka Alibar*?"

"Yes, Inka Alibar. It may sound odd, but I assure you it would be considered a common name on Ipnokia. We're using Ipnokia because it is in an area to which few beings travel."

"So then what?"

"You tell Jarrison you believe his story. You have been told that he may have information regarding the theft of the Tablet of Jakaroo. Tell him we are interested in the person who hired him. Do not mention Dank Nebitol.

We want to see if he brings him up on his own. Your goal is to get him to name Dank and find out where he went."

"Sure. Except, what if he wants money before giving me any details?"

"Good question, but that won't happen. He'll know that you won't have any Kronkian currency or any way of getting some. Once you get the information, you'll calmly thank Jarrison, exit the house, walk back to the Star Hopper, and the two of you will return."

"That sounds easy enough," Danny said hopefully.

"Yes it does, but that's the best-case scenario."

"What are you talking about? What else might happen?"

"Anything."

"Anything? What do you mean, anything?"

"Danny, there is a saying that I've lived by for my entire searching career that I think may serve you well on this mission. Expect nothing, expect everything."

"What the hell does that mean? You said this would be easy!"

"It means, my eloquent, excitable young friend, two things. Expect nothing means that you should not lock an expected outcome into your mind. You can, of course, plan what you are going to do and visualize how you would like a situation to unfold, but you should not rigidly imbed that scenario into your mind. You must be ready to adapt and adjust if something unanticipated occurs, which leads to the other part: expect everything. It means that, when going into any situation, you should try to think of everything that could possibly happen and decide what you will do should it occur. Does that make sense?"

"I suppose."

"In this case, expect everything means you consider that you may run into a neighbor, a law enforcement officer may stop you, Jarrison may not answer the door, he may not be as willing to talk as we believe, or you may have trouble shaking him."

"What do you mean 'shaking him'?"

"Jarrison committed twenty years of his life to acquiring the tablet, probably for the promise of a life of leisure and luxury on an exotic planet. If our theory is correct, instead of such a life he was dumped back on Kronk by Dank, who probably did so with glee. Since arriving back on Kronk, no one has believed his story, and he's become the subject of public ridicule. He's an aggressive, highly trained intelligence officer who is bitter and angry and has little future on his home planet. What do you think he may want to do when you tell him you are going after Dank?"

"He'll probably want to go with me. What the hell should I do if he does that?"

"If you refuse, he probably won't accept that and may become aggressive. With his training and physical superiority, you'd have little chance of stopping him."

"So what do I do?" Danny asked nervously.

"You will enthusiastically welcome his help and ask him to go with you. No one travels without packing a bag, especially if they think they're never returning. When he goes to his room to pack, you quietly but quickly exit the house and run back to the Star Hopper."

"Okay," Danny said, "but what if he doesn't go to a room to pack? What if he's got his stuff right by the door so he can move quickly in case reporters find him? It seems a spy kind of guy would do something like that."

"My God, Kingsley. I think he's starting to think!" shouted Shey as he returned to the table with three small bowls of ice cream covered with fresh berries.

"Yes, I believe he is. Excellent point, Danny. You may very well be correct. In that case, you've only one choice."

"Which is?" Danny asked.

"Have you ever fired a weapon, Danny?"

"Oh no. No, no, no, no. I can't shoot anybody. I might be able to handle asking some questions, but I cannot shoot anybody. No. No way. You didn't tell me I was going to have to shoot anybody."

"I don't think he wants to shoot anybody," Shey said, as best he could with his mouth full of ice cream.

"Danny, your response is understandable. I'm not talking about shooting him with one of your primitive handguns. You're going to have to carry a Zapper MR5 and set it on a level of stun that will render him unconscious for a few minutes. It is a last resort. If he wants to go with you and he doesn't leave the room, you'll have to stun him and then leave quickly. And you'll need to do so when he's got his back to you. With his training and your lack of experience in these matters, he'll probably evade your attack and disarm you if he sees you pull it out."

"Or I could come along and pull it out," Shey interjected proudly. "That would stun him."

"Do you think you can handle that, Danny?"

"I suppose I'll have to," he replied weakly as he stared at the table.

"Good. That's all you need to know for this excursion. You should try to get to sleep early, since you'll be getting up early. When we've finished eating, Shey will take you to the medlab to insert the EZ-Comm. It's a simple, painless procedure. Any questions?"

"No."

"Wonderful. Gracie, can Danny have a glass of wine without it affecting how he will feel for the visit to Kronk?"

"He should feel no ill effects if he has one glass of wine at this point."

"Gracie, Sinatra, random, upbeat," Kingsley said while motioning for Shey to pour Danny some wine. "Yoobie mode, view screen off."

As the jazzy opening of "I'll Be Seeing You" filled the room, the windows revealed a spectacular, multicolor sky highlighted by a breathtaking Yoobatarian sunset. The storm had passed through quickly, leaving the sky covered in rippled layers of clouds, the sun peeking from between their lower edge and the horizon, its rays creating an array of reds, oranges, and pinks as they mixed with the gray, blue, and white of the clouds.

"Glorious," Kingsley said softly. "I'm glad we didn't miss this. Let's get our minds off the mission for a while.

Danny, I'd like to hear more about your family. You have no siblings, correct?"

"Right."

"What was your father like?"

"He was okay. I mean, he treated me pretty good and provided for us. Now that I think about it, I guess I wasn't very close to him though."

"Our research said he's no longer with you."

"Right. He passed away suddenly a few years ago."

"You don't seem sentimental about him."

"I'm not. Like I said, we weren't very close. I visited maybe once a month. I'd go up on a Saturday afternoon, we'd get a bite to eat, talk about my job and his day-to-day stuff, watch TV, and then I'd go home Sunday. It was all kind of superficial."

"And your mother?" Kingsley asked.

"What about her?"

"Were you close to her?"

Danny took a gulp of wine and fixed his gaze on his plate. "Yes, I suppose I was. She was the only person I ever felt completely comfortable with, that I could talk to about my problems and worries."

"And what happened to her?"

The contents of the plate became blurred by the moisture accumulating in his eyes. "I was in high school. Sixteen. It was unexpected and happened fast. She was having numbness in her arms. She went to the hospital in Columbus for some tests, and they did open-heart surgery. She died during that."

"I'm so sorry, Danny. That must have been very difficult. How did that make you feel?"

"I was surprised. I mean, like I said, we didn't expect it."

"I didn't ask what your reaction was. I asked how it made you feel."

Danny pondered the question for a moment before realizing that he'd never really thought about it. He had always just thought of his mother's death as something that happened, an almost neutral event that he dealt with logically and unemotionally before getting on with his life.

He thought back to that night. He had watched television all afternoon and evening without having any idea what was going on. His father returned from Columbus and said, "Well, Danny, you don't have a mother," with the same calm despair he might have used to tell Danny the Buckeyes had lost a game. He remembered going to bed and thinking about everything she did for him, day-to-day mundane tasks as well as times she did something special to please him. He replayed dozens of specific moments and conversations, going as far back as he could remember. He thought of the birthday parties with the neighbor kids, of the small presents she would buy him to lift his spirits whenever he was sick, and how he always found every piece of clothing he wanted to wear in his room, cleaned and pressed. He thought of all the work she did to get him to go places and do new things, and he felt bad for having always given her such a battle.

Danny looked up and met Kingsley's eyes, eyes that exuded an inviting compassion.

"It pissed me off," said Danny. "I felt . . . robbed. And kind of abandoned."

"Those are very natural reactions. And sad? Did you feel sad?"

"No, I can't remember feeling all that sad. I think numb would be a better way to describe it."

"Danny, that was a traumatic event, and you didn't let yourself experience it, much less deal with the emotions. It almost sounds like you treated it more as a disappointment than a tragedy. It would serve you well to think more about her. Talk to her some, mentally or out loud. Write her a letter. You may be surprised how good it feels."

"I might just do that," Danny said.

Kingsley glanced at the time. "Why don't you go on up to the medlab so Shey can insert the EZ-Comm into your ear, then head back to your room, relax a bit, get some sleep?"

"Okay," Danny said sadly. He was normally more than happy to be given the opportunity for solitude, but this time he would have preferred staying put. The Kronk trip was looming, but Kingsley, Shey, the food, and the wine were providing a nice diversion, keeping the inevitable pre-excursion jitters at bay. Danny knew he would be overwhelmed by worry once alone.

———————————

Danny was too wired to sleep. The EZ-Comm insertion had been as quick and painless as Kingsley had described. Shey was Shey, a little sassy, a little bossy, but tolerable. Now Danny had changed into his sleepwear and was pacing around his suite.

"Danny, time for you to get to sleep. You've got a big day tomorrow."

"I'm not sleepy. I want a beer."

"It would be alcohol-free."

"I liked you a lot better when you weren't in mother mode."

"Noted. Now get into bed or I will encourage you with tickle rays."

"Oh yeah? Go for it. I'm not tick—"

Danny was cut off by a blue beam that made a tight line from the wall directly to his behind.

"What the hell!" Danny yelled as he flailed at the beam while twirling and stumbling about as if a swarm of bees had attacked. Amid a combination of giggling and profanity-laced shouting, he managed to find the bed and get prone, which brought the barrage to an end. After catching his breath, he immediately began thinking about the looming excursion.

"Danny we are going to prepare you for sleeping. We will review Kingsley's lessons in the form of affirmations," Gracie stated. "I will make a statement, and you will repeat it in your mind exactly as I said it. The intent is that you not just repeat the words but that you also focus on their meaning, absorbing their essence into your being, believing them without fear, doubt, or judgment. Are you ready?"

"I suppose."

"We are going to start with deep breathing to help you relax. Take a slow, deep breath, pulling the breath down into your abdomen, expanding that region as much as possible. Continue that breath, expanding your lungs and chest until they can hold no more. Now pull the air into your upper chest, expanding the area around your collar bone as much as possible. Now pull it into your neck, face, forehead, all the way to the top of your head. Good. Now let it all out slowly from the top down. Excellent. Now breathe in again, lower back, abdomen, chest, upper chest, head. Now out. Continue the cycle."

Danny focused on the breathing, partly because he didn't want to fight with Gracie anymore but mainly because it felt damn good. It required enough concentration that it occupied his mind. It also quickly relaxed his entire body, his almost-always-slightly-clenched body. After eight more complete breaths, Gracie continued.

"I relax every muscle in my body . . . I clear my mind of all worry and doubt . . . I release all of the fear from my body, mind, and soul . . . I speak freely with strong words and a firm tone . . . I am comfortable making eye contact with everyone I encounter . . . I enjoy connecting with all living beings . . . I calmly handle any and all situations."

As Gracie repeated the phrases, Danny repeated the words in his mind, with fewer and fewer thoughts of the mission intruding as they moved through each cycle. By the fifth time, he was thinking only of Gracie's words. By the tenth, he drifted off.

CHAPTER 11

Danny exited his room to find Kingsley waiting in the hall. "Good morning, Danny. Shey's waiting in the garage. Let's head down and I'll see you off."

The words *see you off* set him off. They flipped the switch. Until that moment the situation had seemed a bit surreal, the excursion threatening but distant. His body quickly became numb, except for his stomach, which was doing cartwheels. Kingsley walked briskly toward the front lift with Danny trudging behind like a death row prisoner on his way to the gas chamber. When they entered the lift, Kingsley handed Danny a device. It looked like a large smartphone but was thinner and lighter than Danny's iPhone.

"This is your MPC, mobile personal computer," Kingsley said. "You can use it to see maps, pictures of locations, people, objects, and so forth. It will display the local time and U-time. The voice assistant is Emma. You'll also be able to tap into the planetary network when you're on the surface.

"Shey will park approximately two blocks from the house. We'll both be able to talk to you via the EZ-Comm. Your route to the house will be displayed on the MPC," Kingsley said as he pointed at the device. He stepped into the garage and continued. "Once you get Jarrison to open the door, tell him you are looking for information regarding the Tablet of Jakaroo, which has been stolen from the Quilicant family. If he mentions Dank, ask him if he knows where Dank may have gone. Once he gives us all the information he has, thank him and tell him you must be going.

"As excursions go, it's simple," Kingsley said as he stopped by the Star Hopper. "It will be a good one for getting your feet wet. However, it's also crucial. We have to get a lead from Jarrison. If we get no leads regarding where Dank went, we'll be at a dead end. So it is imperative that we leave here with something. Strap the MR5 to your ankle."

Danny stared at the strap and weapon Shey was attempting to hand him. After a moment he gingerly took the MR5, holding it at arm's length with his thumb and index finger as if it were a dirty diaper.

"That's perfect," Shey exclaimed. "You can carry it to the surface like that, and if Jarrison gives you any trouble, you can toss it at him. Enough review and enough with the pep talks. We're just going down to ask a question, for crying out loud. Let's go."

As the door to the transport slid open, Danny's racing mind kicked into overdrive. Kingsley turned to face Danny and was taken aback to see his glistening forehead and panicked expression.

"Danny, calm down. It's going to be over before you know it. Now look at me. Look at me and focus."

Kingsley put a hand on each of Danny's shoulders. "Listen to me. You can do this. Stop the frantic thoughts and focus on the mission. Remember the training. Make eye contact, speak with strong words and a firm tone. Connect with him. No timid actions, no wimpy words. Got it?"

"I guess . . . I suppose," Danny uttered with all the confidence of a high school quarterback about to start the Super Bowl.

"Danny," Kingsley said as he moved his open hand toward Danny's forehead, the tips of his fingers coming to rest on a spot just above Danny's eyes. "Quiet your mind. Stop the frantic thoughts and the speculation of negative outcomes. Envision positive results."

Kingsley placed his right hand, palm open, fingers together, on Danny's chest. "Calm your heart, pull your energy in, let go of the fear, trust your instincts, flow with the universe."

Danny's eyes fluttered open. "I can do this," he said softly.

"Great! Remember, you can talk to me at any point, and I'll help you along if need be. Now join Shey on the Star Hopper."

Danny stepped into the transport and took a seat beside Shey. Kingsley stuck his head in after Danny had entered and yelled toward the front. "Shey, shenanigan ban!"

Shey responded to the command with a yeah-whatever wave without looking up from the control panel.

The moment the door slid shut, Shey laid the groundwork for the trip.

"Okay, sport, here's the deal. I'm the excursion lead. You'll follow all my orders without question. I'm not going to baby you like Kingsley does. That timid crap won't cut it on my watch. You'll be smart, bold, and fearless or I'll kick your butt up between your ears. You'll do what I say the way I say to do it without giving me any—"

"What?" Danny asked, placing his hand over his left ear. "You're supposed to shut the hell up and drive the damn ship."

As the Star Hopper slowly dropped from the open belly of the *Aurora*, Shey scoffed and followed the directive, but only for a couple of minutes. He started up again, shifting from brash bossiness to relaxed chatter, recounting in detail everything he had learned from Gracie about the Kronkian people and their culture, dropping in random thoughts about the mission and musings on the sexual appetites of Kronkian women as he went.

Danny processed bits and pieces of what he said. He sat quietly, staring out the window, trying to focus on Kingsley's parting words of wisdom. He closed his eyes and focused on his training with all the mental might he could muster while placing his hand on his chest. Eye contact. Talk firmly. Connect with him. Let go of the fear. Focus on the goals. Quiet my mind. Calm my heart.

Danny was jarred from his meditation by the Star Hopper's rapid descent being stopped as it touched down on the planet's surface. He opened his eyes and looked around to find what appeared to be a country road and fields, no different than those found outside of Columbus. The sun was down, but he had no trouble seeing his surroundings. The area was illuminated by moonlight, which cast an eerie glow on everything.

"This looks kind of spooky. Everything looks blue."

"It's the light of the Kronkian moons. There are three of them, so when it's clear, it can be very bright. Now we head for Vee Jimpa and hope we're not stopped by law enforcement."

"Law enforcement?" Danny said. "Nobody said we may be stopped by police!"

"It's not likely, but possible. Expect everything, sport. But don't worry. If that occurs, let me do the talking. Just sit there and don't say anything, which shouldn't be difficult for you."

The headlights came on, and the transport slowly accelerated, much too slowly for Danny's taste.

"You do drive like a Maroovian swamp sloth," he said.

"Shut up and focus on the excursion."

"I don't think Kingsley would approve of the way you're . . . oh, yeah . . . Kingsley?" Danny waited for his defender to put Shey in his place but heard nothing. "Is this thing not working? Kingsley?" His query was met with the unmistakable sound of snoring. "What the hell? He's snoring?" Danny shouted. "Kingsley!"

"What? Where am . . . hmm . . . yes . . . oh yeah . . . yes I'm here, Danny. Is there a problem?"

"Is there a problem?" Danny yelled. "I'm just about to get out of this thing and go to the house, and you're asleep? You said you'd be in constant communication! What the hell are you doing?"

Shey let out a muffled snicker, garnering a glare from Danny. "What's so funny?"

"Danny, I guess I've been hanging around Shey too long. I thought I'd try my hand at a little comic relief. I wasn't asleep."

"Great. Now I have to put up with this stuff from both of you."

Ten minutes later, Shey broke the silence as he surveyed the suburb they had entered.

"We're getting close to Jarrison's neighborhood. Looks a lot like where you live, doesn't it, Danny?"

Danny concurred. Seeing the Earth-like surroundings relaxed him a bit. He had been half expecting a weird, exotic setting, despite Kingsley's description of the planet. The transport came to a halt sooner than Danny had hoped.

"Why'd we stop?"

"Well, Danny," Shey said. "I decided that you and I really need to get to know one another better, to spend some quality time together, to share, to laugh, perhaps cry a little, to form what I hope will be a lifelong bond. And I thought this might be a good time and place to do it."

"We're at the drop-off spot, aren't we?"

"Yep. Hit the pavement, sport."

Danny wanted to move, or at least told himself he should move, but couldn't. His body felt numb and disconnected from his mind. It felt foreign to him, as if it belonged to someone else and his head just happened to be sitting above it. "I'm sorry, but I don't think I can do this," Danny said, bracing himself for some verbal abuse.

"Sure you can," Shey said, his tone more soothing than sassy. "It's a simple excursion. You knock on a door, you listen, you leave. There's nothing to be afraid of. To the contrary, try thinking of it as fun."

"Fun?" Danny asked incredulously.

"Yes, fun. And exciting. Think about it. You've heard this fabulous tale about a queen, a queen who may lose her throne because one of her top security people was really a spy working for her planet's most devious villain. They pulled off the elaborate heist of a mystical artifact and are racing to create a tool that will help the villain rise to power. Now you get a chance to meet his cohort and hear about it all firsthand. It's an adventure that could easily be in one of those movies you watch and you're actually part of it!"

Danny thought for a moment before responding. "I suppose you're right. But I think I'd rather be back in my apartment watching it on TV."

He gingerly stepped from the Star Hopper onto Kronk's surface, scanned his surroundings, and pulled the MPC from his pocket. After telling Emma to display the map to the house, he reviewed the route, turned left, and saw that the street they were on dead-ended into another about a hundred feet or so away. After taking a deep breath and exhaling, he started down the street. When he reached the end, he turned and continued without hesitation.

Kingsley's reassuring voice came through the EZ-Comm. "Danny, I'm concerned that you're preoccupied with negative outcomes. Be in the moment. Nothing could be more important than what you are in the middle of doing. Slow your thoughts, absorb the moment, release the fear. This is one of the most important moments of your life. Don't miss it by being back on the ship while your body is going through it. Be present. Now let's focus back on the task at hand. Sensors show you should be close to Jarrison's street."

Danny approached an intersection and looked up at the street sign. Wyndoggle Way. He passed three houses, 4220, 4224, 4228, his anxiety growing along with the numbers. He froze when he saw the target dwelling, 4232, a contemporary-looking stone and cedar house. He gulped, exhaled deeply, made his way up the curving walk, and, once at the front door, pressed the doorbell without pausing. He waited in the silence, his entire torso reverberating from his heart's pounding. No answer. He pressed the button again.

"There's no answer."

"We didn't expect there to be. Yell that you are looking for Chase Claxon."

Danny cleared his throat and managed a less-than-booming "I'm looking for Chase Claxon."

"Louder. I could barely hear you," urged Kingsley.

"I don't want to bother the neighbors."

"You're going to have to take that chance."

"I'm looking for Chase Claxon," he shouted through cupped hands.

The door swung open rapidly, sending Danny a step in retreat. When he regrouped, he saw a man who appeared to be around fifty, physically fit and powerfully built but haggard, disheveled, and a bit frenzied. His gray-streaked black hair was badly in need of a brush, his face in need of a razor, and his clothes looked in need of an iron.

"What did you say?" asked the figure, his voice smacking of desperation and anger.

"I . . . I . . . I said I'm looking for Chase Claxon."

"Get in here," he shouted as he reached out, grabbed Danny's forearm, and pulled him into the house, flinging Danny into the foyer and slamming the door simultaneously. Danny turned to find him looking through the peephole.

"Are you alone? How do you know that name? What are you doing here?"

"Yes, I'm alone. I've been hired by the Quilicant family to find the Tablet of Jakaroo, and the evidence points to you knowing something about the theft. I'm looking for clues as to where it may be," he said, looking Jarrison directly in the eyes. His voice was surprisingly strong, only wavering once.

"Who are you? Where are you from?"

"I'm Inka Alibar from the planet Ipnokia," Danny said, extending his hand.

"Inka Alibar from Ipnokia, huh? You look like someone from Ipnokia, but you don't look like a searcher. Who are you working for?"

"I, uh, I have a partner, but I'm sure you don't know him. He's also from Ipnokia. We're fairly new at this, but the Quilicants hired us because we've already had several successes and they wanted someone who wasn't well known." Danny felt his voice and confidence growing stronger as he went.

"I suppose that makes sense. Come on in."

Danny followed the man past a wide staircase into the main living space. The vaulted ceiling was covered with dark wood beams and housed several canned lights. The back wall was all glass, exposing a well-lit swimming pool. A huge stone fireplace dominated the right wall of the room. Danny looked up over his shoulder to see that the staircase led to a bridge that overlooked the room they had entered. The host plopped down on one of several pieces of overstuffed, earth-toned furniture and signaled for Danny to do the same.

"You are Jarrison Opal, aren't you?" Danny asked as he sunk into a sofa.

"Yes," the man said wearily. "I'm Jarrison Opal . . . though at the moment it may serve me well to change my name."

Danny decided to play dumb. "Oh yeah? Why is that?"

"Why is that? Because everyone on this planet thinks I'm nuts." Jarrison had melted into his chair, his head against the top of the chair back, rolled to the side to see Danny. His aggressive edge had been replaced by pure fatigue, a condition that he made no effort to hide.

"I'm sorry to hear that. You are the person who posed as Chase Claxon on Yoobatar?"

Jarrison chuckled. "Yes, I'm Chase Claxon. I actually feel more like Chase Claxon than Jarrison Opal. You can't absorb yourself in an identity for twenty-three years and then just drop it. My troubles all relate to the fact that I found myself back on Kronk and I couldn't keep my mouth shut. People wanted to know where I was for all that time, so I told them. Look what it's gotten me. It's only been a couple of days and I'm fed up with it. I'm sure the media coverage will abate, but I'll have scandal linked to me forever. I'll never be able to work in the intelligence field again. What else can I do? I trained my whole life for that."

First goal achieved. This was Chase Claxon.

"Maybe you could become like a private detective or something," said Danny.

"Yeah, maybe. I'm sure someone would take a chance on me. Who knows, if I had a few successes it may become stylish to hire me. I just need to wait a while and let things settle down."

"So what can you tell me about the Tablet of Jakaroo? Were you involved with its disappearance?"

"Ah yes, the tablet. The thing I wasted twenty-three years of my life for. Disappearance? That's a nice way of saying it. It was stolen, and I'm the one who took it."

Goal two accomplished, Danny thought. "Can you give me any clues as to where I might find it?"

"Clues? You bet your ass I can give you clues. Find that bastard Dank Nebitol and you'll find the tablet."

Goal three achieved. Danny's anxiety had been completely replaced by excitement. "Any idea where I can find him?"

"Well, not exactly, but I'd be more than happy to tell you where he went," Jarrison said, sitting up in his chair and raising his voice. "He showed up a couple of months after I was let go from the Falcon Force for supposedly leaking information and messing around with the senator's daughter. He said he was from another planet and offered me a chance to start a new life in government security. My long-term mission would be to gain the trust of the planet's ruling family so that one of them would tell me if this mystical tablet existed and, if so, where it was stored."

"Wow. You must have been skeptical. I mean, Dank saying he was an alien." Danny was eager to get the information and leave, but he didn't want to do anything to rile Jarrison.

"Of course I was, but he quickly proved his claim. If I found the tablet existed, I was to steal it, get the hell off the planet, and meet up with him. Dank's goal was to overthrow the government with the help of some trinket he could make from instructions on the tablet. In return for my years of service, I had my choice of either being the head of security for his government or being dropped on the planet of my choice with more than enough money to live out my life in luxury. I chose the latter. I waited until I became a Trog, the highest level within the security force, and went to work. I became very close to the queen's sister and ended up finding out the location of the tablet from her. Hey, can I get you a beer or something?"

Danny was about to accept out of habit but caught himself. "Oh, no thanks. I would, but I have a lot to do tonight."

"Look at me, rambling on about my life when you're obviously on a mission. You're being very patient, Mr. Alibar. I'll get to the point. So, the sister and I really hit it off and had secret meetings, often in the caves under the Quilicant compound. I not only got her to show me the location of the tablet room, but she even took me in to see it, which is how I acquired the codes to get past the security system. After that it was easy. I stole the tablet, hopped in a transport, and rendezvoused with Dank, who was waiting in orbit."

"And then he brought you here?" asked Danny.

"Yes, that's when the bastard dropped me here," said Jarrison raising his voice while rising to his feet. "He said he was going to give me the equivalent of millions of U-bucks and take me to an exotic planet. He even showed me several and let me pick. When we were supposedly en route to the planet I chose, he locked me in my room and told me he was taking me back to Kronk. He was laughing at me. A couple days later he knocked me out and I woke up in a field. The son of a bitch dropped me back here."

Jarrison was getting agitated, his voice thundering as he paced around the room. Danny was starting to feel uneasy again.

"I, uh, I'm really sorry to hear that. Do you know where he went?"

"Oh yes, but Dank doesn't know that I know. The tablet is written in an ancient language called Quontal. Almost no one knows how to read it. Dank thought he pulled off a real coup by getting this Fraleezian linguist to help him. Dr. Jillian Falstaff's her name. He found out that she knew a good deal about Quontal, so he offered her a ton to help him. She accepted. What he didn't know is that she had no intention of helping him. She not only knew Quontal, but she's a Yoobaphile. She loves everything about Yoobatar, the people, the culture, the geography."

Jarrison had stopped his harried pacing and calmed down to some degree. "So, unbeknownst to Dank, she knew who he was and what he was all about. When he told her he needed a Quontal expert, she guessed that he had or was going to acquire the tablet, which she always suspected existed.

She agreed to go, but to hinder his mission rather than help. She thought she could either slow Dank down by feeding him poor translations or by leaving clues as they went in the hopes they'd be found by pursuers. She thought it might be dangerous but saw it as a chance to help the planet she loves. She called me in my room one night when we were in transit and told me everything in the hopes that someone looking for Dank would find me. When Dank left here, he headed for a planet called Dabita Bok in search of a crystal called marzical. It's the first ingredient required for making the amulet."

Danny felt a rush upon hearing those words, a rush that was coupled with relief. Mission accomplished. He glanced around the room and began plotting a graceful departure.

"Danny," Kingsley whispered in Danny's EZ-Comm, "Gracie says that marzical is very common on Dabita Bok and that there are many varieties. Ask if he has any more details."

"Did she give you any specifics on where on Dabita Bok to find the type that is needed?"

"I was just getting to that," replied Jarrison. "She said that the tablet gave a cryptic clue rather than naming the specific location. It is supposed to be the marzical taken from the place where one can *walk on fire while underwater*. Find that place, and you find where Dank went."

"I want to thank you for your time. You've been extremely helpful. I have to get going now."

Jarrison looked disappointed. "Wait. Take me with you."

"What?"

"Take me with you. I've got no life here, no future. Don't worry, I won't ask for part of your fee. But I will ask that you leave Dank to me once you get the tablet. The thought of getting a crack at that devious bastard is enough reward for me."

"Remain calm, Danny," Kingsley whispered. "There's nothing to get upset about. Thank him for offering, but turn him down."

"Thanks for offering to help, but I think we've got it covered. Plus, our ship is small. We really don't have room for another crew member."

"That's nonsense," Jarrison barked, his mood quickly turning darker and more aggressive. "You couldn't have traveled as far as you've traveled in a small transport. I want to go with you. In fact, I insist that you take me."

"He's getting agitated, Danny. Don't refuse him again. Welcome him along and hope he goes to get a bag. When he does, run for it."

Danny pretended to mull over Jarrison's offer. His stomach knotted as he thought about the MR5.

"You know, I think you're right. With your background you'd be perfect for searcher work. I have to admit I was only thinking of having to split the fee another way. If you don't require any of it, you're welcome to come along."

"Great. Then it's a deal. Wait here. I'll go up and throw a few things in a bag. It'll only take a couple of minutes," Jarrison said.

Danny listened closely to Jarrison trudging up the steps behind him and glanced over his shoulder to see him heading down the bridge toward a doorway. The moment Jarrison disappeared, Danny was off the sofa and making a beeline for the front door. He was relieved that the rubber-soled shoes Kingsley had provided made no sound as he scooted across the foyer's tile floor.

"Go, Danny. Now!" Kingsley shouted in his ear.

"I'm going!" Danny replied. His tone wasn't loud, but sound traveled well through the open floor plan.

"Did you say something?" Jarrison yelled as he exited the room and looked down to the living room. Danny froze with his hand on the doorknob.

"Inka? Where the hell are you—"

Danny didn't wait for the end of the question. He flung open the front door and dashed down the walk toward the street. He sprinted the length of Wyndoggle Way and then looked back as he made the right turn at the end of the street, just in time to see Jarrison running down the walk in front of his house.

"Wait! You're not leaving without me!" he screamed.

Picking up his pace, Danny sprinted like he'd never sprinted before. He was so caught up in fleeing that he neglected to make the appropriate left turn at the next intersection.

"Where are you going, Danny?" Kingsley yelled. "You were supposed to turn left back there."

"Damn!" he yelled as he came to a stop, panting heavily from the running and the panic.

"Don't stop! Keep going and turn left at the next intersection," Kingsley ordered. Danny obliged and made the left turn. He was winded, but Jarrison's continued shouting pushed him on.

"Take the next left. You'll come up behind the Star Hopper. Shey will be waiting."

Danny turned at the next corner and could make out the silver transport ahead on the right. The site of his getaway vehicle coupled with the sound of Jarrison's pounding feet on the pavement pushed him into another gear. As he neared the Star Hopper, he heard a rustling in a cluster of bushes off to the right. He glanced over to see Shey sashay from the shrubs, smoothing back what little hair he had and whistling while looking quite pleased with himself.

"What . . . the hell . . . are you doing? I'm being . . . chased," Danny gasped.

"Yes, I know. I've been listening on the EZ-Comm. We'd better be going, don't you think?" Shey climbed into the transport.

Danny glanced back to find Jarrison closing fast, only a hundred or so feet away, and Shey was still clogging the entrance. Danny decided to clear it. He gave Shey a push on the back and flung himself in, sending both into a pile.

"He's coming!" yelled Danny.

"Max, close the door," Shey said calmly while looking up from the floor.

Danny sat up, holding his breath. The door slid shut just in time to prevent Jarrison's outstretched arm from entering and sending him into a door-pounding, cursing tirade.

"We've got to get out of here. He's pounding on the door. What if he breaks a window?"

"Relax. This thing's designed for space travel. He can pound on it all night and it won't do a thing. You did a great job out there. We'd better get back to the ship." Shey made his way to the front and plopped down in his seat.

"Really? You really think so?"

Shey didn't answer. As they took their seats, Jarrison moved around to the front and started pounding on the tinted windows while screaming at them.

"Damn it! Let me in. Now! Don't leave me here. If I ever track you guys down, I'll kill you!"

Danny was frightened despite Shey's confidence in the ship's construction.

"Why Danny, I think your new friend is a bit fussed up. Hi, Jarrison," he said, waving and blowing him a kiss, sending Jarrison into a hysterical rage.

"Stop it! You're pissing him off even more," implored Danny.

"So what?"

"So what? So what if he gets a ride off this planet, finds us, and beats the crap out of us, or worse?"

"He can't hurt me. I'd flick him away like an irritating insect," Shey said gleefully as he rose, turned, and dropped his pants, establishing a fourth Kronkian moon and inspiring Jarrison to pick up a sizable rock and wing it into the windshield.

"Oh God," said a cringing Danny as the rock harmlessly bounced off and landed on Jarrison's foot, sending him into a one-legged, circular hopping pattern. "That's fine for you, but what about me? What if he finds me?"

Shey pulled up his trousers and took his seat. "Well, there is that. I keep forgetting that people I'm with don't have my freakish strength and unrivaled combat skills. My mental lapses in this regard have unfortunately resulted in several acquaintances getting into rather ugly skirmishes. Yes, you'd better keep an eye out for him the rest of the mission. Okay, I've had enough fun. Let's go."

Danny was happy to hear those words and ecstatic to feel the Star Hopper start moving forward. He looked up to find Jarrison stumbling to the side to avoid being run over, only to recover and continue his assault on the side of the transport as it pulled away. Shey was whistling again.

"Will you be in touch?" Jarrison yelled as the Star Hopper pulled away. "What about my foot?" he shouted before limping back toward his house muttering assorted obscenities under his breath.

The end of the commotion brought more rustling from the bushes as a short, perky brunette emerged, smoothing her hair back, straightening her clothes, and grinning from ear to ear from having been the recipient of a Glemanthian Rhythmic Mindblower.

CHAPTER 12

THE DOOR TO THE STAR HOPPER slid open, revealing the waiting Kingsley and Abby. Danny stood in the doorway and waved, feeling like the astronauts returning from Apollo 13. To him, what he'd been through was no less of an ordeal.

Shey wasn't terribly interested in Danny's soaking up the moment. "Move it," he said as he gave Danny a kick in the ass, literally.

Danny yelled an expletive but quickly refocused on his welcoming party. "What did you think? How'd I do?" he said, arms outstretched as he stepped onto the garage floor.

"Congratulations, Danny, you are officially a searcher!" Kingsley exclaimed as Abby jumped on Danny, lapping at his face with her tail wagging at the speed of light. "You were fantastic. A flawless performance." He approached Danny, his hand held high, ready for a slap.

Danny obliged. "Yeah, I thought it went great. And it wasn't so bad. I thought about all the things you told me, and I think it helped. I mean, I was nervous, but I think I held it together pretty good. Oh, yeah, what the hell were you doing in the bushes while I was running for my life?"

Shey nonchalantly strolled past the group. "I was giving a young Kronkian lass an experience she will never forget . . . and one I won't likely either. I must say, she was an eager little thing."

"Sex? I was about to be beaten to a pulp and you were in the bushes having sex?"

"*Sex* is much too mundane a term for what I was doing. I was painting a carnal masterpiece."

Danny turned his attention back to Kingsley in search of more praise. "So I did okay, huh?"

"Okay? My boy, you were wonderful. You achieved all of the goals and handled the situation flawlessly. We're en route to Dabita Bok. You're probably exhausted. Do you want to get some rest?"

"Actually, I'm kind of pumped up. I don't feel like sleeping."

"That's certainly understandable. I must admit, when I was listening in, I was yearning to be there with you in the thick of things. It's difficult to be a searcher for sixty years and then sit on the sideline. You certainly must be hungry, though. How about getting a bit of breakfast and then finally playing that round of golf I promised you? Shey?"

"You two go ahead. I'm going to work out."

Kingsley and Danny, with Abby prancing along, headed up to the living room, where they partook of a light breakfast while watching UNN. Danny felt a strange sensation as he sipped coffee, played with Abby, took in the beautiful Yoobatarian morning displayed all around them, and basked in the satisfaction of his success. He was actually happy.

"Oh, bull! Turn it off, Gracie. Pardon my outburst, Danny, but I get so sick of the politics that play out in the PUPCO senate chambers and then hearing Huppa Nanstrom put this spin on it like everything's fine. Sometimes I think I'd be better off if I just ignored it all and watched only sports. Are you ready for that round of golf?"

"Absolutely."

"Why don't you go change and freshen up a bit if you like, and I'll meet you in the arena in about thirty minutes. If I'm not there when you arrive, tell Gracie you'd like to hit some balls. She'll help you pick out some clubs and tell you what to do. Danny, have you thought about what exactly you accomplished on Kronk?"

"Like I said, I think it went well."

"Yes, but it will serve you well if you reflect on your successes. Let the experience soak into your soul. Absorb it. Then pull it out when you are preparing for other future excursions and have self-doubt. It will make you stronger and more confident."

"Okay. Sure."

"Seriously, think about what you've accomplished, Danny. A short time ago you were sitting in your apartment on Earth, hibernating from everything you feared. Now you've traveled about the galaxy, met people, and learned new technology. You've actually gone into an unpredictable situation on an alien planet as part of a mission to help save a civilization, and you know what? You've handled it all marvelously. See what you're capable of if you set your mind to something?"

"Yeah, I suppose I have done a lot."

"And done it successfully, without panicking or passing out or exploding or whatever it is you fear will happen in such situations. That's what you need to engrain in your psyche, not just that you did it, but that you did it while keeping your head. It tells you that you can control your thoughts and your emotions and handle any situation presented to you. Reflect on this success when you have time."

"I'll try. See you in the arena," Danny said before striding, almost bounding, from the room.

When the door to the arena slid open, Danny's heart soared. It was something so near and dear to him that its mere sight gave him an adrenaline rush, something onto which he hadn't set foot in many years. It was a basketball court. A hardwood-floored, brightly lit, full-length basketball court with a ball sitting at mid-court, begging to be put into action.

As he made a beeline for the ball, he was flooded with memories: the thousands of hours he spent honing his craft on the cement court behind their house, the power he felt when he scored in pickup games with his schoolmates, the exhilaration of running onto the court with the team on Friday nights, and the respect he got around school and the town for being a basketball player. By the time he picked up the ball and rolled it around in his hands, he was choked up. With the possible exception of solving software problems, this was what he had done better than anything else in his life.

It dawned on him that what he was doing was exactly what Kingsley had just been talking about, reflecting on his success and accomplishments, absorbing them into his soul, and thinking of them when he needed a boost. He realized he'd been doing it for years without realizing it. He'd been doing it when he solved difficult support cases in the form of saving complimentary emails and periodically reviewing them to pump himself up. He stood, holding the ball with eyes closed, replaying the Kronkian excursion in his mind from start to finish and soaking in the fact that he really hadn't been all that anxious.

Danny began his assault on the basket. Starting from the right corner, he fired away, chasing down the ball after each shot, moving out to his range, and letting another one go. After making eight of the first eleven, he became slightly more adventuresome, dribbling a few times and making moves as if trying to beat a defender before pulling up for a jump shot. He then moved on to crossover dribbles, spin moves, drives to the basket, and turn-around jump shots. All but a few of the shots found their mark, with most of them never touching the rim. Danny stopped and picked up the ball as it rolled back to him. Breathing heavily, he held the ball in both hands and stared up at the basket, amazed at his accuracy after not having shot a ball for ten years.

"You're quite good, Danny."

Danny turned to find Kingsley leaning against the arena doorway.

"Thanks."

"And how did you come to be so adept at it? Were you born with that ability?" Kingsley asked as he strode to the middle of the floor.

"Born with it? No. I mean, I might have been born with hand-eye coordination that helped and maybe some natural athletic ability, but that's it."

"So one day you just woke up and found you had this amazing knack for shooting a basketball?"

"Don't be ridiculous," Danny scoffed. "It's from practicing. Thousands of hours."

"I see. So you didn't quit the first time you missed a shot?"

"Of course not."

"But you failed."

"That's a bit harsh. You don't view something like missing a single shot as a failure. You just keep shooting."

"Did you have particular practice sessions during which you missed an abnormally large percentage of shots?"

"Sure, once in a while."

"You didn't decide to give up the game?"

"No," Danny said slowly. "If anything, it made me mad, and I went at it harder."

"And if you had sessions that were particularly good, in which you made almost every shot?"

"It pumped me up and made me more confident. And it showed me the practice was paying off."

As Danny walked off the court, Kingsley threw him a towel. "And when you missed a shot or made a turnover in the game, were you embarrassed, or did you have an anxiety attack?"

"No," Danny replied as he wiped the sweat from his forehead. "It's part of the game. It's just a mistake. Everybody makes them."

"I see. So your philosophy for this endeavor was to not quit after your first failure and to practice for hours on end in order to become better and better and keep your skills from eroding. You did not become discouraged and give up the game after a particularly poor performance, and you gained confidence by a strong showing. Before performing you were excited rather than anxious, and during the games you didn't panic or have an anxiety attack if you made mistakes, because you knew that no one is perfect. Is that about right?"

"Yeah, I suppose."

"It seems to me you may want to try applying the same principles to talking in front of people," Kingsley said before turning and heading back toward the arena door.

Danny stared at the floor for a moment before chasing after him. "But I had some natural skills for shooting a basketball."

"And you don't for speaking to people?"

"Nope."

"I beg to differ. You're intelligent and articulate, which are the two essential traits. Plus, you're polite, pleasant-natured, amicable, and you have a good sense of humor. You just need to get over the fear. Danny, don't expect to wake up one day and be a magnificent public speaker. That doesn't happen to anyone."

"Well, I hate to admit it, but like most of the stuff you've told me, that makes some sense."

"Most of the stuff?" asked Kingsley with an impish grin.

"Okay, it's all been pretty good so far. So how do I get over the anxiety?"

"That, my boy, is what we will be working on. However, you've already taken some big steps in the right direction," Kingsley proclaimed as he extended his arms toward Danny with his palms facing outward.

"So was this another training session?" Danny said as he bounced Kingsley the ball.

"Danny, I'm going to let you in on a secret. Life is a training session. You weren't done learning when you left school."

Kingsley motioned Danny to follow him into the hall as the door closed behind them. "Now, what type of course would you like to play?"

"How about an ocean course with some rocky shoreline? Something like Pebble Beach would be great."

"How about Pebble Beach?"

"You have Pebble Beach? How do you have Pebble Beach? I've played it a thousand times on my computer golf game. I've always wanted to play it for real."

"We have all the great courses from most planets, even those that aren't aware. Iggies do topographical scans and photograph every inch of the course. Gracie, set up the arena for golf. The course is Earth's Pebble Beach."

Danny was champing at the bit to see how realistic it would appear. The doors slid open with a nearly silent hiss as an awestruck Danny entered, gawking.

"Wow," he said softly.

Though the same technology was at work, the room put the Ped-Rite screens to shame. Every inch of the room was dedicated to the simulation. The floor was a carpet of rich, green grass, the ceiling a gorgeous shade of blue with puffy clouds hanging about, the walls a seamless, three-dimensional display of mature trees, multimillion-dollar houses, and the Pebble Beach clubhouse. The entire scene was bathed in brilliant sunshine. A slight breeze carried the scents of the native flowers and trees. Danny felt like he was really on the Monterey Peninsula.

He approached what appeared to be a tee box and glanced to his left. Having seen the scene hundreds of times on his computer, he immediately recognized it as the first hole of Pebble Beach. After standing on the tee and taking it all in for a few seconds, he turned to Kingsley.

"This is unbelievable," he said as he bent down and ran his hand over the artificial grass.

Danny followed Kingsley to the wall behind the tee as a door in the wall slid open, revealing a large service bay which contained two sets of golf clubs and two pairs of shoes.

"Grab the clubs and shoes on the left. They should work for you based on Gracie's scans," Kingsley said.

Danny obliged and followed Kingsley onto the first tee. Kingsley was standing at the back of the tee box, clubs at his side, staring down the fairway. Kingsley wore light gray slacks and a black golf shirt, Danny a white shirt and navy pants.

"Here's how this works. We stay in this general area the entire time, and the course comes to us. The view is depicted on all of the walls around us. Anything that would be within thirty yards in front of us is created holographically, including undulations in the terrain, water, bunkers, and trees. The system creates the images with concentrated particles and then slows them down to a point at which they have the mass of real trees, so don't think you can hit through them any more easily than a real tree. When hit, the system will capture the trajectory, velocity, the amount of spin on the ball, and the direction of the spin."

"That sounds like golf simulators we have," Danny interjected.

"Yes, well, the concepts are similar, but our technology is much more advanced. Ready?"

"I haven't played for years. Can I hit a couple before we start?" Danny asked.

"Certainly. Driving range, Gracie." The surrounding scenery faded and was replaced by the Pebble Beach driving range. A small area of the floor opened, and a large container with dozens of balls rose from beneath. Kingsley dropped several onto the turf and started swatting them with a five iron. Danny watched the fluid, elegant, seemingly effortless swing and was slightly jealous. He turned to draw the driver from his bag, teed up the ball, addressed it, and took a mighty whack at it, a whack that resulted in a low screaming shot that rapidly sliced.

Kingsley sighed deeply. "You looked like you're having some sort of seizure. If you swing just a little harder, you may be able to pull a few muscles and dislocate a couple of joints. And your tempo was atrocious."

"Give me a break. I haven't played in a long time."

"That's got nothing to do with what I just witnessed. Put the driver away, get your pitching wedge, and put another ball down. Now, address the ball and relax your body. The more relaxed and supple your body is, the more effortless club speed you can generate. Concentrate on shortening your backswing and then move back and through the ball. Think pendulum. Smooth and fluid."

Kingsley stood back and watched as Danny hit several crisp iron shots and then some drives, all much straighter and farther than his pre-lesson efforts.

"Much better. Let's hit the course. Don't worry, I won't be pestering you with instruction and reminders during the round. We want to have fun, enjoy the scenery, and take in the beautiful day. Lead us off, Danny."

The driving range faded and was replaced by the first tee. Failing to heed Kingsley's advice from the range, Danny tensed his body from head to toe and took a rip at the ball, sending a hard-slicing, 210-yard drive into the trees in the right rough. He picked up his tee and shuffled slowly to the back of the tee box while Kingsley teed up his ball, glanced down the fairway, waggled his club head once, and launched a gorgeous, 260-yard, gently fading drive down the middle. The surroundings changed to depict the view from Danny's ball in the right rough.

He proceeded to pitch his ball back to the fairway and hit a slicing but reasonably well-struck six iron to twenty feet short of the green, while his playing partner capitalized on his perfect drive by hitting a nine iron fifteen feet to the right of the pin. Danny hit a sloppy chip and two-putted for a six. Kingsley's perfectly paced birdie putt singed the right edge of the cup, leaving him a tap-in for par. Kingsley took a par and bogey on the next two holes while Danny carded a triple and double bogey.

Unfortunately, his play didn't match the beauty of the surroundings. He doubled the fourth, lifted his spirits a bit with a bogey on the fifth, but then quadruple bogeyed the par five sixth after hitting two balls into the ocean. A bogey on the short, downhill, par-three seventh was little consolation at that point.

"Hold it, Danny," Kingsley interjected. "I can't take it anymore. I know I said that I wouldn't be pestering you with instruction during the round, but this is too painful to watch."

"What's the problem?" Danny asked.

"What's the problem? Hasn't it occurred to you that you're playing rather poorly? I can tell you have natural ability, but your muscle tension and swing speed are keeping it from coming out. Remember our discussion about flowing with the universe rather than fighting it?"

"Sure."

"Well, you should try applying that to your golf swing. You've been fighting the game up to this point—clenching your body before swinging, taking violent, herky-jerky rips at the ball, cursing your bad shots, obsessing about your score, and being much too emotional about it all. Get into a flow frame of mind. Relax your body and take a smooth, fluid swing. Relax your mind. Visualize the shot you want to hit when addressing the ball. If you post a bad score on a hole, let it go. Focus on the next hole, on the next shot. If you do that, the good score will come."

Danny addressed the ball, exhaled, and made what was by far his best swing of the day. He finished with a perfect turn, holding his pose as he watched the ball soar down the left side of the fairway and gently fade to the middle.

"Wow. That felt like . . . I've never had a shot feel like that."

"There you go. You relaxed and didn't try to kill it, and you probably hit it thirty yards farther than you have been. Now maybe you'll believe me. Lesson's over."

Danny followed up his drive with a lovely six iron and two putts for his first par of the day. Four good shots sandwiched around a poor chip gave him a bogey on the difficult par-four ninth. They moved to the back nine with Danny in a bit of a huff after Kingsley and Gracie refused to tell him his score for the front.

"Focus on your next shot, Danny," was all Kingsley would say.

They played the back with little being said. No more lessons were given. The mission wasn't discussed. They simply played the game and took in the glorious surroundings, with the only dialogue being compliments on good shots. Danny worked at staying relaxed and in the flow, with remarkable results. By the time they stood on the tee of the eighteenth hole, the approach to the game he'd adopted for the back nine left him in a state with which he was unfamiliar. He stared out over Carmel Bay with a serenity, a sense of inner tranquility that he'd never felt before. No stress, no pain, no fatigue. He felt slightly energized, and his senses seemed sharper. And, for the first time in his life, he didn't have a clue how many over par he was on the back nine.

"Feels pretty good, doesn't it?" Kingsley asked after hitting his drive.

"What?"

"The state you're in. I can tell from your posture and stance, from the look in your eyes. Feels good, doesn't it?"

"Yeah, it does. It's certainly a different way of approaching the game. I feel like I'm in a zone, a really peaceful zone. It's a shame it can't last."

"Danny," Kingsley chuckled, "it can last. Apply the same principle to your day-to-day life. Keep your mind clearer, keep your body unclenched, let go of the past, don't obsess about the future, focus on what you are doing at the moment, and let go of fear." Kingsley launched a booming drive over the edge of the bay and into the fairway.

Danny swatted another fine drive. He followed that up with a solid three wood that came to rest eighty yards in front of the green while Kingsley's two iron found the putting surface. Danny's next shot, a softly hit pitching wedge, hit next to the hole and released, stopping twenty feet past. After Kingsley two-putted for a birdie, Danny drained his putt for one of his own. As he reached into the hole for his ball, Kingsley waited a few feet away.

"Great finish to a fine back nine, Danny," Kingsley said while shaking his hand. "How about we go brag about our great shots and lament all the what-ifs over a beer in the yard?"

"That sounds great," Danny said while taking one last look at the sun glistening on the ocean.

———————————

Kingsley returned from the service bay and sat two beers on the table.

"So what did you shoot on the back?" he said.

"I don't know," said Danny.

"That's good to hear. Scores, Gracie?"

"Danny shot a fifty-two on the front and a forty-two on the back for a ninety-four. You shot thirty-seven, thirty-eight for a seventy-five."

"Wow," Danny exclaimed softly. "I know you were hitting a lot of good shots, but I didn't realize you were playing that good. Nice round."

"Thanks," said Kingsley after taking a swig of his beer. "So, I've been wanting to talk more about your exam results. Do you really agree with Shey's evaluation?"

"I do," he replied, after taking a large gulp from his frosty mug.

A look of curiosity and compassion came over Kingsley. "What happened to you, Danny?"

"What happened? What do you mean?"

"What happened to make you so fearful of everything?"

"I don't think there was any single event that made me the way I am, if that's what you mean."

"So you've always had these issues?"

Danny stared into the distance and thought for a moment before responding.

"As far back as I can recall. When I was little, I didn't like going new places or meeting people. School was a challenge every day. I remember hating any situation where I was the center of attention, any time I felt people were looking at me. The worst was when I had to talk in front of other people. If it didn't go perfectly, my throat would tighten up, my stomach would knot up, I'd have trouble breathing, and I'd feel like I was on fire. Stumbling on my words while talking to a girl, giving a wrong answer in class, even trying to talk in front of a bunch of my friends. That stuff also kicked in any time I felt I might get into trouble or had to deal with any conflict or confrontation. There were a dozen things every day that caused me to feel anxious or to have a minor panic attack. And there were a few specific incidents where I had a real meltdown. The worst was when I had to give some speeches in a high school class. I actually thought I was going to die."

"I'm sorry you went through all of that. It must have been demoralizing."

"It was. Every incident just beat me down a little more."

"Did your parents try to help with that?"

"I don't think my dad really got it. As I recall, his stance was always that I was just shy and I'd grow out of it. I think my mom understood and did what she could. I remember a lot of pep talks, but I think she was in over her head."

Kingsley had strolled over to the service bay again and returned with two plates, each containing a sandwich and some chips. "And after high school you attended The Ohio State University. We researched that institution when reviewing your history. Interesting that you would go to a school with such a large enrollment. I would think the number of people would have bothered you."

"I was a little worried about that, but you know what I found there? Anonymity. There were lots of people everywhere, but no one knew me or cared who I was. I didn't talk to anyone, and no one bothered me. It went pretty well for three years; then I found out in order to graduate I would have to take a class that included a group project and presentation. I couldn't do it and dropped out."

"Interesting. So how did you end up being the support guru for a software company?"

"After dropping out, I was too embarrassed to move home. I couldn't get a job as a programmer without a degree, but a small software company hired me to do phone support. I didn't like talking on the phone . . . I'd get nervous when I called to order a pizza . . . but I didn't think I had any other choices. It turned out that talking on the phone bothered me a lot less than being in front of people. Within a couple of months I got used to the phone work and was really good at the job. Really good. I had a knack for solving problems and explaining complex topics to customers. I did great for a couple years, but then the company started growing and I became more high profile. That meant talking to customers who were visiting the company, working with other employees who needed my help, and tons of meetings. I was having meltdowns almost daily. I'd be coasting along just fine, then one of those things would come up and out of nowhere the switch would flip. It would feel like a presentation and bam, a pretty severe panic attack. It was worse than high school. Much worse."

"And how did you extricate yourself from that?"

"I unloaded on my boss one night over a couple beers. He was stunned. I had hidden all of that from everyone. He proposed that I work from home, which I've been doing the last two years. It's been great. I created a life where I don't have to deal with people anymore."

"And no more presentations."

"Right. My boss shielded me from ever having to do them. Until now. The night before you guys showed up, the president of our company decreed that I was to teach some employee-training classes, and I kind of lost it. I drank a bunch, and then you found me the next morning. This must all sound pretty pathetic to you, huh?"

"Not at all, Danny. I think you'd be surprised how many people feel like you do. It's just not as severe with most. You were clearly a very sensitive child who went through a lot of demoralizing experiences that continued into adulthood. After struggling with it your whole life, you decided you'd had enough, and you created a life that required very little human interaction. I suspect the more you isolated yourself, the worse your social phobia became. Do you have any recurring dreams, ones that are unpleasant?"

"Actually, I do. A couple of times a week. I had one the other morning, just before you got me up to do yoga. I'm always being chased. I might be in the wilderness, running through fields and woods, or in an empty sports arena or office building, racing up and down stairs, hiding behind furniture. But it's always the same. I know I'm being chased, I hide a while and feel safer, then I know they're getting close and I start panicking, and I take off again. The strange thing is I never see who's chasing me. And they never catch me. I just know I have to keep moving."

"Interesting. That's probably the easiest dream analysis I've ever encountered."

"What do you think it means?"

"Seriously? Danny, you're running from something. You're staying just ahead of it, but it's always there. What have you been avoiding all your life?" Kingsley asked.

"The fears and issues I described? The ones Shey found in the exam?"

"Of course that's it. If you do the work we need you to do for this mission—especially if you embrace it and really want to overcome some of this—I think the dreams will stop. I think the work we do for this mission will help you a great deal in your life back on Earth."

"For being a searcher, you sure seem to know a lot about human behavior."

"It's just wisdom that comes from exposure to principles of human nature along with observation and experience. My exposure came, and is still coming, from Shanna Var."

"What's Shanna Var?"

"Not what, who. Shanna Var is my mentor. She has been for over forty years. Shanna is an incredibly advanced being who has had a tremendous impact on who I am today."

"It seems strange someone like you needs a mentor."

Kingsley chuckled. "We all need to keep learning and growing, Danny."

"I suppose," said Danny. "Hey, you know what sounds great? A nap. The golf and beer and rehashing my past has wiped me out."

"I'll tell you what. Consider the next few hours personal time. Finish your beer, relax, take a nap, find a book to read, or watch a movie. We'll meet back in the living room at say, seven o'clock. Shey's been researching what we've discovered so far and what our plan of attack will be for Dabita Bok. He'll get us up to speed at happy hour. See you tonight," Kingsley said before heading down the path to the lift.

Shey entered Kingsley's office to find him leaning back in a chair, facing the screen, with his feet on the conference table. "What's up?"

"Shhh."

When Shey realized what Kingsley was watching, he quietly slid into another of the chairs and gave the screen his full attention.

A handsome, sandy-haired teenage boy sat on the edge of a bed staring at the round yellow pill sitting on his nightstand, not changing his expression or breaking his gaze when the silence was broken by a woman's voice.

"Brisby, make sure you eat something, and don't stay up too late."

The boy looked around the room, gaze momentarily coming to rest on a large view screen mounted on the wall to his right. Still expressionless, he rose from the bed and made his way into a massive walk-in closet, where he slowly disrobed and put on a shirt, a pair of pants, and socks. He then shuffled into the bathroom, where he brushed his teeth, combed his hair, and reviewed the state of his complexion. He stepped in some water that he'd splashed onto the floor while brushing, causing him to return to the closet to change socks.

Back in the bedroom, he made his way over to the wall of windows that gave him a panoramic view of a pristine property, an enormous pool, sculptured hedges, countless flowers, and manicured lawn as far as the fading daylight allowed him to see. Returning to the edge of the bed, he hesitated before glancing down at the yellow pill. He made one more methodical trip to the bathroom for a cup of water and returned to the edge of the bed, where he sighed and stared off into space.

"Music. 'Blue Flame' by Maleena Zeena. Repeat . . . ten times."

As a haunting melody filled the room, he closed his eyes and appeared to lose himself in the music, softly singing along, nearly inaudibly, to random parts. When the song started for the second time, he opened his eyes, wiped away a single runaway tear, went over to a monitor, typed several letters, and returned to the bed, where he quickly picked up the pill and popped it into his mouth. He took a gulp of water and stretched out on the bed.

Kingsley and Shey watched in silence as the young man disappeared in the darkness that took over the room.

"That's enough, Gracie," Kingsley said softly.

"Sorry about the intrusion. I didn't realize what you were doing," said Shey.

"No problem," Kingsley sighed deeply. "I just keep watching it and hoping for a different ending. No matter. I suppose it's best if we just focus on the task at hand."

CHAPTER 13

"GRACIE, HAPPY HOUR. Have a seat, Danny. Shey, how about some drinks?"

Danny followed orders and eagerly picked up the beer that Shey set in front of him after the chairs had slid into happy hour position.

"Cheers, everyone," Kingsley said as he raised his martini glass. Once Shey and Danny followed suit, he continued. "Danny, do you have a toast?"

"Uh . . . no . . . I wouldn't know what to . . . I mean, no . . . I can't . . ." Danny sputtered as he stared at the two men holding their drinks in midair.

"Good God, boy, I didn't ask you to address the PUPCO senate. Calm down. I'll do it. Here's to a successful start to the mission, to Danny's excellent work on Kronk, and to our continued success. Cheers," Kingsley said as they clinked glasses and took a sip, in Danny's case a gulp, from their drinks. "Now, Shey, what do you have so far on Dabita Bok?"

"Yeah," Danny added. "Are they aware?"

"Oh my, yes," Shey answered. "Dabita Bok is an extremely advanced planet that has had traveling status for hundreds of years. Their CUSTAR is currently . . . what is it, Gracie?"

"One hundred and seventy-two."

Shey continued. "Their planetary network has many references to the phrase 'walk on fire while under water.' It is in a cave that is on the personal property of a gentleman by the name of Durbin Carbindale. He has an estate in the countryside on the outskirts of a city called Valteema. Durbin is from a very wealthy, powerful, and well-respected family that has great influence in both business and politics. However, Durbin is considered the black sheep of the family. He's never had a career of his own and has lived off the family fortune, though there is speculation that his funds are running low. He has lived on his current estate for twenty-seven years, where he has become a recluse and developed a reputation of being ill-tempered. He reportedly has more than a little disdain for visitors."

"Would approaching him be dangerous?" Kingsley asked.

"I don't believe so, at least based on what I've read about him. He may be surly and gruff, but I don't think he'd become violent."

"Danny," Kingsley said. "You'll go to Durbin's estate and request to speak with him. You're going to have a different alias on each planet we visit. Doing so will make it more difficult for anyone to track our activity. You will tell him you are Darkus Murmak from the planet Emulox and would like access to his cave. If he asks why, tell him you'd rather not say but that it's an urgent matter, one of life or death, and you'd greatly appreciate it if he would accommodate you."

"What if he says no?"

"Then you will bribe him," Kingsley said. "I've set up a new U-bank account and put a hundred thousand U-bucks in it. There's an app on the MPC that will allow you to transfer funds to his U-bank account. Start with twenty-five thousand. If he seems interested but still won't budge, you can bump up the offer. Okay?"

"Sure, I think I can do that."

"Once you get to the target location, you'll need to get a sample of marzical for analysis. Then you're going to examine the area for any other clues. Don't forget that we apparently have an ally in Jillian Falstaff. I expect that she may have tried to leave us some information regarding where they are headed next. So the plan is that we'll park the *Aurora*, you'll—"

"Park?" Danny asked. "I didn't think this ship ever landed."

"It doesn't. We park in space. Most planets that travel have a sophisticated system of parking for visiting ships. Any ship over a certain size must use a space spot. Think of it as your system of roads, exit and entrance ramps, and parking lots. There are designated coordinates where you are allowed to park. There are orbit lanes and paths that you have to use for moving around the planet and taking your smaller crafts to the surface and back.

"So the plan is we park the *Aurora*, you'll head down to the surface, go to the Carbindale estate, get some marzical, look for clues, find out if anyone else has been there, and then return to the *Aurora*."

"Got it," Danny said, mustering more confidence than he felt.

"Well, I think we're ready for Dabita Bok. Let's relax a bit, shall we? Gracie, Sinatra, random, mostly upbeat swing with an occasional ballad, volume at four."

With "Almost Like Being in Love" providing a festive background, Kingsley and Shey clinked their glasses, took sips, and simultaneously smacked their lips. After twenty minutes of lighthearted banter, Shey headed to the kitchen to finish dinner. "One of my damn-near-universally famous pizzas," Shey shouted as he left the kitchen carrying a very large, very hot pizza.

"What's on it?" Danny asked as he plopped down in a chair.

"Chicken, mushrooms, asparagus, red peppers, pine nuts, and goat cheese, with an olive oil and garlic sauce," replied Shey, returning from the kitchen again with a bottle of wine and three glasses.

The three of them attacked the pizza with the only conversation being Kingsley telling Shey about their round at Pebble Beach and then the high points of the PUPCO broadcast that had upset him so that morning. Danny was happy to sit quietly and enjoy the food, wine, and ambience. They were surrounded by a rainy Yoobatarian summer evening. The sound of the steady shower, audible above the Sinatra music, coupled with the soft lighting, provided a soothing setting. Danny once again found himself in a serene zone, reflecting on his success on Kronk, the breakfast he had enjoyed with Kingsley, the thrill of shooting baskets again, and the wonderful time he had playing golf.

He took another small sip of his wine and looked across the table at Shey and Kingsley, engaged in a debate about something PUPCO had done, and it struck him how much he truly liked them. Odd, he thought, how three days ago he hardly knew them and now he felt completely at ease in their presence, how he thought of Kingsley as a father. In fact, he felt he was closer to and already had learned more from Kingsley than his own father. And Shey as . . . a brother? He actually liked having him around and missed him when he wasn't, even though he alternated between wanting to affectionately slap him on the back and thoroughly beat the crap out of him.

Once the pizza was finished, Kingsley distributed the last of the wine, and the group sat without speaking, listening to "In the Wee Small Hours of the Morning" accompanied by the softly but steadily falling rain. As the song came to a close, Kingsley spoke up.

"Well, we probably should break this up. It is an excursion night. We can't stay up until the wee small hours of the morning drinking wine. We'll get to Dabita Bok around eleven, so we don't have to get up too early. We'll have a briefing at nine. I'm going to my room to read a bit before I turn in. I've enjoyed our evening. Good night, gentlemen." Kingsley rose and exited the room with Abby close on his heels.

Danny sat and thought about the prospect of another excursion while Shey made two more round trips to the kitchen to clear the table.

"You know you're allowed to help with this," Shey said as he picked up the three empty wine glasses, the last items to be cleared.

"I'm just thinking about the excursion."

"Tonight you should just be concerned about getting some sleep. You have a big day ahead of you."

"You mean *we*," Danny replied.

"I do?"

"You said that I have a big day tomorrow. I'll be doing the questioning of Carbindale, but you'll be down there with me."

"Not this time, sport. You're on your own."

Shey had just thrown a large rock into the placid pool of Danny's serenity. "What do you mean? I can't go down there by myself," he said, agitated.

"Can't? You not only can, you will," Shey replied with a touch of glee.

"Oh no, I'm not ready for that," Danny said, his agitation clearly growing. "If he thinks I can take the Star Hopper down to a planet and then go everywhere I need to go by myself, he's crazy."

"He doesn't think that at all."

"Oh, good. Don't screw with me on this stuff, Shey."

"No, there's no need for you to take the Star Hopper. You'll take a Solo Trek."

"What? I can't fly one of those little things down to a planet. He didn't say anything about this."

"He will in the morning. Why are you so worked up? It shouldn't be a surprise. He told you before Kronk that I can only go if the planet isn't aware."

"No, no, no, no. He has to let you go with me. I can't . . . I'm going to go talk to him."

"It won't do you any good, but go ahead."

Danny was up in a flash, knocking his chair over backward and practically running from the room. His mind was racing faster than his body as he flew across the foyer and down the main hall toward Kingsley's room.

"Gracie, where's Kingsley?"

"Kingsley is in his suite."

When arriving at Kingsley's door, Danny stopped and pressed the panel to request admittance. He was breathing heavily, partially from the brisk trip and partially from the anxiety. When the door slid open, Danny burst into Kingsley's suite to start pleading his case, but what he found in the room left him speechless.

Kingsley was sitting on a large sofa that faced the left wall, a wall that was home to a fireplace and a massive view screen. In the chair to his right sat a woman, directly facing Danny. She appeared to be around fifty, an attractive woman with shoulder-length blond hair that was pulled back, and kind, brown eyes. She wore a turtleneck and slacks, both black, but was barefoot. She smiled warmly but said nothing as Danny stared at her in shock.

"Well, hello, Danny. Come on in," Kingsley said as he turned to Danny. "I'd like you to meet someone. This is Shanna Var."

"Hello, Danny. I've heard a lot about you. I'm glad to finally meet you," she said in a voice that was soft but loaded with charm and confidence.

"I . . . uh . . . I . . . yeah, hi. It's nice to meet you."

"I mentioned Shanna to you this afternoon, Danny. She's my mentor. We were just having a chat about some things. What is it I can do for you?"

"Oh . . . um, nothing. It can wait until tomorrow."

"No, it can't," Shanna said.

"You can say anything you like in front of Shanna, Danny. Now what's on your mind?" Kingsley said.

"Okay. Um, Shey said I was going to have to go to Dabita Bok by myself tomorrow."

"That's correct."

"But I . . . I'm not ready for something like that. I can't do it."

"Of course you can. This shouldn't be a surprise. I told you that I'd let Shey go with you only if the planet isn't aware, and to tell you the truth, I'm rethinking that."

"I can't fly a Solo Trek or land it or drive it around. And what if I get in trouble or something? No way."

"Danny, you're getting upset over nothing. You don't have to fly, and there's no driving involved. Stella is the computer on the Solo Trek you'll take. She will take care of the trip to the surface. When you land, she will get you to the Carbindale estate using the highest speed and most efficient path possible. And you're not going to get into any trouble. Dabita Bok is an advanced, peaceful planet. I will again be connected constantly with the EZ-Comm so I can direct you through any situation that arises."

"I just don't want to be alone down there. Look at what happened on Kronk. Shey got me out of there when Jarrison was after me."

"Danny, the point is moot, because there is no way we can risk having Shey go with you. You knew he wasn't going to be able to on most excursions. You'll feel better about it in the morning."

Danny was defeated and dejected. "I'm going to my room," he said before turning to leave.

Once the door slid shut, Kingsley sighed deeply and looked over at Shanna. "You could have helped."

"It's your game. I'm just a spectator. Besides, you were fine."

"Was I? I don't know. I'm making a lot of this up as I go. I was close to going back into military mode, raising my voice, ordering him to do it, threatening him with some sort of punishment. I don't know how many times I can do that or how effective it really is."

"And if you did all of that to get him to perform, what would his motivation be?"

"Fear, I suppose."

Shanna folded her legs into a lotus position. "So you want him to agree to do what you say out of fear of punishment? Sounds like you just want to have him conquer one fear by replacing it with another."

Kingsley chuckled. "You're right, as always. Deep down I know that's not the way to go, but I'm running out of ways to motivate him."

"Fear isn't the answer. It may work in the short term to get someone to do something that they are resisting, but in the long run it fails. There comes a point where the thought of facing the threatened punishment is more appealing than facing the impending situation. Then you have nothing. Plus, motivating using fear builds resentment and anger."

"I know all of that. I suppose I was abandoning my principles out of desperation."

"Which is when you need them most. You just needed to be reminded. It's easy to get so caught up in trying to teach someone your principles that you lose touch with them yourself."

"I'll try to remember that. We've come so far. I'd hate to muck it up at this point."

"Do I also have to remind you of the one absolutely necessary ingredient for getting someone to change?"

"I know, they have to want to change."

"And you think Danny wants to change?"

"I'm not sure," Kingsley said, stroking his beard. "I think he's slowly shifting from doing all of this out of fear to doing it to help Yoobatar and Queen Quilicant. Has he made a clear proclamation that he wants to change, that he wants to conquer all of his issues and become a certain type of person? No. Not yet."

"Working to overcome his fears in order to save an alien planet or to meet a pretty girl is only going to take him so far. He will face issues that will make those things seem irrelevant. In the meantime, they may help pull him along until more drastic measures are required."

"Drastic measures? What exactly are you proposing?"

"I'm proposing nothing. I'm saying that for him to achieve what you want him to achieve, he needs to be committed to changing, to firmly resolve that he does not want to live his life the way he has to this point. If he doesn't do that, you have no chance. When the going gets tough, he'll simply give up, regardless of the perceived consequences or expected payoff."

"And how exactly do I get him to commit to changing?"

"You'll figure it out. Perhaps Danny isn't the only one meant to grow from this experience."

Before Kingsley could reply, she was gone.

As the door slid shut behind Danny, he looked around his room for something to throw. Failing to find anything that he felt would give him satisfaction, he ripped off his left shoe and flung it against the wall.

"Damn it, Gracie!" he yelled as he walked across the living room awkwardly. "Just when everything was going good and I was having some fun, this comes up. I can't go to a fucking strange planet by myself. No way. I don't even like going to the grocery. What the hell am I supposed to do about this?"

"You have an incoming call. Would you like to take in on the main screen?"

"What? A call? I think you're mistaken, Gracie. It must be for Kingsley. Let him know that there's a—"

"The call is most definitely for you."

"Who is it?"

"Vivitar Quilicant. Shall I notify her that you are available?"

A shocked and panicked Danny looked around the room. His mode quickly shifted from agitated and angry to overwhelming anxiety with a little excitement sprinkled in. He felt like he was in high school again and the best-looking, most popular girl in the class was approaching him in the hallway. He hurriedly ran his fingers through his hair and tried licking his lips, but his arid tongue failed miserably.

"Danny, will you take the call?"

"Oh, uh, yeah. Sure," Danny stammered as he tried taking a couple of deep breaths. In the middle of a second gulp of air, he stopped moving, breathing, blinking, and thinking as the blank screen was filled with the Yoobatarian royal beauty. Sitting on a sofa in a simple, black V-neck sweater, her appearance was much less official-looking than on the previous call.

"Hello, Danny."

"Hello, Your Highness," he managed after clearing his throat.

"You can call me Vivitar, Danny."

"Uh, okay . . . Vivitar." Danny felt a rush just saying her name. "Do you want me to get Kingsley?"

"Absolutely not. I want to speak with you in private. Do you have a problem with that? You are a member of his crew. I don't want you to feel disloyal having this conversation behind his back."

"Oh, no, that's not a problem," he blurted. Danny most definitely did not want the moment to end.

"Wonderful. I wanted to speak with you in private because I want your opinion without Kingsley's influence or interference. Tell me, Danny, how do you feel the mission is going?"

"Really good . . . so far."

"Kingsley has kept me up to date per my request. I want to hear your version. My concern is that Kingsley's desire for his fee is causing him to perhaps put a bit of a spin on the state of the mission. What has happened since we last spoke?"

Danny quickly described what occurred on Kronk and what he had learned about his next excursion. "So now we're on our way to Dabita Bok and should get there in the morning."

"Excellent. That's exactly what Kingsley told me. It's good to know he's being honest with me. Do you mind if I call you from time to time during the mission?"

"No," Danny replied, almost before Vivitar had finished the question.

"Splendid. I'm counting on you, Danny."

"I won't let you down," he said confidently.

"I'll look forward to thanking you in person when this mission is complete. Good night and stay in the flow," she said before the screen went blank.

"Wow," Danny said softly as he stared at the screen. "I think she likes me, Gracie."

"While I cannot read her mind, the tone and content of her speech would lead me to believe that she does not dislike you. Now get into bed, and I'll lead you through breathing exercises and affirmations."

Danny reluctantly followed her direction and was prone in a couple of minutes.

"Tonight we are going to work on slow, rhythmic breathing, inhaling and exhaling with no pause after either. Focus on your breathing and not thoughts about the mission or Vivitar. If a thought enters, let it go and refocus on the breathing."

Within a few minutes Danny fell into the described rhythm and was listening to and thinking only of his breathing. When Gracie's readings indicated he was completely relaxed but not asleep, she began the affirmations.

"I speak freely with strong words and a firm tone . . . I enjoy connecting with all living beings . . . I calmly handle all situations . . . I expect nothing . . . I expect everything . . . I am willing to learn and change . . . I freely and confidently express opinions and make decisions . . . I focus on the present and remain in the flow of the universe."

CHAPTER 14

As Danny stood on his yoga mat beside Kingsley, he tried to get his bearings and fix his bedhead, both with limited success, while waiting on the instructor du jour to appear on the screen. He was on the verge of whining about not having had any coffee yet when a tall, slender brunette appeared and introduced herself as Tamber. She proceeded to lead them through a program that started out very gently but quickly grew in difficulty, so much so that Danny had worked up a sweat by the time they finished.

"I asked for a rigorous routine to really get your juices flowing for the excursion," Kingsley said as he threw Danny a towel. "Let's get some breakfast."

They arrived in the yard to find a refreshingly cool Yoobatarian morning and a dining table that was home to bowls of fruit-smothered oatmeal, a basket of muffins, a carafe of coffee, and a jovial Drimmillian who was sipping coffee and watching UNN on a large screen that interrupted the landscape.

"Good morning, gentlemen," said Shey. "Beautiful day, isn't it? How was your session? Invigorating, I hope. Sleep well? I certainly did. Do you feel the excitement in the air, that electricity that always seems to be present on an excursion day?"

"What the hell got into you? You get laid last night?" Danny asked, amid disturbing mental images of what Shey may have done with Shanna Var.

"Not exactly. Ask me if I did any laundry last night."

"What?"

"Just ask."

"You do any laundry last night?"

"No, but I did a load by hand," Shey yelled before bursting out in gleeful laughter. "Isn't it great to start our day with humor?"

"Yeah, it is. We ought to try it sometime," Danny deadpanned while pouring himself some coffee and trying to fend off the even-more-disturbing images of Shey pleasuring himself.

"Did you hear that, Kingsley? Danny tried to be funny. With emphasis on *tried*, of course."

Kingsley was paying attention to the view screen, not the sophomoric banter. He was again disgusted by the goings on in the PUPCO senate.

"Mute that, Gracie."

As they sipped and ate, Danny's thoughts settled on the impending excursion and the previous night's events.

"What's the deal with Shanna Var?"

"I told you, she's my mentor."

"I know that. I mean, why didn't you tell me she was on the ship? What room is she staying in?"

"She doesn't have a room."

"What, she just wanders around?"

"Basically," Kingsley replied between forkfuls of food.

"I don't get it. Where is she now? Why didn't I see her before last night?"

"I don't know where she is right now. She comes and goes as she pleases."

"Why are you being so evasive?"

Kingsley was taken aback by Danny's assertive attitude. "Because I don't know if you're ready, or open-minded enough, to hear the truth."

"Sure I am. You have to tell me now. You can't leave me hanging like this."

"Oh, tell him for crying out loud," Shey interjected. "He's watched enough science fiction that nothing should surprise him. And besides, he may see wilder stuff on this mission."

"I suppose," said Kingsley as he took a big swig of coffee. "Shanna Var is a member of a highly evolved race called Calizians. The Calizians are so advanced they can dematerialize, travel anywhere in the universe in an instant, and rematerialize at will. Shanna shows up when she feels I need counseling and, annoyingly, not always when I want her to."

"Dematerialize? Does she have some kind of device that makes her invisible and zips her around?"

"No, Danny, she has no device. When I say the Calizians are highly advanced, I don't mean technologically. Shanna's abilities come from being spiritually advanced. She has the power, as does her entire race, to raise the vibration of her cells to the point her body can be converted to a higher form of energy. With a thought she can transport that energy anywhere she likes and then reconvert it, or slow it down, so that it again takes the form of her physical body. Actually, she can take any form she likes."

"How does she do that?"

"Do you remember when I was explaining the phrase Vivitar used about staying in the flow? I said that everything in the universe is energy."

"Yes."

"Okay, so what is energy? It's molecules, molecules that take on various forms based on their makeup, their density, and primarily their rate of vibration. The same molecules make up ice, then become water, then evaporate into thin air. The human body, as well as your mind and spirit, is made up of molecules that are vibrating at a certain rate at any point in time, a rate that is constantly changing based on a number of factors. Spiritual development is increasing the rate of vibration of your body, mind, and ultimately your soul, or spirit."

"And how do you do that?"

"First, it helps tremendously to prepare your body. You have to make it more conducive to an increased cellular vibration and, in turn, increased energy flow. You start by improving your diet, limiting toxins, getting adequate sleep, drinking lots of water, and getting exercise. Next is oxygenation of your cells, which is achieved through proper breathing. Gracie has been working with you on that at night.

"Which leads me to where all spiritual development begins, the mind. Thoughts are energy, Danny. Very powerful energy. They impact your mood, attitude, and emotions. They control everything you do, everything you don't do, and everything you say. Thoughts, actions, and speech are all supercharged by emotion. Emotions have a vibration just as thoughts do. Strong emotion behind thought impacts the vibration of everything significantly more, many times more, than a thought with little or no feeling. Emotions such as resentment, jealousy, intolerance, anger, hatred, malice, and, most importantly, fear lower your vibration dramatically. All negative emotions have their basis in fear. On the opposite end of the spectrum, positive emotions such as joy, delight, peace, happiness, acceptance, and, ultimately, love elevate your soul. Your attitude is also important. Being optimistic, enthusiastic, positive, passionate, and having a zest for life greatly increases your vibration as opposed to wallowing in pessimism, doubt, worry, and despair.

"Learning to avoid negative thoughts, emotions, and actions, moving away from fear and toward love, is the key to spiritual advancement, also known as *ascension*."

"All of this sounds like a lot of work."

"I've got some things to take care of before the excursion, so I'll let you gentlemen continue this scintillating conversation," Shey said as he sprang up and headed toward the lift.

"It's a process, Danny. You start slowly and build. There are tools to help. Meditation is the most important. It clears your mind of clutter and puts you in touch with spirit. Affirmations are a powerful tool that become more effective the more frequently you use them and the more feeling you put behind them. Along the same lines are visualizations, in which you picture how a future event will play out or the lifestyle you desire.

"Two simple tools that most beings don't use nearly enough to their advantage are contemplation and introspection. Contemplate things such as why something happened to you, why a certain person entered your life, what you've accomplished, and what you'd like to accomplish, even the purpose of life and why you are alive. Introspection, or self-examination, is just as important. Look inside yourself. Examine what kind of person you are, identify your issues, evaluate your thoughts, feelings, and actions, and determine in what areas you want to improve. Through contemplation and introspection, we gain insight. Insight gives us the power to grow. It identifies what we need to work on."

"Okay, so that's it? You think right and act right and use these tools, and you'll be able to disappear?" Danny asked.

Kingsley chuckled. "You make it sound like a magic trick."

"Well, isn't it kind of?"

"Not at all. It is simply the elevation of your spirit. Your spirit, or soul, is the immortal pure energy that is your true essence. Development of the spirit is why we're here. The true nature of our existence is that our soul exists on a spiritual plane that is commensurate with its rate of vibration, one of an infinite number of such planes or states of vibration. We take a physical body in order to learn lessons, to grow, to help others, and ultimately to advance spiritually by raising our vibration. I'm sure you've heard of reincarnation. It's the mechanism we use to develop. When we're in the spiritual plane, we choose the situation into which we will be born. The rest is up to us once we get here.

"Think of the universe as a school, with each lifetime being another grade. You're required to go to school, but how much you learn and how fast you learn it is up to you. The difference with reincarnation is that a soul goes through dozens, possibly hundreds of lifetimes and, because of free will, it doesn't always advance. If you get caught up in negative patterns and don't recognize them, do what you know is right, or get help, you certainly may leave a lifetime at a lower vibration than you entered it."

"I like that reincarnation thing," Danny said. "It never really made sense to me that we are born, live our life, die, and then spend eternity in heaven or hell based on the way we lived in that one lifetime. That would be an awful lot riding on one life."

"Yes, it would be. In reality, you live many lifetimes with your vibrational state ebbing and flowing based on what you do in each one. You make some mistakes or get caught up in some negative patterns, and you regress a bit. In general, though, you are moving forward or advancing. Think of it as your stock market. It goes up and down from day to day, but in the long term the trend is for it to grow."

"And Shanna?"

"I'm getting to that. Over the course of perhaps many, many lifetimes, you can ascend to the point that your mind and soul are so advanced that you can actually control the vibratory rate of your body. You can speed up the vibration of your cells so that they are moving too fast for the human eye to see, to a frequency at which they are converted to energy that can be moved about the physical plane with just a thought, and then slowed down again to take the form of a body. The Calizians have achieved that state. Shanna is a spiritual master, a master of her spirit."

"So Shanna's that advanced and all she does is mentor you?"

"Heavens no. I'm just one of her pupils. I suspect she can actually split her energy, converting to her physical form in different places while a portion of her being remains in the spiritual plane. Shanna first showed up about forty years ago and started giving me advice, unsolicited advice, I might add. I don't know why she picked me. She only shows up occasionally to give me what she considers guidance. Sometimes what she says and does is more infuriating than helpful."

"Kingsley," Gracie interjected. "We are two hours from Dabita Bok."

"Thank you, Gracie."

"What?" Danny exclaimed. "Two hours? We're only two hours away?"

"Yes," Kingsley said as he pushed back his chair, rose, and stretched while scanning the Yoobatarian countryside. "Ready to visit Durbin Carbindale?"

"No, I'm not. We haven't done any prep work. I don't know what I'm supposed to do."

"There isn't a lot to cover, but we will review what you're supposed to do before you leave. Go shower up and meet us in the garage in an hour. Standard excursion garb."

"But . . ."

Kingsley stood up and strode briskly toward the lift, leaving Danny alone with Abby and his unfinished objection. He looked down at the large canine sprawled out on her side, looking up at Danny with her head still on the floor.

"Damn it, Ab! I'd be having a good time if it wasn't for this mission crap."

Danny set down his coffee mug and rubbed his forehead. The symptoms were back. He hated the symptoms. Passionately. He was sick of them, sick of a lifetime of not being able to control them, sick of them swooping down on him out of the blue and taking charge of his body every single time something unpleasant lay before him. All he wanted was a life without them, a life that had thus far eluded him.

Danny took a deep breath. "Well, I guess I better get going before Gracie starts zapping me with tickle rays."

"Perfect timing, Danny," Kingsley shouted as Danny entered the garage. "I love punctuality."

"Yeah, well, it's not voluntary. Your thug would have made sure I was here."

"It's early afternoon in Valteema. You'll take a Solo Trek down to the planet's surface, to the spairport that is closest to the Carbindale estate."

"Spairport?"

"Space and airport. It's used for all arrivals and departures of both visiting alien ships and native flights. Most planets don't permit ships to simply land and take off from anywhere they desire. As I described, when you touch down, the Solo Trek will take care of getting you to the Carbindale estate. Durbin Carbindale is probably not interested in chit-chat, so get right to the point. Request access to the cave. If he refuses, offer him the money. Get to the cave, get a sample of the marzical, then get back to the Solo Trek. The Solo Trek will get you back here."

"So what do I do if I run into Dank? What's he look like? I mean, you don't know how far behind him we are."

"He's around seventy, dark hair with some gray, about my height, usually some stubble. But I don't expect that to happen, at least on Dabita Bok. Based on when he left Kronk, we're still probably a day behind him. But it could happen on one of the planets we visit. If and when it does, you'll terminate the excursion immediately and let us know. Shey and I will then deal with Dank. Now follow me."

Kingsley led the group past the Star Hopper to the row of Solo Treks on the left side of the garage's back wall. He stopped at the one on the right end. It was a small craft; seven feet high, six feet long, and five feet wide, with a short nose that protruded from below a window that spanned the front.

"Gracie, Danny will be the owner of this Solo Trek. Danny, that means that you and only you will be able to open the door and fly it. Go ahead."

"Open Solo Trek?" Danny said, causing the door to almost silently slide open.

Shey exited the weapons room and handed Danny an MR5 that was attached to a strap.

"Here you go, sport."

"Kingsley, we have arrived at Dabita Bok, and I have brought the ship to rest in a space spot," said Gracie.

Kingsley turned to Danny. "Hop in."

The Solo Trek's interior was dominated by a high-backed seat into which Danny settled before checking out the rest of the interior. It was comfortable but certainly not spacious, with windows on the front, each side, and the ceiling. In front of him was a row of three slanted display screens in a semicircular pattern. The screens were home to a list of options such as *system status*, *navigation*, *life support*, and *weaponry*. Above the panels and below the front window was a small view screen, approximately three feet wide and two feet high.

Kingsley continued. "Stella will take care of getting you to the surface and back and driving to and from Durbin's estate. You just sit back, enjoy the ride, and focus on the task at hand. Any questions about the transport or the excursion?"

"Nope," Danny replied, taking a big gulp as the thought of actually departing on his own became more real.

"Danny," Kingsley said, leaning in and putting his hand on Danny's shoulder. "You're doing a great job. I have confidence in you. I know you can handle this. You have all the tools. Remember everything we worked on before Kronk. Just let go of the fear. Simply refuse to let it in."

Danny looked up at the wise, weathered face. A wave of confidence washed over him as he stared into Kingsley's eyes and let his words sink in. "Thanks. I feel pretty good about it."

"That's my mission lead," Kingsley said as he gently punched Danny's shoulder and backed away.

"Close the door, Stella," Danny said firmly. As the door slid shut, he felt a slight tremor of anxiety from being isolated, but it was quickly quashed upon seeing Kingsley's big grin and thumbs-up sign through the window.

"Are you ready to depart, Danny?" Stella asked. The voice sounded like a Midwestern young lady, about Danny's age.

"I guess so," he replied after a deep inhale and even deeper exhale.

A small door opened beneath the transport, and Danny saw Kingsley, Shey, and Abby slowly rising before disappearing, their comforting images replaced by the black of space.

CHAPTER 15

DANNY'S *EXPECT EVERYTHING* TRAINING came in handy as the Solo Trek glided from under the belly of the *Aurora* and stopped just past its nose. He had the preconceived notion that at that point he would find nothing but star-speckled space and the planet below him. What he saw instead resembled a massive, multilevel parking garage with countless rows and layers of parked spaceships. Between each two-deep row of parked vehicles, other ships were traveling in an organized fashion through wide stretches of open space.

"Wow. This is amazing," he said softly.

Stella explained. "This is the standard space garage system used by a large majority of highly advanced planets. Each space spot is defined by a set of coordinates. The space spots and the lanes are displayed on the screen."

"Thanks," Danny said as he looked down at the screen to find lines defining thousands of box-shaped parking spaces and lanes, both vertical and horizontal. The transport moved from the *Aurora*'s space into a lane and turned left. Danny glanced back over his shoulder to get a last look at the mother ship before starting his adventure.

"This is freaking unbelievable," he said as the Solo Trek glided past dozens of mostly occupied spots. "A couple of days ago I was sitting in my apartment watching TV, and now I'm in a transport flying through a space parking garage."

The Solo Trek slowed before making a sharp right turn and continuing on. After a few moments of flying by ship after ship, they emerged from the garage, entered open space, and accelerated. The planet was finally visible below. Danny leaned over and strained to see as much as he could from the window.

"Stella, it seems like we're just kind of in orbit. When will we start going down?"

"We are about to turn from an orbit lane into an exit lane and then into a service lane that will take us down to the surface."

The transport slowly veered to the right while rotating ninety degrees forward and continued its flight, leaving Danny facing down toward the planet.

As the Solo Trek drew nearer the surface, Danny could see a sprawling urban area that he assumed was Valteema. He looked for a distinguishable downtown, but instead saw numerous small groups of skyscrapers spread throughout the city. The transport made a beeline for a massive building on the outskirts of the city, a building that was surrounded by thousands of parked vessels. The Solo Trek wasn't slowing down quickly enough for Danny's taste. The ground rushing toward his face made him tightly grasp the seat's armrests and brace for what seemed to be inevitable impact. Just as he was about to let out a yell, the Solo Trek abruptly but smoothly slowed, rotated back to an upright position, gently touched down in their assigned spot, and immediately started moving through the parking lot. As the transport made a turn onto a ramp, its speed increased. Danny looked to his left and cringed at a steady stream of traffic. To his relief, the Solo Trek merged flawlessly, gliding in between two other vehicles without slowing down.

"Are you okay, Danny?" Stella asked. "Your vital signs are slightly elevated."

"I guess I just have to get used to the speed of everything. I could have sworn we were going to crash a couple of times."

"The transportation is all computer controlled, and the system is accident-free. The movements of all ships are perfectly orchestrated."

"How fast are we going?"

"In Earth terms, one hundred and twenty-seven miles per hour."

Danny whistled as he tried to take in the scenery that was flying by, a task that became much easier when the Solo Trek suddenly veered off of the main road onto an exit ramp and slowed. After passing under the just-exited highway, Danny got his first good look at Dabita Bok. The mostly residential area, decidedly more urban than that which surrounded the spairport, was relatively Earth-like, only much more futuristic. As on Earth, there were streets and sidewalks and parking lots, old buildings as well as new, grass and trees, traffic and pedestrians. The vehicles that shared the roadway with the Solo Trek were different shapes and sizes, but all had an ultramodern appearance. The older buildings reminded Danny of old buildings on Earth, made of stone or brick with interesting architectural details.

After passing through several blocks of freestanding homes, apartment buildings, and businesses, the Solo Trek slowed slightly as it entered what appeared to be a small downtown area. There were a handful of skyscrapers surrounded by dozens of smaller structures. Each was constructed mostly of glass held together by gleaming metal frames. Everything was spotless, from the buildings and grassy areas to the streets and sidewalks. The traffic, both pedestrian and transport, was the heaviest Danny had encountered. He was very glad that he wasn't driving.

"Stella, is this the downtown?"

"The layout of urban areas on Dabita Bok, as with most advanced planets, is slightly different than on your planet. Rather than having one large, central downtown area surrounded by suburban areas, cities have areas called redcomm clusters, one of which we are passing through at the moment. In the middle of a redcomm cluster is a group of buildings that are both residential and commercial, typically called the *center*. Also, near the center there will typically be an entertainment district with shopping, restaurants, and sporting venues. As you move away from the center, you'll find some smaller businesses, manufacturing facilities, more residential structures, parks, golf courses, and other recreational areas. Such a layout allows the inhabitants to live close to their place of employment and reduces the traffic problems that develop with one large downtown. The effect is that of many small cities bordering one another. Valteema consists of twenty-seven redcomm clusters."

Within moments the transport was clear of the urban district. Danny turned his attention to the beautiful, almost breathtaking, Bokian country-side through which the transport was swiftly gliding. Much of the rolling terrain was covered with tall, wild grasses. The fields were framed by a forest of towering pines a few miles to his right and by some rather impressive mountains in the distance on his left. It was all bathed in brilliant sunshine. Despite the surrounding natural beauty, Danny put his head back, closed his eyes, and heeded Kingsley's advice. Expect nothing. Expect everything. He repeated it over and over, like a mantra, until Stella interrupted.

"Danny, we've arrived at the Carbindale estate."

They were stopped in the middle of a country road, about fifty feet from a driveway that was framed by two large brick columns. Stretching between them was an electronic screen that displayed the words "Visitors Are Not Welcome." The grounds were heavily but not densely treed. Danny peered past the brick columns to see the drive winding and eventually disappear-ing through the trees. No house was in sight. He looked down the property line each way, expecting to see a wall or fence, but found only a tall black pole every couple hundred feet.

"So where's this great security?" Danny asked. "It looks like you can just walk onto the property."

"Danny," Kingsley said. "It's all done with energy fields that are emitted from the poles you see surrounding the grounds. I'm sure it's very difficult to penetrate, and it probably has sensors that let Carbindale know if anything touches it with significant force. There is likely a comm station outside the gate. Pull up to the gate and ask for entry. Ready?"

Danny swallowed hard and was about to say that he wasn't, out of habit, when he realized that was not the case. He actually felt ready. He was on edge and a little nervous, but he wasn't terrified. The blanket of dread that so often smothered him was absent.

"Ready," he replied firmly.

As if on cue, the transport moved up to the driveway, turned in, and came to a rest next to the monitor. The window to Danny's left slid down, giving him a good view of the panel. It contained a camera lens and a keypad in addition to the screen.

"I'd like to speak to Mr. Durbin Carbindale, please," Danny said pleasantly.

No answer.

"I said I'd like to speak to Mr. Carbindale," he repeated.

"I heard you, I heard you," replied a sophisticated, albeit irritated, voice. "What do you want?"

Assuming the voice was that of a servant, Danny restated his request. "I'd like to speak to Mr. Durbin Carbindale, please."

"So quit repeating yourself like a Villabar bird and speak!"

"I . . . I mean I'd like to see Mr. Carbindale. Are you him?"

"What do you want?" The man was obviously getting more annoyed with each exchange.

"I need to speak with you on an extremely urgent matter, a matter of life and death. I won't take much of your time."

The man chuckled, and his voice softened a bit. "Not good enough. You know how many tourists try to get onto my property? I've heard it all. Life and death? You'll have to be more specific. Who are you and what do you want?"

"My name is Darkus Murmak, from the planet Emulox. I can't tell you more. I mean, I'd prefer not to over the speaker. I can't stress enough how important it is."

"Try."

Danny decided to play his hole card. "I'm prepared to offer you twenty-five thousand U-bucks if you'll meet with me."

"Twenty-five thousand? I suppose I can spare a few minutes for twenty-five thousand U-bucks. The field covering the entrance is now down. Drive to the house, park in front, leave your weapons in the transport, turn off your communication devices, and come to the door. You'll be scanned before entering. If any weapons or active communication devices are found or if you fail to pay me the U-bucks, you will not be permitted entry, and my dogs will make certain you return to your transport and leave . . . in how many pieces I can't guarantee."

"Thank you," Danny replied as the window slid shut. "Kingsley, what about the EZ-Comm?" Danny asked as the transport passed between the columns and moved down the winding drive.

"His scanner will probably detect it, but don't worry. Such devices are quite common on most advanced planets. He wants to make sure no one else is listening, so you'll have to turn it off before going into the house."

"You mean we'll be out of touch while I'm in there? I don't think I like that idea."

"Danny it's our only option. You'll probably only be in the house for a few minutes. In case of an emergency, just turn it back on so I can hear what's going on."

"Emergency? If there's an emergency, you won't be able to get here fast enough to do anything about it."

"True, but if he knows someone is listening, it may impact his actions. As I said, it's our only option."

"I suppose," Danny said as he laid his open palms on his now-queasy stomach, a queasiness that was exacerbated by the Solo Trek's arrival at the front door of the Carbindale home. It was an impressive structure with a two-story central section and two single-story wings. The architecture had a classic, traditional feel. The exterior was weathered stone, the roof slate shingles, and the windows were flanked by black shutters. Large blocks of cut stone outlined the black double doors.

Danny sat in the motionless transport and took a deep breath.

"Danny, pull in your energy; remain centered and calm. And keep breathing. That's important. Remember the basics: eye contact, speak firmly, and connect with him. It will show him that you're not afraid. You are an intelligent, articulate, powerful being, Danny. Exude your strength. Remember the mission goal. We're doing this to help Vivitar and all of Yoobatar. You know what to do. You have to get to that cave, and you have to find out if Dank has been here."

"Okay, let's do it. EZ-Comm off," said Danny. He removed the MR5 from his ankle and headed to the front door. Before he could find a way to notify the owner he had arrived, the right of the two doors slowly opened. Danny peered inside without moving.

"Come in, come in. Don't stand out there gawking like a Villabar bird. You seem to have several of their traits. You're not part Villabar, are you?"

The voice was disarming, almost playful, and drew Danny through the door and into the foyer. It was a sizable, two-story space with a beautiful multicolored rug covering most of the limestone floor and a massive iron chandelier hanging overhead. The walls were adorned with pieces of art. A round table, home to a gorgeous red vase that held a brilliant arrangement of flowers, sat in the middle of the space. On each side of the area, a wide staircase dramatically curved up to the second floor. Between them was an opening into a large room that was home to a wall of windows. On either side of the foyer was another doorway. Through one to his left came the voice again.

"I asked, you're not part Villabar, are you?" The voice was quickly followed by its owner, a dapper, silver-haired gentleman who made his way across the foyer and held out his hand. "Durbin Carbindale. Nice to meet you, Mr. Murmak." He wore charcoal slacks, a white shirt, and a deep red velvet jacket.

The alien's appearance and pleasant tone left Danny stunned, speechless, and staring at the extended hand. He had been expecting a nasty, intimidating villain. What he got was Cary Grant.

"I imagine you find my demeanor surprising, particularly if you were privy to my reputation. I established that reputation intentionally in order to discourage the throngs of tourists that regularly besiege my property. You see, my estate is home to this unusual cave that has become quite well-known. Now, are you going to shake my hand?"

Danny regrouped and shook the outstretched hand.

"Do you speak? Let's start with something simple. Were any of your ancestors Villabar birds?"

"No, no they weren't," Danny finally managed to utter.

"How fortunate for you. Before we begin, we have some business to finish. I believe you are going to pay me twenty-five thousand U-bucks?"

"Oh yes," Danny replied as he pulled the MPC from his pocket and followed Kingsley's instructions on how to transfer funds after Durbin supplied his account number.

"Splendid, now what is it I can do for you exactly?"

"I need access to the cave where you can walk on fire while under water."

"I must not have heard you correctly, young man. Given what I've already told you, you can't have the gall to be telling me that you're nothing more than a tourist. Though I must admit, until recently no tourist has ever offered more than a couple thousand U-bucks to see it. Is there something else, or should I have Zerba and Zelda escort you from the property?"

Two massive dogs trotted in from the back room and took their places on either side of Durbin. They looked like Great Danes, only stockier.

"Hello, ladies. Please be seated," Durbin said. Each dog immediately sat. "Now, was there something else? The U-bucks bought you some patience, something I normally don't have, but it is wearing thin."

Danny managed to pry his gaze from the powerful dogs and look Durbin in the eyes.

"Yes, yes there is. I need to see the cave, but I swear I'm not a tourist. I desperately need a small amount of marzical, and I need the marzical that's in your cave."

"Marzical? Why in the world would you need a worthless crystal—which, by the way, you can find anywhere."

"There's something special about the marzical in that cave. Please, it's a matter of life or death."

Durbin crossed his arms and stroked his chin as one of the canines let out an impatient growl. "I'm listening."

"My mother has a disease that our doctors can't cure. We got the help of a healer who said that the marzical in your cave has some sort of magical healing properties and that I need to get some. So I'd appreciate it if you let me get a small piece. I won't be long. I'll get it and leave."

"I don't believe your story. I've lived on this property for close to thirty years, and I've never heard of such a thing. I don't believe that my marzical or any other has magical properties. Unless you've got something better than that, I insist you be on your way."

"I'll pay you more. How about fifty thousand U-bucks?"

"Fifty thousand? Just to get some marzical? I suppose I can spare some for that price. However, you must first tell me why it's so important."

"I told you why I need it."

"And I told you I don't believe you. Why do you need it?"

Danny stuck to his guns. "Why do you need to know?"

"Mr. Murmak, I have a fair amount of leisure time, but I don't like to play games. That's the deal, the U-bucks and the reason. Take it or leave it."

"Why do you want to know so badly?"

"Let's call it curiosity. When I have two individuals offer me a sizable sum just to see my cave after not having had such an occurrence in thirty years, I'm naturally curious."

Danny had forgotten to ask Carbindale if he'd had any other recent visitors. The thought that it may have been Dank sent Danny's heart racing. "Two? Someone else paid you? Who? When?"

"Well, well. It appears I'm not the only curious one. It was early yesterday morning. A rather imposing individual who called himself Ben Kindolta offered me fifty thousand U-bucks to visit the cave. I took it with no questions asked. However, since this is the second such occurrence, I can't help but think they are related. I therefore cannot oblige you without knowing what in the world is going on."

"What did he look like?"

Durbin sighed. "In terms of a Dabita Bokian he would be around seventy. He was tall, probably a good three inches taller than both of us, and his hair was long, almost shoulder length, and was mostly dark brown with a little gray. He was also very good-looking in a rather rugged, outdoorsy sort of way. And he had what was probably three or four days of facial hair growth. I've dealt with a multitude of beings in my day, and I must say he was one of the most confident and charismatic I've met."

Oh, great, Danny thought. Dank's got all that going for him without the amulet. Vivitar doesn't have a chance if we don't stop him.

"He entered my home by himself, but when he started out to the cave, a very attractive young lady emerged from his transport and joined him."

Dr. Falstaff, Danny thought.

"So can I see your cave?" asked Danny.

"Reason?" Mr. Carbindale was not giving in.

Danny didn't know what to do. He wished Kingsley could whisper him some guidance. If he stuck to his story, he may not get into the cave, which could mean the end of the mission. But he certainly couldn't divulge the true mission. He decided to compromise.

"All I can tell you is that it truly may be a matter of life and death, perhaps even the death of a civilization," he blurted out.

"My, my. That sounds both overly dramatic and intriguing at the same time. What civilization, and why do you need to go into my cave to save it?"

"I might have exaggerated a bit. If I don't get into your cave, an entire planet's society may be harmed. I absolutely can't tell you the planet or why that may happen. I just told you that to show that I'm not joking around," Danny said.

"While your claim is dramatic, it's much too general. I'm afraid I need more detail."

Danny took a deep breath and chose his words carefully. "Okay. I'm looking for the guy that was here yesterday. He stole something, and I'm trying to get it back from him."

Durbin strolled around Danny, looking at him pensively. "Young man, I like you. I don't know why, but I do. And as far-fetched as I find your claim, I believe you . . . or at least I believe that you believe it. You can visit the cave for the same price the other fellow paid, fifty thousand U-bucks. One of my companions will lead you there and will wait outside. You will have fifteen U-mins inside. If you don't come out by then, she will come in after you, which, I can safely say, you will not want to happen. Deal?"

"Deal," replied Danny as he made the second transfer to Durbin's account.

"Mr. Murmak, Zerba will escort you to the cave and wait for you outside. I will see you back here," Durbin said as he made his way to the door and touched a panel beside it.

"Thanks. Thank you, Mr. Carbindale," Danny replied before scurrying out the door after Zerba.

A grinning Durbin Carbindale addressed the remaining canine. "Isn't that something, Zelda? Daddy's earned 125,000 U-bucks in two days just for letting people see that ridiculous cave. And there may be more. Much more. I think our Grugnok friends would like to hear about this."

Zelda rose and followed her briskly striding master through the opening on the right side of the foyer and into his spacious, elegantly appointed study. Durbin sat at his massive ornate desk in his massive leather chair and punched a button on a keypad, causing a slim, twenty-inch screen to rise from a slot that appeared in the desk's surface.

"Call Val Cheznik," he ordered. "Tell him it's very important." After several minutes passed, during which time Durbin impatiently tapped his fingers on his desk, his voice assistant replied.

"Val Cheznik is on the line."

The screen came to life and displayed the image of one of the rare species that deviated from the common humanoid look that dominated the inhabited planets of the universe. Durbin always cringed a bit at his first glimpse of Val Cheznik. Only his broad shoulders and large, square head appeared, the latter of which seemed to sit directly on the former with no connecting neck. His greenish-brown skin was thick and creviced. His face was home to a small mouth, two holes where most beings had noses, and narrow eyes with bright red pupils. Durbin had often speculated that the Grugnok race had been formed by a normal humanoid being stranded in the wilderness and eventually mating with a Skabian Hurba monster.

"Val, my good friend! What a pleasure to see you again. It's been too long."

"Yes, and each time we meet, I have to tell you that I'm not interested in pleasantries, Durbin," Val replied. "And we are not good friends. We do business. Period. What is it you want?"

"Val, your sparkling personality goes wonderfully with your twinkling red eyes and impish grin. The charisma flying from my screen is staggering. Have you ever considered a career in the entertainment industry?" Durbin replied. He was well aware that Val hated pleasantries, but he always liked playing with him a bit.

"This communication is over in five seconds if I hear nothing to change my mind."

"Okay, okay. I've got something I think you'll find intriguing and which could lead to something quite profitable. You're probably familiar with the rather famous cave that's on my property?"

"Yes."

"Well, it's common knowledge how I feel about tourists, so I've had no one attempt to visit it in several years. That is, until recently. In the past two days I've had two separate individuals offer me substantial sums just to visit the cave."

Val wasn't impressed. "So two wealthy individuals knew of your disdain for visitors and paid their way into the cave."

"That's what I first thought, but now I think there is more to it. The first person came yesterday morning. His appearance and attitude were not that of a tourist. It was as if he was on a mission. He said his name was Ben Kindolta. A second person showed up a short time ago, a young man who called himself Darkus Murmak. He was an innocuous-looking young man, but he had a sense of urgency about getting to the cave. He then offered me a substantial amount of U-bucks, and when I mentioned that another person had done the same yesterday, he was quite interested. When I mentioned the person's name, Darkus became very excited."

"So it was two wealthy beings who know each other. Is this all you bothered me for?"

"I'm not finished. I think that hearing the name of the first visitor made the second all the more determined. When I pushed him for a reason, he finally told me that if he didn't get there, an entire society may be harmed and it could perhaps even lead to the death of a civilization. He also admitted that he was after the Kindolta fellow because he had stolen something that Mr. Murmak needed to retrieve. I got the impression he needed to do so quite desperately."

"What does that have to do with me?" Val asked.

Durbin often did business with the likes of Val, but he found his lack of wit and insight to be annoying and tiresome. But he had little choice. One must do what one must do to maintain the lifestyle to which one has become accustomed, he frequently told himself.

"Think about it, Val, two people, one being pursued by the other, both giving the impression they are on an important mission, both willing to pay a ridiculous sum just to enter my cave, with one saying a civilization depends upon him retrieving something the first had stolen. I don't know what they were after in my cave, but the assumption one may arrive at is that they are after something of great value or which will give them incredible power. If someone were to pursue and find these beings, they might be able to acquire it. Correct me if I'm wrong, but I was under the impression that the Grugnok were interested in such things. For the small fee of two hundred and fifty thousand U-bucks, I can tell you how to find Mr. Murmak."

Val picked up on Durbin's tone, which was close to that an adult would use when trying to explain something to a child. "You know, Durbin, a person should be careful how he behaves during business dealings. Someone may lose their temper and decide that the satisfaction of eliminating such a person would far outweigh the loss of potential profits."

"You're right. Please accept my apologies. I've been under a bit of stress lately, and it's affecting my manners." Durbin hated apologizing to anyone for anything, even if he was wrong, but he knew Val was right. The Grugnok was one of a handful of species in the universe that could still behave violently with little provocation.

"That's better. I am interested in your proposition. I'll give you a hundred thousand U-bucks. How will I know where to find these beings?"

"Your offer is generous, but I believe that what they may lead you to may be so valuable that I should receive at least two hundred and fifty thousand U-bucks. If you're not interested, I'm sure Hank Malvern would be." Durbin was sure using Hank's name would seal the deal. The Grugnok were an extremely competitive race. Hank was the captain of another Grugnok ship and one of Val's biggest rivals.

Val let out a low growl before turning to speak to another square-headed, thick-skinned Grugnok who was standing nearby. He turned back to Durbin and continued. "We have a deal. The funds are being transferred to your account."

Durbin focused on another section of the display for a moment before looking back at Val. "Thank you. And I just sent you the signature of the tracking devices and a video of Darkus."

"Receipt confirmed. Durbin, if this turns out to be fruitless, I may be back to pay you a visit."

Durbin swallowed hard before answering. "Now Val, you know there are no guarantees in this business. You're accepting the deal knowing the risks. Otherwise I can't agree."

"I know, I know. I just wanted to see my *good friend* squirm a bit," Val said before the screen went dark.

Danny couldn't wait to share what had transpired with Kingsley. "EZ-Comm on. Kingsley? You there?"

"I'm here, Danny. What's going on?"

"It went great. He wasn't at all what I expected. He was really sophisticated and really nice."

"Yes, well, he's from a wealthy family, so that's not too surprising. So he's letting you go to the cave?"

"He sure is. He didn't want to let me, but I talked him into it. Plus I had to pay him fifty thousand U-bucks, in addition to the twenty-five to get onto the property."

"That's fine. Are you on your way to the cave?"

"Yep," Danny said as he started forward again, picking up his pace to keep up with Zerba. "I grabbed the MR5 from the Solo Trek, and now I'm following one of his dogs to the cave. I have fifteen minutes to . . . oh my God, I forgot to tell you the best part. I think Dank was here yesterday!"

"He was?"

"Yeah. Carbindale said a guy paid him fifty thousand U-bucks to see the cave."

"How do you know it was Dank?"

"His description fits. The name he gave Durbin was Ben Kindolta." Danny gasped for air. Zerba's pace was taxing Danny's conditioning.

Kingsley chuckled. "That's an anagram for Dank Nebitol. Dank needed an alias. He has such an incredible ego that he probably thought he'd have some fun with anyone who may have found Chase and followed him to Dabita. And because the tablet will tell him the next destination, he probably thinks there is no chance anyone would be able to determine where he's going. What time was he there?"

"Durbin didn't say. He just said it was yesterday morning."

"That means we've already caught up quite a bit. He dropped Jarrison off nearly three days before we found him, and he was here less than a day and a half ago."

Danny silently followed his canine leader down the path over what had become rather rugged terrain and into a heavily treed area. After a few more moments of traipsing through the trees, they came up alongside a sizable stream. While it was at least fifty feet wide, it was not more a couple of feet deep. Danny could see the bed through the crystal clear, briskly flowing water. The trail dove downward and away from the stream so quickly that Danny had trouble keeping his footing. When it leveled out, they were a good twenty feet below the level of the stream. The trees had thinned and the surrounding terrain had become rocky when Zerba abruptly turned to the left toward a collection of smooth, massive boulders that sat in front of a high wall of solid rock, spun to face Danny, and sat down.

"The dog stopped."

"You must be near the cave entrance," Kingsley said. "Do you see it?"

"Nope."

"Look around. Use the camera on the MPC and tell it to transfer the video back to us."

"Emma, give me a camera and transmit everything back to the *Aurora*," Danny said as he lifted the device. He turned to get a shot of Zerba waiting patiently.

"Danny," Kingsley said. "Don't do anything to upset that dog. That's a Ralkian razor hound. They're extremely intelligent, possibly the brightest dog in the universe—sorry, Abby—and very obedient. They are also extremely powerful and unrelenting when they decide to attack."

"And the name has something to do with their teeth?"

"Correct. But they don't attack unless provoked or they have specific orders to do so."

After weaving his way through several boulders that were all taller than him, Danny came to a stop at the wall of rock and stared at an opening that was at least eight feet high but no more than three feet wide.

"That looks like the entrance, Danny."

Danny looked back to make sure Zerba wasn't following him and exhaled loudly. He again took stock of his situation. It all seemed unreal yet incredibly real. It seemed like weeks since he got the email about the training class from his boss. He stared at the black crevice.

"It's so dark and, well, it's a cave."

"And?"

"And I really don't want to go in there."

"You said Durbin gave you fifteen minutes. When do you think they started the clock?"

"Damn. You're right," Danny exclaimed before taking a deep breath, placing a hand on each side of the entrance, and stepping into the darkness.

"Danny, there's a very strong light on the MPC."

"Now you tell me? Emma, flashlight."

The area was flooded with light. The passageway was a good eight feet wide just inside the narrow entrance. He was relieved not to find any critters in the cracks and crevices of the cave. The farther he went, the faster he walked, partially due to his comfort level increasing but mainly because he was getting excited to see his final destination.

"There's some light up ahead." Danny continued on, with the glow becoming brighter as he went. After another hundred feet or so the path turned sharply to the left. "Wow," he gasped as he turned and gazed at the scene before him.

"What is it?" asked Kingsley.

It was truly dazzling. Danny had entered a large, round space, fifty feet in diameter and unlike anything he'd ever seen. The entire surface of the room, every inch of the floor, walls, and ceiling, was covered in a clear, glistening crystal. The floor and ceiling were level and smooth, almost polished looking, while the walls had angles and imperfections. The room was flooded with light that bounced around, creating a brilliant multicolored display that reminded Danny of the kaleidoscopes he had as a child. The light, Danny realized, was coming from both above and below. Clearly visible through the transparent floor were several dozen flames, individual fires that somehow survived beneath the surface. From above came sunshine, strong, brilliant sunshine, so bright that Danny had to squint to look directly at the ceiling.

"I can see why it's a tourist attraction."

"Show me."

"Oh yeah. Sorry." Danny held up the MPC and directed the camera around the room.

"That's marzical on the walls. The floor is something else, probably quizintine. You need to get a marzical sample and then quickly but thoroughly look around for clues of any type. Keep the camera up so I can also look and so we can record all of it."

Danny walked into the middle of the room and looked up. Through the ceiling he could see that the cave was directly under what he assumed was the stream he had walked along earlier. The water flowing over the stream's crystal bed was so clear and shallow that the sun's rays weren't impeded. If anything, the water and the crystal helped diffuse them, adding to the brilliance of the cave's perpetual light show. Danny was walking on fire under water.

"Get some marzical using the MR5, as we discussed. A small sample will do."

Danny went over to the wall, found a small area in which the marzical was jutting out a bit, pulled out the MR5, adjusted the setting, aimed, turned his head, and blasted off a chunk, which he proceeded to put in his pocket. He then went about looking for anything that might remotely be considered a clue, slowly walking the room's perimeter while scanning the wall from floor to ceiling, all the while holding the camera in front of him.

"I don't see anything that looks unusual," said Danny. "I don't think Dr. Falstaff left us anything."

"It would be difficult for her to in that room with the hard surfaces. You don't have much time left. You'd better get going."

Danny headed for the cave's entrance. The brown and gray rock walls were rough and crusty, and the floor was mostly dirt. He moved slowly, scanning both the walls and the floor for several feet in front of him before advancing.

"There's nothing here," Danny said when he saw the light at the end of the tunnel. "What are we going to do if we don't find any clues?"

"We'll deal with that later. Focus on the task at—"

"Wait!" Danny interjected. He had stopped his scanning and was pointing the camera down at what appeared to be some writing in the dirt near the wall to his left.

"Move in for a close-up, Danny," Kingsley said.

"It looks like someone scratched something into the dirt with a stone or something. It's kind of crude, but it's definitely writing. It looks like it might be a combination of letters and dashes. 5T4KT/MN-JF. Yeah, I think that's what it says. This is our clue, isn't it?" Danny was excited, and his voice showed it.

"Let's hope so. If that is a JF on the end, it could be Dr. Falstaff's signature. Let's not celebrate yet. You've got about four minutes before your time is up. Wipe out those letters so no one else finds them, and scan the rest of the tunnel for anything else interesting."

Danny complied and stepped out into the Dabita Bokian sunshine. Zerba was waiting on him but had no reaction to his arrival other than taking off down the path from which they had come. They arrived back at the house to find Durbin Carbindale and Zelda standing on the front porch, the former with a glass of red wine in his hand.

"Mr. Murmak, did you get some marzical so you can help your poor, ailing mother?"

"I did. Thanks again."

"You're welcome. It was a pleasure doing business with you. Good luck in your pursuit of Mr. Opal," Durbin said, extending his hand.

Danny gave it a firm shake, thanked him again, and headed toward the Solo Trek. Once the transport's door was closed, Durbin Carbindale reentered his mansion, instructed his computer to play his favorite Manikor symphony, settled into his favorite chair with wine in hand, and dreamt of how he would spend his massive influx of U-bucks.

CHAPTER 16

DANNY ENTERED THE CONFERENCE ROOM to find Shey and Kingsley sitting at the table, staring at the room's view screen, which displayed text on the left and a map of outer space on the right. The monitor on the table was frozen on the image Danny had found in the tunnel, the 5T4KT/MN-JF scratched in the dirt. Kingsley rose to greet him.

"Another fantastic job, Danny," Kingsley said, raising his hand for a high five. "Keep performing like this and I'll put Shey out to pasture and hire you as my full-time assistant."

Shey scoffed as Danny smacked Kingsley's hand. "Yeah, I think I'm getting the hang of this. That one was actually exciting . . . and kind of fun!"

"Have a seat, Danny. You can set the marzical on the table. We're starting to work on what the code might mean. Speak up if you have any thoughts on the matter as we discuss it. Shey?"

"We have to assume that the 5T4KT/MN are references to the next planet and the next ingredient," Shey said as he stood and walked toward the screen. "The first question is, what do each set of letters tell us? That is, which set of letters refers to the location and which refer to the next crystal. We're assuming that the digit *4* is shorthand for the preposition *for*, so she was telling us to go to this planet *for* this ingredient. That would mean the

5T refers to the planet and KT to the crystal. At this point we're also assuming that the slash is a separator. With the following two characters, she is perhaps trying to tell us where on the planet to go. Would you agree with that assessment?"

"Uh, yeah, sure," Danny replied.

"So, we must determine to what planet she was referring," Shey continued. "She may have been trying to convey that the planet's name is one word that contains five Ts. Gracie, are there any planets that have five Ts in their name?"

"There are three known planets that have names that include five occurrences of the letter T."

"Do any of them have a crystal that would be abbreviated KT?"

"None of these planets are known to have deposits of any such crystal."

Kingsley jumped in. "Gracie, are there any other planets that would relate in any way to having five Ts in their name?"

"Quintawba. Quin is a prefix meaning five, while the remaining portion of the name begins with the letter T."

"What about crystals on Quintawba?"

"The planet Quintawba is home to the crystal karbolite, common abbreviation KT."

"That could be it!" Danny shouted.

Kingsley had been leaning back in his chair, pensively taking everything in. "Gracie, do the letters MN refer to any regions or specific locations on Quintawba?"

"On the continent on which karbolite is found, there are two regions, eighty-six cities, and a mountain which could be referred to by the letters MN."

"What do you have on the mountain?"

"Mount Nobistad is thought by some to be a spiritual vortex, one of twelve on Quintawba. It is home to significant deposits of a large number of crystals, their abundance and variety of colors so great that the mountain sparkles from a distance."

"Spiritual vortex?" Danny asked.

Kingsley responded. "A spiritual vortex is an area on a planet where the energy is such that it is conducive to spiritual development, exactly the kind of place where a crystal with mystical properties would be found. Gracie, is karbolite found on Mount Nobistad?"

"In abundance."

"Gentlemen, I think we have our destination. Gracie, set a course for Quintawba at maximum cruising speed. Danny, it will take a couple of days to get to Quintawba, so we'll take the rest of the day and evening off from mission talk or training. The afternoon is yours to do with what you please. The ship's amenities are at your disposal. We will meet back here at seven for drinks and dinner. How does that sound?"

"Good. I'm going to start by taking a nap," Danny replied as he rose. "Maybe I'll play some golf after that. See you later."

Kingsley waited for Danny to exit the room, cross the foyer, and enter the main hall before speaking. "Gracie, let's see what Brisby is up to."

After a minute had passed, the lighting dimmed, and the conference room's view screen was filled by the scene of a handsome, sandy-haired teenage boy sitting on the edge of a bed. He was staring at a round yellow pill sitting on his nightstand, not changing his expression or breaking his gaze, when the silence was broken by a woman's voice.

"Brisby, make sure you eat something, and don't stay up too late."

He looked around the room, his gaze momentarily coming to rest on a large view screen mounted on the wall to his right. Still expressionless, he rose from the bed and made his way into a massive walk-in closet, where he slowly disrobed and put on a shirt, pair of pants, and socks. He then shuffled into the bathroom, where he brushed his teeth, combed his hair, and reviewed the state of his complexion. He stepped in some water that he'd splashed onto the floor while brushing, causing him to return to the closet to change socks.

Back in the bedroom, he made his way over to the wall of windows that gave him a panoramic view of a pristine property, an enormous pool, sculptured hedges, countless flowers, and manicured lawn as far as the fading daylight allowed him to see. Returning to the edge of the bed, he hesitated before glancing down at the yellow pill. He made one more methodical trip to the bathroom for a cup of water and returned to the edge of the bed, where he sighed and stared off into space.

"Music. 'Blue Flame' by Maleena Zeena. Repeat . . . ten times."

As a haunting melody filled the room, he closed his eyes and appeared to lose himself in the music, softly singing along, nearly inaudibly, to random parts. When the song started for the second time, he opened his eyes, wiped away the single runaway tear, went over to a monitor, typed a few letters, and returned to the bed, where he picked up the pill. He rolled it around between his thumb and forefinger for a few seconds and placed it back on the nightstand beside a photograph of his parents. He picked up the framed picture and stared at it for a minute.

"Sorry," he said softly before setting it back down. He picked up the pill and popped it into his mouth. After hesitating for a moment, he took a gulp of water and stretched out on the bed.

In a few moments the screen went dark. The lighting in the conference room was dim, but Shey could still make out the smile on Kingsley's face.

When Danny finally opened his eyes, he knew he had been out for quite a while.

"Gracie, what time is it?"

"Four fifty-seven."

"Oh, man," he groaned. "I was out for two and a half hours. Damn. I was hoping to golf before dinner."

He considered pushing himself up but thought better of it. This was his free time. He didn't have to be anywhere or do anything. He'd been pushing himself enough lately. He deserved to lie in bed all afternoon if he wanted. Danny instructed Gracie to put his room in Yoobie mode, put his hands behind his head, and relished the moment. He felt good. He felt rested, relaxed, and in general quite pleased with himself. He was enjoying his new life and had no desire to go back to his old one. The fear, anxiety, and timidity that dominated the latter were being replaced with confidence, assertiveness, and a glimmer of inner peace. It felt like it was part of his being rather than a surge that would soon dissipate. He felt powerful.

"Gracie, where are Kingsley and Shey?"

"Kingsley is in his suite, and Shey is in the living room's kitchen."

"Is it okay if I go for a run?"

"As Kingsley indicated, all of the ship's amenities are at your disposal."

Danny rolled off the bed. After changing into some exercise clothes and shoes suited to running, he exited his room with a spring in his step and boarded the lift.

"Level?" Gracie asked.

Danny paused. The excursions had made him bolder. "I think I'd like to explore a little. Let's go to the basement."

"Main kitchen or garage?" Gracie asked once the lift came to a stop.

"Kitchen."

The door slid open, and Danny stepped into a large, dimly lit room that could have been the kitchen of a world-class restaurant. The walls were lined with commercial stainless-steel appliances, three six-burner ranges, six ovens, and four large sinks. The middle of the room was dominated by two massive, rectangular islands, one stainless steel and the other butcher block. To his left was a glass door through which Danny looked to find a sizable greenhouse of some sort. It was lit by simulated sunshine and was home to an array of growing herbs, fruits, vegetables, and flowers. Danny continued along the wall to a steel door, which he opened to reveal a freezer that was nearly as large as the greenhouse.

"Wow. They could feed an army."

Danny exited the kitchen into a hallway. It was so quiet and dimly lit that Danny developed a bit of an eerie feeling.

"Gracie, am I allowed to be here?"

"Yes. If you didn't have access, you wouldn't be where you are."

"What are these rooms on this side of the hall, opposite the kitchen?"

"This area is used by the staff. In addition to the main kitchen, there is a den, which is directly across from you, a common living and entertainment area, and eight guest rooms."

Danny entered the den, a richly paneled room that was home to a sofa, two chairs, each with an ottoman, and several tables and lamps. He wandered over to the wall of built-in bookshelves and started scanning the titles: *A Stately Feast* by Nabir Haph, *Night Is Dark* by Umber Chamuka, *The Serious Farce* by Wimsal Trindle.

"These aliens sure have some funny names," Danny said to no one in particular. He glanced down at another shelf to find a row of novels by someone he recognized. Danny hadn't read any of his books, but he certainly knew the name.

"John Grisham?" Danny said as he scanned the titles, familiar to him since he had seen all the resulting movies. *The Firm . . . The Client . . . The Pelican Brief . . . Tater Torts.*

"*Tater Torts?*" Danny picked up the book and read the back of the dust jacket. 'In John Grisham's thrilling, no-holds-barred look inside the potato industry scandal of 2035, Frank Stevens is an attorney turned struggling potato farmer who takes on . . .'

"2035?" He said, before opening the cover and flipping through the first couple of pages. "Copyright 2038? What the hell? Gracie, how can this *Tater Torts* book have a copyright with a future date?"

"I have no information on that book."

Danny put the book back on the shelf, left the library, glanced into the living room, and entered the garage. "What's through that door between the Solo Treks, Gracie?"

"The storage rooms, engineering, and the rear lift."

Danny made his way through the door and down the hall, stopping at the entrances to the storage rooms, one on each side. The door to the room on his left slid open when he touched the access pad. He was slightly disappointed to find that it looked like nothing more than a storage room.

Pieces of furniture were pushed together along the wall to his right, and the back wall was lined with shelves holding rows of containers. To his left was a row of thin vertical slots in the wall.

"What's in the wall over here?"

"Paintings."

"Why are they being stored here?"

"Kingsley has a sizable collection—more pieces than can be displayed on the ship"

"Can I look at them?"

"Your guest level will allow that. Press the button next to a slot, and the painting will partially slide out. You can then pull on the frame to slide it out farther. The beams will keep it suspended until you pull it completely out. To replace it, gently push it in."

Danny pushed one of the buttons and slightly backed up as a painting emerged from its cave. He carefully grabbed the frame and gently pulled it toward him. The painting smoothly slid out, revealing an abstract work that was such an unstructured splash of harsh colors that Danny actually cringed.

"I don't get it," he mumbled as he quickly pushed the painting back into place, noticing the name Froktum in the bottom right corner.

He opened two others before he found one he liked. It was an impressionist scene of a lovely garden and pond. Danny was immediately drawn to the softness of the strokes and brilliance of the colors. After staring at it, mesmerized, for a few minutes, he started guiding it back into place when he saw the signature in the corner.

"Monet?" Danny asked incredulously. "He's from Earth. Gracie, the artist of this painting is from Earth, isn't he?"

"I have no information regarding the home planet of that artist."

"What? That's ridiculous. I know this is him. I had an art history class in college. I know the name, and I recognize the style."

Danny selected another painting and stopped pulling on it before it was halfway out. It was a sea of swirling strands of color in a style he recognized from a movie he had watched.

"Oh my God. This is Jackson Pollock."

He quickly pushed it back and looked over his shoulder. "Gracie, how did Kingsley get these paintings from famous Earth artists?"

"I have no information regarding the acquisition of the works to which you refer."

Danny considered the likely options. Kingsley had told him that the recruiting trip had been his first time to Earth. That would mean that either he had been there before or had arrived on Earth earlier than he had led Danny to believe. If his claims that they had no Earth currency were true, he either paid for them with fake money or, worse yet, stole them. Or they hadn't been to Earth but bought the paintings from someone else who had been. Even then, they had more than likely been stolen by that party. Whatever the scenario, it involved lying or stealing or both.

Danny backed away from the rack, his world slightly shaken. The man he held in such high esteem, the man he completely trusted, who he respected and admired like no other person he'd met in his life, was quite possibly a liar and galactic criminal. He grew concerned over what Kingsley and Shey were actually capable of if they knew what he had discovered. After wiping the sweat from his forehead, he scanned the shelving to make certain each painting was in place and left the room. Jogging was the last thing on his mind as he plotted the best course back to his room.

———————

At 7:00 p.m. sharp, Danny entered the living room to find Shey in the kitchen and Kingsley sitting at the bar with a martini that looked as though it had yet to be sampled. Since exploring the basement, he had been pacing in his room, contemplating his next move until changing into dinner attire—a black shirt and light gray slacks.

As he strolled toward the bar, Danny reminded himself that everyone is innocent until proven guilty. Nevertheless, the discovery of the art had shifted his perception.

"Danny, my boy, belly up to the bar!" Kingsley, dressed in black slacks and a dark blue, long-sleeved polo, was obviously in a good mood. "Shey, get Danny a beer. Or would you like to try a martini?"

Danny slid onto a stool two down from his host. "Umm, yeah, sure. Why not?"

"Excellent. Shey, get Danny a martini."

"Coming right up," Shey replied as he headed to the bar area of the kitchen. He was dressed in charcoal slacks and a deep red shirt.

"I have a toast, so get yourself one too."

"Here you go, sport," Shey said, as he placed a beer on the counter.

"Danny," Kingsley began as he raised his glass, "we didn't take the time to reflect on the Dabita Bok excursion when you got back, so I'd like to now congratulate you on yet another job well done. You handled each part of the trip with the skill, determination, and fortitude of an experienced searcher. I can now say that I believe the mission is in good hands."

"Thanks," Danny said as he touched his glass to Kingsley's and took the type of gulp he normally would of a beer, a gulp that left him coughing and gasping, half bent over.

"Kingsley," Shey said. "I dare say we failed to give young Mr. Kerrigan the proper training for drinking a martini."

"Danny, it's not a beer. You don't gulp, slurp, or chug it. You sip and savor, rather like fine wine. Perhaps even more slowly."

Danny had recovered enough to speak. "Thanks for warning me. It tastes like pure alcohol."

"There's a reason for that. It's pure alcohol. It's also an acquired taste. Try a couple more sips, and if you don't like it, you can get a beer."

As Danny stared at Kingsley, he realized there was no way this man could be a criminal. Shey perhaps, but not Kingsley. There was one other possibility Danny had been considering. It would still mean that Kingsley hadn't been completely honest with him, but Danny was certain if that were the case, there had to be a good reason.

"Are you guys from the future?" he blurted.

CHAPTER 17

Kingsley stopped mid-sip and locked eyes with Shey for a second before setting down his drink.

"Danny, I think maybe the martini experiment has failed. From the future? I think you'd better switch to beer. Or better yet, stop drinking."

"I'm not drunk, and I think it's a reasonable question."

"Reasonable? That's not the word I would use. How about irrational, ludicrous, or absurd? You've been watching too much science fiction. The possibility makes for interesting stories, but time travel simply isn't feasible."

"Then maybe you can explain some things for me?"

"Certainly. That would probably be a better approach than assuming we're time travelers."

"Earlier in the trip, the day of the OSU game, Shey told me the score."

"I remember."

"Well, I went to my room a couple hours later and checked my watch, and it wasn't even eight o'clock yet. The game wasn't even scheduled to start until then. There's no way it would have been over by the time Shey told me the final score."

"Why do they call it a watch when you really just glance at it occasionally?" asked Shey.

"Good one, Shey," Kingsley said. "Your wit grows sharper with each passing day. I'll bet that by the time—"

"Stop it," Danny said firmly. "If you're acknowledging his jokes, I know you're hiding something."

Kingsley scoffed. "I told you not to bother bringing your watch, that it wouldn't function properly in space."

"Mine seems to. The time and date still look right, and I've done several tests counting seconds and comparing my count to the watch. They seem very close."

"Both unscientific points. Just a coincidence, Danny."

"Okay, how about that Grisham book that says the copyright was 2038?"

"What are you talking about? What book? Where?"

"I went down to the lower level earlier to look around. I went into the den and was looking at the books. There's a John Grisham novel that I've never heard of that says it's about something that happened in the year 2035. The copyright is 2038. And how did you even get a hardcopy of a book from Earth if you've never been there?"

"You went down to the staff area of the lower level? Shey, how long before dinner is ready? Not too soon, I hope. I was counting on having a short happy hour down front," Kingsley said.

"You didn't answer my question."

"I don't know, Danny. I have no idea what all the books are the staff has put on those shelves or how they acquired them. They probably visited Earth at some point. Regarding the dates, perhaps this Grisham fellow set his book in the future, and the publisher played among by printing that copyright date just for whimsy. That sort of thing happens, you know."

"I would think that kind of thing might be illegal. I think copyrights are pretty serious."

"I appreciate your imagination, but you're making a huge leap from a couple of insignificant items. Tell him, Shey."

"You're making a huge leap from a couple of insignificant items," Shey said. "What you are asserting is posterous. No, it's worse than that. It's before posterous. It's preposterous."

"Didn't you tell me that the recruiting trip was your first trip to Earth?"

"Yes."

"And you arrived on Earth just the day before you came to my apartment?"

"Yes."

"And you didn't do any shopping?"

"Shopping? We didn't have time for shopping. Besides the fact that there is nothing on Earth we would want, I told you that we have no Earth currency."

"Did you steal anything while you were there?"

"Steal? We do not steal. Why would we? I can afford to buy whatever I like."

"Would you buy stolen merchandise?"

"Of course not! Danny, what are you getting at?"

"I was wondering how you came to have paintings from famous Earth artists, painted before my time, in your storage room."

"You went into the storage room? Why were you in the storage room?"

"I was exploring. I'm a searcher, remember?"

"They are probably works from artists that have the same names as some artists that have lived on Earth."

"Two artists from different planets, both named Claude Monet, with the exact same style of painting? No way. And another looks like a Jackson Pollock."

"I don't know anything about those paintings. We have a lot of guests on the ship, and they often ask if they can keep things in our storage room while aboard. They must belong to one of them and they simply forgot them when—"

"I don't buy it," Danny said. "Could it be that you're from the future and that you've visited Earth before and in your time Earth uses the universal currency and you bought those paintings?"

"Danny, I don't think the martini could have done this. Did you bring along some hallucinogenic drugs that you've been taking in your room?" Kingsley chuckled before he picked up his drink, spun away from the bar, headed toward the room's lower level, and plopped down in one of the high-backed chairs. "Gracie, happy hour. Sinatra, random, upbeat swing. Shey, hold dinner for a half hour."

Danny chased Kingsley to the front of the room and stood across from him just after the table rose from the floor and the chairs slid back.

"You're not getting out of this that easy. What the hell is going on here?" Kingsley turned toward the kitchen.

Shey shrugged. "Your call."

Kingsley leaned forward, set his drink down, and fell back into his chair. "Calm down and sit down. Gracie, lower the music."

Danny followed directions, taking the seat across from Kingsley, who pensively stroked his beard. "Your assertions are all correct. Shey and I are from the future."

"I knew it! That is so cool. What year are you from? How did you do time travel?" Danny asked as he edged to the front of his seat.

"We are from what on Earth would be the year 2198. In that time, Earth is extremely advanced, with a CUSTAR of 196, a prominent member of PUPCO, and a great friend of Yoobatar. That explains what you've seen. I've been there many times and have purchased artwork. I normally have it on display but put it in storage before you came aboard. I didn't think you'd ever explore the storage rooms, and I honestly didn't know we had books from Earth down there. The staff must have left them. Regarding how we achieve time travel, I couldn't begin to explain it. Gracie could probably give you the details, but they'd be meaningless to you. Any other questions?"

Danny's mind was reeling.

"So Dank also has the technology, and you chased him back through time? How did you know what year to go to? Why did he go back in time? Did the tablet tell him to?"

"Not exactly. Dank didn't go back in time."

"I don't understand. Then how are we chasing him?"

"Because we returned to our time after picking you up."

"What?" Danny shouted. "I'm in the year 2198? Are you kidding me?"

"Yes, you are, and no, I'm not," Kingsley said calmly.

Danny's stomach knotted. He suddenly felt much farther from home than the actual distance. "What the hell am I doing here? What if I get separated from you guys? How will I get back to my time?"

"I realize it's a shock to your system, Danny, but you don't have to worry. In the first place, you're not going to get separated from us. When the mission is over, you'll have options. You can either stay on Yoobatar in the current year as we planned, or we can return you to Earth, either in the current year or back to the year you were in."

"I feel sick," Danny said as he set his drink down.

"Nonsense. Time is irrelevant. You're the same being you were when you were back in your time, the same collection of molecules, the same spirit, the same energy. It doesn't matter where you perceive yourself to be in what you view as linear time."

"So why didn't you tell me before?"

"When we were recruiting, getting you to believe we were aliens and convincing you to go along was hard enough. We didn't tell you then because we assumed you wouldn't go if we told you we were going to move you through time," Kingsley replied.

"You got that right."

"And we didn't tell you before now because you were adapting to being in space, getting used to the ship, and most importantly, working on being the mission lead. We didn't want to add anything that might have made the situation more difficult."

"I guess I can see that. I just . . . hey, why in the world did you go back in time to recruit someone when Dank was in your time?"

Kingsley smiled broadly. "I was wondering when you'd get to that question. We needed a third crew member, and, as I told you in your apartment, we wanted someone who would do it without demanding a large piece of the fee. I'm really counting on this one to allow Aurora and I to live well for the rest of our lives. We were en route from Yoobatar to Kronk. It would have been extremely difficult to find anyone on an advanced planet who would do it for nothing. The nearest planet that didn't travel was a few days out of our way, and we didn't want to add that much time on top of the recruiting itself.

"We were going to be fairly close to Earth. Shey came up with the idea to use our time travel technology to go back in time and recruit an earthling. We assumed it would be fairly easy to find a recruit if we went back to a time when Earth was aware but didn't travel. The process only takes an hour or so. We recruited you and moved back to 2198. We did it when you went to take a nap after I gave you the tour."

"Aren't you guys worried about me going back and then changing history based on things I see or learn? Or that you being on Earth back in my time might change something?"

"Not at all. We did nothing but recruit when we were there. And what are you going to change? You're not going to see anything that could have the slightest impact on Earth's evolution."

"If you're from the future, then you can tell me things like how Ohio State does in football for the next thirty years and what happens to me the rest of my life, can't you?"

"We could. But we're not going to. We're not really concerned about you changing anything using the information, but it would be unethical to tell you. If it was bad, that you are going to die in three years, for example, you'd probably either give up on life or quit your job and spend all of your money on frivolous material possessions, trying to make your remaining days happy ones. If it was good, you may end up not making the choices that lead you to what we currently know as your future. Besides, it would be meaningless, since that can change."

"What do you mean by change? If you're from the future, can't you look back at records and see what happens to me?"

"We can, but that's the future that plays out based on how you are right now. Time and space are much more complex than beings perceive them to be. We know of a future you have based on who you are right now, but that can change if you change, which in turn causes you to make different choices."

"Sounds confusing."

"It can be for our minds. I will tell you, however, that Earth's future is much more positive than is depicted in most of your science-fiction movies. There are no cataclysmic wars or horrible natural disasters that wipe out civilizations. The planet makes tremendous leaps, especially spiritually, and becomes a model for others to follow."

"That's good to know. As long as you're being honest, can I ask you something else?"

"Absolutely."

"I've been wondering about this for a while, and now that I've heard all of this, I'm even more curious. You weren't recruiting a third person to be a gofer; you were looking for someone to lead the mission, weren't you? You knew that there was a good chance word would leak out about you and the Quilicants and that you wouldn't be able to lead it, so you recruited someone in case you needed a different lead. You could have found a gofer in your time for a little money, but to recruit someone to be the lead would have cost you a lot."

"Now you are getting far-fetched. Why in the world would . . . oh, what the hell. Yes, Danny, we weren't recruiting for the reasons we gave you in the apartment. We have at times done that, but only if the mission wasn't terribly urgent and our plans definitely called for a third person. For this mission, I decided to recruit someone who would be a safety net, someone who could lead the mission if necessary. Someone from our time would have demanded a large part of our fee to take on that role. Vivitar doesn't know that we went back in time to get you and doesn't know what we discovered once on the ship . . . that you had none of the required qualities. So there, I wasn't completely honest with you, but if I'd have told you either of those things, you wouldn't have come along. I didn't like not being completely forthcoming, but it was all done for the good of the mission."

"I understand," Danny said. "But I do feel like I've been manipulated a little."

"That's expected, but I hope, actually I need, an assurance that you still trust us and are still completely committed to leading this mission. Nothing has changed in that respect. Are you still with us?" Kingsley asked, raising his glass.

Danny looked to the kitchen to find Shey giving him a thumbs-up. "Yes, I'm still with you," Danny replied as he broke into a smile and tapped his glass to Kingsley's.

"Splendid. Now, enough of this serious talk. Let's relax and have some fun this evening."

"I couldn't hold dinner any longer," Shey shouted from the kitchen. "Kingsley, take a seat. Danny, please come here and help carry some things to the table."

"Shouldn't we discuss our plan for Quintawba?" Danny asked as he entered the kitchen.

"We'll have plenty of time for that tomorrow. It's a two-day trip. Tonight, no more mission talk. Gracie, we need some atmosphere. Yoobie mode for the room, dim the lights, and some jazz for background music. No vocals. Maybe Coltrane."

Danny and Shey joined him at the table, Danny carrying two plates and Shey a plate and a bottle of red wine. As they settled into their chairs, Kingsley looked delighted. Danny looked disgusted.

"Shey, I'll pour the wine if you describe what you've prepared."

"Grilled Tebitolian drussik with hybano chutney, on a bed of Banganese wild grains, with sautéed vegetables discovered in the most exotic spot in the cosmos, the Vortex garden on Yoobatar."

"Drussik? What the hell is that? And what are these weird-looking vegetables?" Danny asked as he scanned the plate.

"It's a fish, similar to your swordfish. Shey has been preparing meals common on Earth as you became acclimated to the situation. We didn't want to throw too much at you too quickly, but now it's time you started sampling delicacies from around the universe. Trust me, we're not going to serve you anything you'll find unappetizing."

Kingsley raised his wine glass for another toast. "Here's to clearing the air and getting everything out in the open."

The group proceeded to sip wine, dine, and enjoy the lush surroundings of the Vortex estate depicted around them, all of which had a positive effect on their moods and stress levels.

"Danny, I want to say again how proud I am of what you've accomplished. You've gone from someone we thought had none of the traits we needed, with no chance of succeeding, to someone who, I dare say, reminds me a bit of me when I was just starting out as a searcher."

"You know, I really don't know anything about you other than you're a famous searcher from Yoobatar. Tell me about your life."

"You know what? I'm going to do that," Kingsley replied while Shey rolled his eyes and took a sizable gulp of wine.

"I was born in the city of Xanawalt in the Yoobatarian year of 3550. My parents were Jackson and Elizabeth Vortex. Xanawalt is in the Ontaga region, where I still live today. What you see around you is my country estate in Ontaga. My father was a searcher, and my mother was an architect. They've both passed on after long, happy lives. I've mentioned my sister, Kayla, and that she's the director of the Mermetec agency. I also have a younger brother, Marquin, who is a medical researcher.

"I had a gloriously happy childhood. I wanted for nothing; my parents were quite comfortable financially. I had a knack for searching from a very young age. I have vague memories of my father hiding things about the house and sending me on little scavenger hunts when I could barely walk. When I became slightly older, he used our entire property, which stretched for miles with woods, caves, and a variety of terrain. He then expanded my training, creating elaborate fake missions for me around Xanawalt and hiring actors to play roles in some cases. I didn't turn away from any challenge. The ones that seemed unsolvable only gave me more resolve. If I heard my father say it once, I heard him say it a thousand times . . . 'He's going to be a great searcher someday, the best that's ever lived.' Who knew at the time he was right?"

Shey sighed and poured himself some more wine as Kingsley took a deep breath and continued.

"School bored me, but I still achieved stellar marks, because I was, honestly, close to brilliant. I also played and excelled at several sports. I begged my father to take me on his missions until finally—I think it was the summer of my sixteenth year—he called me into his study to tell me he wanted me to be part of his crew. I went on three missions with him that summer and amazed everyone with my intuition, instincts, and assertiveness. I was relentless and fearless in my pursuit of our mission goals. He normally traveled with a crew of two, a Drimmillian and another Yoobatarian, but it didn't take long before I went from being a kid in the way to his right-hand man."

Shey rolled his eyes for the third time. "Okay, any more and I'm going to have trouble keeping down this meal I worked so hard to prepare. I've heard you tell this at least a dozen times, and each time you become more and more dazzling at a younger and younger age."

"Don't mind him, Danny. He's a little fussy since he's been relegated to mostly being a chef on this mission. I trust you're not bored?"

"Not at all," Danny replied. "I like hearing about this."

"Splendid. I attended the University of Danaril and rather effortlessly acquired dual degrees in investigative studies and interstellar archaeology. I spent my college years absorbed in my class work and, on the side, studying the missions and methods of the greatest searchers in the universe. In the summers I continued to serve as an apprentice to my father. When I finally earned my degrees, my father was so confident in my abilities that he let go of the other Yoobatarian, and I became part of his crew along with his Drimmillian assistant, Yarmo Laznik."

"Excuse me, assistant?" Shey said after clearing his throat loudly.

"Assistant, partner, comrade. It's just semantics."

"Semantics my ass! Yarmo Laznik was one of the most renowned, respected searchers in Drimmillian history. He was my idol growing up.

I wouldn't be here if it weren't for him, which means you wouldn't be either, because, as I've pointed out many times, you'd have been nothing but a third-rate, bottom-dollar searcher looking for lost dogs and teenage runaways!"

"Okay, okay. Calm down. Danny, Yarmo was as invaluable a member of my father's team for many, many years, as Shey has been to me. Happy? Now pour me some more wine, you egomaniacal son of a bitch, and don't interrupt my story again. Now, where was I? Oh yes, so I joined my father's crew out of college, and we spent the next twenty-two years working together. It was a marvelous experience for me. When I was forty-three, my father retired, so I set out on my own. That's when I hired Shey.

"I had no trouble getting jobs. People knew the Vortex name and had heard good things about me, so they generally didn't hesitate to hire me. I —we—did quite well. Nearly every mission was a success, and we had established a reputation of being a team that could get the job done.

"The mission that cemented my reputation in the searcher community came when I was fifty-eight. The crown jewels of the ruling family of Swenta Rigas, the Glenveema family, were stolen. We found and recovered the jewels in under three weeks with a clever and daring strategy. I achieved my celebrity among the general population several years later when I located and safely retrieved the beloved president of the largest country on the planet Tebitol, Mibby Jankar, who had been kidnapped and held for ransom by a group of Maroovian pirates. It was a case that drew immense interest from around the cosmos, with daily coverage on UNN. That is when I made the biggest, possibly the only, mistake in my career. Rather than accept my fee and quietly walk away, I gleefully soaked up all of the praise and limelight they threw at me."

"Even though I repeatedly warned you against doing so," chimed in Shey.

"Yes, even though Shey strongly warned me against doing so. While it was very rewarding in the short term, it also turned out to be the beginning of the end of my career. You see, Danny, one thing a searcher doesn't need is celebrity. I knew that, but I let my ego get the better of me. From that point forward I started acquiring parasite searchers, beings that fancy themselves to be searchers but who can't get any real jobs. After a while they end up spending their time looking for real searchers on missions and then kind of riding along, following the searcher in order to determine what they're after.

"They started hindering my missions and eventually even my ability to get hired. I got fewer and fewer jobs over the years until I retired three years ago. Now I spend my days playing in charity golf tournaments, endorsing products, making an occasional public appearance, and even a speech now and then. Then I got a call from Vivitar about this mission. And here we are."

"You're married, right? You didn't mention your wife."

"Oh my, you're right. See? I get so excited talking about searching, I forget everything else. I lived the life of the carefree, swashbuckling bachelor for many, many years. That all changed when I met Aurora, in a bookstore, when I was home between missions. She was, and still is, a very accomplished poet and novelist and was also considered a bit of a philosopher. I knew who she was, but she didn't know of me. I thought I'd try to sweep her off her feet, but she beat me to it. I was putty in her hands from our first conversation, and I still am today. We married three months after we met and have been together ever since."

"Sounds nice. You've had quite a career."

"My adventures give me a lot to reflect upon . . . the ploy I used on Mooligan Five to recover the sensitive files stolen from the government, the daring and dangerous mission into the jungles of Swacka Moor to find the kidnapped wife of the king of Kipaldi, the—"

"Danny," Shey interjected, "how about a big bowl of hubris for dessert. We have plenty."

"You know, we're passing by a lot of planets. I could drop you off on one, and Danny and I could complete the mission."

"You two? Give me a break. I'm the brains and the glue. Without me you two would fall apart like a book without a binding. Don't try to intimidate me with your shallow threats."

"Fall apart?" Kingsley boomed. "Flourish is more like it. Flourish unencumbered by your negative attitude and sophomoric sense of humor."

"Oh yeah? Well maybe I'll take the Star Hopper back to Yoobatar and we can find out how much you flourish. But if I do, I won't rejoin the mission unless you double my part of the fee."

"Double it? And you think I have hubris?"

Their volume was increasing with each exchange.

"Come on, guys," Danny interjected as Kingsley cocked his ear toward the ceiling. "Let's just get back to—"

"Quiet! Both of you!" Kingsley yelled as he stood up and raised his hands in front of him.

"Father?" came a voice from the room's speakers.

"Yes, princess?" Kingsley replied while remaining motionless. Danny looked stunned.

"Father, will you come see me?"

"Absolutely, princess. I'll be right there," he replied before dashing from the living room without another word to his crew.

Danny turned to Shey, who had nonchalantly returned to eating. "Who the hell was that?"

"That," Shey replied, "was Kingsley's daughter."

"His daughter?"

"Yep. His daughter. Vicki."

"And she's calling him from Yoobatar?"

"Not exactly."

"Then where is she?"

"She's on the ship," Shey replied as he took a sip of wine.

CHAPTER 18

"She's on the ship? Where?" Danny asked incredulously.

"In her room."

"What room?"

"The guest room across from Kingsley's suite."

"And she's been on board the entire mission?"

"Yep."

"How come I haven't seen her?"

"Because she doesn't leave her room."

"Ever?"

"Gracie, has Vicki left her room since Danny joined the mission?"

"She has not."

"How old is she?"

"Thirty-two."

"Why hasn't Kingsley told me about her?" Danny was still somewhat bewildered.

"Probably because he didn't want you bothering her . . . trying to talk to her or, worse, trying to wank her if you got a little horned up."

"Wank her? Yeah, right. Like I'd try to wank Kingsley's daughter. I don't try to wank anybody."

"He also thought that you knowing she was there may have distracted you from the business at hand."

"I suppose that's possible. Why doesn't she come out of her room?"

"Because she doesn't have to. She's got a service bay for food."

"But why doesn't she at least come out to just get out of her room or to see Kingsley?"

"Let's just say she has some issues."

"What do you mean, *issues*?"

"What I mean is that she makes you look like Darple Winstack."

"Gracie?"

"Darple Winstack is a gregarious Yoobatarian celebrity, known for singing, dancing, and comedic performances as well as hosting large parties at his estate."

"What exactly is wrong with her?" Danny was growing concerned.

"She's extremely shy and sensitive, so much so that she can't handle interacting with people. When she's on Yoobatar, she stays in her suite in whichever property the family is residing. Kingsley drags her along on missions from time to time because he thinks it would be good for her to get out, but she just stays in her room the whole time. She's been that way her entire life."

"Is she . . . like a zombie or something?"

"Heavens no. She's extremely intelligent, articulate, and attractive. If you go see her, she will talk to you, pleasantly and politely, but it's obvious she's uncomfortable and would prefer you weren't there. Most of their communication with her is done via text messaging. Kingsley and Aurora visit her a lot, but even that makes her mildly anxious."

"Kingsley seemed pretty excited when she called."

"With good reason. This is the first time, to my knowledge, that she's ever called and asked him to come see her."

"What does she do all the time?"

"We aren't sure. She probably watches a lot of television and movies and sleeps a lot. We know she exercises, since she's in good physical condition.

She's basically just terrified of dealing with people. You two would probably get along great."

"Sounds like I probably won't meet her." Danny was both relieved and disappointed.

Their conversation was interrupted by Kingsley striding back into the room with a spring in his step. He returned to his seat, freshened his wine, and glanced at the both of them. "Now, gentlemen, where were we? Oh yes, I just wrapped up telling you my life story. Any questions, Danny?"

"Shey was just telling me about your daughter. I can't believe she's on board."

"Yes, well, I didn't see how telling you would serve anyone. But now you know."

"He said she doesn't ever call you. Is she okay?"

"Yes, she is. Best I've ever seen her, actually. Shey, do you believe she called? She said she just wanted to see me. She asked how the mission was going, and she even asked about you, Danny."

"About me? Why did she ask about me?"

"Because she knew we picked up a third crew member, and she wanted to know what you were like. Shey, how about some dessert?"

"Sounds great. Will Vicki be joining us?"

"Let's not get carried away."

"Vicki Vortex," Danny blurted. "Kind of sounds like a stripper."

"What did you say?" Kingsley asked, his voice dripping with restrained anger as he rose from his chair.

"Uh-oh," said Shey.

"Um, nothing. I was just making a bad joke. Forget I said anything."

"Danny, did I mention that Kingsley has no sense of humor when it comes to his daughter?"

"I'm sorry," Danny stammered. "I didn't know. I'm really sorry. I think I just had a little too much to drink. It won't happen again."

"Kingsley, we need him, remember?"

"Yes, I suppose we do," Kingsley replied as he dropped back into his seat and sighed. "I'm sorry if I overreacted, Danny. Actually, I'm going to pass on dessert and turn in. I'm tired, and I think I may have imbibed a bit too much myself this evening. Good night, men. Tomorrow we will map out our Quintawba strategy."

———————

Danny stared at the ceiling of his room and struggled to get his mind around all he had learned in three hours. Kingsley and Shey were from the future, he was currently in the year 2198, and Kingsley's daughter was on the ship. While knowing he was in another time was a shock to his system, it was the knowledge of Vicki's presence that was occupying most of his thoughts. Even though Shey said she never left her room, there was always the chance Danny would run into her. Shey telling him that she was good-looking only added to his desire and terror.

Danny got up and aimlessly moved around his suite. He was tired but not sleepy. In addition to his unsettled mind, his body was reacting poorly to the mixture of gin and wine to which it had been subjected. He was hot and had an upset stomach. He thought of getting another beer and finding a golf tournament, but he decided it might make matters worse.

"Where are Kingsley and Shey, Gracie?"

"They are both in their suites."

"Is it okay if I walk around the ship for a while? I need some fresh air."

"The air is of the same quality in all areas of the ship, but you are free to walk as long as you like."

"Why aren't you telling me that I need sleep and start zapping me into bed? And you let me get a little tipsy tonight."

"Kingsley turned off mother mode when you were returning from Dabita Bok."

Danny exited his room, stood in the center hallway, and contemplated where to go. He remembered that the yard had a walking path around its perimeter. When he stepped from the lift, he knew he had made the right choice. The only sound was the foliage rustling from the gentle wind that came from the left. The breeze was cool, cooler than in the rest of the ship, and felt rather refreshing. Danny strolled down the path toward the dining area, surveyed the scene, and considered how much it did feel like he was outside. It was surprisingly bright, much brighter than it should have been, given that the only artificial lights were small ornamental lamps placed every so often along the paths. Danny walked down the path to the left, curving back toward the rear of the ship, when he found the source of the light, the biggest, brightest full moon he had ever seen.

"Wow," he said as he stopped and stared.

"Incredible, isn't it?" said a female voice from behind him.

Danny whirled around and put a hand on his heaving chest. "You scared the hell out of me! Shanna, is that you?" He strained to make out the figure sitting on the bench tucked in the foliage a few feet from the path.

The figure slowly rose and started toward Danny. When she emerged from the cover of the tree limbs and into the moonlight, he could tell it was definitely not Shanna Var. She was a few inches shorter than Danny and was wearing a black V-neck top and black slacks. She stared at the moon while approaching Danny and turned when she arrived next to him. The stomach churning that had started a moment before kicked into high gear when the light hit her face. Danny's first coherent thought was that Shey had terribly understated Vicki's beauty. Dark, softly curving, shoulder-length hair framed her face and puddled gently on her shoulders, with random strands gently blown about by the breeze. Her skin appeared flawless and light in complexion. Her face, though void of makeup or a smile, was stunning. But her most striking feature, the one that Danny's gaze had quickly locked on, were her eyes. They were a mesmerizing shade of blue. They were eyes that conveyed both sadness and intelligence as they looked directly at him.

"It's so large and beautiful. It looks like it's only a short distance away, like you could almost reach out and touch it," she said as she glanced back at the moon.

Danny tried to swallow to no avail and decided he'd better say something, anything, quickly so she didn't think he was an idiot. "Yeah, it's a . . . it's really, really big."

As she continued staring at the moon, he searched frantically for something else to say, something charming and sophisticated, something that would immediately endear him to her—something that was at least better than what he had just said. He found no such phrase.

"I'm Danny," he blurted, mangling it as much as you could mangle two words.

She looked back at him, locked eyes again, and gave him a barely perceptible smile. "Yes, I know," she said before turning and walking down the path.

After hearing the door at the back of the yard open and slide shut, Danny exhaled deeply.

"'It's really, really big.' What a moron!" he said with disgust. It's always the same, he thought. He'd reacted the same way around good-looking girls, panicking and struggling to utter something more suave than a five-year-old would say, ever since he was five years old. He headed back to his room, where he fell into a deep sleep after replaying the encounter and berating himself for his performance.

––––––––––––

Danny felt surprisingly good when he awoke, so much so that he was slightly disappointed that Kingsley didn't grab him for a walk or yoga. He headed to the living room, where he found Shey whipping up what smelled like a great breakfast.

"Morning, Shey. Where's Kingsley?" he chirped as he pulled up a seat at the bar.

"He's visiting with Vicki again. What the hell has gotten into you?"

"I met her last night."

"Who?"

"Vicki."

"No, you didn't."

Danny looked confused. "Yes, I did."

"You met Vicki last night?" Shey stopped his work.

"Yep."

"Where?"

"In the yard. I got up to take a walk, and she was there."

"And you talked to her?"

"Yep. Actually, she spoke to me first."

"Are you sure it wasn't Shanna? She can change her appearance to what-ever she likes."

"Five-nine, dark hair, blue eyes, really good-looking."

"Sounds like her. And it sounds like you already have a crush on her. Sounds like Danny's got a new girlfriend. Or at least he wishes he does."

"I do not!"

"I hope not too, for your sake. If Kingsley found you're trying to diddle his daughter, he'd put you in a Solo Trek and jettison you into an uninhab-ited corner of space."

"I'm not trying to diddle or wank anybody! I'm just saying I thought she was really pretty. Anyway, we just talked for a minute. It startled me. You said she never leaves her room."

"That's because she doesn't. Gracie, did Vicki leave her room last night and go to the yard?"

"She did."

"Hmm. What did you say to her?"

"That's not important. Sorry I brought it up."

Shey went on about his business while Danny surveyed the orange, yellow, and blues of the Yoobatarian sunrise. He was in a chatty mood, so much so that even conversing with Shey had some appeal.

"So how do you guys do time travel?"

"You wouldn't understand."

"Just explain the basics, at a high level."

Shey sighed and again stopped his food preparation. "It's new technology, still experimental really. The government developed it, and they control it. I'll try to explain it in terms your mind can comprehend. I assume you're familiar with the concept of measuring speed of travel in relationship to the speed of sound or light."

"Sure."

"Well, our scientists have created a propulsion system called a temporal zip drive that enables a ship to go faster than the speed of time."

"The speed of time?"

"Yes. All conventional modes of transportation move much slower than time. That's why, in your mind, it takes a certain amount of time to travel from one point to another. How much slower you are moving than the speed of time determines how long it takes to get from place to place. For example, it takes longer to travel a hundred yards if you walk than if you run, so running is closer to the speed of time than walking. Our scientists started getting ships to move at speeds so great that they approached the speed of time. Are you still with me?"

"I think so."

"The first major breakthrough was when they reached a travel speed of zero elapsed time, or ZET, which is the speed at which you could actually travel somewhere and arrive at the same time you left your point of origin. They then improved the technology so that the speed generated was practically limitless. They quickly confirmed what they suspected, which is that if you move faster than ZET, you arrive at your destination before you left your point of origin. You actually go backward in time, because you are moving faster than time. The current state of the technology is that you pick the date, and it calculates how long you'd have to go at what speed to hit that time."

"And Kingsley was willing to go through that just to find a lead that wouldn't want part of his fee?"

"You've obviously never seen Aurora's shoe closet."

"Good morning, gentlemen," came the booming voice from the hall, just before Kingsley appeared.

"Morning, Kingsley," Danny said as he turned his attention to his mentor.

"And how does this beautiful Yoobatarian morning find you two?"

"I'm pretty good. Shey was just . . ." Danny lost his train of thought as Vicki emerged from the same hallway.

"Danny?" Kingsley asked. "Oh yes, Vicki will be joining us for breakfast this morning. Did you make enough, Shey?"

"If no one has seconds," Shey said as he started bringing over plates loaded with scrambled eggs, crispy potatoes, and sausage patties.

"Then no one shall have seconds. Danny, help bring everything to the table," Kingsley said as he took a seat at the round dining table. "What were you two talking about?"

"Shey had just been explaining to me how you guys achieve time travel."

"Oh, he was, was he?" Kingsley asked as he glanced at Shey. "And what did he have to say about it?"

"Well, he told me about how the key is to go faster than the speed of time and how your scientists invented the temporal zip drive that could make a ship do that."

"He told you about the speed of time?" Kingsley asked.

"Yeah. He told me about getting to zero elapsed time, where you were going so fast that you arrived somewhere at the same time you left."

"Zero elapsed time?"

"Yeah. And when they broke through that barrier, going faster than the speed of time, you actually arrive before you left. You go back in time."

"Temporal zip drives, zero elapsed time, moving faster than the speed of time," Kingsley said as he took a bite of his breakfast and looked over at Shey, who was also working on his food with his head down. "Tell me, Shey, did you come up with all of that on the fly, or have you been working on it for a while?"

"On the fly."

"What are you talking about?" asked a confused Danny.

"Danny, Shey's made up a rather elaborate explanation and, I'm sure, is taking great delight in the fact that you bought it. He was pulling your leg."

"What?" Danny asked as he shot glances around the table.

"Those concepts don't exist. Going faster than the speed of time? How can you go faster than something that isn't measured in relationship to movement? I don't blame you, Danny. It was a decent story. Shey preyed on your lack of knowledge of physics and our technology."

As everyone, including Vicki, had a good laugh, Danny looked over at Shey and wanted to strangle him. He had trusted Shey for a serious explanation, and instead he was the butt of a joke. And now he was the target of laughter. In front of Vicki.

"Danny, you look upset," Kingsley said. "He was just having some fun. It's no big deal. Most beings in your position would have bought it. Don't take it so personally."

Shey got up to get something from the kitchen.

"Danny," said Shey, "maybe later I'll explain where the voice you know as Gracie is really coming from. There's a woman who moves around in the walls of the ship and talks through the holes in the speakers."

Danny wanted to spring from his chair and tackle the little bastard. He again managed to control his impulse. "What about all that you told me about Shanna Var? Was that all true, or did you make that up?"

"That was all true," Kingsley said. "A good rule of thumb to follow is that anything I explain is the truth and anything Shey explains probably isn't."

"I'm glad you all were entertained at my expense." Danny glanced at Vicki to find her looking down with a slight smile as she started on her meal.

"Gracie, turn on UNN."

Kingsley turned in his chair to get a good view of the UNN anchor, a blond-haired young man with a chiseled face. "The newly formed PUPCO commission for rapid CUSTAR development announced just three U-hours ago that they have, after an exhaustive search, picked the first three planets to take part in their Accelerated CUSTAR Approval program, otherwise known as ACUSA. These planets were selected based on the balance of their CUSTAR components, their desire to be PUPCO members, and their willingness to give PUPCO unregulated access to their people, planet, and information systems. PUPCO spokesperson Huppa Nanstrom said that the commission is confident that—"

"ACUSA my ass!" Kingsley shouted. "They finally won out. They should call it the Artificial CUSTAR Approval program."

"Who?" asked Danny.

"The PUPCO senate members who think it's a good idea to help planets achieve a CUSTAR of one hundred. It's a very controversial matter. A lot of people, including me, think that you should not get involved with the cultural, spiritual, and technological development of a planet. Those senators think they are good-hearted missionaries. I think they're overbearing meddlers who are interfering with planets' natural development. Well, it looks like they won."

"Yeah, I see where that could be a controversial issue. I'm not sure—"

"Quiet, Danny!" Kingsley shouted as he leaned toward the screen.

". . . and will gladly cooperate," the anchor continued. "Nanstrom indicated that the ACUSA representatives will begin visiting the planets in the near future in order to begin full-scale evaluations. Once again, the three planets selected for the ACUSA program are Branwak, Hargitoz, and Quintawba."

Kingsley rubbed his beard, looked at Shey, and raised his eyebrows.

"Interesting," Shey said.

"What?" Danny wanted to know everything that was going on and was no longer afraid to ask.

"Gracie, do you have access to information about the ACUSA emissaries?"

"Yes, that information was made available on the PUPCO U-net site. Three days from now a large ACUSA delegation will visit each planet for the evaluation period mentioned on the newscast."

"What's going on?" asked Danny.

"I'm just gathering some information that may help us on the

Quintawba excursion," Kingsley replied. "It's nothing for you to be concerned about now. I'm still formulating the plan."

For the remainder of the meal Kingsley and Shey chatted about the PUPCO senate while Danny ate in silence, stealing frequent glances at Vicki. She ate quickly with her head down and excused herself.

"How about that, Shey? I suggested to Vicki that she join us for breakfast, and she agreed without putting up any resistance." Kingsley's eyes were moistening.

"That's fantastic. It was great having her here."

Kingsley cleared his throat. "Well, then. Let's meet early afternoon, say two o'clock, in the conference room to discuss our strategy. Once you're done with breakfast, you'll have free time until the meeting."

"Want to play a round of golf after breakfast?" Danny asked.

"I'd love to, Danny, but I need to spend the time thinking about Quintawba. Why don't you and Shey play?"

Danny looked over at Shey, grimaced slightly, and decided playing golf with him would be better than not playing at all. They decided to meet in the arena at nine thirty. While heading through the foyer back to his room, he glanced into the guest gathering room to find Vicki sitting in the back right corner. She was staring out a window into space, apparently unaware of Danny's presence. He felt conflicting urges to go in and talk to her or to run like hell for his room before she saw him. He decided upon the former.

Vicki swiveled her chair toward him. "Hello, Danny."

Danny couldn't decide what made him melt more, her eyes or hearing her say his name. As his tongue fattened, throat tightened, and mind went blank, he suddenly wished with all his being that he hadn't entered the room. "Hi" was all he could manage.

"Have a seat."

"Okay." Danny sat in the chair to her left and faced the window. "How are you?"

"I'm fine, thank you. Yourself?" Vicki was also staring out the window.

"I, uh, I'm okay, I guess. Actually I'm kind of hungover. I had a little too much to drink last night. Your dad talked me into trying a martini. I'd never had one. Have you?"

"A couple. I drink mostly wine."

"I'd never had wine either until this trip. It's pretty good. I've always been a beer drinker. You like beer?"

"Not much."

"Kind of neat looking out there, isn't it? I've never been in outer space before. I mean, I've seen it on TV and in movies, but it really feels different being out in it."

"Yes, it is. It's often compared to the feeling of being on a boat in the ocean or flying in a shuttle for the first time, only space travel is worse because you're separated from land by much greater distances."

"That makes sense. Well, I should get going. I'm playing golf with Shey."

"Good luck."

"Thanks." Danny was up and headed for the door without looking at her. He was relieved to be out of the conversation but was sorry it was over. He entered the foyer to find Shey leaning against the wall just outside the door.

"Someone should put that exchange in a romance novel."

"What? You were listening?"

"Relax. I'm here to help. Good God, Danny. Telling her you're hungover? Asking if she likes beer? Saying it *looks neat* out there? All while acting like you've just seen a Jankovian screaming zombie. It's a wonder she didn't break down and throw herself on you."

"Knock it off. I'm not very experienced at talking to women."

"That's painfully obvious, but you've made progress. I'm guessing that before this mission there's no way you would have approached a good-looking woman and start a conversation, correct?"

"Correct . . . but it didn't go very well."

"But it's a start. I told you, I'm here to help."

"Yeah, right. Thanks, but I don't want to learn about a Maroovian Twisted Inversion or whatever the hell you do."

Shey chuckled. "I'm not talking about astonishing sexual techniques.

Those are for pros. What I can give you is some advice on how to talk to a lady. You could use the experience, and Vicki could use the companionship. She's been a recluse her entire life, and I feel sorry for her. I'd like to see her have a friend or two, even if it's you."

"Thanks," Danny said, feigning appreciation. "Okay then, what the hell? I can listen to some advice. If I don't like it, I don't have to follow it."

"Great. Let's talk about it on the golf course. See you at the first tee."

CHAPTER 19

"Good recovery," Shey commented as they walked off the sixth green. Danny had just made his second par in a row after playing the first four holes six over. They were playing a mountainous course with breathtaking scenery, the Cliffs at Knobby Ridge. Shey had been so pleasant, serious, and gentlemanly during the round that much of Danny's pent-up anger toward him had melted. He also was quite a player. Danny estimated he was under par. After they hit their tee shots on the seventh, Shey turned to Danny.

"So, you fancy Miss Vicki, do you?"

"Well, yeah, I guess I do a little. But what's the point? You said Kingsley would kick my ass or something if he thought I was trying anything."

"I may have been exaggerating a bit. I think he's always been saddened by the fact that Vicki has never had a relationship and would be open to the idea of her spending some time with you. Don't tell him I said this, but he's very fond of you, Danny."

"That's good to hear. Then what should I do?"

Shey replied after both had hit their approach shots. "First, you have to calm down. Why do you think you get so agitated?"

"I suppose it's because I'm worried about blowing it, about saying something really stupid or doing something that looks goofy."

"There's the problem. You're more concerned about how you look and sound than you are about connecting with her and actually getting to know her. Your focus is on yourself when it should be on her."

"That's true," Danny said. "I guess I'm too worried that she won't like me."

They putted out in silence, with Danny two-putting from about thirty feet and Shey draining a twelve-footer for birdie. After Shey hit his drive on the next tee, he continued.

"My opinion is that they have less chance of liking you when you're all bottled up in your pleasant android mode. People are drawn to people who are at ease with being themselves, those who are interesting, authentic, and exhibit a strong life force. Why do you think you hide who you are?"

"I don't know, but I'm sure you have some thoughts on it," Danny replied after hitting a respectable drive and picking up his tee.

"Of course I do. It's because it would hurt you more to think they don't like who you really are. If you show your true self, it's all out there and you're vulnerable."

"I suppose that's possible," Danny panted as they climbed the steep fairway of the uphill eighth hole.

"You need to let your guard down, express opinions and emotions, be animated, and connect with who you're talking to. Be yourself and let the chips fall where they may. Some people will like you and others won't. No one is universally liked. Even me."

"I don't know if I can do that."

"Like everything else, it just takes practice. The next time you encounter Vicki, be your true self and don't worry about what she thinks of you or if she senses you like her. Focus on her."

Danny pulled a six iron from his bag, stood over his ball, and looked up after taking a couple of practice swings.

"Okay, but then what do I talk about? That's my biggest problem. I don't know what to say."

"Why do you want to talk to her?"

"I guess I'd like to get to know her," Danny replied before striking a smooth iron shot that stopped just short of the green.

"And what's the best way to get to know someone?"

"Ask them questions?"

"Right again. You don't get to know someone by talking about yourself. You need to ask questions that will lead to you finding out what her interests are, how she feels about things, and what kind of person she is. Who knows? You may not like her at all," Shey said with a grin as he whacked another fine shot that hit twenty feet past the pin and backed up to within ten.

"Like what should I ask?"

"That, my boy, is for you to figure out. Converse with her. Conversing involves listening to the other person intently and then responding to what they say. Also, compliment her and let her know what you think of her, but only if you're sincere. Be yourself, ask questions, and be sincere, and you'll be fine."

"I can try that. Thanks, Shey, for being serious for once."

"It was painful, but I muddled through. I don't know how people do it all the time. Let's make these putts and pick up the pace so we can get the full round in before the Quintawba meeting."

What little conversation there was for the rest of the round focused on the course or their games. Danny continued solid play throughout the back nine while Shey continued to be stellar. As they walked off the eighteenth green, Shey complimented Danny on his eighty-seven while Danny gushed over Shey's sixty-nine. As they stepped into the hallway, Kingsley broke in over the intercom.

"Gentlemen, I trust you enjoyed your round. I've decided to bump up the meeting time and hold it over lunch. Let's assemble in the living room in twenty minutes."

Danny thanked Shey for the round and hurried off to his room, where he quickly showered and got into some fresh clothes. He was confident he could handle anything as he strode into the living room to find Kingsley and Shey at the table dining on hearty salads.

"Quintawba will present our greatest challenge to date and will require a creative excursion plan," Kingsley began. "The difficulty will come in gaining access to the planet. Not long after they became aware, the people of Quintawba discovered that aliens had secretly been visiting their planet for some time, doing research and gathering information—which, as I have explained, is typical. However, it's not always accepted well. Some planets find that to be a bit invasive and deceitful, but they generally get over it. Well, the Quintawbans have not. They told PUPCO that no one would be allowed on their planet without first appearing at their newly formed Center for Alien Registration and Tracking, known as CARET."

"And PUPCO agreed?" Danny asked.

"Oh yes. PUPCO realizes that when planets become aware, it is a sensitive time for their civilization. Their population is often scared, paranoid, and generally intimidated by the prospect of life on other planets. They may suspect it for decades and be eager to know for certain, but when they do, it is often quite sobering. PUPCO decided to play along in the hopes that the Quintawbans will loosen up their visitation policy once they become acclimated to aliens."

"So what do I do, go to this center and register and then do my thing?"

"Not exactly. They now broadcast a message to all approaching ships that they must register at CARET, but doing so doesn't guarantee access. You have to have a good reason for wanting to visit. If you do get accepted, your movement is monitored closely while there."

"Okay," Danny said as he explored his salad with his fork. "So how am I going to get access?"

"It's a salad, Danny. Lots of vegetables and a little protein . . . something similar to chicken. I had been struggling with that ever since we decided that Quintawba was our next destination, trying to come up with some story that would be believable and that would explain your going to Mount Nobistad. This morning's UNN broadcast gave me the idea. The ACUSA delegation that will be visiting Quintawba is scheduled to arrive in three days. Once they arrive, they will have to register at CARET but then should be given unfettered access to the planet. You are going to pose as a member of that delegation who is traveling solo and arriving early due to your schedule and the location of your home planet."

"I'm just going to show up, tell them I'm early, and they're going to believe me?"

"Not exactly. Julky Hinderthal is the head of CARET and is in the group of Quintawban officials who have been working with the ACUSA team. Ira Batoosa is the director of the ACUSA program at PUPCO. I'll send Julky a U-mail that will appear to come from Batoosa. It will explain that one member of the ACUSA evaluation team, Tavit Nanby from Calixum, will be arriving on Quintawba two days early to begin his work. Assuming Julky approves, you will register with CARET and tell them that your assignment is to visit a small town. There is one called Dralia that is a short distance from Mount Nobistad. You will tell them that is where you have been instructed to visit and that you must interact with and study the town's population without anyone knowing who you are.

"Once there, you will go to Mount Nobistad. It should take no more than an hour or two to find the karbolite deposits and look for any clues as to where Dank may have gone next. Mount Nobistad is a fairly popular tourist attraction, so there may be a lot of natives around. Ask a few if they've seen someone who looks like Dank. Once you've finished there, you need a tidy exit. We want to avoid sending you back to CARET, so you'll call Julky Hinderthal and explain that you just received word that your grandfather is very ill and failing quickly. You'll apologize and ask if you can depart the surface from Dralia since you need to get home as soon as possible. That's the ideal scenario."

"What's the less-than-ideal scenario?" Danny asked warily.

"Well, for example, before allowing you to go to Dralia, they may feel the need to . . . to . . . interview you, to ask you questions about your mission, your background, and so forth. But don't worry, they wouldn't dare mistreat you as a PUPCO representative. It will probably be a formal, polite conversation. It might just be Julky, or it could be several CARET team members. To be prepared you'll need to spend a few hours studying the Calixum geography, culture, and customs. Danny, are you alright?"

"These people may grill me? I may have to answer a lot of questions and talk a lot? In a room with a bunch of them?"

"Danny, what did you think, that you were just going to drop down on each planet, travel to a spot, and find a clue? The first two excursions went well, but they were hardly typical searcher work. You have to play roles, be cunning and bold, work to get information from people, and occasionally take on mildly dangerous situations. Trust me, you can do this."

"I . . . I don't know. It's been going so smoothly. What if I panic and they don't believe my story? It sounds like these people may throw me in jail or something. What if they torture me?" Danny yelled.

"Calm down, Tavit," Shey deadpanned.

"Danny, they are not going to torture you or throw you in jail," Kingsley said. "No matter what they may suspect, they wouldn't risk harming an ACUSA member. If you stumble badly, you simply explain that this is your first mission for ACUSA and that you are little on edge about it."

"I don't know. I don't do well when a bunch of people are focusing on me."

"There you go again. You're envisioning the worst-case scenario with little regard for its probability or rationality. What's more than likely going to happen is that a CARET representative or two will very pleasantly greet you, ask you a couple of questions, and allow you to go on about your business. Once they do, you will return to the Star Hopper and—"

"The Star Hopper? I'm not going down in a Solo Trek?"

"Oh, I neglected to mention that part. Given their current paranoia, they will scan ships that are close to their planet. Therefore, we cannot get close to Quintawba with the *Aurora*. We can't risk them identifying it as my ship. So we will keep our distance, and you will take the Star Hopper. They would know you wouldn't be able to travel from Calixum in the Solo Trek."

"How far away will you be?"

"I don't know yet; probably a couple of nunsecs."

"Time wise?"

"Maybe an hour or two."

"Wait a minute. Will the EZ-Comm work from that distance?"

Kingsley looked down and rubbed his forehead before lifting his head to answer. "Probably not, but even if it does, I don't think we'd be able to use the EZ-Comm. The chances are too good that they would be able to pick up the signal. We can't have that happen."

Danny was starting to look as though he was holding onto the rails of a sea-going ship that was being tossed about violently. "Tell me you're not telling me that I have to go to this planet under these circumstances and that I won't be able to be in contact with you?"

"Yes, Danny, that very well may be the case."

"I think we need a new excursion plan. I am not going down to that planet not knowing what they are going to do with me or to me if they suspect something, without being able to contact you."

"Danny, you can do this. You performed brilliantly on the first two excursions, and you doubted your abilities before each. This is simply a different situation. Remember, you will be protected by the fact that they think you are a PUPCO representative. Worst-case scenario is that they decide to hold you until the rest of the delegation arrives. They wouldn't harm you. If you don't get back in a reasonable time, Shey will come for you. We'll just have to risk being discovered."

Danny wasn't comforted.

"Let me get this straight. The best-case scenario is that I go to a suspicious if not hostile planet, get interrogated, lie about who I am, hope they buy it, travel to a remote mountain if they let me, look for clues and ask locals questions about Dank, and hope they allow me to take off from there. And if any of that doesn't work and they lock me up, I have to hope that he can get to the surface undetected, break into what is probably a high-security building, and rescue me. Is that about it?"

"Yes, that's about it," replied Kingsley.

"Are you insane?" Danny shouted. "There are only about ten things

JOHN ARNETT

that can go wrong with that, and if anything does, I'll have to decide on my own how to deal with it."

"Well, pardon me if you have to deal with a little stress in order to save the rule of a family and possibly the civilization of an entire planet!" Kingsley boomed. "We need you to rise to the occasion, Danny. We need you, Vivitar Quilicant needs you, and all of Yoobatar needs you. Do you want to call Vivitar and tell her that the mission has failed because you were scared? Gracie, get Vivitar on—"

"Stop. Just stop!" Danny yelled. He glanced at Kingsley and Shey, exhaled deeply, and continued. "Okay, okay. I'll do it. What the hell."

"Splendid," Kingsley said. "I'd like you to start studying Calixum. Gracie, prepare for Danny what you think would be a good overview of the planet, basic information that would cover what he may be asked on Quintawba, including what you can find on Tavit's personal history. We will reconvene for dinner."

Val Cheznik stood inches from the mirror in his brightly lit bathroom, closely scrutinizing his crusty, green face. He didn't like what he was seeing. He didn't like that his skin was becoming less supple and more deeply creviced. He especially didn't like that the rich, warm shade of green was starting to devolve into a mundane brown. He knew it was perfectly natural, but he didn't like it one bit. He tried to focus on the bright side of his aging, which was that he would be able to retire soon. After fifty-eight years of unscrupulous scrounging about the cosmos for every little trinket of value upon which he could lay his rigid little fingers, he was tired. He was ready to quit, but his situation wouldn't allow it. The last of his twenty-seven offspring was still in college, and tuition was high, even straining the income of a successful Grugnok captain. Ten more months; then he could dock his ship for good and spend his golden years with his lovely wife, Mary. He was shaken from his melancholy thoughts by a voice over his speaker.

"Captain, Dave here. We have a development. I think you should come to the bridge." Dave Wilcox had been Val's first officer for over thirty years.

He sighed. He was just about to crawl into bed and catch a movie. "Yes, Dave. I recognize your voice. I'll be there in a few minutes."

Val made his way from his cabin to the bridge as fast as his aging legs would carry him. He entered the room to find three of his ten crew members busy at control panels. He would miss his crew. Most of them had been with him for decades.

"What is it, Dave?"

"We've gotten close enough to the trackers to identify the type of ship they're on. It's a QC class star cruiser!"

"QC? Are you sure?"

"Positive. It looks like it might be a 900 series. Do you want to continue our pursuit? We'd be no match for a QC 900."

"Yes, continue our course, but keep your distance so we don't get their attention. This is actually wonderful news. Ships such as that are normally owned by either heads of state or by very wealthy individuals. Let's see if Darkus leaves in a transport again. If he does, we'll go after him. If we can acquire him, we'll get the specifics of why he wanted to see Durbin's cave so badly and perhaps trade him to the ship's owner for U-bucks or some of their technology."

"Yes, sir. Good night, sir."

"Good night, everyone," replied Val. He patted Dave on the shoulder and headed back to his room, where he crawled into bed with visions of an early retirement dancing in his big, square head.

CHAPTER 20

"LIST THE CONTINENT, country, region, and city in which you reside on Calixum," Gracie asked.

Danny sighed. "Gracie, I don't think I can do this excursion." He was sitting at the desk in his suite, studying maps of Tavit's home planet.

"You can do it. The question is how well you will do it."

"I think you know what I mean."

"I think what you are trying to avoid saying is that you are afraid."

"Well, yeah. I'm afraid to go to Quintawba."

"How did that feel?"

"Not very good. For some reason saying it out loud made me feel a lot more like a wimp."

"Why are you afraid? What do you think may happen?"

"So now you're a therapist?"

"I have complete knowledge of all behavioral methodologies in the universe and have a clear understanding of the mission. So yes, I'm qualified to give you advice. What do you fear will happen?"

"Like I said, I might lose it and have a major meltdown and they'll throw me into prison or torture me or kill me or something."

"Kingsley has explained to you that the worst that would likely happen is that they grow suspicious of your behavior and want you to stay at CARET until the rest of the group arrives. In that event, the odds are very high that Kingsley and Shey will be able to extricate you. You know what I think?"

"No, but I'm sure you'll tell me."

"I think you know what you are describing is extremely unlikely and that you simply don't want to deal with how you will feel while having to interact with the Quintawbans. You're worried about being tortured alright, but not by them. What you'll go through emotionally and physically when talking to them is the torture you fear."

Danny rose from the desk, went over to the window, and stared pensively into the deep void of space.

"Now, list the continent, country, region, and city in which you reside on Calixum."

"I am from Ladifer, which is a large city in the Savim region, which is in the country of Janrus, which is on the continent of Mullitan," Danny mumbled without turning away from the window.

"You are correct. My only hope is that you will show more enthusiasm and less apathy if asked by the Quintawbans."

"We've been going over this stuff for two hours. I'm tired."

"Not quite the warrior attitude we would expect given your position on this important excursion."

Danny turned and looked at the ceiling. "Warrior? Who the hell said I was a warrior?"

"No one has made such a statement, but perhaps you would benefit from taking that approach."

"I thought Kingsley said there was little chance of violence or danger on this mission."

"By warrior attitude I mean taking an approach that is anchored by courage, boldness, and a belief that you can rise to any occasion, that you will do whatever it takes to assure the mission is a success. That includes not whining about what is excursion-critical preparation. Warriors may feel fear, but they do not let it rule their behavior. Have you ever been brave, Danny?"

"Huh?"

"Have you ever been brave?" Gracie asked. "Can you think of any situation in your life where you have been courageous?"

Danny was a bit taken aback by the question. "Sure. I've done things I really didn't want to do."

"But why did you do them? It's not being brave if you do something because you feel you have no choice. Or because it's the lesser of two evils. Have you ever done something difficult, something you feared, because you really wanted to, because doing it would help someone else or improve yourself? Or because it would be for the greatest good of all involved?"

"Of course. There have been lots of times when I . . . uh . . . when I . . ."

"When you what?"

"No. No, there haven't. I can't think of a moment in my life when I felt brave," Danny said sadly.

"You ought to try it. It's never too late to start, and this would be the ideal situation. Being brave would serve you well on this excursion and on the rest of the mission. Now, on with the preparation. Tell me about your education and career."

Danny took a moment to reflect on the mission. It dawned on him that courage is often something you find when others are counting on you. He perhaps could determine the fate of Kingsley, Shey, Vivitar, and all of Yoobatar.

"Gracie, I think it's time for me to be brave. Where's Kingsley?"

"In his office."

Danny strode down the hall to Kingsley's office door, requested admittance, and entered.

"I want to apologize for how I acted at the meeting. I realize the importance of the mission and that everyone is counting on me, and I want you to know I'll do whatever you need me to do. My behavior was immature and unprofessional, and it won't happen again. You've got enough to worry about without dealing with me being a wimp every ten seconds."

"I appreciate that, Danny," Kingsley said from behind his desk. "I know that was difficult for you."

"Thanks. Gracie and I had a talk about bravery that really hit home. I just want to be a help, not a hindrance. I think I'm going to go take a nap before dinner."

"Hold on. There has been a slight change in how the Quintawba excursion will likely play out."

"How slight?"

"I've traded U-mails with Julky. He's fine with Tavit showing up early, but he's going to need you to participate in some festivities."

"Festivities? What exactly?" Danny asked warily.

"He wants you to have lunch with several CARET executives when you arrive, then tour the facilities to meet more of their people and learn about their culture. Also, they are in the middle of series of formal galas surrounding their inclusion in the ACUSA program. Tomorrow's is for all Quintawbans who have contributed to the ACUSA selection effort. He wants you to be the guest of honor at tomorrow night's event, then have breakfast the next morning with the ACUSA team before you head to Dralia."

"Guest of honor at a gala? What the hell does that entail?"

"Well, it will involve meeting a lot of politicians and dignitaries and, um, possibly saying a few words to the attendees."

"A speech?" Danny yelled. "I can't give a speech."

"It's not a speech, it's just a few sentences about how happy you are to be there and thanking them for their hospitality."

Danny's chest was heaving. "No way. I can't do that. And meet all those people? No fucking way. Can't you get me out of it? Send him another message and tell him I can't do all of that."

"I already tried that, gently, since they don't totally trust PUPCO. He said that you will be expected to attend each event."

"This isn't the normal searcher stuff you described when I agreed to be the lead!" Danny yelled.

"That's true, and I'm sorry it's taken this turn. I didn't plan on it. I tried explaining that you were not in the ACUSA leadership group and were not cut out for that type of thing, but he was adamant. You were just saying that you'd do whatever we needed you to do. What about this newfound bravery?"

"I . . . I don't know," Danny mumbled.

"This is news to you. Go back to your room, get some rest, and get used to the idea. You'll be fine."

Dejected and numb, Danny turned and shuffled from the office without responding and headed for his room.

Kingsley exited his office, grabbed a beer from the service bay, plopped on his living room couch, shut his eyes, dropped his head onto the back of the chair, and threw his feet onto the coffee table.

"You must be tired," came a voice from the other end of the table. Kingsley hardly reacted. He had been surprised in his suite too many times to be jumpy.

"Did you guess that because you're omniscient, or did my posture give it away?" he replied without bothering to open his eyes. He knew Shanna Var had just materialized and was sitting in the chair opposite him.

"It's not surprising. You've been working hard, and you're not as young as you used to be."

That got Kingsley to open his eyes. Shanna was sitting crossed-legged in the chair, also drinking a beer.

"I've never thought about it before, but that must be one of the downers about being omniscient; there are no surprises."

"Sure there are. I'm surprised all the time by people. I don't know how people are going to react to things, how they are going to handle situations."

"Why are you drinking that? Alcohol has no effect on you."

"True, but I do like the taste, and it brings back memories of my past lives when I really enjoyed a couple of beers now and then."

"Any cryptic nuggets of wisdom regarding the mission?"

"Sure. Getting Danny to Quintawba is going to be a challenge."

"There you go flaunting your omniscience again. I'm tired and Danny doesn't want to do the Quintawba excursion. You're amazing. Tell me something I don't know. I know, how about that this whole thing was a stupid idea."

"Is that what you think?"

"I'm starting to."

"I'm not. I'm more convinced than ever that this was the right thing to do, that you're doing some of your best work, and that Danny is going to shine."

"Is that why you're here, to give me a pep talk?"

"I guess you could say that. I thought the timing was right since some doubt seems to be creeping in right at the time you need to have the most resolve. Your most challenging work is yet to come."

"Oh, that's abundantly clear. It would be nice if you pitched in once in a while."

"What do you think I'm doing here?"

"I was hoping for something a bit more direct."

"If the situation arises in which I feel that's warranted, I'll consider nudging things in the right direction." Shanna took another sip from her bottle and set it on the table. "Danny doesn't want to go to Quintawba, but I'm guessing you underestimate his resolve. He's playing along because he doesn't want to upset you, but the thought of going terrifies him."

"Like I said, tell me something I don't know. I'll work him through it."

"Like I said, you underestimate his fears. I'm here to warn you that if you face resistance, getting angry about it will serve no purpose. His frame of mind is now such that he would rather face most any punishment you could conjure up than do the Quintawba excursion, so yelling or threatening will do no good."

Kingsley leaned forward in chair. "What do you suggest?"

"I'll leave that to you. My point is that you are going to have to be creative, dramatic, and perhaps even drastic. The key is to keep in mind what must occur for all of this to work."

"I know. I know. He has to want to change," Kingsley said before Shanna turned into a gently glowing mass of white light and slowly faded away.

"Danny, my boy! Come in and bend an elbow," Kingsley boomed.

Danny entered to find Shey scurrying about the kitchen and Kingsley sitting at the bar, a glass of white wine in hand. In the past two hours Danny had detached from the situation and shut down emotionally, turning into a not-so-pleasant android. He was so numb that he was oblivious to the glorious Yoobatarian evening that was visible through the windows.

"You're a bit late, so we decided to start without you. Take it easy tonight. You've got a big day tomorrow."

The last sentence made Danny flinch slightly. He took a seat on a bar stool without speaking and wrapped his hand around the mug of beer Shey had set in front of him.

Kingsley hopped up from his seat and bounced down the two levels to the front of the living room. "Gracie, happy hour. I'd like upbeat tonight. Sinatra, *Come Swing with Me!* followed by *Come Dance with Me!* Down here, men."

Kingsley was joined by the rest of his crew around the table.

"Vicki isn't feeling well this evening, so she won't be joining us."

Danny simply nodded and sipped his beer. Being around Kingsley and Shey again instead of being curled up back in his suite was stirring the pot. The emotion he had worked so hard at shoving down was starting to simmer.

"A toast to the mission, gentlemen. We're making up ground on Dank, and we have a solid plan for Quintawba. It will take a little longer than we thought, because of the festivities, but I think it will work."

Danny had been so consumed with fighting his fears that he hadn't given Dank much thought.

"Wait a minute," he said. "What if Dank is there? What will I do then? I won't be able to contact you."

"That's not likely. We missed him by a day at Dabita Bok. Unless he has problems getting through CARET, he will probably be long gone before you arrive. This is only the second planet, and there are five crystals. Anything is possible, but I expect we will close the gap to twelve to fourteen hours by the time we reach Quintawba and probably catch up to him by the third or fourth planet."

The lump in Danny's throat was not being washed away by the frequent, sizable gulps he was taking from the mug. It was all piling up. He was trembling a bit and starting to take on the look of a caged wild animal.

Kingsley was softly singing along with Sinatra's high-powered version of "Almost Like Being in Love," which filled the room. Shey was keeping his eyes on the volcano he sensed was about to blow.

Danny was looking so distraught, Kingsley could no longer ignore it.

"Danny, are you okay? You look a bit space sick. I would think you'd be used to—"

"I can't do it!" he yelled.

"What is it exactly that you believe you can't do?"

"The Quintawba trip. I can't do what the plan we've got . . . all that stuff they want me to do. I can't and I won't!"

"You can do whatever you put your mind to. What you mean is that you don't want to do it."

Danny wasn't appeased. His considerable anxiety was quickly shifting to anger. "Can't, won't, don't want to. Call it whatever you want. I'm not going to do it. Period. I've had enough of this. Either come up with a different plan or one of you do it."

"Danny," Kingsley sighed, "how many times do we have to go through this? You've been anxious about both prior excursions, but with the proper preparation and frame of mind you got through them splendidly. This will be no different."

"Yes it will, because I'm not doing it. This isn't even close to what I had to do on the other two planets. If I'd have known this kind of stuff was part of being the mission lead, I wouldn't have agreed to do it, and you know it. I am not going to Quintawba. Got it? It ain't gonna happen!"

"That's enough!" Kingsley bellowed. "You will do the Quintawba excursion, and you will do it as planned! You committed to being the mission lead three days ago, and you told me not two hours ago that you would do whatever it takes without complaining. Not to mention the fact that the future of an entire planet's civilization hangs in the balance. Doesn't that mean anything to you?"

"I don't care anymore! I don't care about Yoobatar or the fucking mission or what I said before. You just care about your fucking fee. Well, find a way to earn it without me, because I'm done."

Kingsley collected himself and took a sip from his wine.

"Danny, forget the mission for a moment. Don't you want to tackle your issues, to conquer your fears?"

Danny stared at the table in silence.

"Answer this: since you agreed to be the mission lead, have you had any more of the dreams where you're being chased?"

Danny thought before replying. "No. No, I haven't."

"That's the result of you deciding to tackle your issues. You've made tremendous progress since we plucked you from your apartment. Think about how far you've come and what you've been able to do so far. And think about how great you've felt after the other excursions. Don't tell me you didn't feel tremendous pride and accomplishment both times. With my training and some determination on your part, the sky is the limit."

Danny had calmed down, but he was still breathing heavily.

"You're not listening. I can't. Yes, I've done some things I never thought I'd be able to do, but the Quintawba trip is totally different. I'm tired of fighting it."

"Tired of fighting what?"

"I don't know. You know. All this. Everything. Everything I've had to do in my whole fucking life. It's just not worth it anymore. It's too hard and I'm tired. I've had enough."

"You're giving up?" Kingsley asked sadly.

"I just want to go back to my apartment."

"And do what? Watch television and drink beer until you die?"

Danny stared at his mug and thought for a moment. "I suppose."

"I see," Kingsley said as he walked over to the service bay and back, set a round, red pill on the table in front of Danny, and returned to his seat.

"What's that?"

"Mylateraglocitine."

"What's it do?"

"You're ready to give up? Okay then, why don't you really give up? You're tired of fighting it? Take the pill, Danny. You won't ever have to deal with new people or strange situations or unusual foods again. It will put you out of this misery you call your life."

"Wait a minute. Are you saying this will kill me?"

"That sounds so . . . violent. It's completely painless. Take it and you will become drowsy and fall asleep in a matter of minutes. Just like when you go to bed at night. The only difference is you'll never wake up. All of your problems will be gone."

The song in the background, "Sunny Side of the Street," was a stark contrast to the somber mood that had suddenly blanketed the room. Danny stared at the pill for a minute before glancing at Shey, then Kingsley, then back at the pill. Kingsley was making it easy. All he had to do was swallow the pill. He found the offer tempting. He was so tired. The idea of falling asleep, of never having to battle his demons again, held great allure. Danny picked up the pill and held it between his thumb and index finger. All he had to do was pop it into his mouth, wash it down with a gulp of beer, and there would be no more training classes, no more Quintawba, no more whatever else awaited him.

Danny moved his hand slightly closer to his mouth as his eyes grew watery and his focus on the little red pill grew more intense. He couldn't feel his arm move as he pulled his hand close to his mouth and inhaled deeply. He paused, waiting for someone to stop him, but Kingsley and Shey simply stared at him in silence. He wanted to place it in his mouth, but he couldn't. He slowly lowered his trembling hand and placed the pill back on the table.

"I . . . uh . . . I can't do it."

"But you wanted to, didn't you?"

"Yes, I guess I did."

"So why didn't you?" Kingsley asked.

Danny blinked rapidly a few times and looked up at Kingsley. "I don't know."

"Think about it."

"I don't know," Danny repeated.

"You have a tremendous fear of unknown situations. There is no greater unknown than death. Is it possible you didn't take it because you don't know what would happen afterward?"

"Maybe. Yeah, I guess that's it. If I knew for sure what would happen . . ." Danny's voice trailed off.

"Interesting. You have a chance to escape from facing all of your fears, but you can't because of one of them. A bit ironic, don't you think?"

"I suppose," Danny muttered. He was too numb to engage in banter.

"Well, it's your choice. I thought I would give you the option in case you wanted to put yourself out of your misery. I guess that's settled. How about another beer, Danny?"

Kingsley made a trip to the service bay and set a fresh mug down on the table. "Well then, I frequently speak of evaluating a turn of events and adapting. I suppose we'll have to do that now. Shey will become the mission lead. It will make things more difficult, and our risk of being identified will increase greatly, but we will make do. I'm not going to eject you into space. You can ride along for the remainder of the mission. We'll drop you back on Earth when it's over."

"Okay, thanks," Danny said as he took a drink from the beer. The crisis had passed, but he didn't feel better. He felt nothing, empty, void of any thoughts or emotions. He had hit rock bottom. All he could do was sit and take drinks from his beer every few moments. The conversation in which Kingsley and Shey were engaged didn't register with him. After drinking over half the beer, Danny set it down on the table and placed a hand on his forehead. He looked around the room to find everything becoming slightly

---

blurry. He felt like he'd had five or six beers, though it was only his second.

"I don't feel good," he blurted.

"What is it, Danny?" Kingsley asked.

"I feel really woozy, and everything is a little out of focus."

"Yes, well, mylateraglocitine will have that affect."

"What are you talking about? I didn't take the pill."

"Yes, I know. I put a powder form of it into that beer you're drinking."

"You what? What the hell are you talking about?"

"I put a substantial dose of mylateraglocitine in your beer while I was at the service bay. You should fall asleep in about five minutes, give or take a minute."

"What?" Danny yelled. "Why did you do that?"

"I was just trying to help. It was clear you wanted to take the pill but that you were too weak to do it. You said yourself that you were giving up. What would be the point of continuing? So you can watch more television and drink more beer, sitting in your apartment waiting for some fatal disease to rescue you? Well, I've saved you a lot of time and misery. If you aren't going to try to deal with your issues, you might as well just move on. Not to mention the fact that I don't want you around here if you aren't going to lead the mission. This isn't a pleasure ship, Danny. I really don't want you eating my food, drinking my beer, and breathing my oxygen if you aren't going to contribute. And I certainly don't want you around my daughter. Anything you'd like to say? You probably have about three minutes."

Danny was frantic. "You can't do this! It's murder!"

"I suppose some might say that, but who's going to know? No one on Earth knows where you are. We'll just vaporize your body, and that will be that. Vivitar is the only person who knows you are on board. We'll just tell her we had a parting of ways and that you left the mission."

"I can't believe this! Quit fucking with me!"

"I'm doing nothing of the sort. If you'd have just given me a reason why you didn't take the pill other than being afraid of death, I might not have helped you. But if that's the only reason you can think of to keep living . . .

let's just say that I wanted to help you get past a fear one last time. By the way, there's nothing to fear. You'll move into the spiritual plane occupied by souls between lives. You'll be at peace, free from all of the worries and fears that have burdened you so in this lifetime. You will experience freedom and bliss."

"Goddamn it, Kingsley! I mean it. This isn't fucking funny," Danny yelled, his speech becoming slurred.

"What's the problem? You should be relieved. You're avoiding your issues once and for all. Actually, I shouldn't say that. You'll just be getting a break from dealing with them. You'll have to deal with them in your next life or the one after that. Your lifetimes are the school years, and the time between are your summer vacations. Remember how much fun those were? Well, that's what this will feel like, only multiplied by a thousand."

Danny wasn't appeased. "You son of a bitch," he slurred as he tried standing up.

"That's probably not a good idea," Kingsley said as Danny tumbled back into his chair.

"Give me the fucking antidote! Now!"

"Antidote? I don't think there is an antidote. Is there, Shey?"

"No, I don't believe there is," Shey said somberly.

"Gracie, is there anything that will prevent ingested mylateraglocitine from working?"

"Yes, betamethatrylazone will reverse the effects if taken before the person loses consciousness."

"Do we have any on board?"

"We do."

"Give it to me!" Danny screamed hysterically, as he fought to stay awake.

"No, I don't think so. You just want it because you're still afraid of death. Just sit back and let it happen."

"No! That's not it."

"What else could it be?"

"Goddamn it. I don't want to die," Danny screamed as tears rolled down his cheeks.

"Why not?"

"Because I want . . . I want to be better. I don't want to be afraid of everything. I want to be normal and have friends and get married and have kids and all that."

"Now you're saying you actually want to deal with your issues?"

"Yes, I don't want to be like I am! I want to fight. I'll work on it. Just give me the fucking antidote," Danny was sobbing and screaming as he fell from his chair onto his knees. He grabbed the tabletop with both hands.

"You'll understand if I don't believe you, Danny. People say anything when faced with the great unknown. I think you need a summer vacation to regroup. Better luck next life."

Danny lost his grip on the table. He slumped to the floor and rolled onto his back.

"No, no, no," he muttered softly before losing consciousness.

CHAPTER 21

THOUGHTLESS CONSCIOUSNESS. Consciousness without self-awareness. Just a pure perception of existence with no thoughts, worries, fears . . . no mental clutter. It was a peaceful, blissful sensation of complete harmony with . . . with everything. The state was eventually disturbed—as if someone had thrown a tiny pebble into a still pond—by slowly rising thoughts of self-perception.

He thought about who he was, about the identity with which he associated himself.

Danny Kerrigan. I am Danny Kerrigan.

That realization was closely followed by a rapid, emotionally detached review of all that entailed, of everything he had experienced as Danny Kerrigan. His family, childhood, school years, work life, and friendships all passed through his mind along with the fears, anxieties, and worries that had accompanied it all. He didn't feel the emotions. He thought about them objectively, what an impact they had on his life, how almost everything he did and all of his interactions had been skewed by them.

He then focused on the last thing he could remember, and the events of the prior few days came flooding back. The training class. The mission. Outer space. Kingsley. Shey. Vicki. The Quintawba excursion, the little red pill, and Kingsley drugging him. He recalled pleading for his life, which led him to wonder about his state and whereabouts. Was it the spiritual plane of which Kingsley had spoken? He certainly felt different, and he was aware of a brightness, or illumination, but he had no other sense of being in such a place. He saw no other spirits. Still, it felt wonderful. A feeling of physicality crept in. He sensed his body. He heard birds chirping and trees rustling in the breeze.

He slowly opened his eyes, raised his head, and looked around. A beautiful Yoobatarian summer morning was depicted in his bedroom windows.

"Good morning, Danny," came a familiar voice from the living room. Danny turned to watch Kingsley enter the room, grab the desk chair, and sit down after placing it next to the bed.

Danny allowed his head to drop back onto the pillow. "I'm still alive."

"Yes. Very much so. Though I can see how you may have been confused. Gracie was monitoring your state of consciousness. She told me that you were in a wonderful place, one that I imagine you've never been."

"No, I don't think I have. What was it?" Danny propped himself up on his elbows.

"What you touched, ever so lightly and briefly, was a state of pure consciousness, of being pure spirit. You had shed your ego, along with all the negative thoughts and emotions that typically go with it. You were in, or very close to, a state of pure existence, of being, in which you were connected to all things. It's what you strive for when meditating. It's the goal of spiritual development . . . to be in tune with the universe and to live more in the spirit and less in the ego. Felt pretty cool, didn't it?"

"Yeah, it did."

"Multiply how you felt by a hundred. It's a crude analogy, but that's what enlightenment feels like, and when you achieve it, you feel like that all the time."

"So how did I get there?"

"My guess is that what I gave you led you into a deeper rest than you normally get, perhaps deeper than you've ever had. That, coupled with your subconscious probably being convinced that you had passed on, allowed you to release your ego and just experience existence. Typically, someone who has such an experience takes on spiritual development with more enthusiasm, since they know what's waiting for them. You didn't feel any fear when you were lying there in that state, did you?"

"No. At one point I actually thought about the things that have always really bothered me, but I didn't get worked up. I just thought about them."

"Exactly. What I want you to know, to truly understand and believe, is that the more you pull that pure spirit into your day-to-day existence, the less things will bother you. You will live, act, behave, and think from a place of calm, centered peace. You felt it to some degree on the back nine when we were golfing."

"That would be awesome." Danny looked directly at Kingsley. "You made me think you had drugged me and I was dying last night."

"Actually, what I gave you was called weeping quamatine. It's an herb, not a drug, so technically I herbed you. But, yes, I did."

"And?"

"And what?"

"No apology?"

"Danny, one apologizes for something if they regret having done it or they feel they've wronged someone. Neither is the case in this situation. In fact, you should be thanking me."

"Thanking you?"

"Yes. What I did was drastic, but it was what you needed. It took believing you were actually dying for you to realize how much you want to live and, just as important, that you really want to conquer your fears. If you'd have taken the pill yourself and passed out without getting upset, it would have meant you didn't want to continue our work, that you had closed your mind to the concept of moving any further forward, and the mission would probably be over now. The only thing I'm sorry about is that it got to that point."

"I suppose you're right. I had pretty much given up."

"And now you realize that you want to continue. Actually, that you need to continue."

"I suppose so."

"Good. Now, let's get some breakfast. Shey is setting it up in the yard. I'd like to start the Quintawba training at ten in the conference room. I assume I will see you there?"

Danny stared into space for a moment before turning his head back toward Kingsley. "You will."

"Splendid," Kingsley said as he rose and started to leave.

"One other thing," Danny shouted.

"Yes?" Kingsley replied, sticking head back into the room.

"Thanks."

"Another reality show?" Kingsley asked as he entered his room. Shanna Var was ensconced in his sofa with her feet on the coffee table, staring at the large screen on the wall.

"It is," she replied without moving her gaze from the screen.

"It never ceases to amaze me that someone so advanced can watch that garbage. That amazement is always followed by my amazement that someone like you would watch television at all."

"I'm a student of humanity. Why zip my molecules all around the universe to study how beings behave when I can plop down on this comfortable sofa and let this wonderful screen bring it all to me?"

"And put your feet on my antique coffee table. What's the premise of this one?" asked Kingsley as he sat in one of the adjacent chairs.

"They found ten people with about the same cellular vibratory rate and are seeing who can raise theirs the most in the span of three months. The winner gets ten million U-bucks."

"Develop spiritually and win a ton of money," Kingsley said while shaking his head. "Something about that rubs me the wrong way."

"Of course it does. That's the twist in this one. To actually make much progress, you have to let go of the competition and money and commit yourself to developing for the right reasons." Shanna turned her attention to Kingsley. "He seems to have made a bit of a breakthrough."

Kingsley took a deep breath. "I've been waiting for this. Go ahead and lecture me on how my methods were unethical and immoral."

"Ethics and morals are subjective. Some people would be appalled by what you did. I happen to think it was exactly what he needed. It's precisely the type of thing I was referring to when I said you had to take drastic action. What approach are you planning on taking to prepare him for Quintawba?"

"I'm going to take each of the aspects of the excursion about which he is anxious and give him some pointers for getting through."

"Basically what you've been doing."

"I suppose."

"That's worked splendidly to this point, but now you need something else."

"Which is?"

"In addition to your wisdom, advice, and tools, he needs to understand why he is the way he is. You need to show him how he got to this point."

"Before Quintawba? That sounds like a tall order. How exactly can I do that?"

Shanna chuckled. "All these years and you still ask me how exactly you should do something when you know I never tell you that. Perhaps Danny isn't the only one who would benefit from such an exercise. Appeal to his logical, analytical, problem-solving side."

"But I don't have time. We're having breakfast and then the training."

"Don't start getting whiney on me. Skip the breakfast, huddle up with Shey, and come up with a plan."

Her form was replaced with a glowing mass of energy.

Kingsley stared at the coffee table for a few moments, bemused and deep in thought.

"Gracie, tell Shey to meet me in my office."

Danny fell back on his pillow after watching Kingsley exit. Such a shock to his system was exactly what he needed to see the big picture more clearly. He knew that he eventually would have to confront his issues. He wasn't looking forward to it, but he knew it had to be done. Avoiding it was just prolonging the inevitable.

After cleaning up and getting into a fresh set of clothes—navy pants, a white tee, and a black quarter zip—he entered the main hallway. He felt different. Every other time he stepped from his room he had felt a slight apprehension about where to go, what to do if something out of the ordinary happened, whether he would get in trouble if he went the wrong way or to the wrong place, and how he would interact with the people waiting for him. That was all replaced with . . . nothing. No anxiety, apprehension, worry, or fear. Just the simple thought of going to the yard for breakfast. It felt foreign. He felt solid, for the first time in his life.

Danny made his way to the forward lift, which took him up to the center of the yard, where he was surprised to find clouds had rolled in. It was a cool, completely overcast setting, the first Yoobatarian day he had seen that wasn't mostly sunny. Danny strolled down the path toward the nose of the ship. He emerged from the foliage to find only Vicki, clad in a cobalt blue V-neck sweater and black slacks, sitting at the table.

"Good morning, Danny," she said cheerfully. It was the most lilt he had heard in her voice.

"Morning. Where are Kingsley and Shey?"

"They're tied up in a conference. Father said we should go ahead without them. Shey brought up the breakfast he made before going into the meeting." Covered plates sat before each of them. "I guess we can start."

Danny followed her lead by removing the covers, revealing an omelet on one and fruit and a muffin on the other. He poured each of them a cup of coffee from the carafe. After several bites of food and a couple of gulps from his cup, Danny realized that it was the first time in his life he had sat down for a meal with a female other than his mother.

He turned his focus to Vicki. He looked at her directly for the first time since entering the yard and was slightly taken aback. Her dark brown hair was the same, and her blue eyes were still stunning, but she looked different. Her face had a life force, almost a radiance, that Danny hadn't seen before. He began his typical search for something to say when he thought of his discussion with Shey during their round of golf. Focus on Vicki, stay in the flow of the conversation, compliment her, tell her what he feels, and let his true personality out. That last point would be the most difficult. Being himself in front of a woman after a lifetime of smothering such an urge would not be easy.

Something about that thought seemed strange to him. It dawned on him it was the word *woman*. Because most of his thoughts about having a relationship with a female had occurred when he was in high school, Danny had always considered himself interested in girls, not women. He realized that thinking of pursuing a woman felt strange, almost inappropriate, because it implied that he was a man or, more precisely, an adult. Bingo. Danny did not think of himself as an adult. Years of shunning responsibility, running from fears, avoiding any action or interaction that seemed uncomfortable, and not having any true relationships with other adults, male or female, left him feeling like he was still a teenager. The reality was like a bucket of cold water being tossed in his face. He was twenty-eight and felt like a teenager.

I am a man, he thought. The phrase felt foreign to him, as if he had thought . . . I am a giraffe.

"Your dad said you weren't feeling well last night," Danny said.

"I wasn't. Just a little down. I didn't feel like being around people."

"I can understand that. And today?"

"Much better, thanks," she replied. She smiled slightly and made eye contact with him for the first time. It was a connection that filled Danny with strong emotion for the first time since he had awoken. His heart started racing and his stomach started churning, but not from anxiety. It was exhilaration.

"That's great. The ship is a much more pleasant place to be when you're around." Not bad. It wasn't going to make her swoon, but at least it was authentic.

"Really? Thank you, Danny. That's one of the nicest things anyone has ever told me." She took a sip of her coffee. "I have a confession. This is the first time I've ever sat down for a meal with a man."

"Really? Me too. I mean, with a woman."

"I find that hard to believe. You're so handsome and charming and sweet. I would think you would have had countless dates."

Danny swooned. "That's very nice of you to say, but I've never really had a date. If fact, this is the closest thing I've had to one."

"Me too, but that shouldn't surprise you. I'm sure Shey or Father have told you how I've spent most of my life in reclusion. So why haven't you dated?"

"Honestly? Because I've always been afraid to talk to girls. I just get really nervous and say stupid things and feel out of control, especially when I talk to girls I'm attracted to."

"I know exactly what you mean. You seem to be doing fine now."

"For some reason, I'm more comfortable talking to you than any girl I've ever talked to."

"Perhaps that's because we're so much alike. So did I miss anything interesting last night?"

"Oh, uh, no, not really. Well, actually yes. I don't want to get into the details, but let's just say I was pretty adamant about not doing the Quin-tawba excursion, and your dad helped me understand that it would be best for everyone if I tried."

"So you're going to do it?"

Danny sighed. "I am. I'm meeting him in a little bit to start my training."

"That's very brave. I can only imagine what it must feel like to be faced with this excursion. I really appreciate what you are doing for us."

At that moment, Danny realized his motivation had changed. He wasn't doing it for anyone else. He wasn't doing it to impress Vicki or to be Vivitar's hero. He wasn't doing it to prevent Kingsley from launching him into space in a Solo Trek. He was doing it for himself.

"So what made you come out of your room? Shey said you never do that."

"I'm not sure. Perhaps a greater force is at work, one that's difficult for us to understand. Perhaps I was supposed to meet you."

Danny's confidence was growing with each exchange. "Would you like to try more of a real date? With me?"

"I'd like that."

"Great. How about dinner tomorrow night?"

"I'd love that. You know, you'll have to let Father know and get his approval. He's very protective of me."

Danny gulped hard. "No problem."

Danny had a bounce in his step as he exited the lift and entered the conference room.

"Have a seat, Danny. Down here near the screen. We're going to utilize it."

Danny took a seat and spun slightly in his chair so that he was facing Kingsley and the large screen. Kingsley, in turn, stood up and began pacing.

"You've made tremendous progress since you joined the mission, and for that you should be commended. All things considered, your performance on the first two excursions was nothing short of amazing. I would have to label the mission to this point a success. We obviously haven't caught Dank yet, but we've made the right decisions, and we're hot on his trail. All in all, you've done a great job."

"Thanks."

Kingsley continued pacing with his hands clasped behind his back. "Though I'm sure you haven't been thinking if it in these terms, your rate of spiritual growth has been phenomenal. You've worked through many layers of fears and self-doubt in a short time. However, I believe that for you to move to the next level, to successfully break through another layer of fears, we will need to do some deeper analysis of your issues. That must be done before we start preparing you for the Quintawba excursion."

"Didn't Shey already do that?"

"Shey did a thorough job of identifying your issues, but we didn't spend any time analyzing them. He and I have taken his findings, grouped them, and classified them, creating a roadmap of how your issues have led you to where you are today. What we need to do is go the other way, go deeper. We need to determine why you have those issues. I think getting to the source of your fears, blowing the lid off of them, is imperative for significant advancement at this point. I think it would help if you slightly detached from yourself and thought about your issues from a purely analytical perspective, as if part of you were a therapist and the other were the patient. Are you game?"

"Yeah, sure. Why not? I guess it couldn't hurt."

"Splendid. Let's get going. All I want from you, Danny, is honest answers. Really think about what I ask and respond with no fear of being judged. Can you do that?"

"Sure."

"Gracie, screen on. We'll start with a review of Shey's findings and the roadmap we created. The approach we took was to name the major issues he discovered and define how each has contributed to forming who you are and how you live. We're going to call this analysis *Danny's Plight.*" That heading appeared at the top of the screen.

"That's a little bleak."

"It's only bleak if you don't do anything about it. Let's start by listing your major issues under a category called Primary Fears. Gracie?" *Primary Fears* appeared near the top left corner. Under it was a list.

"As you can see in the list, what we are calling your primary fears are those of public speaking, unfamiliar situations, getting into trouble, confrontation and conflict, expressing opinions, making decisions, failing, expressing emotions, and intimacy. It's important that you understand and agree with all of this."

"That looks about right."

"Shey and I feel that these primary fears led to your fear of connecting with people. That general fear has resulted in several compulsive behaviors: you avoid eye contact, do not talk much, get flustered easily, panic when you are the center of attention, and avoid human interaction whenever possible." Kingsley paused and scanned a second list that had appeared onscreen with the heading *Traits and Behaviors*.

"When you do deal with people, you are shy, indecisive, risk averse, timid, and distant to the point of appearing cold. You show no emotion, let no one close emotionally, avoid physical contact, try nothing new or different, and are afraid to ask people for things, especially authority figures. Oh yes, you express few opinions and do not stand up for your views if they are challenged. Are you still in agreement?" Kingsley asked.

"It's right on."

"Good. Now, we feel that all of those interaction fears and behaviors have resulted in what we will call *Self-Issues*," Kingsley continued as a third column appeared. "What slowly developed, over many years of facing these issues, was abysmal self-esteem, low self-confidence, little self-worth, ample self-loathing, suppression of your true self, and a feeling of being powerless.

"Those slowly engrained self-issues in turn resulted in the personality traits we see in the last column, *Personality and Lifestyle*. You were depressed, apathetic, passionless, pessimistic, angry, sad, anxiety ridden, and void of charisma. They also resulted in your current lifestyle. You have no goals, no friends, no dates, no sex life, and no fun. You stick to your routine, trying nothing new and doing nothing spontaneous. You hate your life but do nothing to change it. Your lifestyle has led you to the state in which we found you, which is . . . Gracie," Kingsley said as a large box appeared on the far right containing the words *Withdrawing from Life*.

"That, we believe, was your plight. Do you agree, from a clinical perspective?"

Danny scanned the lists for a few moments before responding. "Yeah, that all makes sense. I like the way you laid it out. Very logical."

"So, you see where this group of primary fears has led you. Or, more precisely, where you were when we recruited you. However, as I said, you've made tremendous progress. But it's time to go deeper. Gracie, give me some room to the left on the screen."

"What goes over there?" asked Danny.

"That, my young friend, is what you are going to tell me."

"I am?"

"Yes, you are. We identified these primary issues early on and went about trying to address them with no thought given as to why you have them. Have you ever thought about that?"

"No, I guess I haven't. I've always been too busy dealing with them or avoiding them."

"That ends. Now."

CHAPTER 22

"I'm going to pick issues from the list and explore them. First, public speaking. Why do you think that makes you so anxious?"

"That's easy. It's because I'm afraid of messing up."

"So if you messed up, what would happen then?"

"I'd look ridiculous."

"That's not a fact. That's an assumption. You are making the leap that the people involved will think you look ridiculous."

"Well sure. I'm assuming they'll think I'm not very smart or articulate, or they'll think I don't know what I'm talking about."

"So what?"

"So," Danny said slowly, "they won't think much of me, and maybe they'll ridicule me behind my back."

"I see. What about the fear of failing?"

"I guess some of the same things . . . looking silly or incompetent."

"Anything else? If someone expects something of you, what would happen if you didn't succeed?"

"I'd let them down. Yeah, that's part of it too. I don't like to let people down."

"And why is that?"

"Because they wouldn't think much of me."

"Okay. How about expressing opinions? Why are you reluctant to do so?"

"Probably the same thing. I don't want it to come out as silly or not very bright."

"Making decisions? Same thing?"

"Partly. I think part of that too is making a decision that affects others and then having the situation not work out or have bad things happen. Then they'd think badly of me, and I could even get into trouble."

"Good segue. What makes you so anxious about the thought of getting into trouble?"

"I think the thought of being yelled at or scolded or reprimanded makes me extremely uncomfortable. Yeah, that's it."

"And why do you think that makes you uncomfortable?"

"Because I'd be disappointing them and they wouldn't think much of me. This is easier than I thought it would be."

"Yes," Kingsley said. "We're certainly seeing a common thread. Expressing strong emotions?"

"I don't know about that one. Part of it probably is that I might look ridiculous. I mean, you can look silly expressing strong emotions."

"Plus you expose more of yourself. You let people see more of who you really are. And, depending on what they see, they may not think much of you, right?"

"Yeah, sure, that probably has something to do with it."

"I would imagine the same is true with intimacy, that you'd be exposing so much of yourself?"

"Probably."

"Confrontation and conflict?"

"I think I'm worried it would escalate to the point I wouldn't be able to control myself and my emotions and that they may not want anything to do with me afterwards."

"And they may not think much of you?"

"That's what I mean," Danny replied.

"And unfamiliar situations?"

Danny thought for a moment. "I think it's what you said a little bit ago. If it's something I've never done before, then I don't know exactly what is going to happen. It could lead to a situation where any of those things on the list may come up."

"I agree with your assessment, and I believe that we've peeled away a layer, that we've moved a little closer to the source. I think we've established that those primary fears developed because of a short list of acute fears, which include the fear of being ridiculed, the fear of being rejected, and the fear of disappointing others. Gracie, put those to the left of the primary fears. Would you agree, Danny?"

"Yes, I think I would. The thought of any of those makes me really upset."

"And why do you think that is? What is so bad about those happening?"

"Like I said, then people wouldn't think much of me."

"You keep using that phrase. That's an interesting way of saying what I think you are extremely uncomfortable saying."

"What do you mean?"

"Danny, what would happen if people didn't think much of you?"

"They wouldn't like me?"

"Precisely! Gracie, put that above the acute fears. Fear of not being liked. That's it, isn't it Danny? Danny?"

Danny sadly looked at the screen and fought back the lump that had suddenly formed in his throat. "Yes, I suppose it is."

"And what is it about the thought of not being liked that bothers you so much? What would happen if no one liked you?"

"I don't know. I guess then I wouldn't have any friends or a girlfriend and . . . and . . . I'd be alone," Danny said as he continued fighting the strong emotion that was building up quickly.

Kingsley returned to his chair and looked pensively at Danny.

"So let me get this straight. You avoid all of the primary fears because if you did all of those things, in the worst-case scenario, no one would like you. You'd have no friends, no mate, and you'd be alone, living a nearly reclusive life, never doing anything new, interesting, fun, or exciting. And you'd probably be depressed, passionless, pessimistic, angry, apathetic, and withdrawn from life. More than a bit ironic, wouldn't you say?"

"What do you mean?"

"What do I mean?" Kingsley bellowed. "Danny, by spending your life avoiding your issues you've created the exact worst-case scenario that you feared would occur if you'd have faced them! Don't you see that?"

Danny looked stunned. "Oh my God. You're right."

"And, since that worst case more than likely wouldn't have occurred, you've missed out on many of the positives that would have come from the experiences you've not had."

"Yeah, but I didn't have to go through all of the stress, anxiety, and humiliating meltdowns."

"Ah. The other shoe drops. You were ultimately afraid of not being liked and being alone, but you were also avoiding the discomfort."

"Discomfort?" Danny yelled. "That's the understatement of the century, whatever the hell century it is. You don't know what it's like. It's horrible, horrible anxiety. My stomach burns and churns so bad I think I'm going to throw up. My heart pounds so fast and strong I think it's going to explode. My throat is so tight I feel I can't breathe, and my head is spinning so fast I think I'm going to pass out. You'd probably give up too if you went through that a few thousand times."

"You're right, Danny. I'm sorry. I didn't mean to minimize your experience. But back to my point: by avoiding your issues you've created the exact situation you believed would ultimately occur. So what it comes down to is whether it is worth working through the issues, dealing with the anxiety until you learn how to reduce or eliminate it, in order to emerge from your cocoon and really experience life."

"I suppose."

"You suppose? What do you have to lose? If you fail miserably, the worst that will happen is that you end up back in the life you had when we found you. You don't really consider your life to be ideal, do you?"

Danny's eyes were welling up with moisture, which he wiped away before answering. He was finished deluding himself. "No. No, I don't."

"Great. We established last night that you don't want to die, and we just established that you don't like your life. Sounds to me like your only option is to try and change it."

"I suppose so . . . but you keep talking about my life. Isn't this really about the mission?"

"The two are not separate. The same issues that led to your lifestyle are responsible for your reluctance to do what is needed for the mission. I'm just trying to show you that if you work through those issues in order to lead the excursions, you will not just be helping Yoobatar and the Quilicants. You will ultimately be helping yourself."

"I guess I can see that," Danny said as he stared into space. "Okay, we got to the source of the issues. Now what do we do?"

"We got close to the source. Being alone and not being liked are side effects. There is one more level to go. Let's call it the *base fear*."

"Base fear. What's the base fear?"

"Your base fear, Danny, is a fear of not being loved."

"Loved?"

"Yes, loved. It's quite common, actually. However, it is now obvious that your fear is more deeply engrained and more acute than in most people."

"Wait a minute. You're saying my fear of having a girlfriend is responsible for all of this?"

Kingsley rubbed his forehead before answering. "You've got to stop thinking of love as being the giddy rush you feel when you are around a female you find attractive."

"Okay then. What is it?"

"Love, in its perfect form, is pure energy, the Source, the Infinite Intelligence, what some people call God. It is the state of enlightenment for which spiritual people strive. Think back to my explanation of Shanna Var and how I discussed the spirit's rate of vibration. Love is at the opposite end of the spectrum from fear. As you move toward fear, your vibratory rate decreases. As you more toward love, it increases.

"We find love within ourselves, or move closer to love, doing all the things I discussed when telling you about spiritual advancement. We also experience love through our relationships. It is the energy that is shared between two people, the bond that is formed when positive interactions occur. Haven't you ever had an interaction with someone and for a short time afterwards you felt exhilarated, where the encounter lifted your spirits?"

"Maybe a few times." Danny immediately thought back to breakfast with Vicki.

"Well, it probably quite literally did. It increased the vibration of your spirit. For that moment, you experienced love with that person, though many beings do not think of it in those terms. At a certain point, after sharing many encounters in which you connect, in which kindness, compassion, praise, gratitude, and admiration are exchanged, you start thinking of the person as someone you love. It's really just that the energy shared between you is that of a higher vibration than it would be if the person was, for example, pessimistic, bitter, jealous, nasty, condescending, angry, egotistical, or self-centered.

"In any event, your base fear is that you will be cut off from all of that, that you will not have people in your life who treat you in the fashion I've described, that you will not be loved."

Danny had been listening quietly, his left elbow on the table with his chin on his hand, quickly processing everything Kingsley said. "Okay, so what do I do about it?

"You've got to conquer that base fear. You will then no longer have the primary fears, and, in turn, the other fears and issues will melt away, and you will be able to handle anything that arises for the remainder of the mission."

"I think you're making it sound easier than it is."

"Don't think of it as difficult. Think of it as an adventure, an interesting and exciting adventure with a fabulous reward awaiting you should you succeed."

"I'll try, though exciting may be a bit of a stretch."

Kingsley rose and began pacing again with his hands behind his back. "Fear of not being loved. The first thing that jumps out at me is that, again quite ironically, you have a fear of *being* loved, even an aversion to being exposed to love. It is such a powerful emotion, one that evokes such strong feeling, that you are probably extremely uncomfortable even thinking about it, being in its presence, feeling it. Is that not the case?"

"That's the case."

"Have you ever told anyone that you love them, Danny?"

He didn't have to think about it. "No. At least, not that I remember. I might have when I was a little kid."

"How sad. Not surprising, but sad. If you did want to tell someone, you would probably be mortified at the prospect, correct? Think about it. Think about telling someone you love them."

Danny's throat tightened as he closed his eyes and envisioned saying it to the people he had been most fond of in his life.

"I think I'd I have trouble saying it."

"And why do you think that is?"

"I think it's the vulnerability thing you mentioned. I'd feel like I'd be totally exposed, and it would really feel awful if I thought they didn't want to hear it or didn't say it back. I'd feel ridiculous."

Kingsley resumed his pacing. "I sense that for this discussion you'd be more comfortable if we came up with a different word. We need a word that encapsulates this fear of dealing with, connecting with, and sharing positive moments with people. Let's see, what can we use . . . how about *bonding*? Yes, I like that. What we are dealing with is your fear of bonding with someone and your fear of people not bonding with you. How does that sound?"

"I like it."

"Good. The first thing you need to understand and believe is that bonding with someone during an interaction is pure good. Nothing negative can come from it, so you need to eliminate the negative connotations. If you are present, genuine, and open to connecting, if you enter each encounter with only good intentions, a positive experience will generally be the outcome. The frame of mind you need to maintain is that there is truly nothing to fear, and absolutely no reason to panic, and that you can deal with any and all situations.

"There is a difference between living alone and being alone. Your fear, being alone, is being cut off from all bonding. You are never alone, Danny. We are all connected. We are all made from the same molecules. We all come from the Source. So your base fear of not being loved, of not bonding with people, is really a fear of being cut off from the Source. That condition, Danny, is what is meant by what some religions refer to as hell. Heaven represents being connected to everyone and everything, being in a state of love. Hell is being cut off from all of that. You, Danny, have been living in hell."

"It's felt like hell. How do I get out?"

"You change your frame of mind. Open yourself up to connecting and bonding with everyone and everything. If you focus on what you want, if you visualize and affirm the situations and relationships you desire, they will be drawn into your life. It all goes back to the vibratory rate of your body, mind, and soul. Thoughts are energy and have a vibratory rate. Your frequent, earnest thoughts regarding your desires and your actions are energy that has a certain vibration and that will attract things of a like vibration. But there is one prerequisite we've yet to cover."

"Which is?"

"You must bond with yourself. Do you like yourself, Danny?"

Danny thought for a few moments before answering softly.

"No, I don't believe I do. I think I tell myself I do and that I like the life I lead, but I really don't. It's like I put up a front, to myself, but behind it is this kind of sickening feeling, a kind of dull dread, that if I thought about it too much I'd realize how much I don't like myself. It's kind of hard to explain."

"Actually, you did so quite well. Your fear of bonding keeps you from taking a deep, honest look at yourself because you won't like what you see. You don't love yourself. And why do you think that is?"

"Because I'm disgusted with myself for being the way I am and not dealing with it. I've been running from it for most of my life. I tell myself that I don't need to face all of these things, that the anxiety is a sign that I'm not cut out for doing the things that make me anxious and that I should simply create a life in which I avoid all that. That's what I've done, but I think that, below the phony surface, I think of myself as a wimp and a loser, like I don't respect myself, so how could anyone else?"

"So you're not cut out for interacting with people, feeling or showing emotion, expressing opinions, making decisions, trying anything new, doing anything that has a chance of failure, or being close to anyone? That doesn't leave a lot, does it?"

"I guess it doesn't."

"Well, guess what? You no longer have that reason. You've been dealing with your issues since we picked you up, and now you have a clear realization that you want to beat them. You have to like, love, and respect yourself. Once you bond with yourself, if you are open to bonding with others, you will develop relationships.

"But what if I feel someone doesn't like me? That makes me feel so wounded," Danny said.

"That's what you need to get over. What people think of you is irrelevant. If you sense someone doesn't like you, let the experience fall away. Don't cling to it and obsess about why they didn't like you. Tell yourself they are just on a different level, at a different point on their spiritual path, and move on. Sound doable?"

"It actually does. So how did I get like this?"

Kingsley returned to his chair and thought for a moment before continuing. "From our previous discussions, it sounds like you have had lot of experiences in which you felt embarrassed or humiliated."

"Oh yeah. A lot."

"Sensitive souls are easily and deeply affected by events in their life. You were probably a very sensitive soul who had these unpleasant experiences at a young age, resulting in a deeply engrained fear of not being loved."

"I think you may be right."

"I think I'm right too. I also think we've done enough work for now."

"I agree. What about Quintawba?"

"What about it?"

"When am I going to get trained for it?"

"You just did."

"No, I mean training for each thing I may have to do."

"Gracie prepped you on Calixum and gave you a history for Tavit, correct?"

"Correct."

"Then you're ready."

"But aren't you going to prepare me?"

"As I said, I just did. Between now and the excursion, work on liking yourself. Bond with yourself. Realize what a good soul you have. Really feel it. Go deep within, get in touch with your spirit, your essence, and you'll feel that you are pure good. Absorb it into your being. Once you've done that, prepare yourself for interactions, prepare to show the universe that goodness. Affirm that you will enter each interaction and all situations from a position of centered, relaxed, peaceful, powerful calm, and that you are open to connecting and bonding with everyone you encounter. Visualize positive outcomes, but know that whatever occurs you can handle. And you must decide that whether the beings you encounter like you or not is irrelevant. You are never alone. All you can do is be your true self, deal with each being with kindness, respect, compassion, and love. Sorry, the L word just can't be avoided sometimes. If you can do all of that, you will raise your vibratory rate, like energy will be drawn to you, and the excursion will be a success."

Danny let Kingsley's words soak in before responding. "That all sounds good and feels right, but it's a lot to accomplish before the excursion."

"Such change is not like flipping a switch. It takes effort and perseverance to shed old, deeply engrained thought patterns. The sooner you start, the sooner you'll get results. It's not all or nothing, but you can make progress in a short time if you enlist great focus and determination. One other thing."

"Yes?"

"I love you, Danny," Kingsley said matter-of-factly.

Danny squirmed in his chair, and his throat tightened.

"Danny, do you like me?"

"Sure."

"Do you care about me?"

"Yes."

"Do you respect me?"

"Of course."

"Do you feel a connection with me?"

"Absolutely."

"So you feel close to me, and all of these feelings are deep and genuine?"

"Yes . . . and they are . . . but I just can't say it."

"You just did. Now get out of here."

Danny rose and started to exit but stopped and turned before reaching the door. "Thanks for the training."

"You're welcome, Danny."

He took a few more steps toward the door before stopping again, this time speaking without turning. "Kingsley?"

"Yes?"

"I bond you."

Danny hurried from the conference room, leaving behind a smiling, misty-eyed Kingsley.

CHAPTER 23

DANNY STRODE ACROSS the *Aurora*'s foyer a changed man. The shift in his perspective, in the way he felt at the core of his being, was not subtle. Kingsley's training session had had an immediate and powerful impact. The analysis of Danny's issues and explanation of what he needed to change rang true and clear. He felt good about himself. He knew he was a good person and no number of less-than-perfect interactions would change that. Prior to the session, Danny knew that he wanted to conquer his issues, but he still dreaded actually doing it. Now the dread was gone. He wasn't looking forward to the excursion, but he no longer had angst-ridden, sickening thoughts that spiraled out of control with worst-possible outcomes. They had been replaced with a relatively calm, rational frame of mind and a whatever-happens-happens outlook. He wanted everything to go well and would do his best to make it so, but he wasn't fretting about what might happen if it did not. It was a strange feeling of faint indifference.

"How soon do we get to Quintawba?"

Kingsley was taken aback by the question. He was sitting in the lower level of the living room chatting with Shey and Vicki as Danny practically barged into the room. It was the first time Kingsley got the impression that Danny was attacking rather than fearing an excursion.

"Good afternoon, Danny. All rested and refreshed?"

"Yes, I had a good nap. When do we reach Quintawba?"

"We'll reach the point where you should depart in the Star Hopper in about an hour. It sounds like you're ready."

"As ready as I'll ever be," Danny said.

"Fantastic. Wear what you have on to the surface. It looks less like a searcher than the normal excursion garb. Let's review what might happen when you get to Dralia."

"Kingsley, Vivitar Quilicant is calling for you," interjected Gracie.

"On screen, Gracie," Kingsley said. Vivitar appeared, sitting at her desk, wearing an elegant purple and black paisley jacket.

"Hello, Kingsley. It's time we had a frank discussion."

"Certainly, Vivitar. What is it?"

Vivitar paused upon seeing Vicki seated at the table. "Kingsley, did you acquire a new crew member?"

"I did not. This is my daughter, Victoria. She decided to join us on this mission."

"Oh yes, I knew you had a daughter but had never met her. It's good to meet you, Victoria."

"Hello, Your Highness. It's an honor to meet you."

"The purpose of your call?" Kingsley asked.

Vivitar focused on Kingsley and quickly turned serious. "A lot of untrue rumors about our family and me in particular are being spread. We think they are being started by Dank's followers. The latest polling shows my approval rating down to 82 percent, and the satisfaction election is in less than three weeks. I do not need to see Dank publicly surface in a week or two and woo another 12 percent, which he could easily do with an amulet. Losing the satisfaction election would likely be the end of my rule."

"I agree," said Kingsley. "I can assure you that we are taking this mission very seriously and are doing everything we can to regain the tablet before Dank can create an amulet."

"I'm sure you are, but I'm afraid your assurance is no longer good enough. How close are you to catching Dank, and what exactly is your next step?"

"As I explained before, it's best that you don't know the details of how we are proceeding."

"Because you're trying to protect me, or because you think I'll find your methods unacceptable and try to stop you?"

"Both."

"I appreciate that, but I want to know what's going on so I feel more confident that Dank will be caught. Believe me, at this point what I would consider to be acceptable tactics has been expanded dramatically."

"Your Highness, I have been doing this a long, long time. You are well aware of my competence and reputation. I'm asking you to trust me, to trust my judgment and my skills, as well as those of my crew, to accomplish our goal," Kingsley said.

"Kingsley, why is it that when you're trying to charm me or convince me of something, you start calling me Your Highness?" Vivitar paused. "Okay, fine. You can keep your plans to yourself."

"A wise decision."

"But I cannot wait much longer. You have three days to find Dank. If in that time you have not acquired the tablet or given me evidence that you've at least found Dank, you will turn over to me what you have done and all of the information you have regarding where he may be. I will then release a Yoobatarian security force, which will start a massive hunt for Dank using that information."

"I don't think that would be wise. If the searcher community or the Grugnok found out, it could be chaos in the cosmos."

"I'll have to take that chance. Three days from now, Kingsley. I'll be in touch. Remain focused, fearless, and in the flow," Vivitar said before fading from view.

Kingsley stared at the screen before rotating in his chair to face everyone. "Well, that certainly changes things."

"How so?" asked Danny.

"We can't afford to waste any time," Kingsley replied. "We have to alter the Quintawba excursion plan."

"Isn't it a little late for that?" Danny said.

"Correct," Shey chimed in. "We can't alter the setup. However, we can't afford to waste an entire evening, and we certainly can't wait until tomorrow for you to go to Dralia."

"So what do we do?"

"What we now have to risk is at best offending the Quintawbans and at worst really getting them aggravated."

"So we're sending Shey in my place?" asked Danny.

"While I agree that would do it, that's not what we're talking about. I think you should have lunch with the CARET team to appease them, but then you will need to convince Julky that you have to head to Dralia instead of attending the gala and spending the night."

"How am I going to get him to agree to that?"

"By being confident, charming, assertive, and unwavering in your resolve."

Danny sighed. "Sounds like it's right up my alley."

———————

Danny stepped from his room, took a deep breath, and started toward the foyer lift when he was stopped in his tracks by a voice from behind him. He turned to find Vicki walking toward him.

"I thought I'd walk you down," she said as the two of them turned and headed toward the foyer. "How are you feeling about the excursion?"

"Actually, pretty good. A little on edge, but good. I think I'm ready."

They rode the lift in silence before stepping into the entrance hall. Vicki turned and looked him in the eyes. "Good luck down there. I have faith in you. You're such a different person than you were when Father recruited you. Your energy is much more peaceful and powerful."

"Thanks. I really do feel different."

"Maybe we can have that dinner when you get back," Vicki said.

As Danny gazed into her eyes, he realized his feelings had changed from a giddy schoolboy crush to something deeper, more sincere, and more genuine.

They turned toward the garage door, and each took a deep breath as the door opened. Kingsley, Shey, and Abby were waiting by the Star Hopper.

"There you are," Kingsley said. "We're getting close to the point where Quintawban sensors may be able to detect the *Aurora,* so it's time we split up. Abby is going with you."

"Abby? Won't that cause a problem with the Quintawbans?"

"She'll stay in the transport while you're with Julky and then explore the mountain with you. She can be very protective."

"Actually, that sounds pretty good. I'd feel better having her along."

"The Star Hopper is now under your command. Max will take care of getting you to CARET, then to Dralia and Mount Nobistad, and then back to this point, where we'll be waiting. You seem, I'm proud and pleased to say, quite calm and confident. Your presence is more solid."

"Thanks. I feel more solid. But all of that stuff isn't gone. I've got some butterflies."

"There's a huge difference between being nervous and having a major meltdown with runaway fear and anxiety. Some nerves are good. Are you comfortable with the plan?"

"I am. What's this Julky Hinderthal like anyways? We really didn't cover that."

"You're right, we didn't. It may help your comfort level if you knew a little more about him. Shey, what exactly is his position?"

"It varies. He's usually sitting at a desk. At times he crosses his legs or gets up and walks around. Sometimes he even lies down."

"That's hilarious. Seriously, what's his background?"

"It depends on where he's standing."

"I should have traded you to the Grugnok for an android long ago."

"Yeah, and if you had, you'd be working as a greeter at Yoobiemart, old man."

"Old man? You arrogant, disrespectful, self-important, annoying little—"

"Hey! Knock it off!" Danny yelled. "We've got an excursion to do. Forget about Julky. Let's get this thing going. You two can fight all you want once I take off."

"Sorry, Danny. You're quite right. We'll be here waiting for you," Kingsley said as he stuck out his hand.

Danny felt like a fighter pilot going off to battle as he firmly shook Kingsley's hand.

"Thanks." Abby trotted past Danny and jumped into the Star Hopper.

"I guess it's time. I'll hopefully see you all later tonight." Danny took his place in the driver's seat and gave them all a quick salute while locking eyes with Kingsley, who returned his gaze and his salute. They all watched silently as the Star Hopper dropped from the *Aurora*'s belly and disappeared.

———

Dave Wilcox stood outside the door to the steam room and hesitated before entering. Val Cheznik did not like being bothered while he was relaxing with a steam, so much so that he had all communication devices removed from the room. Nevertheless, Dave had to speak with him about a development, and he knew Val might be in there for hours. The moist heat helped soften his Grugnok skin, which grows stiffer and tougher with age. The fact that he was impervious to temperature extremes allowed him to remain in the room for as long as he liked.

Dave finally entered and attempted to locate Val in the steam and dim lighting. "Captain, are you in here?"

A grunt and a grumble came from a back corner of the room. Val had fallen asleep. "Yes, what is it?"

"It's Dave. There has been a development with the tracking signals."

"Okay, okay. What happened?" Val asked as he sat up and toweled off his face.

"The transport tracker is still in the QC 900. It's taken a position five nunsecs from Quintawba. The other tracker, the skin sensor, is now in a multi-person transport and is taking a course that appears to be toward Quintawba. What would you like us to do?"

Val sighed. His was fond of his crew. They had always been loyal and obedient, but he frequently lamented their lack of insight and initiative. They rarely made any decision without first consulting him, no matter how obvious the course of action.

"Well, Dave, we want Darkus Murmak, and we'd prefer not to engage the QC 900. We know he's headed to Quintawba. I think we should follow him there. What do you think?"

"I think that sounds like an excellent plan."

"Of course you do. Let me know when we arrive at Quintawba. We'll take a Grugpod down to the surface and find our little friend. Off you go. And no more interruptions until we get there," Val said as he returned to a prone position and closed his beady red eyes.

Danny stood outside the door to Julky Hinderthal's office and hesitated before entering. He took several deep breaths in a last-minute attempt to relax. He wasn't out of control but felt he could get there with little provocation. Danny reviewed his training, took a few more slow, deep breaths, and asked for admittance.

"Come in, Mr. Nanby."

Danny cautiously stepped through the door and found himself in a spacious, nicely furnished office. The walls were covered in a combination of rich, dark paneling and bookshelves, while a sofa and two chairs filled the space directly in front of him. His eyes quickly moved to the left, where he found the source of the voice. Julky was in the process of moving out from behind a large, impressive desk.

"Welcome to Quintawba," he said as he stopped a few feet from Danny and stuck out his hand. He was a tall, slim man, several inches taller than Danny, with black hair and a tanned face. He wore a charcoal suit and a white, open-collar shirt. "I'm Julky Hinderthal, director of CARET. I trust you had a trouble-free trip?"

"Uh, yes. Yes, it was fine, thanks."

"Have a seat, please," Julky said as he motioned to one of the chairs flanking the sofa and took a seat in the other. Danny obliged and let out a sizable exhale. "You seem a bit on edge. Is there a problem?"

"Oh, uh no, not at all. I'm just a little uncomfortable in these situations."

"Uncomfortable? I know the PUPCO ACUSA program is new, but I would have expected you to be experienced at interacting with and study-ing alien cultures. You are a sociologist, correct?"

"I am, but I've never been in a situation quite like this one. Plus, I'm a bit nervous about tonight's plans. As you said, I'm a sociologist. I'm not used to that type of attention." Danny replied with an effort to look Julky in the eyes.

"So, Tavit, tell me a little about yourself."

Danny froze. It was time for his presentation. He still needed time to catch his breath, so he decided to redirect.

"What is it you'd like to know?" he managed to utter.

"What's your background?"

"It depends on where I'm standing," Danny replied. From the moment the words left his mouth, he wished he could reel them back in. He made a mental note to thrash Shey . . . if he ever saw him again.

Julky furrowed his brow and looked a bit perplexed, or perhaps mad. Danny clenched. Julky's face softened and he let out a lengthy chuckle. "That's very good. I like that."

Danny exhaled loudly. "I'm so sorry. It just came out. It was very unprofessional."

"Not at all. Can I get you something to drink?"

"Water would be great," came the reply from Danny's dry, pasty mouth. He made a mental note to hug Shey when he saw him again. The ice had been broken. "I live in Ladifer, which is a large city in the Savimoor region in the country of Janrus, which is on the continent of Mullitan. I have a large, close-knit extended family, but I'm not yet married and have no children. My career has occupied much of my life for the past ten years."

"Balance, Mr. Nanby. Balance," Julky said as he handed Danny a glass.

"Excuse me?"

"Balance and moderation are the keys for a fulfilling, healthy existence. They are the motto by which Quintawbans live."

"That makes a lot of sense. And it's a good thing to know about Quintawba from a sociological perspective," Danny said. Julky's words of wisdom put Danny even more at ease. He was starting to feel like he was talking to Kingsley.

"So why did you become a sociologist?"

"When I was young, I was always intrigued by differences in people and cultures. Plus I loved to travel, and I loved to interact with beings, to really get to know their views, their customs and habits, just how they approach life in general. After school I worked on Calixum for a few years, but my real interest was in working with alien cultures, so I took a position with PUPCO. The thought of not only studying a culture but having input on what they can do to grow and improve is exciting." Danny didn't know where it was coming from, but he was on a roll.

"Well, it's certainly great that you have a passion for your work. I can see why you were selected for this program. I assume Director Batoosa forwarded you the agenda. We'll have lunch shortly with a handful of CARET executives, followed by a tour of the facility. Tonight will be a gala that will kick off ACUSA week. Tomorrow you'll have breakfast with the entire ACUSA team. That will be followed by a session with some media people. The people of Dralia are expecting you early afternoon."

"I need to talk to you about this schedule," Danny interjected.

"What about it?"

Danny took a deep breath, quickly reviewed what Kingsley had told him to say, and let loose. "I really appreciate your hospitality and being your guest of honor, but I'm not really cut out for that type of thing. I'm an observer, more along the lines of an academician or a scientist than a politician. I have no experience in public relations. We have people in the delegation who are designated as liaisons. It's their job and they are trained for it. I'm not. I'd hate to be presented as the face of the ACUSA delegation only to disappoint your people due to my lack of experience in those situations. At best I would be less than impressive. Worst case, I say or do the wrong thing and give your people doubts about the program. This is an important time for your planet. Do you really want to risk making a bad first impression by putting me in front of everyone?"

"You make a valid point, Tavit."

"Also, I have a personal reason for wanting to start my work immediately. My grandfather is very old and is failing. I was just visiting him on Calixum, which is why I traveled separately from the delegation. I'd like to return to Calixum as soon as possible. So, with your permission, my preference is to head directly to Dralia."

Julky looked pensively at Danny for several seconds. "You know, ever since we were selected for the ACUSA program, we've been excited for it to start. That's why we're having these events and balls. You are correct that the people trained for such matters should be the ones that participate. I too am close to my family and can understand your desire to be at your grandfather's side. Tavit, I like you. I like you and I trust you, and I'm going to allow you to begin your work this afternoon. But first, I would like you to have a quick lunch with our team."

"Yes, absolutely. And thank you for accommodating me."

"Certainly," replied Julky. "How long will your work in Dralia take?"

"Probably no more than a couple of days. It depends on how long it takes me to gather everything I need."

"I'll get you one of our communication devices so that we can keep in touch and track your whereabouts. As agreed to in our negotiations with

PUPCO, we will also supply you with a preloaded currency card. It should provide for your food and lodging during your stay. Is there anything else I can do for you?"

"No, sir. That's it. I really appreciate everything you're doing."

"Part of my job is to be accommodating and to do whatever is necessary to make sure this program is a success," Julky said as he rose from his chair and started toward the door. "If all goes well, I'll see you back here in a few days. Now let's get that lunch."

Julky led Danny down the hall to an elegant, glass-walled conference room. It was home to a twenty-foot-long, dark wood table surrounded by navy blue chairs. Two steel and crystal light fixtures hung above the table. Danny swallowed hard at the sight of the three men and three women seated along the far side, all dressed in very Earth-like business attire.

"Have a seat, Tavit," said Julky. He motioned to a chair opposite his team and took his own seat at the head of the table. "Everyone, this is Tavit Nanby, the ACUSA delegate from Calixum. His assignment is to spend some time in Dralia."

Danny's heart was racing as they all stared at him in silence. The mood was not light. Danny braced for the interrogation he feared.

"Dralia?" scoffed a large, red-faced man directly across from Danny. "Why in the world would you want to waste your time in Dralia? It's a small, unextraordinary town."

"Brankle!" Julky shouted. "Is that any way to greet our esteemed guest? Forgive Brankle's demeanor, Tavit. He's new to the world of diplomacy, and he doesn't trust PUPCO."

Brankle didn't soften his glare.

Danny inhaled and exhaled deeply. "That's perfectly understandable, given what your planet has recently been through. It's often a shock to learn aliens have been among you for some time," Danny said, looking directly at Brankle. "To answer your question, in order to determine if Quintawba is ready for the ACUSA program, PUPCO wants to learn about your planet from its people, not just from literature or presentations. And it wants to learn from people in all cultures, of all races, from all types of environments and socioeconomic levels. Dralia was targeted as a typical, rural small town."

"Mr. Nanby, I'm Yarta Peshkin. Welcome to Quintawba," said a young, red-headed woman on the far left. "So tell me, how many PUPCO representatives have been here without our knowledge? Were you one of them? Why should we trust PUPCO, and you, now?"

Danny glanced at Julky, who was still smiling.

"I can't tell you how many were here. I am not privy to that information. I can assure you that I was not here before today. Regarding trust, PUPCO is a respected organization dedicated to assuring that people from all planets live in peace while exchanging ideas and helping member planets when they are in need. The organization has no ulterior motives. I'm confident that your trust will quickly grow once you start working closely with PUPCO."

A woman to the right of Brankle chimed in. "So do you think you're superior to us? That you're superior beings? That we're your science project?"

"Not at all. We're all the same. We have just acquired more knowledge than Quintawbans to this point. Every civilization is at a different point in its development and evolution. Having more knowledge doesn't make a species superior. We're excited to share what we know . . . with permission of course . . . in order to help you in any way we can."

Danny was on a roll. He spoke confidently, with nary a crack or waver in his voice.

"Everyone, lunch has arrived," Julky said as several servers poured into the room and placed plates of sandwiches and salads in front of the group.

As everyone started eating, the group continued to pepper Danny with questions about his job, his family, his home planet, and the ACUSA program. Julky stepped in and deflected some. Danny handled the rest perfectly. The mood in the room slowly softened—so much so that Danny's mild attempts at humor even generated some laughs.

After lunch everyone wished him well, and Julky led him from the room.

"Excellent job, Tavit," he said as they strolled down the hall. "I think you might be better at diplomacy than you think. Perhaps with a little more experience you'll move into a higher-profile role with PUPCO."

"Perhaps. I like my job, though. I'm ready to visit Dralia. I do have one other request. I've heard so much about the beauty of Mount Nobistad. I know it's near Dralia. I'd like to make a short stop at the mountain to see it up close."

"Of course, let's get you on your way."

"I'm getting tired just watching you. Sit down already," said Shey. He and Vicki were sitting at the living room island.

Kingsley ignored his request and continued pacing around the kitchen. "How do you think he's doing?"

"No idea . . . but wearing out the kitchen floor isn't going to help him."

"I know, I know. How do you feel, princess?" Kingsley asked.

"I'm okay. A little woozy perhaps," she replied as she took a sip from her glass of white wine.

"With everything you've been going through it may be best if you avoid the effects of too much alcohol."

"I agree. I'll take it easy."

"How about some entertainment? Perhaps a short video before dinner? Gracie, what's Brisby up to?" Kingsley asked. His query was followed by the room's lighting being lowered and the main view screen coming to life. The three of them settled in for the show.

Marsha Flondike stopped digging through her earring box and stared at her husband. After twenty-three years of marriage, he still occasionally managed to make her weak-kneed.

"Did you hear me?" asked Marsha as she refocused on finding her earrings.

"Hear what? Wow, you look fantastic. Great dress."

"Thank you. I said I'm really worried about Brisby. He's been a bit preoccupied and disconnected lately."

"Oh, honey, there's nothing to worry about. He's a teenager. He's just going through normal teenage stuff."

"It may be normal, but I'm not so sure I like it. It's been a few weeks now."

"Okay, okay. I'll tell you what. After I get back from the club tomorrow, we'll sit down and have a serious discussion with him. Like I said, we really have to get going."

Appeased but still uneasy, Marsha gave up on finding the perfect earrings and settled for her second choice. Despite Graham's insistence that she join him in the lift, she stopped at a closed door and touched the illuminated panel to its right.

"Brisby, honey, we're leaving for the evening. Are you okay?"

Her query was met with silence.

"Come on, Marsha," said a perturbed Graham. "He's fine. Let's go."

"Brisby, make sure you eat something, and don't stay up too late."

Marsha finally gave in to Graham's pleading. As she turned to join him on the lift, she heard the door slide open behind her.

"Hey, Mom," said a smiling Brisby as he emerged from his room. "I had my music pretty loud."

"Honey, how many times have a told you? You going to ruin your hearing doing that."

"I know. I know. You guys look great."

"Thanks, sweetie. Brisby, what's been bothering you? You know we give you a lot of space, but I'm starting to worry."

Brisby looked at the floor before answering. "Nothing, really. It's just . . . it's just that I've kind of had this crush on this girl for a long time, and she finally started paying attention to me and, I haven't been real happy with how it's been going. I'm kind of tongue-tied around her."

Marsha turned to Graham, who had returned from the lift. "I guess you were right, honey, normal teenage stuff," she sighed.

"What say we have a chat about it when I get back from golfing tomorrow afternoon? I'll tell you how I wooed your mother," Graham said as he tousled Brisby's floppy mass of dark brown hair.

"Sounds good, Dad. You guys have fun tonight."

"Are you doing anything, dear?" asked a relieved Marsha.

"Marsha, we've really got to be going," said Graham as he again attempted to exit.

"Kevin and Baylen are coming over to watch the match. That's about it."

"Okay, see you later," said Marsha as she pecked him on the check and joined her husband on the lift. Within minutes they were being whisked away to sip cocktails, laugh politely, and be seen without appearing dreadfully bored at what anyone who was anyone considered to be the social event of the season, the Wanderwill Ball at the Pinclucker Center for the Arts.

CHAPTER 24

"How much longer to the mountain, Max?"

Danny was enjoying the trip. Once he cleared the urban environment and was rolling through the countryside, with Abby curled up in the chair beside his, he relaxed. The flat terrain and the massive fields of what looked like wheat, rippling in the breeze, made him feel as if he were back in Ohio. Being alone in the silence gave him time to reflect. He felt good, even great, about what he had accomplished and who he had become. The tight, trembling mass of fear, dread, and insecurity had transformed into a centered, calm, confident . . . man.

"About fifteen minutes to the park entrance," said Max. His voice had a soothing, sophisticated tone.

"Park? What park?"

"Mount Nobistad is in the Dashmorp Reserve. It's what you would think of as a national park."

Danny soon saw Mount Nobistad in the distance. And what a site it was. Thousands of crystal deposits imbedded in the rock, coupled with the brilliant sunshine, caused the mountain to shimmer and glisten in a dazzling array of colors. It reminded Danny of looking into a kaleidoscope.

"Oh my God, Max. That's amazing. It looks like the whole mountain is crystal."

"The park's network site indicates that approximately eight percent of the mountain's surface is exposed crystal."

"Still, eight percent. How are we going to find the karbolite?"

"The site indicates that karbolite is the least abundant crystal in the mountain, with only one large deposit."

After coasting along for several more minutes, the park entrance was in sight. Danny took several deep breaths and told himself to remain nonchalant as he pulled up to the booth. A uniformed gentleman sat staring at a screen and didn't appear to notice him. Danny sat quietly for several seconds and was preparing to say something when the man finally came to life.

"Welcome to Dashmorp Reserve. Twenty-eight credits please," the man said as he held out his hand while slowly looking up and down the length of the Star Hopper. "This thing new?"

"Fairly new. Why?"

"It's just that I haven't seen anything like it before, and now I've seen two in the same day. The other one wasn't quite as big but looked a lot like this."

"There was another? What did the person driving it look like?"

"It was an older guy, probably in his early seventies, with dark hair. Looked like he hadn't shaved for a few days. Real nice guy. A woman was with him. Said she was his daughter."

Dank and Dr. Falstaff. Danny wondered if they were still in the park. He couldn't face Dank alone. He'd have to take off and get back to the ship.

"What time did they come in?"

"Oh, it was probably around ten this morning."

"Do you know if they're still here?"

"They left around noon. Why? Do you know them?"

"No. I was just curious who else might have a transport like this. Thanks for everything," Danny said as he pulled away from the booth. "Six hours behind Dank, girl. That's exciting . . . and kind of scary. Let's see if we can find a clue about where he went and get out of here."

Danny surveyed his surroundings. He had been so caught up in his conversation with the guard that he hadn't paid much attention to the massive, sparkling mountain looming before him. The relatively flat area around the entrance was covered with long, waving grasses, wildflowers, and a sprinkling of old, massive trees. Once he was a couple of miles from the gate, he hit foothills, and the terrain became much more rugged. Rocky outcroppings and boulders flanked the winding, uphill road. Over the next few miles, the road alternated between flat stretches that wound through groves of pines and uphill climbs that were framed by walls of rock from which spilled more colorful deposits of wildflowers. Danny's excitement grew as the transport climbed the mountain.

"Slow down, Bob," said a fussy Val Cheznik from the backseat of the Grugpod DL300. "The last thing we need is to be pulled over by Quintawban security. I want to do this quietly."

Bob Montgomery, who was driving the transport toward the Dashmorp Reserve, scoffed at his captain's wish. "Who cares? If they pull us over, I'll blast them, and we'll be on our way."

"I care, that's who cares," bellowed Val.

Karen Simpson, the other front seat occupant, cringed. She hated it when Val yelled. Val took a deep breath.

"I'm sorry, Bob. I'm not myself today. I guess I'm getting a little tired of this whole thing. Normally, I wouldn't care, but Quintawba is a high-profile planet right now. PUPCO is watching what goes on here very closely. We're not exactly hard to pick out of a lineup. If PUPCO hears that we've been here wreaking havoc a day or two before their delegation arrives, they might come after us with a zeal and determination we've not seen before. And I don't need that. I want to finish this one and retire."

Bob and Karen exchanged stunned looks. "What? What do you mean, retire?" asked Karen. "You said you weren't going to retire until the end of the year."

"I know I did, but I don't think I have another ten months of this in me. My tank is empty."

"But what will we all do?" she exclaimed. Karen, like the rest of Val's crew, had been with him for years. However, it was more than career concerns that caused her reaction. She and Val had carried on a short, passionate affair several years before, and she still carried a torch for him. His retirement would mean that she would probably never see him again.

"I'll write letters of recommendation for each of you, which should help you find work on another ship," replied Val.

"Thanks, Val," said Bob. "I can understand you wanting to hang it up and spend time with your family. A letter would be great. Looks like we're getting close to the signal. There's security at the entrance to the reserve. What should I do?"

"You know what to do," Val sighed.

As the sleek transport pulled up to the entrance gate, the guard looked up. "Not another one. Hey. Can you lower your window, please?" He held his hand above his eyes and squinted in an attempt to see something through the heavily tinted glass. The driver's window quietly dropped, as did the guard's jaw.

"You seem a bit surprised," said Bob. "Have you never seen a Grugnok?"

"I . . . I . . . uh . . . no, I guess not," the guard replied. He glanced down to make sure his weapon was within reach and to determine how far his hand was from the emergency button.

"Tell me, has another vehicle like ours recently entered the park?"

"Uh, yes. About a half an hour ago." The guard was still trying to get his mind around the fact that he was carrying on a discussion with what looked like a creature that should be living in a swamp.

"How many beings were in it?"

"Just the driver. At least, that's all I saw."

"And could you describe him, please."

"He was a nice-looking young man, probably around thirty, with light brown hair."

"Thank you. You've been most helpful," said Bob as he nonchalantly lifted a weapon from his lap and fired. A small white beam hit the guard and sent him slumping to the ground. Bob jumped from the Grugpod, made sure the limp body was tucked under the counter, and messed with some controls until the sign outside the booth changed from Park Open to Park Closed.

"He should be out for at least a couple hours," Bob said before scanning the area for witnesses, climbing back behind the wheel, and heading off in search of the signal.

"I have Director Batoosa from ACUSA on the line."

"Put it through," said Julky as he put down his mug and swiveled toward his monitor just in time to see the kindly face of the white-haired Ira Batoosa.

"Director Batoosa. Your call is unexpected. Is there a problem?"

"No problem. I just wanted to touch base and make certain everything is ready for the delegation's arrival."

"Everything is going as planned. The excitement level is high among our population. We're anxiously awaiting the arrival of the rest of the delegation."

"Wonderful. I'm sure it . . . excuse me, did you say the rest of the delegation?" A look of concern clouded Ira's face.

"Yes. Everyone in addition to Mr. Nanby."

"Mr. Nanby?"

"Yes. Tavit Nanby. He arrived earlier today and has started his work."

"Mr. Hinderthal, Tavit Nanby is on the ship that is en route to Quintawba. I saw him board it with the rest of the delegation. Now what exactly are you talking about?"

Julky's mind and pulse were racing as he leaned forward in his chair. "I received a U-mail from you that said Tavit Nanby would be traveling separate from the delegation. It said he was coming directly here from Calixum and asked if he could start his research upon arrival. He was here earlier today. He's now on his way to Dralia to begin his work."

"This is Tavit Nanby," Ira said as a picture filled the screen.

"That's not the person who was here."

"And I don't suppose you have any recorded images of this man?"

"I do not."

"It appears that you've been deceived. I would expect better security measures from a planet so eager to achieve a higher CUSTAR. I'd like to know why someone is impersonating one of my delegation. I'd suggest you find this imposter and, when you do, hold him for questioning by our team."

"Certainly, Mr. Director. We will track him down and detain him. I hope this doesn't affect the program."

"I hope not as well. Goodbye."

The moment Ira Batoosa's image faded, Julky yelled for his assistant.

"We need to find Tavit Nanby. Immediately."

The assistant pecked away at his keyboard before responding. "The signal is coming from the Dashmorp Reserve. It appears he is on Mount Nobistad."

"Send two teams of our security people to retrieve Mr. Nanby. Tell them this is urgent, top secret, and that he may try to elude them. Or even become hostile."

"Are we close, Emma?" asked Danny as he pushed aside branches belonging to the dense cluster of pines through which he had been walking.

"The deposit is twenty-five yards ahead, at a forty-degree angle to the right of the direction you are currently facing."

Danny fought through another group of particularly dense branches, bursting through them and falling onto his hands and knees. He found himself in a small clearing with the karbolite deposit imbedded in the mountainside about ten yards ahead. He dropped his head to catch his breath, but what he saw made him hold it instead. Footprints. Lots and lots of footprints. There were clearly two sets, one much larger than the other. Their pattern showed that the people that left them had walked toward the karbolite and then back into the pines. Danny tensed and felt a rush of adrenaline as he thought about the fact that Dank and Dr. Falstaff had been at that exact spot only a few hours earlier.

"Looks like we found it, Ab," Danny said. Abby had an easier time getting through the pines than Danny, but she still had needles clinging to her fur. A vigorous shake got rid of most of them.

After pushing himself up and brushing off the dirt and pine needles, Danny approached the crystal while surveying the area for clues. As he neared the deposit, the pattern of the footprints changed. The smaller set veered to the left, about fifteen feet from the deposit.

"Looks like Jillian Falstaff kind of stood over here watching. She may have been nervous. Looks like she was moving back and forth a little, but all of the prints point in the general direction of the crystal."

Danny then followed the larger set up to the face of the mountain, where he found a sharp-edged depression in the deposit. The prints then turned away from the wall and made a straight line toward the cluster of smaller prints.

"Okay. So, Dr. Falstaff stands over there and waits while Dank blasts off some karbolite. He then brings it over to her, and she reads the Quontal that appeared when they placed it on the tablet. Now we have to look for clues she left."

Danny approached the mountainside and examined the wall for twenty feet on each side of the deposit. He found nothing he considered a clue, so he made a back-and-forth sweep of the entire clearing, looking for anything unusual on the ground. When nothing turned up, he decided to make his way around the perimeter, starting to the right of the deposit and going clockwise, to look for anything hanging on a tree branch or lying on a bush. He once again came up empty.

"I can't find anything, Ab," Danny said as he took a seat on a small, flat boulder to the left of the deposit. Abby was curled up, basking in the sun, a short distance away.

"Emma, now what?"

"I have no suggested course of action at this point."

Danny sighed as he put his chin in his right hand and decided to blast off a piece of karbolite and look for clues on the path back to the transport. As he was getting up, he noticed a short line of the footprints that moved from the cluster facing the karbolite toward a group of small bushes and back again. Danny lifted the lowest branches to find a small silver device, about the size of a credit card and just as thin. It had several buttons below a screen.

"Emma, I found something!"

Danny hit what he guessed was the play button and held the device closer.

"We don't need a very large piece of the karbolite," said a woman's voice.

"I know what we need," came a male reply.

Danny hit the pause button and stared at the device in amazement. "Oh my God, Emma! This is Dank and Jillian Falstaff. It's actually Dank's voice! She must have thrown this thing into the bushes before they left." He leapt to his feet with his heart pounding wildly and hit the button again.

"I just don't want to take any more than we have to. They consider this mountain and its crystals to be sacred."

"Dr. Falstaff, I appreciate that you're trying to preserve some silly superstition for the Quintawbans, but I, quite honestly, don't care."

"Silly superstition, Mr. Nebitol? Kind of like a mystical tablet that tells you how to make an amulet that will boost your charisma?"

"That, doctor, is my silly superstition. What I'm saying is that I don't care about theirs. Here's the crystal. Put it on the tablet and tell me what it says."

There was silence for nearly a minute before the female voice spoke. "It says that the next required crystal is albatarum from the Branora Canyon on Endoophar."

"The Branora Canyon?" Dank asked. "Isn't that a forbidden area?"

"Yes, it is. It's considered a sacred spiritual location with many caves in which a large number of rulers were laid to rest centuries ago, along with their treasures."

"Great," said Dank with disgust. "Another spiritual place we have to get into. Why are all these crystals in spiritual places?"

"It makes sense," Dr. Falstaff replied calmly. "If they have mystical properties, it isn't surprising they are found in places the natives consider special."

"It may make sense, but I'm losing my patience. This is becoming more difficult and taking longer than I had anticipated. Endoophar is probably two or three days away. The satisfaction election is in three weeks. I've got to get back and get into the public eye. Let's get back to the ship."

Danny heard the faint rustle of tree branches and then silence. He hit the stop button and sat back on the rock. He looked around the clearing and visualized the scene he had just heard. "Let's head back to the Hopper, girl."

"You are supposed to get a sample of karbolite," said Emma.

"Oh yeah. I almost forgot." Danny walked over to the deposit, put the MR5 on the correct setting, and pointed it at the crystal. He cut out a piece and began fighting his way through the pines, over and around several groups of boulders and then through the less densely treed area that led to where he had pulled off the road. The moment Danny caught sight of the transport, he froze. Another vehicle, similar to but smaller than the Star Hopper, was parked directly behind it in a position that would prevent Danny from leaving. As he cleared the trees and moved closer to the vehicles, he heard no one and saw no one. Danny stood by the back of the Star Hopper, trying to figure out how he could leave.

"Where the hell are they?" he yelled.

"Are you looking for us?" came a voice from behind him.

Danny spun and was stunned by the sight of three creatures emerging from the trees to his right. They were thick-bodied, square-headed beings with leathery, crusty, greenish-brown skin and tiny red eyes. Each had on dark red, loose-fitting, long-sleeved shirts and black pants with wide belts that carried several small devices. The device Danny focused on immediately was the silver item on each creature's right hip which looked exactly like the MR5 he had carried on the previous excursions. They looked rather beastly, but the uniforms and clear diction of the speaker told Danny they were intelligent. One was about Danny's size, while the other two were much more imposing, surpassing his mass by a substantial amount and his height by a few inches.

"Perhaps you didn't hear me. I asked if you were looking for us?"

Danny thought of making a dash for the Star Hopper, but they were close enough that they would probably catch him or shoot him before he made it in and got the door closed. Even if he made it into the transport, he wouldn't be able to contact Kingsley. He remembered Abby at his side but doubted she would be much good against three heavily armed lizards.

"Uh, yes, sir. Yes, sir, I am if this vehicle belongs to you," Danny managed to utter through his tightened throat.

"You look like you've lost your color, young man. Have you never seen a Grugnok before?"

Grugnok. Danny immediately remembered Kingsley's description of the species. "No, sir, I haven't. But yes, you certainly did startle me."

"I do apologize. My name is Val Cheznik," he said as Karen and Bob fanned out to each side. "And you are?"

"I, um . . . I'm Tavit, Tavit Nanby. From the planet Calixum."

"Tavit Nanby. Interesting. What is it I can do for you?"

"I, uh, I was finished with my sightseeing and wanted to leave, so I was hoping you could move your transport."

"I see. Well, I'm sorry to say we can't do that just yet," replied Val as he stopped within ten feet of Danny and began a slow stroll to the left, stopping briefly to glance at Abby. "You see, we're also looking for you."

"You are? What in the world for?" Danny's voice trembled slightly, a fact that was not missed by Val.

"An excellent question," he said as he stopped and faced Danny. Val was tired of many aspects of his job, but playing with a target was not one of them. "Bob, why would a young man calling himself Darkus Murmak from Emulox pay a visit to Durbin Carbindale's cave and then travel three days to visit a mountain?"

"I don't know, Val. It does seem odd. Maybe he's on vacation and visiting the natural wonders of the universe?"

"Perhaps. But if so, why would he use an alias? Didn't your exhaustive search on the U-net turn up only a handful of Darkus Murmaks on Emulox, none of whom was close in age or appearance to the young man standing before us?"

"Yes, I believe you're right."

"And now he is Tavit Nanby from Calixum."

Val moved closer to Danny, stopping just three feet away before looking down at the karbolite in his left hand. Danny held his breath as Val's laser-like red eyes looked directly into his. "So tell me, young man, why would someone use an alias and tell Durbin Carbindale that he needed to find an earlier visitor in order to save an entire civilization?"

"I made all that up. I just wanted to visit his cave."

"You know what? I don't believe you. No one would pay that sum of money just to see a cave, and there is nothing mystical about Durbin's marzical."

"I was told there was. Maybe he doesn't know."

"And your reaction upon hearing the other visitor's name? What was it, Karen?"

"Ben Kindolta."

"Yes, Ben Kindolta. Durbin said you had a strong reaction upon hearing his name."

"He's my uncle. I was just surprised he had already been there. We must have gotten our signals crossed. I didn't realize he was also going after the marzical for my mother."

"And your real name is?"

"Tavit Nanby."

Val chuckled. "Okay. If you want me to call you that, I'll call you that . . . for now. We also found no one with the name Ben Kindolta who could have been at Carbindale's estate. And you're traveling in a QC 900. You don't act like someone who would own a QC 900. Who are you traveling with? Who owns that ship?"

"I do. It's mine."

"I'm afraid I don't believe that either. Aliases, fabricated stories, large sums of money to see a worthless crystal. And now you've got another piece of crystal, which you've obviously extracted from this mountain." Val moved another step closer as his voice turned less amicable. "My fifty years of experience tell me that you have an interesting story to tell us. I'd like to hear it."

"What I told Durbin is the truth."

Val shook his head, put his thick-fingered hands behind his back, and walked several paces away from Danny. "In that case, you're going to be a guest aboard our ship until you share your true mission. Once you do that, we'll negotiate for your return with the owner of your ship. Hopefully, for your sake, they are very fond of you. Bob, please render our friend unconscious and carry him to our transport."

The other large Grugnok removed the weapon from his belt and stepped forward. Danny was slightly startled to feel the Star Hopper against his back. He hadn't realized he had been slowly backing up as the weapon-wielding Grugnok approached. As Bob stopped and took aim, Danny took a quick look up in the hope that Kingsley and Shey were descending from the sky to save him. He looked in the wrong direction.

A soft glow began radiating from near the front wheel of the Star Hooper. Danny turned to see it was coming from Abby. The glow emanated from under her fur, became more intense, and soon expanded to the point that her shape was no longer visible. The brilliant, golden mass of light slowly but steadily grew to at least twelve feet high, at which point it became less intense and began to solidify. In a matter of seconds a giant creature that looked like a cross between a dinosaur and a gorilla took shape. It had crusty gray skin, enormous arms, and an intelligent but displeased look on its massive face. As the light disappeared, the group stared in shock, each trying to get their mind around what they just witnessed and to decide their next move.

"Drop your weapons," boomed the giant. Bob Montgomery let go of his as if it had suddenly scalded his hand. Val and Karen quickly pulled theirs from their belts and threw them down.

The giant looked down, took a step toward a trembling Val Cheznik, reached down, picked him up by his neck, and lifted him to eye level. "Abort your mission. Now."

"Yes . . . yes, of course . . . immediately," Val said as best he could with his neck being squeezed. "Everyone back to the transport." He didn't need to say it. Bob and Karen were already scrambling for their vehicle. The beast walked over and set Val down next to the door. He fell down in his hurry to climb in.

Once the Grugpod was zooming back down the road so fast that it almost careened over the edge, the giant turned and looked down at a speechless Danny. It gave Danny a gentle smile, and his form quickly changed back to brilliant light, shrank back to its original size, and reformed as Abby. Danny blinked rapidly and stared at her as she dropped to the ground and started licking herself.

"Well, girl," he said slowly. "I guess we should make that call to Julky and get out of here."

Danny gathered himself and pulled the CARET communication device from his pocket. After looking round to make sure the bizarre happenings hadn't drawn the attention of any curious locals, he called Julky.

"Mr. Nanby. What can I do for you?"

"Mr. Hinderthal, something has come up."

"You sound out of breath. Are you okay?"

"I'm fine. Just winded from hiking. The reason I'm calling is that I've received a message from Calixum that my grandfather has taken a severe turn for the worse. I'd like to see him before he passes if at all possible."

"Well, that's understandable."

"I'd like to head back to Calixum immediately, which unfortunately means I'll need to stop my research before it gets started."

"I'm sorry to see you leave, but if you have to go, you have to go."

"Thank you, Mr. Hinderthal. My plan is to depart from my current location if that's okay with you."

"Our tracking system shows that you are deep in the park, part of the way up the mountain."

"That's correct."

"Mount Nobistad is a very peaceful, spiritual place that draws many visitors. I would prefer that their experience not be tainted by a spaceship lifting off from the mountainside. My only request is that you exit the park and drive a few miles away before departing."

"Sure. I can do that."

"Excellent. It was good meeting you, Tavit."

"Thanks. You too. Bye." Danny terminated the call, gave a small fist pump, hopped into the Hopper, and directed Max to leave the park while keeping a close, wary eye on Abby. As the transport headed down the winding mountain road, Danny basked in peaceful satisfaction and took in the beauty of the majestic pines, smooth boulders, and glistening crystal deposits.

He was most of the way down the mountain when he came to a lightly treed area that afforded him a sweeping view of the reserve between the mountain and the entrance.

Sitting at the entrance gate were two large, black vehicles. Two men were looking in and around the security booth.

"Max, can your scans reach the park entrance from here?"

"They can."

"What can you tell me about those trucks sitting there?"

"They are the vehicles used by several Quintawban security agencies, including CARET. There are two beings in the first, four in the second, and two more outside the vehicles."

"Do you think they are looking for me?"

"That is entirely possible."

"Great. They must have figured out that I'm an imposter. Max, can the Star Hopper take off from here?"

"It can."

"Any chance Quintawban aircraft can catch me?"

"My long-range scans do not detect any military aircraft in the area. However, there is no reason to be concerned. The Star Hopper is faster than any Quintawban craft, and their weapons would not be able penetrate our shields."

"Great. Open the door," Danny said as he jumped up, headed to the door of the transport, and threw the CARET communication device into the trees beside the road before retaking his seat. "Now, let's get the hell out of here."

Val Cheznik was fuming. He didn't like being embarrassed, especially in front of his crew. "A Calizian. Durbin sent us after someone who is traveling with a fucking Calizian!" he yelled has he banged his fist against the back window of the Grugpod.

"I'm sure he didn't know," Karen said gingerly. "He would never do that and risk your reaction."

Val tried to regain his composure. "Probably not, but you know what? He's going to get a reaction. I've been wanting to pulverize that little twit for years now. This may not be a good reason, but it's reason enough. I've wasted three days following that kid! And for what? We don't even know if he was after anything we'd want, and I'm out 250,000 U-bucks. We're heading to Dabita Bok to pay Durbin Carbindale a visit. By the time I'm done with him, he'll be more than happy to give me my money back."

"Val, I know you're angry," said Karen. "But if you do what you're saying, word will spread, and no one will want to do business with you."

"I don't care. I'm retiring, remember?"

"Are you sure we don't want to regroup and take another shot at Darkus

Murmak?" Bob chimed in.

Val shook his head with disgust. "Shut up and drive, Bob. The Calizian isn't going to let us touch him."

The group rode along in silence: Bob Montgomery thinking about what to have for dinner, Karen Simpson fondly recalling her fling with her captain, and Val Cheznik dreaming of how to make Durbin pay.

———————

"Danny. Danny."

Danny stirred slowly at first, rolling his head back and forth, and then quickly opened his eyes and sat upright. "What is it, Max? What happened? Are we under attack?"

"We are not under attack. You fell asleep shortly after we left the Quintawban atmosphere. You asked me to let you know when we were in communication range of the *Aurora*. The EZ-Comm can be used now. Would you like to call the ship?"

"Yes. Absolutely. Give me a minute to wake up."

Danny rubbed his face and got his bearings. The departure from Quintawba had gone flawlessly. Once free and clear, Danny had let his guard down and crashed. He felt tremendously refreshed from the hour of sleep and was immediately energized by the thought of being safely back in the *Aurora* with . . . with his new family. He couldn't wait to see them all.

"Danny? Did it go okay?" Kingsley asked.

"Hey, Kingsley," Danny said calmly. "No, it didn't go okay. It was damn near perfect! And I've got the location of the next crystal!"

A cheer erupted from the *Aurora*.

"Fantastic!" Kingsley said.

"The only problem was that some Grugnok found me."

"Grugnok? What? Where? What happened?" asked Kingsley.

"A small group of them confronted me on the mountain after I got the karbolite. They knew everything I had told Durbin. They were going to knock me out and take me back to their ship when Abby turned into this huge monster thing and they took off. What the heck is she?"

"I'll explain when you get back. The important thing is you're okay. We can't wait to hear about the rest of the excursion. See you soon."

For the rest of the trip, Danny reflected on everything that had happened on Quintawba. He shook his head in disbelief as he thought about how he had traveled to a planet alone, persuaded Julky to let him go to Dralia, masterfully handled the CARET executives' questions, somewhat fearlessly explored the mountain, found the karbolite and the recorder, and dealt with a group of nasty reptiles . . . all while avoiding a major anxiety attack.

"I kicked ass, Max."

"Emma filled me in on what I missed. Yes, I believe you did."

Before long Danny saw the *Aurora* in the distance. In a few minutes he was stepping out of the Star Hopper and into the garage.

"There's our mission lead!" Kingsley shouted. Cheers went up from the group as Kingsley moved in and gave Danny a firm bear hug. Shey was close behind to shake his hand and slap him on the back. Before Danny's hand was even free, Vicki swept in and hugged him.

"You said you got the karbolite. Did you find any evidence Dank had been there?" Shey asked.

"That's the best part. The guard at the entrance to the park said that a couple who sounded like Dank and Dr. Falstaff entered the park about eight hours before me and were only there for a couple hours." Danny tossed the karbolite sample to Shey. "Yes, I found the karbolite—and I think you could say I found a clue about where they're going."

"Smugness," Shey said. "Something we've not previously seen from him. Next thing you know, he'll be arrogant."

"Well, what is it?" Kingsley asked.

Danny pulled the device from his pocket and held it up like a trophy. "It's a recorder! I found it in the bushes near the karbolite. It's got the entire conversation between them, including Jillian Falstaff saying where the next ingredient is."

"Danny, that's fantastic! We may be able to catch up to them on the next planet. Where are they going?"

"Endoophar. It told them to go to the Branora Canyon on Endoophar for . . . for . . . I can't remember the name of the crystal. Listen."

Danny played the recording for the group. Kingsley interrupted before it had finished.

"Gracie, take us to Endoophar. Top speed."

"So how did the Grugnok find me?"

"That's a good question. Durbin must have placed a skin sensor on you. Did he touch you?"

Danny thought for a moment. "When I got back from the cave. He shook my hand before I left."

"Gracie, scan Danny's right hand for anything foreign."

"I detect a small sensor film attached to his palm."

Danny stared at his right hand. "What? Can we get it out?" he yelled.

"Relax, sport," said Shey. "I can remove it in the medlab. Gracie, check the Solo Trek he took to Dabita. Durbin would've had a contingency plan in case he couldn't get the skin sensor on you."

"There is a tracking device on the underside of the Solo Trek."

"I'll get that one too," Shey said.

"Are they still tracking us?"

"The Grugnok saw Abby's abilities. They aren't going to continue to pursue us. My guess is that they are headed back to Dabita Bok to visit Durbin. Go to the medlab with Shey, get cleaned up, and we'll reconvene in the living room."

CHAPTER 25

"So, DANNY, let's hear the details of what transpired on Quintawba," Kingsley said as he picked up an appetizer with one hand and his wine glass with the other. "Wait. First, a toast. To another tremendously successful excursion, orchestrated perfectly by the newest sensation in the searcher world, Danny Kerrigan."

Kingsley, Shey, and Vicki leaned forward and touched glasses. Danny, who was already oozing confidence, felt his pride swell even more upon hearing Kingsley's compliment.

"Well, thanks, but it wasn't that difficult. You guys planned it and told me what to say and everything. Julky was really nice and easy to talk to. I told him everything we talked about . . . about how I wasn't cut out for the diplomacy and we want his people to get a good first impression. He bought it all. And the story about my grandfather. He really liked that."

"And the meeting with his team?"

"Well, they were a little intimidating, but it wasn't too bad. They kind of grilled me, but I didn't panic. Julky said afterwards that I was great."

"Fantastic. And you had no trouble finding the karbolite?"

"Not at all," Danny replied. "But I was having trouble finding any kind of clue until I looked closely at the fresh footprints. They led me to the recorder in the bushes."

"Great," Kingsley said. "Now, tell me everything that happened at the Carbindale estate while the EZ-Comm was off."

Danny was about to sip his beer. He froze.

"With Durbin? Why?" he asked without looking up from his mug.

"Why?" Shey interjected. "Because it's obvious that Carbindale put the device on the Solo Trek while you were at the cave, put the skin sensor on your hand before you left, made a deal with the Grugnok, and told them how to track you."

"I told him what you told me to tell him. I gave him the story about needing the marzical because it could heal my mom. He was reluctant, so I offered him the money."

"And then he agreed?" asked Kingsley.

"Yep," Danny replied as he stared back into his beer mug.

"I don't think so. The Grugnok have no sense of humor and do not appreciate being misled. Carbindale would not have brought them in because you needed marzical for your sick mother. What else did you tell him, Danny? We need to know. You are not going to get into trouble, if that's your concern."

Danny squirmed in his seat, took another hit from his drink, and looked at Shey, then Kingsley. Both were staring back with a look of unwavering expectation.

"Okay, okay. I told him more about the mission. I had to. He didn't buy the mother story, and he wasn't going to let me see the cave for just the money. He said that since two people in two days had offered him a lot of money to see it, he wouldn't let me go unless I told him the real reason. I figured if I didn't get to the cave, the mission might be over."

"What did you tell him, Danny?" Kingsley asked.

"I told him that a planet's civilization may depend on me seeing his cave, that an entire society may be harmed."

"Is that it?"

"No. I said I couldn't tell him any details, but he demanded more information, so I told him that I was trying find the guy who was there the day before. I mentioned that he stole something that I was trying to get back."

"I see. Did you mention Yoobatar?"

"No! I didn't give any details. I didn't say anything about you guys or Yoobatar or the Quilicants or the tablet or the amulet. What I just told you is everything I told him. I swear."

Kingsley took a sip from his drink.

"Well, that explains the Grugnok's appearance. Durbin probably does business with them. He knew that they would be interested in what you told him. The Grugnok love knowing about items of great value, particularly ones that have already been stolen. He probably contacted one of their ships, piqued their interest by telling them what you told him, and sold them the signature of the trackers for a handsome fee. Yes, Durbin has made out quite well in the past two days."

Danny had been braced for a tongue lashing and was a bit confused by Kingsley's reaction.

"You're awfully calm about it," he said. "I thought you'd be really pissed."

"Would you say that you did your best under the circumstances?"

"Absolutely."

"There you have it. You did your best. That's all we can ask for. You analyzed the situation and did what you thought was right, what was crucial to save the mission. You gave enough information to get Durbin to let you see the cave without giving any specifics. You showed guts, and you showed that you care about the mission. I like that. And I'm not so sure I wouldn't have done the same in the situation. So the Grugnok appearing was the only issue?"

"Not exactly. I think Julky figured out I wasn't actually part of the delegation. When I was leaving, two CARET security trucks were entering the reserve, so I took off from the mountain."

"Julky must have touched base with Ira Batoosa and found out that you were an imposter," Kingsley said.

"You don't think PUPCO is looking for us, do you?"

"I doubt it. Someone posing as an ACUSA member isn't a big enough deal for them to waste time on it. And besides, there is nothing that could lead them to us."

"So, about Abby. What the hell is she?"

"Abby is a Calizian."

"We've got two of those things traveling with us?"

"We do not."

"I don't understand. You said . . . are you saying that Shanna Var is Abby?"

"That would be correct."

Danny looked skeptically over at Abby, who was stretched out on the floor nearby.

"I'm not so sure I believe that."

"Shanna also has control over the shape, mass, density, and form of her energy. She, in essence, can turn herself into anything. She normally exists around me as Abby. It's an easy way for her to let me know she is present, to observe, and to travel with me. When she decides she wants to have a conversation, she transforms into the female form you met in my office.

"Okay, so if she's so powerful and can zip herself around the universe and take any form, why doesn't she just show up where Dank is, turn into that creature I saw, and take the tablet from him?"

"That would be great, but that's not the way she operates. She is an observer, advisor, mentor, and monitor. She only gives advice when she feels it is appropriate, and she very rarely influences a mission . . . overtly, that is. We can't count on her to do what we think would be the right course of action. She gets involved in situations at her own choice, not when I want or need her to. If I asked her to retrieve the tablet—something that would be incredibly simple for her—she'd laugh in my face."

Danny again looked at Abby and felt a bit of a bond. He felt privileged and grateful that she had stepped in to help him. "Endoophar sounds kind of familiar. Have you guys mentioned it before?"

"Yes, actually I have," replied Kingsley. "Endoophar is the planet of which my old friend Javo Jamison was the ruler for many years. We saw the UNN story about him not running for another term. We'll work on an Endoophar plan tomorrow. Tonight is just for celebration. Gracie, upbeat Sinatra. Mostly swing with a ballad now and then. But nothing sad. Danny, get yourself another beer."

The group proceeded to have the most relaxed, revelrous night since the mission began. As they sipped wine and dined on another of Shey's pizzas, Kingsley told stories, Shey told his version, they argued, and everyone laughed. Danny talked freely and at length, making his own jokes, telling them more about the excursion, describing his pathetic life on Earth, and regaling them with stories of many of the issue-related things that had happened over the years. But it wasn't done with sadness or shame. He was telling them in a detached, comical manner, like it was a past life that he would no longer be living, almost as if it was all something that had happened to someone else. Vicki contributed frequently, showing a playfulness and sense of humor that had previously not been on display.

Shortly after they had finished dessert, Vicki excused herself and retired for the evening. Danny was sorry to see her go but decided it might be a good time to ask Kingsley about their planned date. He didn't get the chance.

"So, Danny, I sense that you've become smitten with my daughter."

Danny tensed up and looked down at the table. "I . . . I don't know what you're talking about."

"I think you're lying."

"No, I'm not."

"Danny, if you are interested in Vicki and want my approval, lying to me is not a good way to start."

With head lowered, Danny struggled to answer. "Well, um, I don't know. I mean, you know . . . I guess I kind of like her, and she's kind of good-looking and everything."

"Expressed with all the eloquence of a ten-year-old with a playground crush. Look me in the eye and tell me your intentions, or I promise that you will have no chance of ever courting my daughter."

Danny slowly raised his head and cleared his throat. "I find your daughter to be very beautiful, nice, and interesting, and I'd like to ask her out."

Kingsley chuckled. "Ask her out? Out where? We're on a ship."

"You know what I mean. I'd like to . . . to get to know her better."

Kingsley looked suspicious. "Oh yes, I think I know exactly what you mean. You've got a lifetime of lust built up, and you want nothing more than to use her as a receptacle for your sperm."

"I do not! I just want to, you know, talk to her, go on a date without you two and Abby around. I was thinking maybe dinner tomorrow night. And I know she's interested in me. We've talked a lot already. We have some kind of connection."

"Let's say I believe you and that she was interested. Do you actually think you're good enough for her?"

Danny quickly turned slightly defiant. "Well, yes. I think I am."

"Oh, really. Let's examine your qualifications. What is it you do for a living?"

"I'm a senior support person for a software company," Danny stated proudly.

"And what is your annual income?"

"Seventy-five thousand," he said more proudly.

Kingsley obviously wasn't impressed. "And your prospects for significant improvements in your career and compensation?"

"Um, I don't know. I really haven't thought about it," Danny said less proudly. "Before this mission there probably wasn't much of a chance of that, but now I think there is."

"Well, that really doesn't matter anyway, since you probably aren't going back. So what is it you think you can do in this century that would give my daughter the lifestyle to which she is accustomed?"

"I don't know. There has to be something. Hey, wait. You're giving me a lot of money for the mission. We'll live off of that."

Kingsley scoffed. "That may support you living your lifestyle for thirty or forty years, but to support both of you, living her lifestyle? It may last ten."

"I'll bet she'd live more like me if she needed to, if she really liked me."

"Proposing that my daughter significantly downgrade her lifestyle hasn't won you any points, but let's move along. Let's talk about your ancestry. What did your parents do?"

"My dad was an accountant, and my mother worked at a travel agency."

"I see. Has there been any royalty on either side of your family?"

"No."

"Any heads of state, explorers, inventors, physicians, world-class athletes, renowned scientists, or pioneers in any field?"

"No, not that I know of."

"Anyone that's done anything exceptional at all?"

"Not that I know of."

"And then there is your personality. Given her nature, my daughter requires someone who is gregarious, assertive, decisive, opinionated, confident, and emotionally available. I dare say you fall a bit short in those categories."

Danny was getting a little perturbed. "Maybe a little, but I've gotten a lot better at all of those things in the past week, and I'm going to continue to improve."

"Yes, but not enough, I'm afraid. Perhaps you've got some other talents that my daughter may find appealing. Tell me about your carnal knowledge and past sexual experiences."

"Wait a minute. You want to know how good I'd be at having sex with your daughter?"

"Danny, on Yoobatar, sex is not a taboo subject. In fact, it's very important and is openly discussed. I'm just trying to find some quality that makes you worthy. Your past experiences?"

Danny was becoming sullen. "I really haven't had any."

"None?"

"None."

"I see. That's too bad. And your carnal knowledge?"

"I suppose most of what I know I've picked up from movies and magazines."

"Well, I suppose it's never too late to learn. Perhaps you have some, shall we say, raw potential. How big is your equipment?"

"Excuse me?"

"Your manhood. How big is it?"

"That would be none of your damned business."

"Okay. I guess you really aren't serious about courting my daughter. You see, I would need to know everything about a potential suitor before I even considered letting him near her."

"Okay. Fine. It holds its own, but it probably wouldn't stand out in a crowd."

"Well, that's okay, since I'm hoping Vicki won't ever find herself in a crowd of penises. But you're being much too general. What's the length and diameter when engorged?"

Danny was getting a little pissed. "I don't know. I've never had reason to measure it."

"Okay then, let's see it."

"Excuse me?"

"You heard me. Get that puppy out. Gracie, roll a few minutes of an erotic film from Sarangia. Those Sarangians have no inhibitions and are very creative. They have an uncanny ability to be innovative and slightly kinky without being distasteful. Once Danny is aroused, scan and measure him."

Danny had had enough. "That's it! I'm not talking any more about my manhood, I don't want to see any porn flicks, and I'm definitely not going to *get that puppy out*. Now knock it off!"

Kingsley looked reflective. "Well then, let's see. We've established that you are physically reasonably attractive, with a body that is in decent condition. On the flip side, you have almost no wealth, the job of a mental laborer with mediocre pay, no goals or prospects for achieving financial security, an unremarkable pedigree, a questionable personality, almost no carnal experience, and a penis that more than likely resembles a piece of used chewing gum. And you want to court my princess? I don't think so. Your qualifications fall woefully short, and I've heard nothing that convinces me that your intentions are honorable. Gracie, notify me immediately if Vicki and Danny are alone together in the same room for more than five minutes."

"Now wait a minute!" Danny yelled.

"What's the matter?" Kingsley asked.

"What's the matter? The matter is that this is all bullshit! What the hell difference does it make if there aren't any ambassadors or doctors in my family? I know she's your daughter, but I'm not asking you if I can marry her. We just want to spend a couple of hours alone together. We just want to talk and get to know each other better. All you need to know is that she's interested in me too and that I'm going to treat her right. It doesn't matter how much money I have or how fucking assertive I am. And by the way, we're both adults. I was going to ask you about this, but only because I thought it was the right thing to do. We could go off and spend time together without your approval. In fact, that's exactly what we're going to do. We won't be here for dinner tomorrow night, because we have a date. Go ahead, tell Gracie to zap the crap out of me." Danny grabbed his half-full beer, chugged the contents, and slammed it down.

"But if your intent isn't to marry her, then what's the point of spending time with her or getting to know her better?"

"What's the point? Haven't you been listening to yourself this entire freaking mission? The point is to connect with her, to share thoughts and concerns and interests, to bond with her. I think we've done it some already, and you know what? I really liked it. It made me feel alive, and I think it raised my vibration. What the hell are you two smiling about?"

Kingsley chuckled. "I think he passed. Don't you, Shey?"

"With flying colors."

"What are you talking about?"

"I was testing you, Danny. I wanted to see if you would stand up for yourself if I grilled you. You've proven again how far you've come. A week ago you probably wouldn't even have admitted that you were interested in her, and you certainly would have backed down after I said what I said. You handled it perfectly. You patiently went along to a point but then stood up for yourself when I went too far. Of course you can have a date with Vicki tomorrow night. I don't think I've ever met anyone who I'd rather have her date. Once again, I'm very proud of you."

Danny gaped at Kingsley.

"It's been a splendid evening, but I'm going to retire," Kingsley continued. "We will discuss the Endoophar strategy in the morning. Good night, gentlemen."

"Night," a stunned Danny said. Shey hopped up, began clearing the table, and directed Danny to help.

"Hey, I told you to help me," Shey repeated.

Danny broke out of his straight-ahead stare and focused on Shey. "My date tomorrow night. Any suggestions on what we should do?"

"How about dinner in the main dining room? I'll even prepare the meal, serve it, and then leave you alone."

"That sounds perfect. Thanks, Shey."

———

"Kingsley Vortex, you old gin-swilling, poker-playing, rabble-rousing, mulligan-taking, anything-inside-three-feet-is-good son of a bitch! How the hell are you?"

"Hello, Javo, my old friend. It's great to see you," Kingsley said to the rugged, tanned, silver-haired image on his office screen. "I'm doing well, but I must take issue with your description. I haven't roused a rabble since I was in my forties, I haven't taken a mulligan in thirty years, and I don't take any putt outside of two feet. I must admit I still enjoy a good card game now and then, and when I bend my elbow, I occasionally find a martini glass at my lips."

"Yes, I suppose some behavior is best left to those not in a position such as yours."

"You know I'm about to join you in retirement," Kingsley said.

"So you've been watching the news."

"I have. So what's the real story? I know you love your grandchildren, but I can't see you giving up your office to chase them around."

"You know me well, Kingsley. Probably better than anyone other than my wife. The Council for Planetary Governmental Affairs, COPGA, thought it was time for a change. It's amazing how you can be tossed aside after serving your planet for thirty years."

"Javo, I know you're capable of doing whatever the hell you want without caring what others think of you. Did you do something that ruffled their feathers?"

"I did not. COPGA said they appreciated everything I had done but that they felt it was time for fresh leadership for Endoophar. What they meant was different, and younger, leadership. I'd been on the fence about running again. I do want to spend more time with my family. COPGA said that if I announced I was retiring, they would treat my departure from office with great fanfare. So I decided it was time."

"We're actually en route to Endoophar."

"You're kidding? Will you have time to play some golf and come over for dinner?"

"I'd love to, but I'll have to take a rain check. I'm on a serious mission. I can't discuss the details, but I need your help. I'm glad to hear you left in good standing with COPGA. There is a young man traveling with me who requires an audience with the council that controls admittance to the Branora Canyon."

"The Branora Canyon? Who is he and what the hell does he need in there?"

"I told you, I can't give you details. There is a lower body in your council system that controls access, correct?"

"There is. That would be COENA, the Council for Environmental Affairs. Kingsley, it takes weeks to get an audience with them."

"Which is where COPGA comes into play. This crew reports to COPGA, correct?"

"They do."

"My request is that you contact COPGA and call in a favor. Tell them that you want COENA to receive a young man three days from now. Late afternoon their time would be best."

Javo stroked his chin and looked pensively at Kingsley. "And you won't tell me any more about what the hell you're doing?"

"I can't."

"I at least need to know who he is."

"His name is Axel Mazikula, and he's from Maroovia."

"Maroovia? What are you doing with someone from Maroovia? That's a million nunsecs from here."

"He's helping me with a special project. I'm asking you to trust me on this."

Javo sighed loudly. "I can probably get you the audience, but you know he has almost no chance of being admitted to the canyon. That council hasn't allowed an outsider in there for decades."

"I know. That doesn't really matter. I just need the audience with the council."

"Now you're making less sense."

"I'll explain it all someday."

"I'll set it up for four o'clock our time."

"Thanks, old friend. I owe you one."

CHAPTER 26

"So did you decide how we are going to get into this sacred canyon?" Danny asked.

The crew, sans Vicki, was having brunch in the yard after sleeping in. They were surrounded by a cool, cloudy, slightly breezy Yoobatarian morning.

Kingsley didn't look up from his plate. "I did."

"And?"

"And there really aren't many options."

"How many are there?"

"One, actually," Kingsley replied, still not looking Danny in the eyes.

"That's not many. I guess it makes what we do pretty clear-cut. What do I have to do this time?"

"You have to go before a council and try to get permission to enter the canyon. Shey, these pancakes might be your best ever, light and fluffy yet firm. I really think—"

"What kind of council?"

Kingsley took a deep breath and sat back in his chair. "Endoophar's governmental structure is comprised of a large number of councils at various levels. The one you need to see is the Council for Environmental Affairs, known as COENA. One of their minor responsibilities is determining who can have access to sacred sites. It normally takes weeks to get an audience with them. Javo Jamison has enough influence that he can get you before them the day after tomorrow."

"So I have to go sit in front of these people who are going to ask me questions?"

"Not exactly."

"Then what exactly?" Danny asked.

"I've, um, I've gotten you an audience with the council."

"An audience? Which involves what?"

"It involves you pleading your case for why you want to enter the canyon."

Danny was starting to tense. "In exactly what type of setting?"

"We're not sure. Probably a large room that is like a theater or a courtroom. The council likely sits at the front, and you would be at, um, at a—"

"At a what?" Danny boomed.

"At a podium," Kingsley said, finally lifting his eyes to meet Danny's.

"Oh no. No, no, no! No way!"

"Here we go again," chimed in Shey.

"Now Danny. Calm down," Kingsley said.

"Calm down my ass. *Plead my case* while standing at a podium in front of a group of people. It's a fucking presentation!"

"It isn't going to be that bad."

"The hell it isn't! And these people are government officials, which means they're probably going to be very serious and possibly annoyed that some young punk is bothering them about getting into a canyon. How many are on this council?"

"Seven."

"And I have to just walk up, and they'll be staring at me, and I have to give a speech about why I want in?"

"Basically, yes."

"Will anyone else be there?"

"Perhaps a few aides or security people. We've asked that the room be cleared of media people and the general public."

"Are you kidding me? You think I'm going to walk into a government auditorium, walk up to a podium in front of government officials, and give a speech? I've got three words for you. Ain't . . . gonna . . . happen."

"Danny, it has to happen."

"There has to be another option. We'll sneak into the damn canyon."

"There is not. Endoophar is one of the most technologically advanced planets in PUPCO. The shield surrounding the canyon is impenetrable."

"So how is Dank going to get in?"

"We're not sure. I'm guessing he also is somehow going to get before the council, perhaps by bribing or charming the right people."

"Oh great, so I'm going to be the second person on the same day to bother them about getting into this canyon. That will improve their mood."

Kingsley, clearly exasperated, rubbed his face and forehead with his right hand. "Danny, think back to everything you've accomplished since you boarded the ship seven days ago. Think of all the things you've done that a week ago you'd have been certain you couldn't do. This is just another new thing that I can get you through with training and preparation. You just dealt with the CARET team beautifully."

"This is different. Much different. There is a huge difference between answering questions and giving a speech."

"It's different, but it's doable."

"No, it's not. No way. I cannot do presentations. No matter how much training you give me, I'll have a meltdown when I go into that room."

"But Danny, Queen Quil—"

"Don't even start again with all this about how Vivitar is counting on me and how I need to save the Yoobatarian civilization. I don't care anymore." Danny pushed his plate away, folded his arms on his chest, and sat back in his chair.

"What about doing it for yourself, conquering your fears like you did before Quintawba?"

"Yeah, well, this is different. A lot of that stuff I needed to be able to do to have a more normal life. I don't need to do presentations."

"Maybe not at a podium in front of people, but you'd still benefit greatly from being able to talk when you are the center of attention without having a panic attack."

"Okay. Maybe that would be good, but I can work on that some other way. I don't need to do this to accomplish that."

"But think how much easier everything else would be if you succeeded at this?"

Danny thought before answering. "You have a point. But seriously, I really don't think I can do this. We're close to catching Dank. Can't you or Shey do it? Wouldn't this council be more willing to let in the great Kingsley Vortex?"

"I considered that. We are getting close to Dank, but we still can't be seen. If we don't catch him on Endoophar, we will have to keep going. This council will absolutely know who we are, and word would leak out about wanting into the canyon. And, actually, we'd probably have less chance of gaining admittance. The council would be less likely to let in a searcher for fear of them trying to leave with something of value. They are much more likely to grant access to a clean-cut, innocent-looking young man."

"Damn it. That makes some sense."

"I'll make a deal with you, Danny. Let me prepare you for the excursion today, and if by the time we get to Endoophar you don't feel you can do it, I won't try to make you. Shey or I will do it in the hope that they grant us access and we capture Dank on Endoophar. Otherwise the mission may be over. We'll just have to risk it. But you have to promise me you will take the training seriously and try your best."

"I guess it wouldn't hurt to go through the preparation. But I still can't see going to another planet alone, walking into a government building, and giving a presentation. What if Dank's actually on the planet?"

"I suppose that's possible. It may be time for Shey and I to go along, especially since we might encounter Dank. What do you think, Shey?"

"As long as we stay out of sight."

"Okay then, we'll go with you to the surface. We'll stay in the Star Hopper, but we'll be close by. If you encounter Dank, we'll hear you on the EZ-Comm and be with you in no time at all. How does that sound?"

Danny looked at both of them and carefully considered the proposition. "Okay. I'll give it a shot. What the hell? As long as you stick to your word that I can back out right up to the point I walk into the building."

"You have my word," said Kingsley. "You can even decide to walk away when you get to the podium. If that happens, Shey or I will step in, and we'll take our chances with the ramifications."

"Okay, so what's the story I'm going to feed this council?"

Kingsley reached into his pocket and pulled out a small, flat device. "I've written what you are going to say to them. You can view it on this. Take it back to your room and familiarize yourself with it. Meet me in the conference room in two hours."

"Have a seat, Mr. Kerrigan."

Danny, holding the portable screen, obliged. He selected a conference room chair that was three from Kingsley's. "Okay, I've got it memorized. Do you want to hear it?"

"No, I don't. I didn't tell you to memorize it."

"Yes, you did."

"No, I didn't. I told you to familiarize yourself with it. Feeling you have to have something memorized and then recite it verbatim simply adds to your performance anxiety. You end up feeling like you have to be perfect. Then if you forget or mangle a word or phrase, you'll get off track, and the performance will be ruined. That just kicks the pressure up a notch."

"And the alternative is?"

"The alternative is to be very familiar with the material, with the information and concepts, and then convey them in a relaxed, almost conversational manner. You want it to appear that you are talking *to* your audience, not *at* them."

"I don't know. It sounds like it would make it more likely that I won't deliver it perfectly."

"That, Danny, is one of your biggest problems. Listen carefully. You don't have to be perfect! You've got to rid yourself of the notion that public speaking has to be flawless. A mistake doesn't make you a failure. It makes you human. Once you realize that, I think you'll see the anxiety reduced dramatically."

"But I can have the speech with me, on the MPC, right? In case I get totally lost or forget a big chunk?"

"No. All you should have are bullet points that list each concept you want to convey. If you need to, look down at the bullet points, find what's next, and tell them what you know about it. If you were going to explain to a customer how some feature works in your company's software, would you write it up, memorize it, and then recite it verbatim over the phone?"

"Of course not."

"Why not?"

"Because I know it so well. I would just explain what I know."

"It's the same idea. You will know the concepts in the speech so well you'll be able to explain to the council what you want. The MPC has a list of bullet points for the speech. Below each are a few words to start that section. That will help get you going if you need it. I want you to work on your speech using that list. Focus on the content and concepts of the words. Absorb the meaning, believe it, and then explain it."

Danny sighed. "I'll try."

"I'm sensing a lack of enthusiasm."

"That's probably because I lack enthusiasm."

"I get that you're not excited to be doing this, but frame of mind is important, Danny. When you practiced shooting a basketball for countless hours, did you do so with enthusiasm?"

"Sure."

"And why was that?"

"Because I wanted to excel at it. I don't have a desire to excel at this. I just want to get through it."

"You should strive to excel at everything you undertake, whether it be sports, your job, household chores, or personal relationships. If you don't strive for excellence, you know what you achieve? Mediocrity. There is nothing special about mediocrity, Danny. Anyone can do it. Mediocrity does not lift your spirit or raise your vibration. Mediocrity smacks of laziness, apathy, and in many cases, fear. Don't be afraid to excel. A phrase I've always liked, which helps me in this regard, is *attack the task*. You can think of everything you do as a task. The goal is to attack each task with energy, focus, enthusiasm, and a desire to do it well.

"Return to your room and practice with just the bullet points and leading words the rest of the afternoon. And remember, attack the task and be excellent! We'll continue the training at ten in the morning."

"Welcome to Chez Gabink," said Shey before leading Danny and Vicki to a small, elegantly set table near the windows. They were both dressed head-to-toe in black. The dining room, which mirrored the size and shape of the gathering room, was easily the most formal on the ship. The deep red walls were accented by several pieces of art with ornate, gilded gold frames. The draperies were elegant, a rich, heavy gold fabric that puddled on the black, white, and gray marble floors. Ornate crown molding topped the walls. Four gorgeous crystal chandeliers were equally spaced across the ceiling. Scattered about the room were several tables, each draped in a gold fabric and surrounded by several elegant chairs.

"I will be your host and humble servant this evening. I will do my absolute best to cater to your every whim. In fact, you may consider me your caterer. This should be an elegant yet festive and lighthearted event. Feel free to express yourself in the incredibly likely event that you find my musings amusing. No need to be reserved. In fact, the time at which you were scheduled to arrive should be your only reservation this evening. Contrary to what you may be thinking at this point, my goal is to facilitate your enjoyment of the meal and one another's company without being too intrusive. I would also like to assure you that I will absolutely not convey anything I hear here tonight to any other sentient being or computing machine. Now, may I start you off with a cocktail, a glass of wine, or a malted beverage?"

"I'll have a glass of white wine," said Vicki. "Select something you think I would enjoy."

"Certainly. And for the gentleman?"

"I'll have that too."

Shey bowed slightly and shuffled off.

The moment Shey stepped away, the reality hit Danny . . . he was on a date. He was sitting at a dining table across from a beautiful woman. The moment screamed for conversation to ensue. Not mundane conversation, but interesting, witty, earth-moving conversation. It felt almost surreal, as if he were in a movie scene. He wanted to say something special and appropriate, perhaps even magical, but his mind was blank.

"I must admit, Danny, this feels really awkward to me. It's a little intimidating when you've never actually been in the situation before."

"I feel the same way," Danny said enthusiastically. "It's like saying something that isn't fabulous or perfect feels out of place with the setting and the moment."

"I think we should jettison those images and just get to know each other. Just talk without any concern for being witty or brilliant or perfect. We did a pretty good job of it at breakfast yesterday morning. Deal?"

"Deal."

"A glass of Polimar from Hunderpa," Shey said as he placed the glasses in front of them. "I will give you some time to relax and enjoy your drinks before I return with the first course."

Vicki waited until Shey was out of earshot before raising her glass. "How about a toast?"

A lump quickly formed in Danny's throat. "I, uh, I've never given a toast before."

"Neither have I. Let's both do one. Just say what's on your mind."

"Okay," Danny said as he lifted his glass, looked down, and closed his eyes to gather himself. "Here's to our first dates. They are long overdue. I've never met anyone that I'd rather my first date be with." Danny clinked his glass to hers.

After they each took a sip, Vicki took her turn. "Here's to us, to our incredible personal and spiritual growth, to the universe—and my father—for bringing us together. I'm not referring to the mission when I say that I know this is the start of a fabulous journey."

Ice broken, at Vicki's prompting, Danny proceeded to talk at length about the Endoophar plan and the day's speech training before Shey approached the table.

"The first course. A lovely lobster bisque," he said, placing two large bowls on the chargers that had been resting in front of them. Like the chargers, the bowls were elegantly simple white china with gold trim. Shey slowly backed away from the table after another slight bow.

"I'm sure you'll handle tomorrow's training well and then the excursion. You may have doubts, but you've had doubts each step of the mission and you've handled them all flawlessly."

"Flawlessly may be a stretch, but each one has gone much better than I thought. I have a tendency to think of the worst possible outcome and then focus on that, as if that's obviously what is going to happen."

"That's human nature, Danny," Vicki said. "I do the same thing. Or I should say I did the same thing. When I was a small child, my parents made me do a lot of things, go a lot of places, and see a lot of people. I dreaded it all and would envision all of the horrible things that were going to happen. Once I got to a certain age, I didn't want to leave my suite. I created a very comfortable life, though not exciting."

"And you never leave you suite back home?"

"No, I leave it. Mostly at night when no one is around, like I did here on the ship the night we met."

"So why do you live like that? If you don't mind me asking."

"Of course not. It's simply that I'm most comfortable, most at peace, when I'm alone. I've been that way my entire life. I've always found being around people to be incredibly exhausting and stressful."

Danny glanced up as Shey swooped in and removed their bowls, placing them on the small cart he had wheeled in. "The second course. Grilled sea scallops in a roasted red pepper cream sauce with assorted greens in a light vinaigrette."

"Thank you, Shey," said Vicki.

"I've always been the same way," Danny said. "When I'm alone, it's like an escape from the battle, a temporary truce between me and my issues before I have to face another stressful situation. I've managed to create a life where I have fewer and fewer of those. I think now I'm seeing that to really be at peace I have to deal with all of this stuff. I'm hoping that maybe then I'll feel happy. So are you happy with the life you've created?"

"Happy? No, I've never been what I would consider happy. My lifestyle permits me to be in a neutral zone—not happy but also not loaded with fear, dread, and anxiety. I can say that since I've met you, I've probably been the happiest I've ever been. Here's to finding true inner peace and the simplicity of being happy," Vicki said as she raised her glass.

Danny reciprocated and took a sip of wine. "So how do you spend your time in your suite? What are your interests?"

"Actually, it's really more of an apartment than a suite. It's connected to my parents' house, but it's quite large. What do I do? I don't watch television all day, if that's what you're wondering. I read and study a lot. I also exercise, and I like to cook. And I love to paint."

"Paint? Really?"

"Yes, I think I've developed into quite a good artist, if I do say so myself."

"Does Kingsley like your paintings?"

"Oh, I've never shown him anything I've done. I couldn't show anyone. Being creative feeds my soul. When I paint, I'm totally absorbed, with no fears, worries, or concerns."

Shey had again approached the table.

"For your entrée this evening, I have sun-dried tomato encrusted Opzillian terwanger, a fish that is similar to your halibut, Danny. It is accompanied by whipped potatoes and assorted grilled vegetables. The wine pairing is a delightful Poratan from Yoobatar. Enjoy."

"He's certainly doing a great job," Danny commented once Shey had left the room. "He can be a pain, but he's okay."

"Yes, he is. Father wouldn't have kept him around all these years if he was more annoying than helpful. Sometimes they bicker like an old married couple, certainly more than my parents."

"What is your mother like?"

"She's incredibly intelligent, graceful, loving, and compassionate, and she has a great sense of humor. She's very strong and independent, which served her well with Father being away on business so much. She's the perfect woman for my father, and she's been a great mother. I know I haven't made it easy on her, but she's handled my . . . my situation, wonderfully."

"And she's a writer?"

"Yes, a novelist and poet. She also spends a lot of her time doing charity work. Like Father, she has a great deal of charisma. So what are your interests? How do you spend your time? Better yet, tell me your life story."

"My life story? Well, there's not much to tell really. As a small child I was quite the entertainer, putting on elaborate shows for family, friends, and neighbors. I'd sing and dance and do skits and play the piano. By the time I was five, I was considered a piano prodigy, so I traveled around the world performing at major venues. At the age of nine I began attending an elite private school where I focused on my music and academics. I was brilliant, actually. It was in junior high that I discovered that I was an even better athlete than pianist, so good that I was the four-time state player-of-the-year in football, baseball, and basketball. I received scholarship offers from every major university for sports and music, but I spurned them both to focus on academics. I got my undergrad from MIT, went to grad school at Harvard, and then to Oxford where I was a Rhodes Scholar."

"And what did you study?" asked a grinning Vicki.

"I ended up with degrees in several subjects—molecular genetics, bio-mechanical physics, quantum economics—but decided I wanted to try something more physical, so after I left England, I became a Navy SEAL. I found the training to be rather easy, so, wanting more challenges, I became a Green Beret, followed by a stint as an Army Ranger. Oh yes, during that time I wrote several well-received piano concertos and a couple of symphonies, worked with some researchers on cures for various diseases, and gave the president economic advice. I was in my apartment in Columbus contemplating offers from several major publishers to write my autobiography when Kingsley and Shey showed up. I decided to go with them because I thought it may add some much-needed spice to my story."

"My, you've certainly had a rich, full life for someone so young."

"Okay, I embellished a bit."

"Just a bit? What's the real story?"

"The real story is that I grew up in a small Ohio town, went to Ohio State, and have been in Columbus ever since, living alone and working from home for a software company. Terribly exciting, isn't it?"

The two continued to chat and laugh through the rest of their meal and dessert. After Shey cleared the table, Danny hoped to continue the evening.

"So, are you up for a walk in the yard?"

"You know, that sounds nice, but to be perfectly honest I think I'd like to turn in. I guess I'm not used to so much activity. I'm exhausted."

"Sure. Absolutely. I'm pretty tired too and have a big day of excursion prep tomorrow."

Danny stood up, pulled Vicki's chair out for her, and followed her from the dining room. They strolled silently across the foyer and down the center hall until arriving at Vicki's door. Danny turned to face her as it slid open.

"Thanks for everything," he said. "I had a great time. I really hope you did too."

"I did," she replied as she put her arms around his neck and laid her head on his shoulder.

Danny gingerly wrapped his arms around her and patted her back before laying his head against hers.

"I like spending time with you, Danny. It feels like home."

"I feel the same way."

"I'll see you tomorrow. Sleep well," she said before turning and disappearing into her suite.

CHAPTER 27

DANNY ARRIVED AT THE ARENA to find "Council for Environmental Affairs" displayed on the panel next to the door. He had spent the morning training in multiple environments. First in the conference room, sitting at the table while Kingsley asked him each section's leading question. That was followed by Danny giving his talk while standing in the great room with Kingsley as his audience. He was then required to recite it multiple times in the theater, at a podium in front of audiences of holographic images. He had handled each extremely well, with only a slight spike of anxiety when confronted with each scenario. Kingsley had then told him to report to the sports arena.

The door slid open. Danny took a deep breath and stepped through. To his left, surrounded by high-backed chairs, was a semicircular table facing the opposite end of the room. About twenty feet in front of it stood a podium. To the right, behind the podium, seats filled with holographic images rose from the arena floor to near the ceiling. Danny's pulse quickened, and his breathing became shallow and rapid. Danny frantically reviewed his training. It doesn't have to be flawless. Get out there and give the damn speech.

Danny briskly strode, screen in hand, past the table and to the podium, and turned to face the council. Each of the seven chairs was occupied. He scanned the group from right to left and found familiar faces sprinkled among holographs. First Kingsley, then Shanna, then Shey, then Vicki.

The image near the middle of the table pressed a button, which led to a loud tone filling the room. The holographic crowd fell silent. The image, an elegant older woman, glanced down at a screen and spoke.

"The council will now hear from Axel Mazikula from the planet Maroovia."

Danny stood in the complete, deafening silence and was temporarily paralyzed by the seven sets of eyes that were focused on him. He gathered himself, looked down at the screen, and read the opening line to himself. He started without looking up.

"Ladies and gentlemen of the esteemed Council for Environmental Affairs, I truly appreciate the opportunity to speak before you today. I know the council has many pressing and important issues to consider, so I am especially grateful that you granted me this audience on such short notice. I only made such a request because of the urgent nature of the situation in which I find myself. I stand before you humble and honored.

"My name is Axel Mazikula, and I have traveled here from the planet Maroovia. I came here today not for selfish reasons or for personal gain. I am here in an effort to save a society, to salvage an ancient and spiritually advanced civilization. I am here as a representative of the Maroovian ruling family, a family that has been honestly, proudly, and successfully leading the planet for more than four hundred years. Their rule has been void of controversy, corruption, and scandal. They have led Maroovia from a crime-laden, war-torn society dominated by unscrupulous, immoral individuals to being an enlightened, violence-free utopia that is both technologically and spiritually advanced.

"But that utopia is now in jeopardy. A force has emerged that is threatening the very fabric, the hallmarks, of Maroovian society. It is a truly tangible and serious threat. A half-Maroovian individual, who is as devious and unprincipled as he is charming and charismatic, has amassed a formidable following, a group of Maroovians whom he has convinced to emulate his treacherous, conniving ways. This individual's desire is to overthrow the ruling family and then take the government and eventually the entire civilization back hundreds of years. While the Maroovian ruling family is not above dealing with challenges, it has been discovered that this person has found a way to artificially increase his appeal to the public, perhaps as much as tenfold.

"It is my task to prevent this being from making this unfair advantage a reality. My quest to do so has brought me here. What I ask of you is that I be permitted to enter the Branora Canyon with the sole purpose of acquiring a very small sample of the crystal albatarum. I am well aware of the sacred nature of the canyon and that it is home to the tombs of your revered ancient rulers. I give my word that I have no interest in that area of the canyon and will do nothing to desecrate those tombs. I am not an archeologist. I am not a criminal. I am simply an honest, pure-hearted emissary from a civilization under siege.

"I realize that my request is unusual and that it may seem incongruous with the problem facing my planet. Planetary security prevents me from giving you specifics. Also, this villain's plans are known of only by the ruling family, and my mission is clandestine. If you attempt to contact the ruling family, they will deny any knowledge of my request. Regardless of your decision, I ask that the information I have given you here today not leave the walls of this chamber.

"So that is my request, to be granted access to the Branora Canyon for the purpose of obtaining a sample of albatarum. The ruling family of Maroovia will respect your decision. They will owe a debt of gratitude to this council and to Endoophar. Thank you for your time and careful consideration of this matter."

The performance was more than adequate. He had started rather meekly, with his head down, clearing his throat between each of the first few sentences, but his voice and posture grew stronger and more assertive. By the midway point, he was standing tall, speaking with great poise and presence. He made almost continual eye contact with his audience, glancing down only to read the first line of a few of the sections. A male image near the left end of the table spoke.

"Thank you, Mr. Mazikula. Please wait outside the chambers so we can deliberate and vote on the matter."

"Okay. Thank you all for giving me this opportunity today."

Danny picked up the device and exited the arena. He was fired up. He had just made a last-second, game-winning shot. But rather than let his guard down he told himself to remain focused and prepared to attack whatever task awaited him.

"The council has requested that you reenter the chambers," said Gracie.

Danny turned, faced the door, and waited to burst through, like a bull waiting to enter the ring. The door slid open, and Danny forcefully stepped forward, almost running over his fan club. Kingsley, Shey, and Vicki, gathered near the door, cheered and applauded as he burst into the room.

"Danny, that was a fantastic performance," Kingsley said. Shey's typical smirk had been replaced with a genuine, ear-to-ear grin.

"Thanks. I'm really pleased with how that went. What's next?"

"We're going to go through it a few more times, trying to trip you up with questions and minor distractions. Now get your butt back out in the hall and get ready."

"Would you like me to request admittance?" Gracie asked.

"Yes," Danny replied. His long day was near its end. The afternoon's practice had been grueling. The group had then reconvened in the living room for a lighthearted evening of food, wine, music, laughter, and storytelling. Once back in his room, Danny found himself to be anything but sleepy. He wanted someone to confide in.

The door slid open to reveal Vicki, looking casual and comfortable in black loungewear and slippers.

"Hey there."

"Hey. I'm tired but a little wired. Can we hang out for a while?"

"Sure. Come on in."

Vicki's suite was much more elegant than his guest suite. Canned ceiling lights gently illuminated the living area. The room was awash in shades of gold, red, and green. The deep red walls were bordered by ornate, white baseboards and crown molding. The seating area was dominated by an oversized gold sofa that was home to several red, green, and gold patterned pillows. On one end of the sofa was a floral chaise lounge; on the other a comfortable-looking, dark green armchair. Also flanking the sofa were a pair of end tables, one round, one square, upon each of which sat a lamp. The grouping surrounded an elegant, substantial coffee table made of dark wood. It also faced a large screen, to the left of which was a fireplace. The dark hardwood floors were covered by several gorgeous rugs. The room was warm and inviting; beautiful without being stuffy.

Vicki plopped down among the oversized pillows on the sofa, wrapped her arms around her knees, and pulled her heels up against her thighs. Danny hesitated and then took a position at the opposite end of the sofa.

"So, you can't sleep?" she asked.

"No. I was so wiped out after the practice in the arena that I crashed for a couple of hours. Now I'm wide awake."

"You look like you have something else you want, or perhaps don't want, to say."

"Don't tell your dad, but I'm starting to get a little worried about addressing the council tomorrow."

"But you were fabulous in the arena."

"I know. I don't know what happened. I was really pumped with the way I handled that. I never thought I'd be able to do the things I did this afternoon. It gave me tons of confidence, but then after my nap this kind of eerie feeling has started creeping in, like something really distant and tiny appeared and started getting closer and bigger. My stomach has been a little upset since dinner, and I don't think it's Shey's cooking. With all of the training and practice and how good I did it, I didn't expect this. I didn't expect the dread."

Vicki went to the service bay, returned with two large mugs of herbal tea, and handed one to Danny. "I think feeling a little dread is natural given your lifetime of anxiety for such events. Patterns that have been repeated over and over with such strong emotion and physical symptoms are hard to break. You know you can do this. You've already done it very well multiple times. You need to focus on those successes, not how you've handled situations in the past. That's ancient history."

"I suppose you're right."

"Here's to you and your success on Endoophar," Vicki said as she took a sip of tea.

Kingsley had no reaction upon seeing Shanna Var stretched out on his sofa eating a box of chocolates and watching television.

"Hope I didn't startle you," she said, without moving her eyes from the screen.

"Startle me? I'm more startled when I come in and you're not here," Kingsley replied as he plopped down in a chair. "So, what semi-annoying nuggets of wisdom do you have for me tonight?"

"None. I just came to hang out for a while."

"Uh-huh," Kingsley said as he caught the piece of chocolate she threw to him. "Things are going quite well, wouldn't you say?"

"Is that what you think?"

"It is. He was much better in all of the practice sessions than I anticipated, and he seems to really be embracing the concepts."

"Yes, he did very well."

"And tomorrow? How do you think he will do?"

"There is a good chance he will fail miserably."

"What? Why?" Kingsley exclaimed.

"The variety of environments you created were realistic and prepared him for surprises, but there was only one problem. They weren't real, and he knew they weren't real. When he walks into those chambers tomorrow, he will know it's the real deal, and it will hit him like a ton of bricks."

"Perhaps, but using my concepts he may be able to adapt and get past that."

"Perhaps. But that's not the main issue."

"And what is?"

"He doesn't want to do it. He says that he does, and he tells himself he wants to in order to save Yoobatar and deal with his issues, but deep down he really doesn't want to. The fear is still stronger than his desire to conquer it."

"So you're saying he has no chance?"

"I didn't say that. I can't predict the outcome of situations or know with certainty how someone will react. I'm just saying that he will likely either bail out before getting there or fall apart when he tries to do it."

"So this has all been a waste of time?"

"Not at all. To the contrary, it has been a perfect use of time. It's just that the mission may be in shambles tomorrow."

"And what am I to do if he fails miserably?"

"I'm in a good mood, so I'll give you a hint. If he fails miserably, you have to give up control. If the mission is to continue, the next excursion must be his idea."

"His idea? What can he possibly suggest that would help?"

Shanna faded away without answering the question.

"We have arrived at the building that houses the COENA chambers," Max said as the Star Hopper came to rest after turning into a parking lot beside a four-story stone building. It was fronted by a large flight of steps and a row of ten columns that stretched almost the width of the building.

"Time?" Kingsley asked.

"Fifteen minutes before Danny is scheduled to appear before the council."

"Danny, you can either wait here until it is time to go in or go in and wait in the building, perhaps even in the audience of the chambers. That might be best so you can get acclimated to the environment."

Danny took a deep breath and did a couple of neck rolls. "I think I'll go in. I guess I'll see you later . . . and then we'll head to the Branora Canyon." He slid from his chair and moved toward the open door.

Shey slapped him on the shoulder as he passed. "When we get back to the ship, I'll kick your butt at golf again."

"Sounds good," Danny said.

Once on the pavement he immediately felt very alone. Danny knew he should enter the building, but he had difficulty moving. His entire body felt tight and numb and foreign, as if it was no longer connected to his head and could not take direction from him. He got his feet moving and slowly walked around the transport, through the sea of parked vehicles, and up to the base of the steps. As he began trudging upward, the dread, a sickening dread, quickly grew stronger. His feet felt like lead as he pulled them from each step and threw them to the next. When he arrived at the top, he was gasping for air, partly from the trek and partly from the anxiety, which had finally appeared. He looked back down at the transport and seriously considered bailing.

Danny entered the building and made his way to the council chamber. He glanced down at his MPC to see he had eight minutes until he was expected to speak. He had decided to wait outside, enter the room, and walk directly to the podium as he had in the arena. The hallway was bustling with serious-looking people briskly walking both directions. Danny spied some people standing outside the chamber doors and assumed they were the reporters. He guessed that they were ready to pounce on anyone who tried entering. He was right. As they chatted, each reporter darted around the hallway looking for anyone who wasn't just passing by. Danny decided to wait down the hall, but it was too late. One of them was making a beeline directly for him. Danny put his head down and started walking away.

"Excuse me, sir. Sir!" yelled the reporter.

Danny froze and slowly turned.

"Are you about to address COENA?" she asked as she raised a small camera and held it between her face and Danny's.

"No comment," he said as he raised his hand to shield his face. Danny decided it would be better to wait inside, so he headed for the chamber door. His actions caught the attention of the remaining reporters, who attempted to cut him off while shouting questions about who he was and what he would be saying to the council. Danny raised his hands and lowered his head while repeating that he had no comment. When he reached the door, he wasted no time entering the room.

The chambers reminded Danny of the courtrooms he had seen in countless movies and television shows. The walls were covered in dark wood. The ceiling contained a massive mural. There were windows along the wall to his left, each flanked by heavy red draperies. Directly in front of him was a center aisle. At the end of the aisle, in front of the seats, was a podium at which someone was speaking. Past the podium, seated around a curved, elevated, ornate desk, were seven somber beings.

Danny's pulse quickened. His stomach churned, and his body clenched. His sweaty hand was wrapped tightly around the MPC. He checked the time again. He had four minutes. He considered bolting. All he had to do was turn around and leave the room, and it would all be over. He would be free. He decided to hang in there for a couple more minutes and took a seat near the back of the room.

As he sat, his mind and body descending into the depths of dread and anxiety, once again he got angry, pissed as hell that he felt as he did. He had handled the training, Kingsley believed in him, Vivitar was counting on him, and here he was having another meltdown. He loathed the way he felt. It was then a new sensation came over him, one he'd never had in all the times he'd been in such a situation.

What the hell, he thought. *Use the anger. Just go up there and give it a shot. If it's awful, it's awful. Just go up and say the damn words and keep going no matter how much they are mangled or how bad you look.*

The physical symptoms hadn't lessened, but Danny had a new resolve. He would not leave.

"Axel Mazikula will now address the council," came a booming voice from the front of the room.

When Danny looked up and saw no one at the podium, his heart almost stopped. He looked back at the door and again considered bolting. Feeling like his body weighed a thousand pounds, Danny pushed himself up from the chair and started down the aisle. When he arrived at the podium, the council members looked up. Their serious looks and authoritative auras added to his dread. He placed the MPC on the podium and stared at the bullet points. His pulse and breathing quickened. He was having trouble thinking clearly. He read the first bullet point and the text below it to himself, but nothing registered.

"Well, Mr. Mazikula," said the gentleman seated at the center of the table. "We're anxious to hear what you have to say. It's not often that Javo Jamison is concerned with what goes on in these chambers. We've never been asked to remove the media. This must be terribly important. Mr. Mazikula?"

Danny struggled to get his breath. He tried opening his mouth and moving his tongue, but both were difficult due to his mouth being dry and sticky. He finally managed to read the first line. "Um, ladies and gentlemen of the esteemed council," he said meekly before pausing to swallow.

"Mr. Mazikula, we cannot hear you. Please speak up and speak into the microphone."

Danny raised his head and scanned the waiting faces. His panic shot into full gear. His chest started heaving as he struggled to catch his breath. A bead of sweat ran down the side of his face. The pounding of his heart felt like it was shaking his entire body. His neck was so tight it felt like steel rods connected his head to his shoulders. Suddenly both of his arms felt numb, a sensation that fueled his panic even more.

"I gotta . . . I've got to get out . . ." he breathlessly uttered. But he didn't get the chance. Everything went black. Danny slumped forward onto the podium. His knees buckled, and he fell sideways to the floor, where he lay motionless.

The stunned council members stared in disbelief.

"Someone call a medical team," shouted the council head.

"No! Wait!" came shouts from the back of the room. Kingsley and Shey came scurrying up the aisle. "We'll take care of him."

They knelt next to Danny. Shey checked his pulse and lifted his eyelids.

"He's going to be okay. He just passed out. I'll give him something to normalize his vitals and keep him out for a while."

Kingsley looked down at Danny and smiled. "At least you gave it a shot, kiddo. Let's get him back to the ship."

Shey picked Danny up and started down the aisle. Kingsley turned to the council. "My apologies to the council for this disruption. We appreciate the audience we were granted here today. Thank you," he said before bowing slightly and following Shey.

The council members looked even more confused. A woman on the far left turned to the man beside her. "Wasn't that Kingsley Vortex?"

"I think it was."

"What in the world is he doing here with everything that's going on back on his home planet?"

CHAPTER 28

Danny opened his eyes and saw a dimly lit ceiling. Reaching about with both hands revealed that he was on a sofa. He heard whispers and turned his head to see four people sitting around a table. Two were Kingsley and Shey. A stranger, a man about Kingsley's age, sat on the far side of the table, facing Danny. A woman sat on the near side with her back to Danny. He was happy to know Vicki was there.

Danny raised his head and looked around. He was in the living room of the *Aurora*, lying on one of the sofas that flanked the circular dining table. He pushed himself upright.

"Kingsley," Shey said as he motioned with his head in Danny's direction.

"Raise the lights, Gracie. Welcome back, Danny. How do you feel?"

Danny squinted as the lights brightened. "I feel a little woozy, but other than that, I think I'm okay." It was then that he got a better look at the stranger. He was about to ask Kingsley about him when the woman turned around. "Oh my God! Queen Quilicant. What are you doing here?" Danny exclaimed as he struggled to his feet.

"Hello, Danny. It's nice to finally meet you in person." Danny was speechless.

"Why don't the two of you leave us to chat with Danny?" Kingsley asked.

"Certainly," replied the gentleman before he and the woman exited. Danny stared at him as he left.

"That guy looks like how Durbin and the park guard described Dank. Who the hell is he? And what is Vivitar doing here? Is she here to cancel the mission because I passed out? I'm really sorry about that. I thought I could do it right up to the time I had to actually talk."

"Why don't you come over and have a seat?" Kingsley said. "There is no need to apologize for what transpired, Danny. Actually, I'm very proud of you. You went to that podium and tried to give the speech despite tremendous anxiety and physical symptoms. You did all I could ever ask. You tried."

"How did I get back here?"

"Shey and I came and got you after you passed out."

"Oh. Sorry about that. I guess that blew your cover. I mean, the council members saw you, right?" Danny asked as he took a seat at the table.

"Yes, they did. But don't be concerned with that."

"Well if you're not, and since Vivitar is here, I'm guessing the mission is over? Didn't you give the speech to the council?"

"That's what we need to chat about. You are correct about the mission being over. However, there are some things I need to explain."

"Such as?"

"Such as the fact that the mission as you know it was not exactly our real mission."

"So you have another twist, like when you didn't tell me that you were from the future or that you really intended for me to lead the mission?"

"It's actually a bit more . . . expansive than that."

"Expansive? What do you mean *expansive*?"

"Expansive as in the entire mission as you know it was fake," Kingsley said calmly.

"Fake?" Danny yelled. "The entire mission was fake? What the hell are you talking about?"

"What I'm talking about is that everything we told you, everything that you think we've been doing, was a manufactured story."

"Manufactured? What the . . . I don't understand. What about Yoobatar and the Quilicant family and Dank and all that?"

"Um, well, there is no such planet as Yoobatar, and there are no such people as Queen Quilicant and Dank Nebitol. The young lady you know as Vivitar is actually my sister Kayla's daughter, Alexandra . . . or Lexi. The gentleman that was here is my brother Marquin, and, yes, he has been playing Dank throughout this production."

Danny blinked his eyes rapidly and stared down at the table. "I still don't get it. You mean everything, the entire freaking mission, was a lie? Everything? Why? What the hell did you bring me along for? Why did you put me through all of this? Wait a minute. Is Vicki really your daughter . . . and is that her real name?"

"That part is real. Vicki is my daughter. My name is Kingsley Vortex, and this is Shey Gabink. Perhaps this would be best discussed over a couple of beers. Shey, will you do the honors?"

"I don't want a fucking beer. I want to know what the hell is going on!" Danny yelled.

"Your confusion and anger are understandable." Kingsley rose and started pacing. "We did not have multiple targets on Earth. We dispatched an iggy so we could observe what was going on in your life, to make certain we were there at the right moment. Once we determined that was the case, we approached you. We needed to persuade you to go with us, so we concocted a story we thought would do so."

Danny was still dumbfounded. "But you went into such detail about the Quilicants' rule, and Dank's life, and Chase Claxon."

"Yes, well, we felt we needed to weave a rich, elaborate tale to keep you interested and motivated."

"What about all the people on the planets we visited? Were they all friends and family of yours?"

"Actually, none of them were. We kept the fake mission going with just Lexi and Marquin. Marquin's ship was traveling ahead of us. Lexi placed her calls to us from there. She's actually an actress in real life, so it wasn't difficult for her. Regarding the planets, we needed someone on Kronk to play along, so Marquin set that up. He found an out-of-work, rather desperate actor and told him he was being considered for a role in a science fiction movie. He said you were the film's young, eccentric director who wanted to see him in sort of a live action scene before deciding whether to cast him. He gave the guy the scene we wrote and told him he had to be in character from the moment you arrived until you left."

"So everyone I dealt with on these planets were actors?"

"No. He was the only person you encountered who was kind of in on it. On Dabita Bok, Durbin Carbindale knew only what you told him. We wanted you to have to explore some remote location that could be identified by a well-known phrase of some sort. We assumed Durbin would let you see it, especially if you paid to do so. Marquin went there first, got access to the cave, and scratched the clue in the dirt for you to find."

"That wasn't Jillian Falstaff?" Danny blurted out.

"There is no Jillian Falstaff. Lexi also played Jillian Falstaff. We knew Durbin had a questionable past, but we were sure he wasn't violent. He probably called the Grugnok because of what you told him about your mission. We didn't count on their involvement. That was really the only bump in the road."

"The Grugnok weren't in on it?" Danny asked. "They were really going to take me back to their ship?"

"Most certainly. But Shanna wasn't going to let that happen. This mission was her idea. She wouldn't have let them derail it. After Dabita Bok, we headed to Quintawba, where we created the story, the double-fake mission if you will, about you being part of the PUPCO delegation. Timing was important there. I've known for some time that Quintawba was going to be part of the ACUSA program and that we had to get there well in advance of that delegation."

"PUPCO is real?"

"Yes, PUPCO is real. No one on Quintawba was in on it. Julky really thought you were Tavit Nanby arriving early to start your work. Marquin had already been there and left the recorder for you to find. Lexi simply used a different accent when they recorded their message."

"I'm having trouble keeping track of who's real and who isn't. Wait a minute. How did Marquin get access to Quintawba and the mountain if they are so strict about aliens visiting?"

"Their security systems aren't actually very sophisticated. Marquin had no trouble getting through undetected."

"And the CARET agents entering the park when I was leaving? They were really going to apprehend me?"

"Most likely. We'd have been in a bit of a bind if they'd taken you into custody. After that we headed to Endoophar so you could give the speech to the council. Javo Jamison didn't know why we needed the audience, but he did set it up for me."

Danny rubbed his face as he tried to absorb everything he was being told. "Okay, so assuming I believe everything you are telling me about this man-ufactured mission . . . why? Why did you travel back through time, why did you come specifically for me, and why did you go to all the trouble of making up such an elaborate story and making me do things on all these planets?"

"To help you conquer your fears."

"Okay, we were clearly working on my issues the entire time. So that wasn't part of the fake mission?"

"Danny, the entire fake mission was created because we needed you to deal with your fears. Let me ask you this. What if we'd shown up at your door and told you that we wanted to help you get over all of your issues?"

"I'd have told you to get lost and slammed the door in your face."

"And if we'd rendered you unconscious, taken you back to the ship, and then demanded you work on these issues? Would you have been cooperative?"

"Of course not."

"So you see, what we did was our only recourse."

"What if I wouldn't have agreed to go with you?"

"We were fairly certain you would. We knew all about the training classes you were being told to do. That's why we showed up when we did. Being from the future, we could have shown up at any point in your life. The moment we chose was optimum. We assumed that, though it was an unknown, the idea of joining us would be more appealing than facing the training classes."

Danny thought back to the early stages of the mission.

"So you didn't need Shey to give me that exam, because you already knew about my problems?"

"Yes, but the exam was still necessary. We knew about your personal interaction issues. We started working on those from the moment we got you on the ship. Once you agreed to be the mission lead, the exam was important. We knew about your fears but weren't certain of their depth. We also needed a vehicle to bring them to the forefront, to give you the impression that we didn't know about them, and most importantly to identify what we had to work on in order for you to be able to lead the mission. It would have been very difficult for us to work on them without you knowing we were doing so.

"While the bulk of the work on some of your issues was done under the guise of the mission, from the time you boarded the ship, we were attempting to address one issue or another. We then tried to create situations that progressively became more daunting for you, with each designed so that you would have to face more intimidating aspects of the various issues."

Danny suddenly looked sad. "What about my relationship with Vicki? It was part of this fake mission?"

"It was not. We were hoping you two would hit off."

"So she wasn't just working me?"

"I can assure you, everything she did and said was completely genuine. Believe me when I say she has very strong feelings for you."

"I'm not sure what to believe any more."

"That's understandable. The culmination of our mission was for you to give a speech in a very structured environment. That was the entire purpose of the Endoophar excursion. Though you trained well and gave a valiant effort, that excursion was obviously not a success."

"You still didn't answer my main question. Why in the world would a couple of searchers travel to the past to help me get over my issues? That doesn't make any sense."

Kingsley sat back down and exchanged a glance with Shey. "Danny, the mission as you knew it wasn't the only thing that was fake. Shey and I are not searchers."

"Oh, great. More deceit. Who the hell are you then?"

"I want to make it perfectly clear that everything, and I mean everything, I've told you since you woke up, and everything I will tell you from this point forward, is absolutely true. Our mission is over. We have no reason to mislead you any longer. Do you believe me?"

"Yes, I think I do."

"For the past thirty years, I have been President Kingsley Vortex."

"Oh yeah? President of what?"

"Earth."

"Earth doesn't have a president."

"Not in your time, but it does now. In 2058, Earth moved from the suspect to the aware stage, and then to the travel stage in 2075. Long before that, the space travel program became a planetary rather than national endeavor. Scientists from around the world worked together, and representatives from various nations formed a committee that oversaw the program. Once we started dealing with other planets, it became fairly obvious that we needed individuals to represent Earth in those interactions.

"By that time the United Nations had become an effective, significant, and powerful organization. It was decided that it would be logical to house this new space agency within the UN. A new branch would be created to handle interplanetary affairs. The existing structure was named the Planetary Affairs Division, or PAD, and the new structure would be the Cosmic Affairs Division, CAD. The new division would have a senate, PUPCO delegates, a cabinet, and a president. It handled any and all issues involving Earth's interactions with anyone or anything that was not from Earth.

There were departments created for such things as travel technology, space exploration, planetary defense, and alien interaction.

"One of the senate's members happened to be my great grandfather, August Vortex. Everyone called him Gus, and everyone loved him. He was brilliant and charismatic. A president of CAD then had to be named. Some members thought there should be a planetary election, but that idea was shot down. There was concern that not enough people on the planet were terribly interested in the formation of CAD and didn't really care who was named president. It was decided that it would be done by way of a vote in the senate. The president would certainly have input on CAD affairs, but their primary role would be that of diplomacy. They would be the face of Earth, both for the rest of the universe and for Earth's inhabitants. Over time the profile and power of CAD grew so that its president became the de facto president of Earth.

"Gus Vortex won the vote in a landslide. That was in 2078. Gus was an immediate success. He embraced the role and quickly made an interplanetary splash, raising Earth's profile along the way. He also became much more visible on Earth than the senate had imagined. He wanted to improve the planet and dove into the task with gusto. In many rousing speeches, he spoke about the benefits of space travel, raising the planet's consciousness, and improving our CUSTAR rating.

"When the senate was formed, they had decided that they would go through the nomination and voting process for president every five years. It was also decided that any given person could serve an unlimited number of terms. As the end of my great grandfather's first term drew near, the senate realized that the election process would be pointless. Nearly every single member loved Gus, and no one nominated anyone to run against him. It was suggested that they appoint Gus for a more lengthy term, an idea that passed overwhelmingly when put to a vote. The term decided upon was thirty years, with the provision that any senator could at any time call for a satisfaction election. If more than forty percent of the senate agreed, a nomination and election process would commence within the senate."

"So that's where you got the satisfaction election thing?" Danny was so engrossed in the story, he didn't even notice Shey placing a glass of water beside him.

"Exactly. A feeling of uneasiness grew in CAD as the end of Gus's thirty-year term drew near. One of his children, Duke, had been serving on the CAD senate for some time. Everyone was quite pleased when he accepted the nomination for and won the presidency. As with Gus and his family, Duke and his family were very high profile and very popular. They truly became Earth's royal family.

"It was during Duke's term that a decision was made by the CAD senate that changed the Vortex family forever. A group of senators proposed that a member of the Vortex family would always serve as president of Earth. After a thirty-year term, one of the president's children, one who had been groomed for the role, would take over. The child would receive a fantastic, broad education, focused heavily on diplomacy and governmental affairs. They would also work closely with the sitting president, observing and absorbing, until it was their time to take over. There was skepticism among the senate, but the satisfaction election provision helped a great deal. Eighty-two percent of the senate voted for the measure, thus establishing, in essence, a monarchy. When Duke's term ended, my mother, Elizabeth Vortex, served a thirty-year term. She passed the position to me. So, as I said, I have been the president of Earth for the past thirty years."

"And him?" Danny asked, nodding at Shey.

"He truly is my assistant, my right-hand man, who served as chief of staff for my entire term. And he actually is Drimmillian."

Danny sat back in his chair and looked back and forth between the two. "That's quite a story. If it is true, you coming to get me makes even less sense. Why would the president of a planet bother with something like that? Why was all of this necessary?"

"Because my term ends in five days."

"You said Vicki is your only child. That means she is the next president of Earth?"

"That is our hope."

"She, uh . . . no offense, but she doesn't seem like . . . she doesn't seem cut out for it."

Shey chuckled. "Your powers of observation are amazing."

"Shey," Kingsley said sternly. "You're correct, Danny. She isn't exactly cut out for it. But she is our only child, so the Vortex dynasty rests on her shoulders. You may recall me telling you that my sister Kayla is the head of the Mermetec agency, which is dedicated to research in the merging of metaphysics and technology. Several years before Vicki was born, they had developed what was called soul request technology. The idea was that before a couple gave birth, they would come up with a list a personality traits they wanted the child to have.

"This technology would then tap into the spiritual plane, the realm where souls exist between lives, and attempt to find a soul that was ready to incarnate and that met the criteria. It had been known for some time that for each lifetime souls actually select the situation into which they are born based on what they need to experience and what lessons they need to learn. The Mermetec agency proposed we could put information out there to attract a particular type of soul. The decision, of course, would still be that of the soul."

Danny looked skeptical but remained silent as Kingsley continued.

"It was tested on many couples and deemed a success. At Shanna's strong urging, Aurora and I decided to use this pre-birth soul request process for our baby. We suspected we might have only one and thought it couldn't hurt to take this extra step. We fed the system all of the traits we thought the president of Earth should have. We wanted our child to be gregarious, decisive, assertive, passionate, powerful, charismatic, and confident. We wanted them to have a gift for connecting and dealing with people. And, most important, we wanted a child that was fearless.

"We had concerns by the time Vicki was two. By the time she was five, we knew the soul request process had not worked. In fact, our child was the complete opposite of everything for which we had asked. She was a sweet, gentle soul, but she was also a trembling mass of insecurity, anxiety, and fear. It almost seemed as though the universe had played a rather nasty trick on us to teach us that we should not be trying to influence such things. Upon seeing how she turned out, Mermetec shut down the project."

"That's too bad," Danny said. "Did you try to get her to work through her issues? I mean, you did it with me."

"Oh my, yes. We consulted with the top psychologists and spiritual advisors on Earth for years. Her mother and I have spent thousands of hours talking with her, but to no avail. Her issues were just too deeply engrained. She ended up spending most of her life in her apartments on our various properties."

"So what about the public? And the senate? Did they wonder where she was all that time and if she would make a good president?"

"I naturally assumed that the rule of the Vortex family was over. But we wanted to keep up appearances in case something miraculous happened. So we told no one about her condition. We couldn't have people thinking she was a recluse, so we've had someone, a double, making most public appearances as Vicki for the past thirty years."

"And that worked?"

"No one has ever publicly questioned her fitness to be president. There have been grumblings about how she hasn't seemed nearly as outgoing and charismatic as those that came before her, but we've managed to keep that to a minimum by explaining that she is very serious and studious and prefers to spend her time preparing herself for her presidency."

"Why can't one of your nieces or nephews take over? That would keep the presidency in the Vortex family."

"We explored that as a fallback plan. None of Marquin and Kayla's children wanted the job. And it's too late now. None of them have trained for it. I have to admit, I didn't push that agenda very hard. I suppose it's my ego, but I always held out hope that my daughter would be able to take over."

"And she's supposed to start her term in five days? When are you planning on telling them that she can't do the job?"

"We're on our way back to Earth now. I'll announce to the senate upon our arrival."

"Why did you wait so long? I mean, shouldn't you have given them more time to find the next president?"

"I probably should have, but I just haven't been able to abandon the possibility that she would come around. A couple of weeks ago I decided I must do something desperate, something that had never been done before, in one last attempt to continue the Vortex legacy."

"And what was that?"

"To recruit you, of course."

"What in the world do I have to do with all of this?"

Kingsley leaned back in his chair and stroked his beard. "Do you believe in reincarnation, Danny?"

CHAPTER 29

"BELIEVE IN IT? I don't know. You talked about it when you were describing Shanna Var's powers. I remember thinking it sounded plausible."

"More precisely, I was describing it when I was explaining spiritual ascension, which is raising the vibration of our soul, our essence. It is to move from negative thoughts, feelings, and emotions toward the positive, to move from fear toward love. As I mentioned, reincarnation is the vehicle for that inevitable process. An important point to remember is that while, in general, everyone's trend is to move forward, you can have downward cycles, possibly long ones, based on your experiences in a given lifetime and how you handle them. That's what happened to you, Danny. When you were a child, your soul was at a certain vibrational rate, but because of all of the embarrassing, humiliating situations you experienced, your rate was lowered significantly. You moved away from love toward fear."

"I think I'd agree with that."

"So you understand that a soul's vibration in a given incarnation can be dramatically influenced by what happens early in life?"

"Sure."

"And that you can actually end a lifetime at a lower vibration than that at which you started it."

"Okay."

"Then it shouldn't be difficult for you to believe a soul's vibration stays with it as you move to the spiritual plane and then into the next lifetime."

"Based on everything you've explained to me it makes sense."

"So, if that is the case, then it would follow that the vibrational level at which you end one lifetime may be the level at which you begin the next. That means, of course, that your experiences and how you deal with them, your thoughts and emotions, whether you are moving toward fear or love in one lifetime, can impact the nature of your being in the next. Do you believe that?"

"In your model, that sounds logical."

"Then you shouldn't have too much trouble believing the nature of our true mission."

"Yes, I'm still waiting to hear what all this has to do with me."

"We needed to convince you to face and conquer your fears so that my daughter can take my place because, Danny, you and Vicki are two incarnations of the same soul."

Danny stared at Kingsley, blankly, blinking. "What?"

"Vicki is a future incarnation of your soul. As I mentioned, I was desperate. A couple of years ago, after many decades of intense effort, our scientists finally became confident that they had been successful in creating reliable, accurate time travel technology. A couple of months ago Shanna had the idea of traveling back in time to work with a prior incarnation of Vicki's soul. The idea was to find the lifetime in which these issues started taking hold and determine a point in that life where it was feasible for us to work with the individual. Aurora was completely against the idea. Hell, even Kayla was skeptical, and she will try just about anything. But Shanna strongly endorsed it, and once I get an idea in my head, I can be a bit stubborn. I was convinced it was our last chance.

"Mermetec recently created what is called the soul tracer technology. The soul tracer is a device that can tap into the past lives of an individual. The person can then see portions of that lifetime the same way you visualize memories. It can also convert that energy into images and sounds from that past life for viewing by others. Without Aurora's knowledge, Vicki and I began working with the soul tracer. Vicki was all for it. She loathed her condition."

Kingsley paused. "Danny, I know this is a lot for you to process, and I'm sure you're wondering if this is yet another manufactured story. I can assure you, it is not."

Danny had slumped back in his chair with his arms folded on his chest. "I'm not sure what I believe."

"We started by looking at the lifetime previous to hers. We found that it was a male, born in Australia in 2124, named Brisby Flondike. He wasn't much better off than Vicki and, unfortunately, took his own life at the age of sixteen after spending much of his life in his room, terrified of the outside world and terribly depressed. We then went back another lifetime and found you. The downward spiral into fear seemed to start in your lifetime. That's when the issues really took hold. We found that as a small child you were shy and timid but a basically gentle, sweet, fairly evolved soul. You then went through event after event during which you were embarrassed and humiliated, each one lowering your vibration and moving you away from love and toward fear, each one a blunt blow to your self-confidence and self-esteem, each one making you more terrified of dealing with people and unfamiliar situations.

"So I decided that you would be the incarnation we should work with and that we could leverage your intelligence, problem-solving skills, and love of science fiction. The main questions were at what point in your life we should appear and what exactly we should do. We saw that by the time you were in your late twenties, you lived alone with no friends and no family, which meant no one would question your absence, provided you could get time off work. The main problem was going to be getting you to agree to leave with us to travel around the cosmos. We then found out about your company demanding you do the training classes, and we saw your reaction. That was our chance. It was the one point at which you might find leaving more palatable than staying."

"That was a good choice," Danny said. "It was probably the only time in my life, up to now, that I would have considered going with you."

"We knew we would then have to craft a story you would find believable. You bought it, at least enough that you agreed to go with us. We had Lexi call you directly as Vivitar to make you feel important and so that you would hopefully develop a crush on her, both of which would make you more likely to work hard at being the lead. Our plan, for the most part, worked fabulously. You seemed to be embracing my advice and demands early on, but Vicki remained in her room and did not contact me. We didn't want to badger her, but we were anxious to know if the plan was working, if the people in future lifetimes were changing as you did, so every day or two we watched soul tracer images of Brisby taking his life.

"Three days into the fake mission, nothing had changed, and we were becoming more than a little concerned. Then on the fourth day, after you returned from Dabita Bok, we saw a slight change. He still took the pill that ended his life, but that time he noticeably hesitated. Later that night was possibly the biggest event of my incredibly eventful life . . . Vicki called and asked me to visit her. We knew we had a long way to go, but that was absolute proof that we were not wasting our time.

"You made incredible progress on all of your issues, and Vicki was changing quickly. By the time you were doing the Quintawba excursion, Brisby no longer took his life. You had made incredible strides and were becoming a normal person. The change in your . . . Danny? Is something wrong?"

Danny looked stunned. "Are you saying that what I've done on this mission kept that Brisby guy from killing himself?"

Kingsley had been so caught up in Vicki's progress that the impact on Brisby hadn't really hit home. "Why yes, Danny, it certainly did. You should be very, very proud of that."

"Great job, kiddo," Shey chimed in.

Danny looked at Kingsley. "But it wasn't a success, was it? The overall mission. Because of what happened on Endoophar."

"You made amazing progress, and Vicki has become a normal person in most respects. However, we did fall a bit short of our ultimate goal. I mentioned that my term is scheduled to end five days from now. On that day, she is to be sworn in and then speak to the CAD senate in an address that will be transmitted across Earth and to all PUPCO planets. The one issue she needed to conquer in order to give the address was her fear of public speaking. That was really the primary goal of the entire mission, to enable her to give that speech. That's why we risked traveling though time and went to all this trouble. I'm afraid that your failu—your inability to give the speech on Endoophar, sealed our fate."

"You can say it. I failed. I couldn't do it."

"No, but you gave a phenomenal effort. You went to that podium despite incredible anxiety and acute physical symptoms. You saved Brisby's life, and now my precious daughter can lead a normal life, just not as president of Earth. As you said at one point during the mission, you don't need to be able to give speeches to live a happy, productive life. I'm extremely grateful."

"And the Vortex family's rule?" Danny asked. "It's done? A hundred and twenty years of being the ruling family, and it's all over because I couldn't give the speech?"

"You shouldn't look at it that way. Everything happens for a reason. Perhaps it wasn't meant to be. Perhaps Vicki not being president will work out best for all involved."

"You said that the Vortex next-in-line got a fabulous education and did all of this training to be president. If she didn't do all of that, even if she gave the address, how was she going to take over for you?"

"She actually did a lot of it. When you spend thirty-some years alone, you have to find something to occupy your time. Despite all of her issues, she is brilliant and has always had a thirst for knowledge. Through self-study, she absorbed as much knowledge as someone who went through the traditional educational system, including what she would have received at a fine university. Also, at my request she rigorously studied diplomacy, inter-planetary affairs, and how my office functions. The only thing she didn't do that the past Vortex presidents did was travel with me to get experience with how the job is really done. But that's all irrelevant now."

"I'm still not so sure I buy the whole Vicki and I being the same soul thing."

"I think you do," Kingsley replied, "which is why you had very little reaction when I told you. You know it's possible because of the immediate bond and comfort level you felt with her. It was a connection unlike any you've had with a human being before."

"It was . . . by far."

Kingsley smiled at him. "Well, there you have it, Danny. That was our real mission in its entirety."

"I don't know. This is all more far-fetched than the Yoobatar story."

"I assure you that what I've told you here is the truth."

"I thought the whole Yoobatar story was the truth. How do I know everything you're telling me now isn't a second fake mission you made up to try and get me to do something else?"

"For one simple reason: we're taking you home. As soon as Marquin and Lexi go back to their ship, Gracie will start us on a course back to Earth. The trip will be about three days. When we arrive, we'll go back to your time and drop you back at your apartment."

Those words hit Danny like a bucket of cold water. What had been his world for a week and a half would be gone. He would never again see the three people to whom he had grown so close. The thought of walking into his empty apartment and watching the Star Hopper drive away made his stomach knot. The realization that he'd then be facing the training class made him nauseous.

"Isn't there something else I can do?"

"About what?" Kingsley asked.

"To help Vicki. Isn't there another speech you can set up for me to do? Now that I know what it's really for, I think I can do it."

"I think it's a little late for that, Danny. You knowing it's a setup would lessen its effectiveness, even if you succeeded. You were fine, for the most part, during all the practice for your speech, mainly because you knew it was practice and that it didn't really matter if you messed up. Once you got into the real situation, you panicked. No, the mission is over."

"But I really don't want to go back to my life. Can't I stay in this time? You said I could when the mission was over."

"And do what for a living? Be a physical laborer? Your computer skills would be of little value. And to be honest, you don't belong here, Danny. It just doesn't feel right. You belong in your time."

"It doesn't feel like I belong in my time."

"Look on the bright side. This mission didn't just help Brisby and Vicki. You are leaving us a much better person than the one we plucked from that apartment. I think your life will be different. You will reverse your withdrawal from life. You'll probably make friends, start dating, and play golf. If you're not happy with your job, I think you have the ability now to find another. After you're back for a time, you'll realize it was the right thing to do."

"I suppose that would be for the best. I just, um, I'm going to miss you guys."

"We're all going to miss you too, Danny. Unfortunately, saying goodbye is part of life. I need to go speak with Vicki. I'm sure you're tired from all of this. Why don't you go to your room and relax and meet us back here at six for happy hour?"

"Sounds good."

As Danny shuffled from the room with his head down, Shey and Kingsley watched.

"Do you really think it would be that bad to keep him around?" said Shey. "You could find something for him to do."

"Why, Shey, have you grown that fond of Danny?"

"Naw, I just feel sorry for the kid having to go back to his life after having an experience like this. Hey, it will be nice not having to hide anything anymore. I was constantly worried about letting something slip and ruining the whole thing."

"I was too. It will be strange not having to keep up the pretense. It's been quite an experience."

————————————

"Hello, Father," Vicki said as she entered Kingsley's office to find him leaning back in his desk chair, staring at the wall.

Kingsley spun in his chair to face her. He had been trying to go to her suite for the prior two hours, but he couldn't bring himself to do so. He couldn't bring himself to hear her say there was no way she could do the address. He couldn't bring himself to hear the words that would bring the Vortex family rule to an end.

"Hello, princess."

"I'm assuming it didn't go so well down there?"

"No, no it didn't. Despite incredible anxiety he went to the podium . . . and proceeded to pass out."

"Oh my. I assumed there was a problem, since I didn't feel any change while you were gone. In fact, I may feel a little worse about it. Is he alright now?"

"He's fine. A little down about what happened and sad the mission is over, but he'll be okay. I told him everything. He's back in his room, resting and digesting it all."

Vicki walked around the desk, leaned against the edge, and took Kingsley's hand. "Father, I'm very, very sorry, but I can't do the address. The thought of doing it is terrifying. Even if I could get through it, the public speaking demands of the job would keep me in a state of constant anxiety. My mental and physical health would deteriorate quickly."

"I know, sweetie. I know. That's fine. I'm just delighted that you've improved so much, and I'm excited to see how you'll spend the rest of your life."

"Thank you, Father, but I know you're very disappointed. You can admit it. You wouldn't have tried so incredibly hard for so many years to get me to change if the Vortex rule wasn't extremely important to you."

"It is. I have tried everything I could think of over the years, but it wasn't just so that you could be president. I wanted you to have a normal life."

"I'm sure you did, especially early on. But you risked time travel, fabricated and played out a fake mission, and brought together a soul from two lifetimes. You can't tell me that you'd have done all that if I had a qualified sibling."

"You have me there. Yes, the family's rule is and has always been very important to me, but you know what? Your well-being is much more important. Everything will be fine. The CAD senate will elect a new president, we will go on, and in time I'll get over it. We gave it a hell of a shot, though, didn't we?"

Danny stepped from the shower with a spring in his step and an out-of-tune song coming from his mouth. He had taken a two-hour nap and woke up a new man. The thought of leaving his new family was not as depressing as before, and he was actually glad the mission was over. He had handled almost everything Kingsley threw at him but was relieved that his work was done. And while he wasn't looking forward to dealing with his employment situation, the more he thought about going home, the better it felt. He stopped his singing when he heard his living room television. He dried off, threw on some clothes, and went to see if he had a visitor.

"That's actually very rude, you know," he said. "Just showing up in someone's room. I would think such a powerful being would have better manners."

"Hello, Daniel," said Shanna. She had been reclining on his sofa but hopped up to face him. "I suppose I could announce myself and come through the door, but that's so low-vibration. I try very hard not to startle people. And admit it, my showing up like this and then just fading away adds to my mystique, doesn't it?"

"I suppose it does."

"Feeling better?"

"I am. The nap really helped . . . with everything."

"Yes, one shouldn't think too much when one is exhausted and emotionally drained. So how do you feel about the real mission?"

"Is it all true?"

"It is."

"And an enlightened being such as yourself supported this charade?"

"I strongly endorsed Kingsley's mission since it helped a struggling soul."

"I thought about his motivation when I woke up. Actually, it was to save his family's rule. He wouldn't have traveled through time and gone through the fake mission just to help me, or Brisby, or even Vicki get over our issues."

"True. Getting Vicki to the point she could take over for him may have been his motivation, but I knew the side effect would be the elevation of a soul, and that's much more important."

"Helping one soul is more important than the presidency of Earth?"

"He didn't just help one. When one soul's vibration increases, there is a ripple effect. Everyone you and Brisby and Vicki encounter going forward will now be impacted differently than they would have been. And, though it's not as obvious, Kingsley has also advanced during all of this. So, how do you feel?"

"I feel good . . . different than I did before, more lighthearted and calm, kind of more solid, if that makes any sense. I'm not afraid of looking for a new job now. It's been an unbelievable experience, but I think I'm ready to go home. I'm going to miss everyone, but Kingsley's right, I don't belong in this time."

"You won't have to look for a new job."

"Well, I'm not going to do the training classes, so I'm assuming I'll get fired."

"I'm going to do something I don't do very often, which is tell you how someone in the past, your future, is going to behave. You're not going to get fired if you refuse to do the training. Nathan Forrester has an ego and a temper, but he isn't stupid. He knows your value to his company."

"Really? Wow. That's great. Isn't that kind of immoral or something, telling me that?"

"If it's for the greater good, it's the thing to do. My telling you that isn't going to cause anyone any harm, and it will free your mind so that you can do what you need to do."

"Which is?"

"I'll let you figure that out. So do you really want to go back?"

"I think so. I kind of miss my world, and I think Kingsley's taught me everything I need to know."

Shanna chuckled. "That's a good one. You've done great work the last two weeks, so I can see how you think that, but you still have a lot to learn, as everyone does."

"I suppose you're right, but I think I'd like to rest on my laurels for a while before I work on any more issues."

"That choice is yours. Everyone is on a path. The pace at which you move along it is completely up to you. I would like to congratulate you on what you achieved on this mission. I really enjoyed watching you change. I especially liked the dynamic between you and Vicki. Did you notice how the more you improved and started liking yourself, the more you felt connected to her?"

"I just figured it was the normal progression of a relationship."

"Part of it was, but you were not going to really like her until you started liking yourself," Shanna said.

"So I suppose you are going to tell me that I love her because I love myself. That seems to be a popular word around here."

"I'm not going to tell you that, because it's not true, is it?"

Danny thought for a moment and looked away. "I feel better about myself, but no, I don't think I'd say that I love myself."

"So you see, you still have some work to do. Don't rest on those laurels too long, sport," she said before playfully jabbing at his chin and fading away.

Danny took a couple of deep breaths as he waited for the lift's doors to open. He was on his way to the yard to see Vicki. It was a potentially awkward, uncomfortable encounter that the old Danny would never have initiated. The new Danny knew it was the right thing to do. He found her on a bench in the far back corner. She was staring at the countryside depicted on the wall and didn't notice Danny's presence until he was only a few feet away.

"Hey," he said softly.

"Hi, Danny."

"Your dad told me everything."

"So I hear."

"You okay?"

"I'm just a little down about letting him down." Vicki sighed. "It's strange how I've always dreaded the day I was supposed to take over for him and now I'm really sad about not being able to."

"Actually, it sounds like I'm the one who let him down."

"From what I hear, you made a valiant effort. I, on the other hand, have never made one. Pretty weird, huh, us being the same soul?"

"I'm still trying to get my mind around it. So you believe it?"

"Oh yes," Vicki said. "I've seen the soul tracer logs and watched you go through a lot of painful experiences. But even if I hadn't, I'd still believe it. I feel a connection with you that I've never come close to feeling with anyone else."

"I feel the same way. Mind if I sit?"

Vicki patted the bench next to her, and Danny obliged.

"So if there is no such place as Yoobatar, what are we looking at?"

"Oh, it's from Earth. It's the area around our family compound in Colorado."

"It's beautiful," Danny said before looking down. "So tell me, did you really want to be president, or were you just doing all of this because your dad was pushing you?"

"Well, the answer to that has changed dramatically in the last ten days. Before that, I was sorry I was letting him down, but I really, deep down, didn't want anything to do with being president. Now I feel different. If it wasn't for my fear of public speaking, I think I would be looking forward to it. I think it would give me a lot of pride and satisfaction to keep the Vortex legacy alive. But things are what they are. Everything happens for a reason."

"So what are you going to do now, with your life, now that you've changed so much?"

"I don't know what I'll do. I've been so focused on the presidency, I haven't considered other options. How about you?"

"I'm not sure. I'll just go back and start doing my job. I'm sure I'll be more social, but it will be hard to meet people, not working in an office or having any existing friends. I'll probably start by going to some department social functions. I haven't been to one in years."

"And perhaps date?"

"Perhaps. I think the time we've spent together is going to help me a lot in that department."

"It was good for both of us." Vicki turned slightly to face him. "I just realized I haven't thanked you. What you've done on this mission has been nothing short of amazing. You absorbed Father's advice and truly raised your vibration through determination and tremendous effort. So thank you, Danny, thank you so much. You've changed my life."

"You're welcome. I just wish I could have finished the job. It's kind of sad that I got as far as I did and then fell short of the goal."

"You did everything you could," Vicki said as she took his hand and placed her head on his shoulder.

Danny stared at the landscape and wondered if he had.

CHAPTER 30

THE MOOD AT DINNER was lighthearted but subdued. The four of them sat around the living room table, sipping wine and chatting casually. At Danny's urging, Kingsley spoke at length about what it was like being president of Earth. Shey was Shey, frequently shifting gears from being sarcastic and caustic to kind and complimentary. Danny and Vicki were peaceful and relaxed, both adding to the conversation and laughing occasionally. The mood was upbeat but tempered by a subtle sadness that filled the room.

"I have a question," Danny declared.

"Certainly," replied Kingsley.

"I've been thinking about the whole time travel thing and Vicki and I being the same soul thing. If her lifetime comes after mine, why wasn't her entire life different once I changed? Why wasn't she over these issues from the time she was born?"

"An excellent question. The answer is that lifetimes are not as linear as you think. The physical and spiritual planes are more three-dimensional. It's a bit difficult for our limited minds to comprehend, but I'll try to explain, given my understanding. Gracie, give me a screen over here on the wall and graphically depict what I describe," Kingsley said as he stood. A large window in the side of the room changed from the Colorado sunset to a sizable screen.

"Give me a line along the bottom. Danny, that line represents linear time, moving from left to right. You think of it as your life starting at a point on the line and ending at another, followed by Brisby's life and then Vicki's. If that were the case, then yes, Vicki's entire life would have been different, meaning we wouldn't have needed to go on this mission, meaning you wouldn't be here right now. Confusing, right? Gracie, give me three lines that start at various points on the first line and move upward, perpendicular to that line. Danny, think of the first line as your lifetime, the second as Brisby's and the third as Vicki's."

"So you're trying to tell me that our lifetimes are kind of going on at the same time?"

"*Kind of* is a good phrase in this instance. These lines are not really lines but planes. Gracie, angle the original line from the bottom left corner toward the upper right and change the vertical lines to planes parallel to one another. Danny, this first plane is a better depiction of your lifetime. Your energy exists in physical form on this plane, along with everyone else who was, or is, alive at that time. Everyone you've ever known is in a lifetime on that plane. The second plane is Brisby's life, and the third is Vicki's. Shey and I are also in this third plane in our current incarnations. The space between these planes is the astral realm. It is where your soul exists between lifetimes. The best way to think of it is that your lifetime begins at the base of this plane and moves up. When you die, you exist in the space between planes. When you are ready to go through another lifetime, it starts at the base of the next plane and moves upward, and so forth. It is all moving along this line at the bottom, meaning the Brisby and Vicki incarnations come after yours, but the lifetimes are, if you will, going on at the same time. I know that is difficult to get your mind around, but, as I said, when in physical form we are limited in what we can understand.

"This all ties into time travel, how you and Vicki can be together, and why her entire life didn't change. The Mermetec agency came up with a way to move beings and objects from one of these planes to another. I don't understand exactly how it works, but basically the ship is encased in an energy field. The vibration of everything in the field is increased to the point it can be transmitted to a different plane, and then it is decreased so it becomes solid again. For this mission, we used the soul tracer on Vicki to pinpoint exactly when you would be informed about the training classes. We then used the technology to move to a day before that point on your plane, observed you for a day via the iggy, recruited you, and then traveled back to our plane when you were sleeping. Does this make any sense?"

"Some, although I think I prefer Shey's explanation about going faster than the speed of time," Danny said, eliciting a chuckle from everyone.

"I didn't think you were ready to hear this at that time. The reason Vicki's entire life didn't change is because she is moving up her plane, living her life, at the same time you are moving up yours."

"When will you take me back? How much time will have passed in my lifetime?"

"The same amount that has passed on this plane. There are concerns that the time travel technology isn't reliably precise. We indicate our desired date and time, and the system does very complex calculations in order to get us as close as possible to that point. We actually showed up to your apartment several hours later than we had planned, but it could have gone either way. We're fairly confident that if we use the exact same settings as before, the same amount of time will have passed on your plane."

"This is starting to feel like Shey's explanation."

"Yes, it can be confusing. It was certainly a daring mission, but it was worth it. That reminds me, we didn't start this evening with a toast," Kingsley said as he raised his glass. "Here's to the success of our mission, to Danny and Vicki and all we've accomplished. Danny, are you going to pick up your glass?"

"No. No, I'm not." Danny's stare didn't leave Vicki as he spoke.

"And why is that?"

"Because I'm not going to toast the success of the mission."

"Danny, as I told you, there are degrees of success. All of our goals weren't achieved, but what you've done for Brisby and Vicki is certainly worth toasting."

"That's not it. I'm not toasting the mission, because the mission isn't over." He was still gazing at Vicki.

"What are you talking about? I told you there is nothing else that can be done at this point."

"Yes, there is."

"And what, may I ask, is that?"

Danny looked at Kingsley and spoke with a calm conviction. "I'm going to go back and do the training class."

"Danny, no," Vicki said. "Don't put yourself through that again."

"It's okay. I don't care if I have another meltdown. I want to try."

"Danny," Kingsley said. "That's very noble and courageous of you, but it's not necessary. I don't know what other advice or training I could provide, so I seriously doubt the results will be any different. And Vicki's right. Why go through all of that again?"

"Because I want to do it. I've made a lot of progress on this trip, but if I don't try, I'll always feel like I ran away, that I couldn't finish the job. I'll always be disgusted with myself if I don't at least try. I want to do it for myself, and I want to do it for Vicki, and I want to do it for you. I can't ruin her future and the Vortex family legacy without at least trying. The training class is a real presentation, the only one available before her speech."

"That's very admirable, but I must say I think that once again your real motivation is fear. You're afraid you'll get fired if you don't do it. If you make the choice out of fear, you'll lose your conviction when the situation becomes difficult."

"That's not it. Shanna has assured me that I will not be fired if I flat out refuse to do it. I'm too valuable to the company. I have four days to get ready for the training class. You'll take me back to my time the day before the class. I'm going to prepare and practice for the next three days. When I get back, I'll have a day to create the materials. The only way you can stop me is if you refuse to take me back. I'm not asking for your help or permission. I'm telling you I'm going to do it. It's a better use of the next three days than sleeping, eating, drinking, and playing golf. If you can think of any other pointers, I'll certainly appreciate hearing them." There was no tremble in his voice, no doubt in his demeanor, no anxiety in his body language. He was solid.

Kingsley glanced around the table. Shey looked impressed. Vicki looked concerned but mildly excited. Danny was unflinchingly staring right at him. Kingsley sighed. "With the time travel technology, you move through time but not space. We'll first have to return to Earth. The Star Hopper doesn't have the time travel technology. I suppose Vicki and I could take it down to Earth while Shey takes you back to your time in the *Aurora*. Think you can deal with Shey for a day or two?"

"If it's for the good of the mission, I'll try."

"Well then, I suppose I better retract my toast. The mission is back on!"

The table erupted in a boisterous celebration.

"Great," Danny said. "I'll start writing the class tomorrow morning."

"And I'll start writing my speech," added Vicki.

"But I already wrote you one that's perfect," Kingsley said. "I worked on it for months."

"It's an excellent speech, Father, but those are your words. I need to use my own."

"A new toast, then," Kingsley said. "Here's to the mission being alive and kicking."

———————

Kingsley was rolling and tossing, exhausted but unable to sleep. He wanted desperately to help prepare Danny, but he knew that rehashing what they had done for Endoophar would serve no purpose. He was on his side, facing the wall, when the room was filled with a soft glow.

"After all these years, you're going to seduce me now?" Kingsley rolled over to find Shanna beside him, flat on her back and staring at the ceiling.

"As tempting as you make that sound, I'm afraid not. I gave up pleasures of the flesh long ago."

"What a shame. I would think that with your vast knowledge it would be quite an experience. It's probably for the best. Aurora would somehow find out, and she wouldn't be pleased. I can't hide anything from that woman. By the way, brilliant move on your part to assure Danny that he wasn't going to be fired. It removed the possibility that he was going to do the training out of fear. With that out of the picture the only reason he would do it is if he wanted to."

"And an excellent move on your part not asking him to do it. That removed any possibility that he would be doing it out of guilt or obligation."

"You said the next excursion had to be his idea. After the Endoophar debacle it dawned on me that the training classes were what you were referring to. It wasn't easy. I was eager to bring it up."

"By not doing so you may have saved the mission."

"Think he can do it?" asked Kingsley as he fell onto his back and also stared at the ceiling.

"He's got a better chance because he wants to do it, but it will still be difficult for him without more help."

"I don't suppose you want to chime in on what that might be? I've spent the last two hours trying to think of a fresh approach. Everything I've told him to this point obviously didn't work."

"Don't think for a second it was a waste of time. It got him through the practice sessions and got him to the podium in the live situation. You just need to go a step further."

"I'm listening."

"This is a critical point in the lives of everyone involved, so I'm going to be more direct than I've ever been with you."

Kingsley sat up. "I can't wait to hear this."

———————

"You wanted to see me?"

"Yes, Danny. Come on in." Kingsley was seated by the small table at the back corner of the guest gathering room, staring into space. "How are you feeling? I haven't seen you all day."

"Pretty good, but a little tired. I got up fairly early and started working on the training class and haven't even taken a nap. I ate breakfast and lunch in my room."

"How is it going?"

"Really well. I should have it finished tomorrow. I can use the next day to review and practice it."

"Great. I have a strategy that I think will help."

"Okay. Shoot," Danny said as he took a seat across the table from Kingsley at the same time Kingsley rose and started pacing.

"First of all, everything we worked on before the council speech still applies. What I'm about to cover does not replace any of that. It builds on it."

"Okay."

"When we've discussed what happens when you feel a situation has turned into you presenting, you said it felt like a switch was being flipped."

"Right. It happens just before a planned presentation or in any other situation in which I suddenly feel like I'm presenting something. When that happens, it's like a switch is flipped, and I lose control."

"I want you to put yourself into one of those situations. What happens the moment you feel you have to present?"

Danny closed his eyes and thought back to a time he melted down in a meeting when asked to speak at length. In less than thirty seconds, he started feeling anxious. He spoke without opening his eyes. "My heart rate increases sharply. I'm having trouble breathing, so I start breathing faster. My throat is tight. So are my shoulders and neck and the back of my head. All so incredibly tight. My mind is racing out of control about what to say, whether I'll mangle it and look like an idiot, and how I can get out of the situation as quickly as possible. My movements become fast and herky-jerky, and my hands are trembling. I'm very physically and mentally agitated. My skin feels like it's on fire, and I'm sweating a lot. I can't find any moisture in my mouth. My stomach is churning and burning and tied up in knots. When I talk, it's fast, and my voice is trembling. Everything escalates. I feel pressure, tremendous pressure, like I'm going to explode. I want to escape." Danny opened his eyes and exhaled deeply. "There. That's what happens."

Kingsley took a seat and spoke. "The key is that you need to stop those physical symptoms before they start."

"Oh, sure. Anything else? How about I split the atom while I'm at it?"

"You're on the right track. You need to control your energy. Danny, your mind is more powerful than you think. Your physical body and your mind are energy. You can control your body and your thoughts. The approach we are going to take is for you to focus on stopping the physical symptoms and controlling your thoughts."

"And how do I do that?"

"As I said, you control your energy. You slow it down. When your switch is flipped, everything becomes fast and tight. *Slow down* and *relax* are your keywords. The moment you feel the symptoms start, the first thing you are going to do is relax. Unclench everything. Drop your shoulders and relax your neck, throat, and the back of your head. Doing a couple of neck rolls will help. Then relax your stomach. Unclench your chest. Your instinct is to tighten up, but you have the power to override that. Relaxing your muscles is a great start, but the concept that is going to help you the most is to *slow down*."

"Slow down what?"

"Everything. First, slow down your breathing. Focus on keeping your breathing slow, steady, and continuous. Affirm that your heart rate is slowing. Remember, you are in charge. Next, slow down your mind. Having frenetic thoughts does nothing but exacerbate your physical symptoms. Slow down your mind and calmly think productive thoughts. Think of what you want to convey, say it, then move to the next thing. You also need to slow down your physical movements. When you are that agitated, you think you have to do everything fast. Lastly, slow down your speech. When you are nervous, you have a tendency to talk very fast.

"So, as I said, your key words are *relax* and *slow down*. You can go through it like a checklist. The moment you start feeling anxious, whether it's five minutes or five hours beforehand, go through the checklist. You may still be nervous, but you can handle the situation if you don't let any one symptom run wild. What do you think?"

"I . . . think . . . I . . . like . . . it."

"That's hilarious. Seriously."

"I seriously like it. You chose the right words. When I get in those situations, everything is tight and fast. If I can keep my muscles at least partially relaxed and slow everything down, especially my breathing, I think I could get through it. Anything else? I want to get more done before dinner."

"Yes. A couple more tools. First, you have to be open to energy exchange with your audience."

"Energy exchange?"

"Yes, when you are about to talk in front of people, you circle the wagons, if you will. It's like you put up a shield, which cuts you off from everyone in the room. It prevents everyone's energy from reaching you and prevents you from extending outward. You make no connection with the people. That creates the feeling of an adversarial relationship, which adds to your fear and anxiety. You need to open your mind and heart to everyone in the room, embrace their presence, and connect with them. You need to exchange energy with them."

"That makes sense. I can work on that."

"One last point. When you approach a task with fear, you feel weak, helpless, and vulnerable. You need to approach the class with a feeling of power—not angry, aggressive power but a positive, peaceful power. If you can do that, you will feel much stronger and confident."

"You're right. I do feel weak and helpless in those situations."

"If you follow these steps—relax, slow down, work from a position of peaceful power, and exchange energy—you'll have a much better experience. I'll let you get back to it. Happy hour is at six-thirty."

———————————————

An uneasy anticipation permeated the ship for the following two days. Everyone was hopeful though not confident, cautiously upbeat but slightly subdued. Danny and Vicki spent the days in their own rooms, preparing and practicing their presentations. As they sat down for dinner on the second night, it hit Danny like a ton of bricks—it was their final evening together. After the next morning he might never see Kingsley or Vicki again. He tried to fight back the quickly welling tears as Kingsley raised his glass.

"To Danny's success," he said. "No matter what happens going forward, he's made phenomenal progress the last two weeks."

"I put forth the effort, but none of it would have happened without all of you," Danny said. "If you hadn't recruited me, I probably would have gone through the rest of my life as a recluse. I'm, uh, I'm going to miss all of you guys."

Kingsley too started tearing up. "And we're going to miss you too, Danny. It's like you've been part of our family for the past two weeks. It seems longer than that, doesn't it?"

"It does. In fact, my normal life seems really foreign now. I know it's where I belong, but a part of me wants to stay in this time with all of you."

"And part of me, a large part, wants you to stay, but I think you need to continue your old life. It will be interesting to see how you do after all that you've achieved. And you know what? We're finding this time travel technology to be safe and fairly accurate. I think we may be able to pop back to your time and visit occasionally. Of course, we'd be difficult to explain to your wife. Oh, there I go again spilling secrets," Kingsley said as he smiled.

"A wife, huh? Wow. You know, I've been so focused on the class that I haven't really thought much about how all of this is going to change the rest of my life. I suppose I will be able to talk to women back there now."

"Of course you will," said Kingsley.

"How's your prep going?" Danny asked as he turned to Vicki.

"I finished it yesterday and have been practicing and tweaking it. I'm very happy with it."

"And she won't let me see it," Kingsley said.

"You know you'll try to make changes if I let you see it. I want these to be my words."

"Did you practice in front of anyone?" Danny asked.

"I don't need to. If you do the class successfully and really feel, deep in your being, that you no longer have the fear, then I'll immediately be able to give the address without major anxiety, perhaps with none at all."

"What's it been like to change so suddenly every time I made a break-through? That must have felt weird."

"A little weird, but actually quite wonderful, almost magical."

Kingsley chimed in. "For the entire mission, we've seen that you conquering a fear had an immediate impact on her. We have no reason to believe that the same won't be true when you have success in that classroom."

It was all Danny could do to hold back the tears. He was in the garage, standing with Shey as Kingsley and Vicki prepared to board the Star Hopper. He was having trouble looking at them as Kingsley shook hands with Shey.

"Take good care of him and the *Aurora*."

"Oh, I'll take care of him. This will be great. I can do and say whatever I want to him without you interfering," Shey said with a grin.

Kingsley stepped up to Danny and put his hands on his shoulders. "I'm not sure what to say, Danny."

"Be sincere and authentic," Danny replied, managing a smile.

"Touché. I think of you like a son, not just because you share a soul with my daughter, but because of everything we've been through in the last two weeks. I want to tell you again how incredibly proud I am of what you've accomplished. I'm going to miss you, Danny."

"I like the idea of you guys using the time travel technology and visiting me at some point."

"We might do that. However, we don't know what the future holds. It would be best if you didn't count on it."

"I understand."

"I'm also proud of you for what you are going to do tomorrow. You are being truly brave. Remember, no matter what happens, you are a fine young man, and nothing can change that. I want you to remember your training and to continue working on your issues for the rest of your life. I'll know if you are. Vicki will change, unexpectedly and inexplicably, if you have a major improvement. If I don't see any such changes, I may have to go back and kick your butt."

"I'm not sure how I'm going to change much without you giving me insights and advice."

"There are a large number of fabulous books on spirituality and metaphysics in your time. Look for the ones that speak to you. And there are a lot of very knowledgeable, attuned beings. If you put out to the universe that you'd like one to enter your life, it will happen. And don't be surprised if Shanna pops in on you now and then. She can move from plane to plane as easily as she can move around physical space."

"That would be cool. It would keep all of this . . . kind of real in my mind and bring back a lot of fond memories. I keep thinking I'm going to go back and wake up some day and wonder if this was all a dream."

"That reminds me," Kingsley said as he reached into a pocket and pulled out a small device. "I wanted to give you this as a going away present. I've loaded it up with pictures of all of us and of every room on the ship. It also holds video recordings of our evening gatherings, rounds of golf, and training sessions. It's yours to take back. If you ever start to doubt that all of this was real, you'll have this to let you know it was."

"Wow. That's fantastic." Danny struggled to get out the words through the building emotion. He looked down, wiped his eyes, and tried to gather himself. "How is this thing powered? I won't be able to recharge it if it dies."

"The energy cells in it will last longer than your lifetime. I'd like to take some pictures now, if you don't mind."

They passed around Kingsley's device and took turns taking pictures of various combinations of the group. Shanna appeared just in time to take one of the four of them. When they were finished, Kingsley turned to Danny once again. The moisture in his eyes matched that in Danny's.

"Goodbye for now, Danny. I love you," Kingsley said before locking Danny in a prolonged hug. When he finally stepped back, Danny looked him in the eyes.

"I love you too, Kingsley."

Kingsley tousled Danny's hair, turned away, and climbed into the Star Hopper. Danny stepped up to Vicki and took her hands in his.

"I guess this is goodbye."

"Yes, I believe it is," she replied as a tear went streaming down each cheek. She threw her arms around Danny's neck, put her face against his, and whispered in his ear. "I'll miss you, but you know we'll always be together."

"I know we will. Good luck with your address."

"There is no luck involved. We will either do it or not do it, and I know you can do it. Thank you for making me functional. Now go finish the job." Vicki kissed him on the cheek, turned away, and quickly climbed into the transport.

Danny again wiped the tears from his eyes and moved to a position from which he could see both passengers. A quiet hum came from the engines as Kingsley powered up the Star Hopper. The floor beneath it slid away. Danny felt a lump in his throat and a knot in his stomach as the transport started dropping slowly. Kingsley saluted him. Danny reciprocated. He locked eyes with Vicki just in time to see her put her hand to her mouth and then extend her palm to him. They were gone before he could respond.

Shey walked up to Danny and put his hand on his shoulder. "Come on, sport. We've got a mission to finish."

CHAPTER 31

Once the floor slid shut, Danny turned and shuffled slowly toward the lift. Though he had known them only two weeks, Kingsley and Vicki had been two of the most influential people of his life. They were gone, and he would likely never see them again. He was feeling something different, something new. He was heavy-hearted.

Danny and Shey walked in silence back to the living room, at which point Danny stopped and looked around. "It seems so weird knowing they aren't on the ship."

"Yes, there is certainly a void when they aren't on board. Let's take a seat up at the table. We're going back to your time now."

"Do I need to buckle in or anything? I mean, is it a bumpy ride?"

Shey chuckled. "It is not. In fact, it's not really a ride at all in the way you think of it. The ship will remain at the same point in this physical plane and will occupy the same space in your physical plane once we slow down. Everything will change to a brilliant white light, and you'll get a feeling of weightless, peaceful euphoria. It is thought to be the way you feel when you move close to enlightenment. Some researchers were thinking the technology could be used to accelerate spiritual ascension, but the metaphysical masters involved with the project assured us that our spiritual and physical bodies are not prepared to handle being in a state of such intense, high-frequency vibration for an extended period. Let's sit in the command chairs."

Danny followed Shey to the front of the living room, where they settled into the front two chairs.

"Gracie, take us back."

Despite Shey's description of the process, Danny braced himself. After waiting in silence for several minutes, Danny spoke up. "I thought you said everything would . . . wow."

It started slowly. Everything in the room—walls, floor, chairs, tables—became brighter and then started glowing. Danny looked down and found the same was true of his body. He was about to shout when a peaceful calm washed over him. Everything in the room became shapeless, changing from a physical state to the brilliant light Shey had described. Danny felt only pure joy, completely free from all thoughts, worries, and fears. He was in a state of blissful ecstasy.

It lasted only a split second. The progression of sensations was reversed, and everything in the room solidified around him. Danny blinked and looked around, disappointed the experience was over.

"Wow, that was unbelievable. But it only lasted a couple of minutes."

"You have no sensation of time when in the astral planes. Gracie, how long did the process take?"

"The process lasted fifty-eight minutes."

"How do you feel?" Shey asked. "You should be experiencing a bit of residual calm."

"I do. I feel really good."

"Unfortunately, that will wear off in an hour or so."

"That felt so amazing. I think if I had this ship, I'd just keep bouncing around through time all day."

"You wouldn't. As I mentioned, your mind, body, and soul can only take it a short time. It's also believed that you can only take doing it so often. The experts recommend no more than twice before taking at least a week before doing it again. Plus, the energy used for that process is of a different type than that used for all other ship operations. We can store enough for five transportations before we have to return to Mermetec and recharge. That was just our third trip. My trip back will be the fourth. Gracie, how long to Earth?"

"We will be in range for your departure in twenty-three minutes."

"Great. More importantly, when are we?"

"In the time zone in which Danny lives, it is five fifteen in the morning on the target date."

"Perfect. We'll be able to land while it's still dark. Go pack and change into the clothes you wore here. Meet me in the garage in thirty minutes."

Shey left ahead of Danny, leaving him alone in the room. Danny started toward the door but stopped near the bar and turned to take one last look around. He felt like he was leaving home.

"This is so strange," Danny said as he looked around his living room. "It's like I haven't been here for years. I don't know if I can adjust to this life again. It all seems so mundane and primitive after what I've been through."

"You'll be fine. You'll reacclimate more quickly than you think."

Danny set down his bag and turned to face Shey. "Well, I guess this is it. Thanks for everything," he said as he stuck out his hand.

"What, are you looking for money? I'm not going anywhere. At least, not yet," Shey said as he plopped down on the sofa and reached for the remote.

"What are you talking about?"

"I'm staying until after your training class, for support and in case you need anything else."

"Okay, well sure. I'm going to go back to my office. What are you going to do all day?"

"Watch television. I can't get enough of twenty-first-century program-ming. What you people put on the air as entertainment never ceases to amaze me. I'll also probably go out and explore a bit. I may expose a few of your local ladies to the wonder and majesty of the Gabinkster. Hey, I could tell them I'm you to start building your reputation around here."

"No! Don't do that."

"Whatever you wish. Now scurry on back and finish the class."

As Shey settled in to watch television, Danny headed back toward his office. As on the *Aurora*, he worked with focus and clarity despite the fact the class was less than twenty-four hours away. He heard Shey leave and return twice. Danny was mildly concerned but asked no questions. He was just relieved that he came back each time without the police or a jealous husband in pursuit. After convincing Shey to eat a delivered pizza instead of preparing dinner, Danny went for a run to clear his head, then went out to get a bottle of wine. By seven they had settled in to watch a couple of serious science fiction movies that Shey assumed were comedies. Shey had a couple glasses of wine, but Danny abstained.

"Think I can do it?" he asked as he lost interest in the second movie.

"What would Kingsley say?"

"He'd say of course I can, and probably tell me to start using the advice he gave me if the symptoms are starting. But he's not here. I'm asking you. As much as I respect him, I think Kingsley sometimes avoids being negative when he feels negative. You don't shovel the sunshine as much as he does."

Shey set his glass on the coffee table and put his elbows on his knees. "Can you do it? Certainly. Will you do it? I have no idea. But it really doesn't matter."

"Doesn't matter? What are you talking about? The Vortex family rule depends on it."

"Yes, but in the scheme of things, it really doesn't matter if the Vortex family rule continues. Trillions of beings deal with situations every day that may seem trivial compared to this but that are really just as important. It's a big deal to Kingsley because he's got some ego issues he needs to deal with, but the universe will continue whether or not someone named Vortex is the president of one of a zillion planets in the cosmos. All issues must eventually be dealt with. Somewhere along the way, whether later in your life,

Brisby's, Vicki's, or one after Vicki, your soul will successfully tackle this issue. No one is on a schedule, and there are no time constraints. It's not like the Source blows a whistle at some point indicating the game is over. If it doesn't happen tomorrow, no big deal."

Danny was surprised by Shey's somewhat cavalier attitude.

"It's not a big deal. I like that. It takes some of the pressure off. But that's big-picture, long-term stuff. If I really blow this tomorrow, I could get fired."

"Do you really think a company would fire their best problem-solver just because he didn't do well leading a training class? That's not what they're paying you for. And even if they did, you'd get another job like that," Shey said as he snapped his fingers. "How many of your customers and business partners do you think would want to hire the foremost expert on the software they are using or selling? I'm guessing a lot of them."

"You're right again. You know, maybe you should have been leading this mission from the start."

"Now you're starting to make some sense. Glad I could help. I think it's about time we turned in, don't you?"

"Yeah, sounds good. Sorry about not having a bed for you."

"I'll be just fine on the sofa."

———

"Danny! How's it going? Did you enjoy your time off?"

Danny stood in the office doorway of his manager, Gary Murphy.

"Hey, Gary. Yeah, it was good," Danny replied. He had slept well, but once he awoke, around five thirty, his racing mind prevented him from falling back asleep. Each time he felt anxiety start to build, he harnessed it by going through the relax-and-slow-down progression. He was on edge but under control.

"Great. Hey, I want to tell you again I'm sorry about you getting roped into this thing, but my hands were tied. I'm glad you're going to do it. You are going to do it, aren't you?"

"I am. I'm not sure how good it will be, but I'm going to do it." Danny turned upon hearing a throat being cleared behind him. "Oh yeah, um, Gary this is my . . . my uncle Shey. He's visiting from out of town and wanted to see our offices."

Gary rose, walked around his desk, and extended his hand. "Shey, it's nice to meet you. I'm Gary Murphy."

"It's a pleasure, Mr. Murphy."

"You should be very proud of Danny. He's one of our most valuable employees. I don't know what we'd do without him."

"Yes, we're very proud of everything he's accomplished."

"I hope you enjoy your visit. Danny, looks like you have about twenty minutes. Anything I can do for you?"

"Not really. I would like to use an empty office or conference room for a little last-minute prep. Is something available?"

"Sure. I don't think anybody is in the conference room down the hall. Go ahead and use it."

"Great. Thanks. See you after the class."

"I can't do it, Father," Vicki said matter-of-factly.

Since arriving back on Earth, the mood in the Vortex compound had been somewhat celebratory. Everyone who encountered Vicki was astounded by how much she had changed. Aurora, the only person privy to the mission other than Kayla, had immediately burst into tears upon seeing her. Aurora could tell she was a different person just from her body language and the look in her eyes. The two had spent most of the previous day together while Kingsley tended to affairs regarding the end of his term. Now Kingsley was standing in Vicki's room, trying to get her out the door.

"You don't know that you can't do it," he said. "You could change dramatically at any moment. It's time to go."

"There's no point. There is no way I can give that address. You might as well call them now and let them know I won't be taking over for you."

"Sweetie, we've gone over this a dozen times. We have to be in the CAD senate building right up to the last minute in case Danny succeeds. If you still say you can't do it at the time of the address, I'll inform them that you will not be assuming the presidency. Your clothes are in the car. You can use the dressing room in my office. There will be people there to do your hair and makeup. Now let's go."

———————————

Danny paced around the conference room while Shey calmly sat and watched. It was five minutes before the scheduled start of the class.

"Danny," Shey said. "Stop. Relax your chest. Unclench and drop your shoulders. Relax your neck, throat, jaw, face, and the back of your head. Do a couple of neck rolls. Okay, good. Now slow down. Deep, slow breathing. That's the most important point. Slow down your thoughts. Visualize everything moving in slow motion. Pull your energy into your center. You have an unlimited amount of positive, powerful energy. Drop your shield. You are going to attack this task with energy, focus, and enthusiasm."

Danny opened his eyes and let out a deep breath. "Thanks. That helps."

"When you enter that room, engage the people immediately. That will keep the shield from building up. Greet a couple of them casually. Exchange energy with them. And don't be afraid to use humor."

"Okay. Those are good ideas. We should probably go."

"One more thing," Shey said as he rose and approached Danny while pulling a small device from his pocket. He handed it to Danny. "Hit play."

Danny did so, and Vicki appeared on the screen. "Hello, Danny. I know what you are about to do is going to be difficult for you. I just wanted to tell you that I have confidence in you. I know you can do it, but not for the Vortex family. For us. We're going to have to deal with it sometime. Why not now? I believe in you, Danny. Now go have fun." Her image disappeared.

"Fun," Danny said. "I never really thought of it that way. I've always thought of it as pure torture. I'm going to have some fun with it. Let's go, Shey."

———————————

"How do you feel, princess?" asked Kingsley.

They were in the dressing room adjoining Kingsley's office. Vicki had changed into a black suit and had her hair and makeup done. For the past hour the room had been bustling with helpers and handlers, but the two of them were now alone, waiting for a miracle. Vicki sat in a large, overstuffed chair while Kingsley paced. She stared straight ahead, expressionless. It was twenty minutes before her address.

"Awful. Worse, the closer it gets. There's no chance. Tell them now, Father. Tell them now so we can just go home."

Kingsley walked over and sat on the ottoman facing her and put his hands on her knees. "You can do it. I know you can. It doesn't matter if Danny succeeds or not. Now pull yourself together and focus on the task."

Vicki's eyes welled up with tears. "No, Father. I can't. I'm sorry. Don't try and make me!" Tears began streaming down her face. The floodgates opened, and she began sobbing uncontrollably. She dropped her head into her hands.

"Victoria, you can do this!" Kingsley yelled as he grabbed both of her forearms. "Our family's rule is at stake. I've been telling myself for a long time that it doesn't matter, but it does. We are the royal family of Earth. The people of this planet need the Vortex family to be leading them. I need you to keep this alive!"

———————————

"Hey, Mark, how's it going?" Danny asked as he strode into the training room. He had entered from the back, glass of water in hand, after pausing outside the door to go through the progression one more time. The first person he saw was Mark Sanders, a developer with whom he had always had a good relationship.

"Hi, Danny. I'm good. How are you? I haven't seen you in the office in ages."

"It's been a long time. I really haven't had a reason to come in. Hey, Joe, how's the golf game?" Danny asked as he continued toward the front of the room.

"I'm playing a lot but getting worse," replied Joe Conroy. "You been playing much?"

"I just recently picked it up again. We'll have to get out sometime."

Danny greeted three others before arriving at the front of the room. The exchanges had kept him somewhat relaxed, but his body clenched, he stopped breathing, and he felt a massive anxiety spike when he turned to face the group. His first reaction was to flee, to run from the room and get the hell out of the building. He dropped his head and closed his eyes. He realized he had been holding his breath. He started taking slow, continual breaths. He went through the relaxation progression and put a halt to his frantic thoughts. The process dramatically lowered his anxiety level, but he was still agitated. He began an inner pep talk. Have fun. These are just people. Drop the shield. Exchange energy with them. Be powerful, be excellent, and have fun.

From seemingly out of nowhere a calm blanketed his being. Danny opened his eyes and did something he'd never done before in such a situation. He looked, really looked, at the faces in the room. They were kind, friendly faces. They weren't the enemy. Everything in the room seemed to be moving in slow motion. He cleared his throat and told himself to slowly and calmly express a thought. He needed some moisture in his mouth, so he slowly picked up the glass of water and took a drink.

"Hello, everyone. I know most of you, but for those I don't, I'm Danny Kerrigan from application support. I feel a little funny doing this since I'm sure some of you know more about this than I do, but somebody in this company obviously thought I have something to offer."

"Don't be modest, Danny. Everyone knows you're the guru," said Mark from the back of the room. His comment drew some chuckles and positive comments from a couple others. The exchange relaxed Danny even more. His voice grew stronger as he continued.

"I'm going to use screen shots from the application and perhaps work on the white board to make some points. We have two hours to cover the material. I want this to be very casual, so I encourage you to ask questions and make comments." Danny brought the first slide up on the room's large screen. After one more deep breath, he began the presentation as planned.

"I'm going to cover the production planning module, starting with the setup and then moving into how everything relating to production flows through the application. I'm going to be referring frequently to the database tables and fields used by each process, transaction, and function. Let's start with the Production Parameters and Options form."

He was on a roll. He was talking firmly and powerfully. As he moved through the material, he became animated and drew diagrams on the white board. He explained each concept clearly, concisely, brilliantly. There was no shield. Danny made frequent eye contact, answered questions perfectly, and even made several successful attempts at humor. His confidence grew with each passing minute. He was connecting with them. They were exchanging energy. He was performing. He was having fun.

"Good God. What have I done? What am I doing?" Kingsley had let go of Vicki's arms and was staring at his hands. "I've placed this office and the family name above your well-being. I've been doing it your entire life. You were right. I wouldn't have done the mission if it was only to help you improve. It was all for the family's legacy. Vicki, I am so sorry. I'll go let them know you won't be taking office, and then we'll go home. Vicki?"

Kingsley hadn't noticed that the sobbing had stopped. Vicki removed her hands from her face and raised her head. Kingsley was stunned. The fear and desperation in her eyes had been replaced with fire and determination.

He was speechless. It was a look he'd never before seen on her face. Vicki smiled slightly, almost mischievously.

"I've got a planet to run. Makeup!" she yelled as she leapt to her feet, so quickly and forcefully it knocked Kingsley backward off the ottoman.

"Victoria? What happened?"

"I think what happened is Danny just nailed his training class."

Kingsley pushed himself upright. "You aren't anxious?"

"Not in the least. I'm looking forward to it. It should be fun."

"Amazing," Kingsley said with wonder and a hint of delight. "It worked."

"It would seem so. Now get off the floor, Father. I've got an address to give. Tell them I'll be there in ten minutes. I've got to fix my face and make a pass through my speech." Vicki sat down at the dressing table as two assistants entered the room and began touching up her makeup. Kingsley rose and headed for the door but stopped and turned to take another look at her.

"Amazing," he whispered. He shook his head and exited.

Kingsley made his way to the CAD senate chambers, where he informed the leadership that Vicki would be slightly late. He then waited in the wings for Vicki to arrive while trying to pace away his nervous energy.

"I'm getting exhausted just watching you, Father," Vicki said as she entered the backstage area. "I daresay you're more nervous than I am."

"You look stunning, my dear. Professional, powerful, and beautiful. How do you feel?"

"Quite wonderful and quite ready. Thank you, Father. Thank you for risking time travel, creating that fabulous fake mission, and most of all for working so diligently with Danny. And thank you for trying to help me the last thirty years. I know it must have been incredibly frustrating."

"I won't lie. It was frustrating, and painful, to see you so paralyzed with fear. Are you ready?"

"I am," Vicki said before Kingsley gave a thumbs-up to the head of the senate, Malikar Bram.

"Esteemed members of the United Nations Cosmic Affairs Division senate," Malikar said. "We have assembled today to witness two historic events. The first is the end of term for a man who has led planet Earth with humanity, humility, integrity, and passion for the past thirty years. Ladies and gentlemen, outgoing president Kingsley Vortex."

The room erupted in a roar that stunned Kingsley. He had been so caught up in the mission and helping Vicki, he hadn't thought about the fact that he would be involved in the ceremony. After receiving a kiss on the check from Vicki, he walked onto the stage to hear the cheers increase in volume. Every senate member was standing, applauding enthusiastically, and most were cheering. Despite his best efforts, Kingsley could not hold back the tears as he stood at the podium and soaked in the crowd's admiration and appreciation. The din continued for several minutes despite Kingsley raising his hands several times in an effort to bring it to an end. When it finally subsided, he looked down and took a few moments to gather himself. Before speaking he glanced up to the balcony where Aurora was seated. She was surrounded by Kayla, Marquin, and their families.

"Thank you. Thank you, ladies and gentlemen, so much for that wonderful greeting. This is a moment I will remember vividly and fondly for the rest of my life. To the esteemed members of the CAD senate, the people of planet Earth, and any of our friends from PUPCO planets who are watching, I would like to express what an honor it has been for me to serve in this position. It seems like only yesterday I was standing in the wings watching my mother's farewell words. My term has been a marvelous thirty-year ride. I have represented this planet and this government with tremendous pride, never taking for granted the privilege it was for me to hold this position. I studied and trained my entire life with the sole purpose of serving in this office. Quite simply, I loved this job. I have dedicated my life to it and can only hope that I left this planet in no worse condition than it was in at the end of my mother's term. If it is at all better, I will feel like my efforts have been supremely successful. Thank you all for your support throughout the years. To the members of this senate, I have enjoyed knowing and working with all of you and I hope to stay in touch with many of you during my retirement. Finally, my only hope as I leave this office is that my daughter

Victoria is treated with the same respect and fairness that I have received throughout my term. Thank you and farewell."

As Kingsley stepped away from the podium, he was greeted with another thunderous round of applause. He nodded and waved several times before taking a position several feet away, near the chair in which he'd be sitting during Vicki's address.

Malikar Bram again approached the podium. "It is now time for the incoming president of Earth to take the oath of office," he said as he nodded toward the wings.

The massive chamber was silent as Vicki calmly and confidently strode across the stage. The senators were curious due to the low profile she had maintained to this point. Vicki arrived at the podium and faced Malikar.

"Please repeat after me. I, Victoria Vortex, agree to serve as president of the United Nations Cosmic Affairs Division for a term of thirty years, beginning this day, the first of April in the year 2198."

Vicki repeated the words firmly and loudly, without a hint of fear in her voice. Malikar administered the rest of the oath, which Vicki repeated flawlessly. He then turned to face the senate.

"Inhabitants of this great planet, I present to you your new leader, President Victoria Vortex."

A substantial but slightly restrained round of applause greeted Vicki as she turned to face the audience. She nodded, went to Kingsley, kissed him on the cheek, and returned to the podium. Malikar and Kingsley took their seats.

"Members of the CAD senate, inhabitants of Earth, and all members of PUPCO, I am excited and honored for this opportunity. From my great-grandfather August to my father Kingsley, the Vortex name has stood for dignity, respect, fairness, honesty, and passion. My desire is to serve and represent this great planet with all of those traits. I have, however, chosen a slightly different path to this point than those who came before me. While the Vortex family has always maintained a high profile, I chose to avoid the spotlight for most of my life. For that reason, I'm certain many people watching this today have concerns regarding my fitness to hold this office. I want to put those concerns to rest right now. The fact that I was less visible than my predecessors will have no bearing on my ability to lead. While I avoided the spotlight, I too dedicated my life to studying and training for this position. I stand here today with no less knowledge of what it takes to hold this office than my father had thirty years ago today. Make no mistake. I can and I will lead our planet!"

The senate broke into boisterous applause. Kingsley stared at his daughter in disbelief. She wasn't just getting through it. The person that hardly spoke to him, who had rarely left her room for thirty years, was speaking with power and conviction. Kingsley loved her approach. There probably wasn't a soul watching who didn't know about her reclusive life. Rather than avoiding the issue and leaving people with concerns, she attacked it head-on. She laid her cards on the table so there were no lingering concerns or unanswered questions. Brilliant. As the din subsided, he stared at her with, for the first time in his life, overflowing pride.

"I would now like to describe my vision for this planet. I will detail my plan for how I believe our inhabitants can achieve new cultural, technological, and spiritual heights and continue to be a leader in the PUPCO community."

"So that pretty much covers it," Danny said as he threw the marker into the white board's tray. "Are there any other questions? Okay then. I've been asked to do a series of these. In a couple of weeks I'll cover production order scheduling and plant capacity management. Thanks for coming."

The room broke into a short burst of applause. Danny was taken aback. He had never seen people applaud at the end of a training class. He glanced at the back of the room to find Shey giving him a thumbs-up. As the attendees gathered their things, Danny headed for the exit amid several comments of what a great job he did and how much they had learned. Shey was waiting in the hall. Danny walked up to him and glanced around at the people moving by.

"You're not going to hug me, are you?"

"It wasn't that good," Shey said as he winked and gently punched Danny on the chin.

"Can you wait back in the conference room? I need to talk to my boss about something."

"I suppose," Shey replied. He looked at Danny suspiciously before heading down the hall.

"And don't talk to any women!" Danny yelled.

Ten minutes later, Danny appeared in the conference room.

"Well, sport, it's time for me to drop you off and get back to my time. I'd love to hang out for a couple days, but Kingsley gets nervous if the ship is away too long."

"I'm going with you," Danny said firmly.

"What?"

"You heard me. I'm going back with you. I have to know how Vicki did. I'd go nuts if I had to spend the rest of my life not knowing. I'm serious. Take me with you, Shey."

"But what about your job? You can't do time travel more than twice in a week's time. You'd have to be there at least a week."

"I know. I've taken care of everything. I just worked it out with Gary. I told him I need more time off since I worked on this class the last two weeks and didn't get much time to relax. I said I wanted it kind of open-ended, like a short sabbatical, and that if I didn't get it I'd probably resign. He agreed with the provision that my pay be stopped if I'm gone longer than my accumulated vacation time. He's going to get my mail and keep an eye on the apartment for me. So I can go with you and return when I'm ready. Can we get back to see some of Vicki's address?"

"I'll see what I can do. The technology is fairly accurate, but not precise. Let's go."

"That is my vision. As you can tell, I'm not planning on resting on what my predecessors have built. Our people are brilliant, industrious, and moving toward enlightenment. Our planet's consciousness has never been higher. Let us keep moving forward together and, above all, remain focused, fearless, and in the flow. Thank you."

The senate members leapt to their feet, almost in unison. The ovation rivaled if not surpassed that which had greeted Kingsley. Vicki took a step back, bowed slightly to both sides of the audience, and waved to her mother. Kingsley waited patiently despite his urge to run to her. With the ovation still in full force Vicki turned and approached her father. He wanted to give her a bear hug and lift her into the air but resisted. He took both her hands and kissed her on the forehead.

"What do you think, Father? Not bad for a fear-laden recluse, huh?" She was beaming.

"My dear, you were astounding. I've never been more proud. How in the world did you come up with all of that, the vision you outlined?"

"You didn't think I was sitting in my room watching TV all those years, did you? I not only studied the job, I critiqued how everyone else in our family had done it and came up with what I would change if I were in the position."

"Even though you had absolutely no intention of taking over for me?"

"Right. I detached from the situation and thought of it as a game."

"A game that you've obviously won. Now let's get out of here."

Kingsley and Vicki turned, waved to the still-applauding senate members, and walked arm-in-arm from the stage. When they neared the wings, they both stopped in shock, then quickened their pace until they were offstage.

"Danny!" Kingsley exclaimed. "What the hell are you doing here?"

Danny didn't answer. His gaze, slightly distorted due to the tears welling up, was locked on Vicki. She stopped in front of him. They locked hands and eyes.

"I caught the end of it. You were unbelievable. To talk like that, in this setting, with all of these senators and billions of people watching, was incredible."

Vicki was grinning from ear to ear. "I couldn't have done it without you. I take it you had a bit of success yourself?"

Danny smiled, somewhat sheepishly. "Yeah, it went really well. With your dad's training and Shey's support, I got through it."

"If you'd have just gotten through it, my transformation wouldn't have been so complete and so amazing. I think you had a switch flip, but not the panic switch. You found peace, didn't you?"

"I did. Right when it was time to start, this calm came over me, and all the anxiety and dread just melted away."

"And that is what paved the way for our performances," Vicki said before throwing her arms around Danny.

"Danny, I can't wait to hear about your training class. It obviously went extremely well—but what are you doing here?" Kingsley asked again.

"I told Shey I couldn't live not knowing how Vicki did, so I demanded he bring me back. I got an indefinite leave from work so I can stay as long as I like," Danny said as he and Vicki broke their hug.

"Well, I must say I'm glad to see you again. I think we deserve some rest and relaxation. Perhaps you'll join Shey and me on a vacation? Now let's head back to the compound. The family is gathering for a small celebration before tonight's inaugural ball."

"You and Shey go on ahead, Father. I need a moment with Danny."

"Certainly," Kingsley replied before he and Shey exited, leaving Danny and Vicki alone.

Vicki again took Danny's hands and looked into his eyes.

"There's something I've been wanting to say to you for a while now, but I just couldn't bring myself to do it."

"What's that?"

"I love you, Danny."

Danny smiled and replied without hesitation. "I love you too."

Aurora Vortex stood in the hallway and stared at the words displayed beside the door: Pre-Birth Soul Request Program.

"I'm having second thoughts about this, Kingsley."

"Second? More like fifty-second. How many times do we have to go through this? It's only natural to be a bit hesitant when using such new technology, but we've been over it and over it, and in the end you always agree. I'm not going to coerce you into it, but I don't think now is the time to get cold feet."

Aurora stood firm and looked annoyed. Kingsley sighed.

"Okay, okay. What is it this time? Do you have a new concern, or are we going to rehash your old ones?"

"Don't minimize my feelings on this. This is our child we're dealing with, and you know as well as I do that it may be our only one. I'm due in three days. Everything has gone perfectly to this point, and I don't want to do anything to jeopardize the baby."

"Jeopardize?" Kingsley boomed. He lowered his voice when he realized people were nearby. "It's not going to jeopardize anything. The technology was developed by the best metaphysical and scientific minds on the planet. The test group of children were an almost ninety percent match to the requested traits. Best case, we put the request out to the spiritual plane and it attracts a match. The probability that this will be our only child makes it even more important that we do this. If it works, we're assured that our child will have all of the traits required of a great leader. Worst case, they ignore it or it never reaches its destination and nature takes over. What is there to lose?"

Aurora sighed. "Okay. Let's do it."

"That's my girl," Kingsley said as he took her by the hand and they entered the room.

"Kingsley. Aurora. It's great to see you both," said Kayla as she quickly moved toward them. "I'm so glad you decided to use our technology."

"Sorry we're a little late," Kingsley said. "Aurora has been a bit hesitant to go through with it."

Kayla took her hand. "That's perfectly understandable, but I can assure you that nothing can go wrong. The desired trait values you submitted are in the system and ready to go. All you have to do is relax in the soul request chair for fifteen minutes, and it will all be over."

"Actually, we've tweaked several of the values since we sent them. I think we were a bit timid before in a desire not to be greedy. These are the values we want to request. Is it too late to change them?" Kingsley asked as he handed her a small device.

"Not at all. I'll have my assistant enter the new values before we begin. Now come along."

Kayla led them down a hallway and into the room that contained the soul request chair. The room was dimly lit and decorated with soothing colors and fabrics. Aurora climbed into the large, comfortable chair and took advantage of both the headrest and the footrest. Kingsley pulled up a chair and sat beside her.

"Is it okay if I sit here? It won't affect the process, will it?"

"No, you're fine there. Just don't touch Aurora while the request is being sent. An energy field will envelop her. That field will be tied into the energy of the request as it is sent to the spiritual plane. It's the connection that conveys which human is making the request. Just relax. I'm going into the control booth over there. You'll be able to see me through the glass. I'll be back when it's over."

Kayla entered the booth and greeted her most-trusted assistant, Trammel Marbury. "We've got a few changes to their desired values. Make these updates as I read them off."

"Sure thing," replied Trammel.

"Assertiveness, eight. Decisiveness, nine. Passion, nine. Risk tolerance, seven. Charisma, ten. Self-confidence, nine. Strength of will, nine. Ability to connect with people, nine. Fearlessness, ten. Leave everything else the way it was."

"You got it, boss."

"Aurora is concerned about this whole thing. I think I'm going to go back in and help comfort her. Make sure the values are correct and start the process," Kayla said before exiting the booth.

Trammel entered new values. Assertiveness, two. Decisiveness, two. Passion, one. Risk tolerance, one. Charisma, two. Self-confidence, one. Strength of will, two. Ability to connect with people, one. Fearlessness, zero. He hit the start button and gave Kayla a thumbs-up. Fifteen minutes later Trammel left the booth and entered the room.

"The process is complete, Ms. Vortex. That's all there is to it."

"Thank you, Trammel," Kingsley said. "Thank you for your help today."

"You're welcome, sir. Kayla, I'm not feeling well. Is it okay if I take off for the day?"

"Certainly. Go take care of yourself. Come on, Aurora. I'll see you out."

Trammel went back to the booth, typed in the settings as Kayla had read them, and saved them in the Vortex file. He exited the building with a spring in his step, climbed into his car, and let the ground transportation system whisk him away to his small but chic apartment. He entered and made a beeline for the bedroom, where he looked down at the real Trammel Marbury, who lay sleeping on the bed. The visitor put his hand on Trammel's forehead.

"When you awake, all you will remember about today is that you went to work, administered the soul request procedure to Aurora Vortex, and then left work early because you weren't feeling well."

As Trammel started stirring, the visitor's shape changed to a glowing mass of light and then disappeared. In an instant the mass of energy traveled to the foyer of the Vortex mansion and became solid again, just as Kingsley and Aurora walked through the door.

"Home sweet home. Hey, Abby, how's it going? We just requested a soul that should assure that the Vortex family rule will continue for another generation. Look, Aurora, I think she's smiling."

THE END

ACKNOWLEDGMENTS

I WOULD LIKE TO THANK Doug Wagner and Toni Robino of Windword Literary Services for their feedback, encouragement, and guidance through the publishing process.

I'd also like to thank everyone at Mascot Books who worked with me on this project, particularly my acquisitions editor, Ben Simpson, my production editor, Brandon Coward, and my editor, Zachary Gresham.

And to my wife, Jill—as a first-time novelist with no creative writing experience, my confidence in the project took frequent, wild swings from thinking I was writing a surefire bestseller to who-am-I-kidding-I'm-not-a-writer. Without her countless pep talks and constant support there would be no *Monarch*.